Readers love the Fish Out of Water series by AMY LANE

Fish Out of Water

"...I will promise you this, you WILL be left with one hell of a book hangover."
—Rainbow Gold Book Reviews

Red Fish, Dead Fish

"I have to give high marks to this book. The writing was sharp and decisive and the story was emotionally charged."
—Gay Book Reviews

A Few Good Fish

"*A Few Good Fish* is a riveting page-turner with high-stakes action scenes, an intriguing plot and two compelling, incredibly likeable central characters."
—All About Romance

Hiding the Moon

"...the author delivers some poetic, tender, heartwarming and heart-rending moments between her amazing cast of characters."
—The Novel Approach

Fish on a Bicycle

"The problem for me with an author like Amy Lane is that she continues to exceed my expectations... Thank you, Amy, you're the best."
—Rainbow Book Reviews

School of Fish

"...for fans of the series this is a must!"
—Open Skye Book Reviews

Fish in a Barrel

"Ms. Lane this was the best yet....10 stars if I could..."
—Paranormal Romance Guild

By Amy Lane

An Amy Lane Christmas
Behind the Curtain
Bewitched by Bella's Brother
Bolt-hole
Bowling for Turkeys
Christmas Kitsch
Christmas with Danny Fit
Clear Water
Do-over
Food for Thought
Freckles
Gambling Men
Going Up
Hammer & Air
With Andrew Grey: Holiday Cheer
Anthology
Homebird
If I Must
Immortal
It's Not Shakespeare
Late for Christmas
Left on St. Truth-be-Well
The Locker Room
Mourning Heaven
Phonebook
Puppy, Car, and Snow
Racing for the Sun • Hiding the Moon
Raising the Stakes
Regret Me Not

Shiny!
Shirt
Sidecar
Slow Pitch
String Boys
A Solid Core of Alpha
Swipe Left, Power Down, Look Up
Three Fates
Truth in the Dark
Turkey in the Snow
The 12 Kittens of Christmas
Under the Rushes
Weirdos
Wishing on a Blue Star

BENEATH THE STAIN
Beneath the Stain • Paint It Black

BONFIRES
Bonfires • Crocus
Sunset • Torch Songs

CANDY MAN
Candy Man • Bitter Taffy
Lollipop • Tart and Sweet

COVERT
Under Cover

Published by DREAMSPINNER PRESS
www.dreamspinnerpress.com

By Amy Lane (cont)

DREAMSPUN BEYOND
HEDGE WITCHES LONELY
HEARTS CLUB
Shortbread and Shadows
Portals and Puppy Dogs
Pentacles and Pelting Plants
Heartbeats in a Haunted House

DREAMSPUN DESIRES
THE MANNIES
The Virgin Manny
Manny Get Your Guy
Stand by Your Manny
A Fool and His Manny
SEARCH AND RESCUE
Warm Heart
Silent Heart
Safe Heart
Hidden Heart

FAMILIAR LOVE
Familiar Angel • Familiar Demon

FISH OUT OF WATER
Fish Out of Water
Red Fish, Dead Fish
A Few Good Fish • Hiding the Moon
Fish on a Bicycle • School of Fish
Fish in a Barrel
A Perfectly Sonny Daye • Only Fish
Devil and the Deep Blue Fish

FLOPHOUSE
Shades of Henry • Constantly Cotton
Sean's Sunshine

GRANBY KNITTING
The Winter Courtship Rituals of
Fur-Bearing Critters
How to Raise an Honest Rabbit
Knitter in His Natural Habitat
Blackbird Knitting in a Bunny's Lair
Weddings, Christmas, and Such
The Granby Knitting Menagerie
Anthology

JOHNNIES
Chase in Shadow • Dex in Blue
Ethan in Gold • Black John
Bobby Green • Super Sock Man

Published by DREAMSPINNER PRESS
www.dreamspinnerpress.com

DEVIL AND THE DEEP BLUE FISH

Amy Lane

Published by
DREAMSPINNER PRESS

8219 Woodville Hwy #1245
Woodville, FL 32362 USA
www.dreamspinnerpress.com

Devil and the Deep Blue Fish
© 2025 Amy Lane

Cover Art
© 2025 L.C. Chase
http://www.lcchase.com
Cover content is for illustrative purposes only and any person depicted on the cover is a model.

Trade Paperback ISBN: 978-1-64108-826-8
Digital ISBN: 978-1-64108-825-1
Trade Paperback published June 2025
v. 1.0

To everyone. Matt, Mary, the kids. Even the dogs. This year has sucked healthwise, and finishing a book is just such a miracle of group effort. Thank you.

Author's Note

ALL FICTION. I mean, these particular characters are fictional. I wish we lived in a world where stuff LIKE this never happened.

Fish Food for Thought

"Dammit, fuck, he's gonna get you, Henry, dodge!"

"To the left, to the left, get your gun—your gun, Jackson, not your grenade launch—oh."

"*Ha*! There we go! Die, motherfucker, *die*!"

"Whew, wow. Okay, yeah." Henry Worrall threw his X-box controller onto the arm of the leather couch with relief. "Well done, my brother. I'll believe you next time when you say you got it."

Jackson Rivers, Henry's PI mentor and friend, set the game to practice, but he didn't shut it off, and he studiously ignored Henry's sigh.

"You should always believe me when I say I've got your back," Jackson said, giving Henry what he hoped was an animated smile.

Henry wasn't fooled. "God, Jackson—have you slept at *all* this week?" he asked, sounding helpless.

"Have you?" Jackson shot back, and he felt a wave of petty satisfaction when Henry winced. But Henry'd had a year to learn how to be a real boy, and apparently he'd passed Jackson up on the emotional honesty scale in that time.

"I'm worried as fuck about Randy," he said dispiritedly.

Just *hearing* it said out loud helped ease the tightwire of stress between Jackson's shoulder blades.

"Burton says there's no sign of the guy," Jackson admitted with a sigh. Abruptly, he was tired, which was an improvement over the manic tired-not-tired that had possessed him since their friend had been spirited away by friends in the military after a close brush with a killer. And not just *any* killer, it turned out. A *special* nutcase, nicknamed "BJ" by the covert ops unit assigned to track him down. Apparently this guy got off on catching—and killing—people in the act. He loved to thrust a knife between the ribs of the person *giving* the blowjob, and then cut the throat of the person *receiving* the blowjob. So far, he'd killed at least five women and six men that they knew about—and he would have killed Randy but, well, Randy was *special*.

Jackson maintained that Randy's job as a *Johnnies* model in adult films made him particularly impervious to shame. Randy hadn't frozen when the 7-Eleven clerk, shamelessly taking advantage of Randy's naivete and love of a good Slurpee, had died in the act. Instead, he'd screamed in the killer's face and taken off running. Fortunately he lived in the flophouse—an apartment that housed a number of guys in the same line of work—and it was right across the street from the convenience store. As far as anybody could figure out, Randy had run fast enough to disappear into the apartment complex before the killer could even recover from what had to be a terrifying bray in his face as he was achieving his own climax, so to speak.

Henry, who admittedly knew Randy better, said that Randy was so loud and so spazzy and so pure of heart the gods simply stuck their hands from the heavens and took hold of the killer, proclaiming, "You shall not pass!"

Either theory held validity, as far as Jackson was concerned. Randy, for all his quirks, was a sweet kid. He needed to do some growing up (not physically, please, he was six five as it was) and get hold of his many neuroses, allergies, and divergences, but underneath all the noise was a gentle giant who wanted to do good *so badly*. He was the first in line to take over a roommate's chores or to go fetch a favorite treat or to lend a book or an article of clothing or an ampule of lube. (Life in an apartment full of young adults who had sex for a living had its own rules.) If anybody deserved to go hauling into the ether, pants around his ankles, to avoid the icy claw of death, it was Randy.

Which was why Jackson had called his contacts in the south with the serial-killer hunters to come take Randy somewhere safe. But getting Randy to safety and assuring themselves that the killer was out of the way and wouldn't track down Randy's brothers in the flophouse were two different things. Henry lived in the same building, and Jackson, Henry, and AJ, another law firm employee, had made sure the security setup from the *last* time something like this had happened was still securely in place. *Everybody* was wired for sound now—the kids who lived with Randy; Henry and his boyfriend, Lance, who lived in the same complex; Jackson; his fiancé, Ellery, a founding lawyer at the law firm; and Galen, Ellery's partner—*everybody* had a cell phone that would alert if a rabbit so much as sneezed in their area. And given that there was a cantankerous neighbor who lived upstairs and liked to stomp loudly on Henry's ceiling when she thought somebody was enjoying too much life, that had pretty much ensured Lance and Henry had enjoyed zero alone time since Randy had been taken away.

So that was one *very* good reason for Jackson's sleeplessness, but he and Henry both knew that wasn't it. Jackson was pretty good at danger—

had gotten damned used to it in fact. This wasn't the first time somebody they knew and cared about was in trouble, and the fact that Jackson was on a first-name basis with a bunch of the serial-killer hunters in the covert ops unit probably said something uncomfortable about Jackson's personal life. But the most uncomfortable thing about his personal life, he thought irritably, was that for one reason or another, it had ceased to be personal.

Fact was, Jackson hadn't slept well in over a decade, for a lot of very good reasons, from betrayal to fear for his person to regret to terror for the people he loved. The hell of it was, Jackson had been working *really* hard to at least be functional, and Ellery had been on board with his efforts. He still spoke to a counselor of sorts every week, and he'd been opening up to his friends and family more since Ellery had come into his life. He wanted to be a real boy almost as much as Randy did, he thought sardonically. But Randy simply had some growing to do. For instance, maybe taking a blowjob in trade for his birthday Slurpee hadn't exactly been prudent. But for Jackson?

The answers were a little less simple.

"Jackson?" Henry asked gently. "Are you having second thoughts about the wedding?"

Jackson actually laughed. "No," he said. "When it gets really bad, I wake up and think, 'I'm getting married in June,' and that actually calms me down. I don't use it too much, though. I need something in my heavy-duty arsenal."

Henry made a sound—a pained sound—like he knew something Jackson didn't, and when Jackson glanced at him, he was massaging the bridge of his nose.

"Don't give me that shit," Jackson said bitterly. "We all play mind games with ourselves to function. You know that as well as I do. I'm sure you've got a list of yours."

This time Henry grunted and picked up his remote control, began scrolling through his character options for a new skin. "Very perceptive. Let's see. My ex-boyfriend will be released from custody in two months. That keeps me up at night."

"I'll add it to the list," Jackson said grimly. Henry's ex was an abusive toxic nightmare, and his role as Henry's brother-in-law had pretty much trapped Henry into an eleven-year stint as an unwilling mistress. Henry's effort to break away from the guy had resulted in a lot of torn knuckles on Henry's part and a stint in military prison on behalf of Henry's ex.

"Naw," Henry said, a twisted grin in place. "He's my boogeyman—let me fight him. Most of yours are *far* more colorful."

Jackson grunted again, but this time in appreciation. He and Henry had started out at odds, but when Henry had lost the chip on his shoulder and Jackson had learned to apply his fully functioning empathy to *everybody*, even rednecks with attitude as it turned out, they could be more than friends. They could be tighter than brothers; they could be *partners* who functioned so well together sometimes it was like Jackson loaned out his brain so Henry could take over.

Henry was giving him a way to talk, and Jackson needed to appreciate it.

"I've let people down in my life," Jackson said simply. "Not on purpose, and certainly not for lack of trying. But…." He swallowed. "When you're about to get married, that's the sort of thing that haunts you."

Henry nodded and kept sorting through the costumes on the screen. "Same," he said softly.

Henry looked young—sounded young most times as well—but he'd survived domestic abuse, and he'd been to war. Something about those experiences gave him weight when he confessed to feeling the same.

"It's… it's nothing I can do anything about," Jackson murmured. "It's not even anything I'd change if I could. But it scares me when I think of who I've failed and how badly I don't want to fail Ellery."

Henry let out a long sigh. "Help, I've been shot," he said without heat or passion—or truth, since his character on the screen wasn't engaged in anything remotely warlike at the time.

But probably with accuracy, Jackson reflected. Henry had betrayed his sister, and whether he'd done it willingly or had been blackmailed, bullied, and threatened into it, he wasn't going to let himself off the hook that easily. But he could make his peace with it.

Jackson had to do the same.

"You're a great kid," Jackson murmured, feeling—wonder of all wonders—tired.

"I'm almost thirty, moron," Henry muttered, prickly as always. He set his remote down and yawned, and Lucifer, who'd always loved Henry best, made an awkward leap into Henry's lap, crashing on his missing foreleg and doing a faceplant into Henry's thigh. Henry stroked the cat's smooth black fur and smiled, and Jackson felt a familiar prickle on his shoulder as Billy Bob, who had been lounging on the back of the couch, reached out and kneaded him some biscuits.

It was a brief, sleepy moment in the evening, not too long after dinner. One that said Henry might crash on their couch for a much-needed nap, and Jackson, maybe—just maybe—might retire to the bedroom and sleep.

Ellery was working late at the office tonight, a thing he did rarely but offered to do *this* night because Jackson's insomnia had been so terribly acute.

"I don't care *when* you sleep, Jackson. If it's after dinner, it's after dinner, but fuck us both, you've got to get some sleep!" When he'd spoken next that afternoon, his voice had dropped, throbbing gently with worry. "Besides, baby, if you fall asleep after dinner, I'll get home just in time for your first nightmare. Timing is everything." He'd given a twisted smile then, and Jackson had been terribly, terribly aware that what hurt *him* hurt Ellery too. Ellery would probably like to sleep uninterrupted as well, and while the first nightmare was almost a guarantee these days, the second, as long as Jackson had Ellery in his bed, was often not. A compromise of sorts, and Jackson understood.

Jackson found himself giving in to it, laying his head on the back of the couch, letting his cat's steady kneading lull him into a sort of somnolence. He was there, almost asleep, when Henry shifted on the couch.

Jackson popped awake in an instant at Henry's muttered oath, his heart pounding with the urgency in Henry's voice.

"I'm up!" he said, struggling for breath. "What do we need to do?"

"Nothing," Henry said firmly, although he was already on his feet and heading for where his shoes sat and his jacket hung in the foyer. "This is a me thing, not a you thing."

"But you don't *have* you things," Jackson complained. "Me, your boyfriend, the law firm—we're the beginning and end of your existence!"

Henry's laugh was warm and rich, and Jackson had a moment to reflect that he was glad Henry had gotten to the point where he really *could* laugh like that. And also that Henry had a full life—he wasn't only liked, he was *beloved*—by his brother, his brother's family, Galen, Galen's husband, John, all the boys he helped to mentor in the flophouse, and by Lance, his boyfriend, who thought Henry was the best man he'd ever known.

"No, seriously," Jackson said on a yawn. "Tell me where you're going. I'll fuss if I don't know."

Henry grimaced. "Actually you'll probably get called in on it too, so I may as well tell you. You know how half the kids who ended up at the flophouse got there because they hit on John or Galen?"

Jackson nodded, because he talked to the kids. "A lot of them were cruising for business," he said frankly. "They hit on John and end up with the world's most ethical porn director, who tries to give them any job but the one they asked for."

Henry inclined his head. "And he only gives them that one if they're over eighteen and are still interested after they've been cleaned up, evaluated, and spent some time off the streets."

From what Jackson understood, John ended up with one porn model in twenty or thirty offers, but he *never* took advantage of his own employees, and he'd helped a *lot* of kids find a way to a different home.

"Did he get another one?" Jackson asked, curious. He knew that sometimes Henry was called in when the kids ended up at John's receptionist's house so he could make sure Isabelle Elaine Roberts was safe when she had a stranger sleeping in her guest room.

"Fourteen," Henry said grimly, and Jackson winced.

"Dear God."

"Yeah. So I'm on to help talk to the kid, but I think Ellery's going to be called in too."

Jackson frowned. "He's fourteen. Has he been accused of something besides solicitation?"

Henry shook his head. "No, I think he witnessed something. John and Galen got the story out of him. I think they're headed here."

"Aw shit," Jackson muttered. "Your gig sounds more fun."

Henry chuckled, but it was a strained sound, and Jackson understood the cost that must be involved with taking care of a kid who'd been out on the streets the way this one had been.

"I'm sorry," he said quickly. "I know it's gotta hurt."

Henry shrugged again. "It's hard. I mean, I'm glad we can get them to someplace good—a shelter, a foster home, someplace *not* the street, but…." He sighed. "My old man was a piece of work," he said. "There was a reason Davy and I had such fucked-up lives before we came out. But we always had food and a place to sleep. Can't say that would have been the story if Dad had known about either of us, but…."

"You're going to see yourself in them," Jackson said softly. "I was one good friend and his mom away from being one. Don't think I don't see that too."

Henry shook his head. "See, *that's* why you don't sleep," he said, blowing out a breath. "Because you know these things—you've already thought about them, and you see them going on in the world, and they scare you shitless. Some of us get surprised every single time."

Jackson chuckled weakly. "Yeah, but you also get to sleep." As he spoke, his back pocket buzzed, and he answered it as he stood and stretched.

Galen and John will be by in an hour or so. Maybe prep them some food.

"And you were right, sensei," he said, bowing in Henry's direction. "Go. Do good things. I'll stay here and make your bosses soup."

Henry grinned. "The wonton soup you fed me was *outstanding!*" he said before heading for the door. He paused, his hand on the knob, and turned. "Jackson?"

"Yeah?"

"Whatever it is you think you failed at, whatever it is you think you didn't do, you gotta find a way to let it go, man. You're a good friend—a good man. Get some fuckin' sleep."

And with that he was gone, and Jackson was fishing the ingredients for homemade wontons out of the fridge again.

JOHN AND Galen arrived in less than an hour, making Jackson glad he'd gotten a move on with the soup. The two of them blew in with a fierce March wind that drifted a few leaves in on their coattails, and Jackson could tell Galen, who used a cane to help him walk, was moving more stiffly than usual tonight, probably thanks to the surprising cold.

"If this is blowing in like a lion," he said acidly, accepting John's help to shed his coat, "I am against it. In fact I think we should boycott lions of every sort."

"We can't," John said practically, hanging both their coats up on the pegs by the door. "Lions are cheerfully homosexual in the wild and possess the world's most amazingly proportioned balls. I think we owe it to our people to give lions a chance."

Galen stared at him. "I don't owe my people the right to freeze my own generously proportioned balls off!" he argued, and John snorted.

"I'm just saying, maybe we shouldn't blame the lions. They didn't make the expression."

"I'll blame whomever I damned well—oh Lord, thank you, Jackson," Galen said, sinking down at the dining room table and accepting the steaming mug of the cocoa Jackson had put on when he was throwing the soup together. Under Galen's planned scruff and the curly hair he grew long to mask the scars from the same accident that injured his leg, Jackson could see white lines around his mouth.

"Would you like to eat?" Jackson asked. "Wonton soup and warm french bread." He grimaced. "Probably an affront to both Asian and European culture, but—"

"Who *cares*." John laughed. He had bright ginger hair and tanned freckled skin, and his green eyes almost disappeared into the lines at the corners when he smiled, which was often. "It smells awesome! Here, you grab your laptop, and I'll dish everything up."

"I already ate—" Jackson began, but Galen overrode him.

"I have strict instructions from Henry to take that for the excrement it is," he said in his acid Southern drawl. "You will eat twice, and you will eat a lot. I for one am *tired* of listening to Ellery worry about you. You will eat to accommodate *me* and for no other reason."

Jackson smiled slightly. Ellery had not been looking for friends when Galen had insisted he be hired at the firm, but he'd found a good one. Galen's dry sense of humor and carefully understated kindness was a good match for Ellery's constant insistence on reason.

As in it was only *reasonable* that they all make sure Jackson was doing well, since Ellery refused to even contemplate a future without him.

"Understood," he said wryly. "He's the boss."

Galen snorted, but Jackson had already busied himself fetching his laptop from the bedroom and trying not to trip on Lucifer, who had a tendency to sprawl any-old-where just to make Jackson's life more interesting.

After swearing at the cat, Jackson returned and set it up at his place at the table, workstation at the ready.

"Okay, guys," he said, trusting John in the kitchen the way you trusted a good friend who'd been over a lot, "tell me what's up."

Galen let out a breath. "Tell *me*," he said, making eye contact with John even as John was fetching bowls from the cupboard, "what you know about the Moms for Clean Living."

Jackson sucked in a breath. "You mean the Stepford Dragons?"

John snorted, and Galen arched a sardonic brow. "Of course. I had no idea they'd rebranded."

"You're talking about those super right-wing scary women who go from town to town ripping books off shelves and screaming, 'Keep those horrible queers away from my babies!' right?" Jackson asked, and while he was going off with his own brand of honesty, his fingers were also walking the talk by pulling up what he knew about the group on his computer.

"We are indeed," John said, and the grin he gave was truly manic. "I'm a soulless ginger porno-making queer—I'm, like, their devil!" He held a hand to his heart. "My nana would be proud."

Galen chuckled fondly. "From what you've told me, she would have been."

"My nana," John told Jackson, "was the most genteel whore you have ever met. She literally told me that's how she met my grandfather, while putting away enough hooch to kill a regiment. But after she married, she rocked a twinset and pearls, scandalized the PTA with her swearing, and—" He swallowed, and Jackson could see genuine fondness for the woman. "—told her entire neighborhood to go to hell after she took me in when my father caught me having sex and beat the shit out of me."

Jackson's mouth fell open, because he had not been expecting that much real emotion.

John shook him off. "No… no. I'm sorry. I'm a little too honest after Galen and I attend our NA meetings. I didn't mean to burden you with that." He straightened his spine, and Jackson could see the genuine strength in somebody with an admittedly odd, albeit altruistic, approach to life. "I *wanted* to say that my nana would have *abhorred* these women, and when my political rage gets acute, I like to imagine her telling them all that she hasn't seen this many twats since she stopped pulling trains in her old brothel." He let out a happy sigh. "God rest her soul. I hope she's teaching the other whores in hell how to cheat at poker and give blowjobs worth a fortune. She was, legit, a hero."

"I'll pour one out for her, next time I'm drinking…?" Jackson let John fill in the blank.

"Irish whiskey!" John said with a grin, indicating his red hair. "What else?"

"Fair enough," Jackson agreed, inclining his head. "To grand old dames." He glanced down at what he'd pulled up on his laptop. "We need more of them," he said with a sigh. White women, most of them with coifed blond hair, many of them with blue eyes, stared back at him.

Galen grimaced. "I don't even need to look," he muttered. "Scary Stepford Dragons?"

"Yep," Jackson said. "And hey, last year they started a chapter in… you guessed it—"

"Sacramento," John said grimly. "I know. They have a small office about two blocks from the church where Galen and I attend our NA meeting."

Jackson frowned at him. "Wait… correct me if I'm wrong, but isn't that only a couple of blocks from Lavender Heights?"

Sacramento's nightlife had made great strides in the past ten years—lots of small businesses, bars, restaurants, and streets people felt safe enough to walk late at night on pub crawls. Lavender Heights was in the heart of all that positive energy and activity, with an LGBTQIA library on one block and a couple of nightclubs three blocks away. It was the kind of place people—any people—could walk hand in hand after dark and mostly only be afraid of traffic.

Putting the office of a bunch of people with an anti-gay or -trans agenda within the proximity of Lavender Heights was like putting nitro and glycerin on the same block.

"It is indeed," Galen said, his mouth tightening. "And this evening, we met a young man who has… well, seen things."

Jackson's eyebrows rose. "Like what?"

John let out a frustrated breath as he brought bowls and such forward to set the table. "That's the hard part. He… well, first he propositioned us—"

"You," Galen said dryly. "He propositioned you. You were standing by the car, waiting for me to catch up, and the young man stuck his head out of the bushes at crotch level and said—"

John gave a pained grimace, and Jackson realized he was embarrassed. "Don't repeat it," he muttered. "Please, Galen. It's so embarrassing. He's a *child*."

Galen's droll smile faded, replaced by gentleness. "I'm sorry," he said softly. "I guess it's only funny to me because I know you're a decent man." He glanced at Jackson and finished the story. "Anyway, he stuck his head out of the bushes, suggested a convenient way John could receive his sexual favors, and then disappeared again as I walked up. John told him he didn't want favors, but we were lost and he'd give the kid a twenty for directions."

"Did it work?" Jackson asked, because it was a good idea.

"Like that," John said, snapping his fingers. "I asked him the way to a hamburger place, and the kid gave me one in two blocks. I said he could have the twenty and I'd feed him if he drove there with us."

Jackson smiled. "Another good idea," he praised.

John rolled his eyes. "Hey, just because the kids I work with are well over eighteen doesn't mean I don't understand what makes them tick."

"Sex and food," Galen said promptly.

"*Money* and food," John retorted. "Street kids really don't want to be doing the sex thing in the first place."

"Or," Galen added, "a place to sleep and food. And sometimes"— the play left his voice, because he too was a decent man—"a place to bathe and sleep and get clean clothes. And a kind voice. And food. Which is why we left him with John's receptionist and called Henry over. I do hope you don't mind."

"Of course not," Jackson said. "I didn't need the car anyway. It's fine."

Henry had driven their shared custody minivan that day when he'd dropped Jackson off at home. Originally the plan had been that Lance, Henry's boyfriend, would come get Henry after Ellery got home, but Lance had been forced to work late—he was a resident at UC Davis Med Center—so Henry got to keep Jennifer, the persnickety crap-brown minivan that only responded to Jackson and Henry and frequently showed her distaste for anybody else at the wheel by doing things like stalling out at intersections or throwing her doors open dramatically. Her previous owner, a perfectly lovely schoolteacher with three kids, told him that once the car had protested a family trip by throwing open her back hatch and vomiting luggage all over the highway—no mechanic on earth could figure out how the latch had opened since it was supposed to be electronically controlled. "Not needing the car" was frequently code for, "Oh God, at least someone else is dealing with her," but not in this case.

In this case, Jackson couldn't think of a more comforting vehicle with which to deal with a kid off the streets in all his probable suspicion and skittishness. Jennifer would feel very real to a kid like that.

"So back to the street kid," Jackson said as John leaned over his shoulder and frowned at the screen.

"I don't see her," he said briefly to Galen, who grimaced.

"Well, fixers aren't usually on the company website," he said acidly, and John stuck out his tongue.

"See *who*?" Jackson prodded, both amused and frustrated. It was fun to see the usually unflappable Galen be cheerfully "flapped" by his significant other, but he was also curious to get to the bottom of this case.

John and Galen exchanged glances, and John was the one who spoke.

"We got the kid a hamburger and a shake," he said after a moment. "And we told him we could get him a place to sleep and a line on a shelter, which was sort of a lie because I'd already texted Mrs. Bobby's Mom. I mean Isabelle." He grimaced. Bobby was one of his models, and the kid had made a lot of sacrifices to get his mom out of the tiny town that had been strangling them both. While she initially had *hated* that her son was in porn, she'd softened when she'd met his friends and they'd all been, well, kind. Sweet young men. And so many of them had been *so* deferential to her as a mother. She still probably disapproved of the porn, but she'd taken the job offer as a receptionist and had become a surrogate mother to the kids. And she'd also helped John and Galen with their effort to help place the young people who most assuredly did *not* belong in sex work, and to find them a shelter, a home, or a system that would keep them safe until they got their feet under them.

"And she, being made of awesome, took him in," Jackson filled in. "And you stole my gaming buddy for the night, and yes, I forgive you too." Jackson made a circling motion with his hands and then stood and placed the laptop on the end table so he could finish helping with the table.

John waved him down. "C'mon," he said with a laugh, bringing a basket of freshly heated bread to set in the middle. "Give me some credit. Galen, who cooks at our house? And don't say DoorDash."

Galen snickered, almost like a kid. "Well, since you've limited my options, you *do* prepare a mighty tasty chicken and rice."

"Thank you," John said. "I'm also hell on a grill, and I have my nana's steak marinade, so there." He sighed and went back to the kitchen. "Anyway, once we got the kid in the car, we started talking to him to make him feel like he wasn't being kidnapped—I always give them street coordinates and bus coordinates, because if they flee, I want them to feel like they can get back to their old spot."

"You would be surprised how many kids don't even know where they *are*," Galen muttered, sounding bitter. "It's like a bus dropped them off and boom! They were suddenly expected to feed themselves. Anyway, John is doing the schtick—'This street is 24th and K, and we're going to stay in midtown. There's some apartment buildings on 30th and L. Can you remember that?' and the kid goes, 'My mom lives on Watt and Whitney, so thanks. I didn't know this part of town until I ran away.'"

Jackson swallowed. "From his mom?"

"That's what we asked," Galen said, "mostly to clarify, and then the kid says, 'No, from the lady who came by to fix me.'"

Jackson shook his head like he'd been shocked. "Say that again?"

John and Galen met eyes, and Galen nodded. John spoke next. "He said, 'The lady who came by to fix me.' And Galen and I were, well, *very* confused to say the least. At that moment we drove by…." He held out his hands in a "gimme-gimme" gesture.

And Jackson got it. "Moms for Clean Living," he said in surprise. "Home of the Stepford Dragons."

John nodded grimly. "The very same. And Cowboy—"

"The kid?" Jackson asked, smiling slightly.

"Swore up and down it was his real name," Galen said, his voice ringing with fondness. "Anyway, Cowboy said, 'She had on one of those jackets.'"

Jackson nodded slowly. "And now we're here, looking up the Stepford Dragons. I get it. Did the kid say anything else?"

Galen shook his head and then sighed. "Well, yes. He was taken in and put in a room with four other boys, one of whom still had makeup on. He said they were… well, sad. He and another boy broke out, climbed out the window and down the trellis, and, well, that's part of the story. But the end of the story is that Cowboy ended up at a shelter—one of the church ones that made a big deal out of homosexuality, and about a week later…." John shuddered.

"Turned his first trick," Jackson guessed sadly.

"Sometimes I'm so angry," John said, sounding tired. "I feel like we've been fighting this battle my entire life, and then I realize how many people we've lost or almost lost to it and…." He shook his head again and gave a weak-tea version of his usual manic grin. "I'm sorry. I'm… you'd think with my job history I'd be jaded now. That I would have learned that sex was a commodity in my teens and gotten over it. But I remember such *joy* in the discovery, you know? Such excitement learning 'What does this button do?' And the kids that walk through our doors? Some of them discover such *power* when they discover themselves. To see that destroyed so horribly by the people who are supposed to protect kids. It's… it's infuriating."

"I can't argue," Jackson agreed, thinking about the way his nightmares chased him down. He and Ellery saw a lot of innocence squandered or destroyed in their jobs. Even the guilty—and not everybody who crossed their threshold was going to be innocent—were often caught by surprise. The eighteen-year-old who went to a party and got busted for party drugs suddenly realizing that he might be kissing goodbye a promising future, not to mention five years of his life. The young mother who did a favor for her boyfriend and got caught up in a trafficking sting. The bodybuilder who threw a hard punch in self-defense and is suddenly wanted for manslaughter. Or the person collecting welfare who got a job and didn't return their next check because it was the only reason they could make rent.

The week before, they'd taken on the case of a fifteen-year-old who had defended his mother from her abusive boyfriend and was being tried as an adult for assault. Jackson and Henry had spent a week listening to report after report of how the boyfriend had been about to kill both the mother and the boy and the police hadn't been able to keep him away. Ellery had brought the boy in for arraignment, face full of bruises and a cast on his arm, and begged a judge not to send him to adult jail while he awaited trial.

Ellery had won, and the boy and his mother were in protective custody—and he was well on his way to getting the case dismissed. But the fact that the small family had been put in this position had been tough on the entire office.

John was right. It sure did feel as though joy was being systematically vacuumed out of their lives sometimes.

A fourteen-year-old kid named Cowboy had needed to run away to defend his right to exist.

"What did you need us to do?" he found himself asking, and at that moment, Jackson heard the garage door open.

"Go greet Ellery," John said gently. "Let's have some of this delicious soup and bread. There's more to tell."

A Defensive Agenda

ELLERY HAD killed the engine when Jackson stepped onto the steps leading into the darkened garage. He turned the light on and leaned against the washer as the garage door closed and Ellery got his briefcase and coat.

Jackson looked tired, Ellery thought critically, but then, he was often tired. He also looked relaxed, which was nice. Ellery had sent him home with the hopes that maybe some relaxation before bed would help him sleep. The case with the kid defending his mother had been a tough one both emotionally and physically. All Ellery had left was paperwork—maybe the time spent killing aliens with Henry helped with that ever-present coiled spring inside Jackson that just waited for him to fall asleep to release.

And then Jackson smiled, the corners of his green eyes crinkling, the grooves around his mouth deepening, and Ellery realized that the most important thing about him tonight was that he looked happy to see *Ellery*.

Ellery drew near and put his hand on Jackson's hip as he leaned in for what he'd planned to be a brief kiss. Jackson, always surprising, took over his mouth, pushing forward, turning, his hands thrusting under Ellery's suit jacket, the heat of his palms burning through his once-starched shirt. Ellery found himself pressed back against the washing machine, trying not to whimper as he thrust up against Jackson and wanted.

Finally Jackson pulled back, and *now* he looked insufferably pleased with himself, and kiss-mussed, and mischievous, and Ellery's chest all but ached with love.

"Evening, Counselor," Jackson said, still preening.

"Hi," Ellery replied dryly. With a meaningful shimmy he stood up straight and maneuvered away from Jackson's highly desirable body. "You're barefoot out here? It's freezing!" Ellery hadn't put his coat on because he'd been planning on a brief kiss, but he shivered now.

Jackson chuckled and flexed his toes. "Well, it's plenty warm inside." He sobered. "John and Galen are already eating, I hope. They briefed me a little, but I think they were waiting for you."

Ellery grunted. "John was pretty cagey when he said we needed to talk. How far have you gotten?"

"To the part right after the kid they took in said he was taken from his home to be indoctrinated by the Stepford Dragons," Jackson said sourly. He shuddered, almost like he was trying to control something inside him. "There's always somebody out on the streets like that, you know. I remember those people. I mean, different names, different alien shells, but always the same shit. 'Do what our God says and you'll be saved, loved, and fed.'" He grimaced like he wanted to spit. "Once, my mom took me there for food and warmth, and after that not even Celia wanted a free ride that much."

Ellery had to fight to keep his breathing even. Jackson didn't mention his mother—drug addict, prostitute, user—very often, and the fact that he did now meant he was far, far more disturbed than he let on.

"I would think," Ellery said carefully, "that a street kid could play the game if they needed to. A lot of money goes to church charities."

Jackson shot him a glare of barely contained fury—but not the kind personal to Ellery, for which Ellery was grateful. "Remember when we worked for Hamster, Hoozer, Pfinster, and Barfly?" he asked, getting the name of their old law firm terribly wrong on purpose.

"It was last year, Jackson, of course I remember," Ellery said. He was trying not to shiver, but this was obviously important.

"Lyle Langdon once had me investigate two street kids. They'd been picked up for solicitation and claimed that they were just trying to keep warm. I asked them if they'd been to the shelters, and the boys—and Christ, Ellery, they were barely legal—looked at each other. They were skinny and cleaned up for court. One of them had been to the dentist and had three teeth pulled up front and not replaced. And that kid looked at his boyfriend and said, 'They wouldn't let us stay, sir.' I… God help me, I was surprised. I mean, I'd *been* to those shelters. I knew what they wanted. But I'd been a kid then, and gay or straight or bi or trans—it hadn't really filtered in. And then the other kid said, 'We're fags, mister. They don't let fags in.'" Jackson shook his head like he was trying to shake off the rage.

"Did Langdon take the case?" Ellery asked, trying to catch his breath. So much damage, he thought randomly. They both knew Jackson had so much damage, but it very rarely opened itself up for scrutiny as it was now.

"Yeah," Jackson said on a sigh. "You know he was good like that."

Ellery nodded. Lyle Langdon, their former supervising partner at Pfeist, Langdon, Harrelson, and Cooper, had been a good guy—and the one dissenting vote in the firing of Ellery himself, which had resulted in, uhm, the less-than-dignified resignation of Jackson and his sister, Jade.

"He would have," he said with relief. Sometimes it was good to know your faith hadn't been misplaced, although Langdon was a businessman. Who knew if he'd defend the Stepford Dragons in a lawsuit if they sent his firm enough money? But then, the group's anti-LGBTQ stance would have been supremely distasteful to Langdon and bad optics for the firm itself, so maybe not.

Little bits of faith. They helped.

"I…." Jackson gave an evil chuckle. "I have to admit, Ellery, I'd be really excited to find a reason to go after these people. I'm in the mood to kick a little ass."

Ellery nodded, although he couldn't keep the trouble out of his gaze as he took in Jackson's hollowed eyes, the slow, almost creaky way he was moving.

"Sure you are," he said soothingly, but Jackson shook his head.

"No, seriously," he said. "A shot of adrenaline to clear out the pipes— I'll sleep like a baby, I swear."

And that *did* make Ellery laugh.

"Then let the mayhem commence," he said lightly and gestured for Jackson to lead the way inside.

JOHN HAD finished setting the table, and Ellery excused himself to change and wash up. He yearned a little to put on his pajama pants and a sweatshirt so he could eat at the dinner table with just Jackson and they could catch up on each other's day. Yes, he'd been the one to show Jackson that a little bit of formality could make a mealtime special, but Jackson had been the one to show *him* that sometimes relaxing with the one person who could read your mind was special all on its own.

Tonight, Ellery contented himself by changing from his suit to khakis and a cardigan, much like Galen was wearing, and he got to the table in time to sit down and start eating. For a moment, there was quiet, and then Galen said, "Ellery, you need to tell him that if he's going to cook this well, he needs to eat. It's unseemly that *we* have to nag *him* about losing weight when I could eat enough of this soup to not move for a month."

Jackson chuckled. "Nice compliment, Galen. Do you need some ice for your knuckles after that backhand?"

Galen glowered at him. "Unseemly," he enunciated. Then he took another bite of soup.

Ellery noticed that Jackson was sopping his bread in the broth and eating that and was actually sort of cheered. Whatever had been gnawing Jackson alive this last month, it seemed that having a case he could sink his teeth into really did improve his hunger.

"So," he said, as the sound of cutlery and slurping died down slightly. "Tell us what you've got for us."

"It's disturbing," John told him frankly after wiping his mouth. "And the source is a hungry, traumatized fourteen-year-old boy. But the boy was scared, and he targeted Galen and me as we left the church precisely because we were a couple—I'm sure of it. Think about that. Whatever hells of debauchery *we* offered, he was thinking at least we were safer than what he'd seen in the hands of the...." His freckled face screwed up in distaste. "Stepford Dragons," he almost spat.

"So what did they do?" Jackson asked. "The Moms for Clean Living," he offered to Ellery, which was good, because Ellery had almost forgotten the real name of the women's group whose claim to fame was stripping school libraries of books about anybody *not* straight, white, and lithium levels of happy.

"Well let's go back to when Cowboy woke up in their place. He said his mom told 'the lying one'—those are his words—that he should go with her, so he ended up in a van with the logo on the side. So whatever is going on, plausible deniability is right out the window. After that he said he was transported to the place near the church and thrown into a room with four beds and a window, and the first thing he did was scale down the window. The part I hadn't gotten to was that the four other kids in the room *joined* him. One stayed behind, one got caught as they touched the ground, and another, according to him, was tackled by a security guard as they were running down the street."

"And nobody said anything?" Ellery asked, incensed.

"The guard was shouting 'Thief' according to Cowboy," John said with a weary shrug. "It was an easy enough mistake to make. So that left Cowboy and Caleb, and Caleb, it turned out, had been living out of dumpsters for a month before the Stepford Dragons got him the second time. He was savvy—led Cowboy toward two blocks of nothing but restaurants and nooks and crannies. The boys stayed there for a day, and they started to fret about the other two boys. They ventured back toward the compound.... Have you seen the place?" John asked suddenly.

"Yes," Ellery said distastefully. "Compound is about right." The building was an old Victorian style, as he recalled, with a stone façade that had probably been added in the sixties, when it was fashionable. The shaded wall was covered in jasmine, which is probably what the boys had climbed down, and the plain stretch of grass in the back was surrounded by a severe-looking but ultimately useless wrought iron fence. The grounds were big enough to cover the front and back of their strip on the block, although the block had been zoned and built to have two houses on either side.

It looked like a security compound, but Ellery had no trouble imagining a bunch of adolescent boys could escape easily.

He glanced at Jackson, who had finished his bread and was now drinking his soup broth with some unexpected zest, and thought of him as a scrawny, angry adolescent. There was no doubt in his mind that Jackson Leroy Rivers would have led a rebellion outside those walls.

John nodded. "So Caleb told Cowboy to stand back, to hide in one of the corners and get ready to run. Cowboy did, and while he was hiding, he saw a woman he called 'Retty' cross in front of his spot. He said he knew her because she'd been the one driving the van that brought him from his apartment to the compound."

Galen made a sound of violence. "His mother kissed his cheek, told him he was going to camp, and they slammed the back door. He couldn't see where he was going. *Fucking. Cowards.*"

Ellery had the feeling there would be a lot of rage going around that night. "Agreed," he said. "So this Retty crossed in front of him and—"

Galen and John shared a troubled glance. "Cowboy gets fuzzy here. He started to cry and say she shouldn't have done Caleb that way, and we asked him where Caleb was, and he… he said, 'On the sidewalk, forever.'"

Ellery put down his spoon, suddenly not feeling so sanguine about food. "Forever?" he asked, horrified.

"Anything else?" Jackson asked. "A sound? Did Caleb say anything? Did Cowboy *hear* anything? A fight? A gunshot? A scream?"

"We couldn't get that far," John said sharply. "Jesus, Jackson—the kid was shaking. We brought him to Isabelle's with the plan of stripping him down and shaving his head for lice and feeding him, which is all pretty fucking traumatizing, and suddenly he was practically fetal in the back of the sedan."

"I shall have to have Henry take it to be decontaminated tomorrow," Galen said, wrinkling his nose. "The boy… well, he'd been on the streets for a good month."

Ellery shared his distaste. It was embarrassing to be thinking about cleanliness in the face of something life and death, but Jackson had come home often enough with clothes that should have been incinerated and not washed—and hair that had needed to be deloused—that at this point he was thinking solely of the hassle.

Jackson had set his bowl down, and he let out a long, slow breath. "So he needs to get his feet under him," he said softly. "Let's give him a night to decompress at least. I'll have Ellery drop me off at Isabelle's place tomorrow, and Henry and I can have a conversation. I'll text him tonight."

"This is… troubling," Ellery murmured. "I-I hate *everything about this*. These women are well off, they're white, and they're being driven by some very powerful money for right-wing causes. Jackson, you and Henry are going to have to be… well, your most dramatic selves, I think, complete with costumes and backstories if you go sniffing around the compound. I'm going to need to get Crystal to do a computer workup—"

"And have AJ go talk to his street contacts," Jackson said. "AJ was under for a little while. You hear more on the street when you're buying drugs or turning tricks. AJ will know who to ask about fake rich white ladies."

Ellery grimaced. "You may have to ask AJ to do that, Jackson. I still scare him."

Jackson chuckled. "Naw, I think he just envies your suits." He shook his head. "But yeah, it's a sensitive subject. I'll ask him."

"I'll call Lyle Langdon," Ellery said. "He's got his finger on the pulse of politics around here—he hates them, but he usually knows who's scratching whose back." He frowned for a moment. "Maybe Arizona Brooks too…."

"Isn't she your sworn nemesis?" John asked.

Well, she *is* the senior ADA, Ellery had to concede. "Yes, but she's also aware of politics. In fact she might know the local politicians who want the Stepford Dragons to clean up the street."

"And I can have Jade run down missing boys," Jackson said, and then, more soberly, "or unidentified bodies."

They all shuddered.

John was the one who broke the silence. "You guys ever think, I don't know, that maybe Cowboy just got scared and Caleb ended up going back to his house as sort of a failed experiment?"

Ellery stared at him, and he knew Jackson and Galen were doing the same.

Galen spoke into the shock. "Baby, I love you because you said that with a straight face. But my God—"

"Don't say it," John muttered, destroyed.

"I can't help it. You are such a—"

"Please?" John begged. "We're in front of friends!"

Galen shook his head. "Kitten on the freeway," he muttered. "Dear God, you have needed somebody to get you out of traffic your entire life."

Ellery watched in surprised fascination as a mottled red crept up John's neck and over his ears, blotching unevenly across his ginger-freckled face.

"It's a good thing I have you, then," he managed to say sulkily, and Galen gave a complacent shark-toothed smile.

"It is indeed."

THEY LEFT soon after dinner—although Jackson was absolutely adamant that they stay long enough for milk and cookies because, he said mutinously, they *all* needed to remember sweetness after that terrible conversation. Ellery insisted on cleaning up since Jackson had cooked dinner *twice*, and Jackson used the time to text Henry.

When Ellery came to bed, after setting out kibble and water for the two miscreants so they wouldn't decide to wake anybody up at fuck-you in the morning, he found Jackson sitting in bed with his knees drawn up in front of his body while he texted with the phone close to his chest.

The pose was very… self-protective. Vulnerable. And Ellery wasn't sure what to do with that. Probe and find out why? Leave it alone unless Jackson said something? Trust that it would come out?

A part of him wanted to laugh at that—the kind of laugh that sounded overhearty and sarcastic—but the part of him that loved Jackson was so impressed with his efforts to take care of himself, to take care of *them* as a relationship that needed constant love and care, thought that was perfectly reasonable.

Jackson got tired of being treated as though he was wounded.

As Jackson texted, oblivious to Ellery hovering in the doorway, Ellery saw his lips twist in that sort of brotherly disdain he and Henry treated each other with. It was only amusing because most of the time they really *were* brothers, as unlikely as that might have been when they started out. But now, after the two of them had watched each other's backs for the better part of a year, Ellery saw the kind of partnership between them that he saw in the best police officers or military units. Give each other shit? Unquestionably. Have each other's backs?

Until they drew their last breath.

"You wish, asshole," Jackson muttered, his thumbs dancing on the keyboard. "As. If."

Ellery's lips twitched, and he went to his dresser to put on his pajamas, first removing his once-worn casual clothes and laying them in a neatly folded pile on top. He was in the process of pulling out a soft cotton T-shirt when Jackson said loudly, "Did I say you should get dressed?"

Ellery's eyes flew open. "I beg your pardon?"

Jackson scowled at him, his fingers pausing on the phone. "Give me five minutes," he said. "Five minutes to finish the conversation, and then you and me have to dance naked so I can keep my faith in mankind."

Ellery was caught at a loss for words.

"I, uhm, thought sex would be off the, uhm, table—"

"Well, we're not having it on the table, are we? We're having it in bed!" Jackson held up a finger and texted madly before turning his attention back to Ellery. For a moment the tension of the conversation drained out of him, his green eyes grew soft, and Ellery knew for certain he had Jackson's complete attention.

"Please?" Jackson asked, his entire demeanor in the here and now with Ellery. "I *really* want to touch you."

Ellery took in Jackson's pose, registering that Jackson was shirtless, and his legs, which he'd thought had been covered with pajama bottoms, were under the covers and very possibly bare.

"Okay," he said softly. "But I warn you, I'm likely to fall asleep if you text for too long."

He slid into bed then and turned toward Jackson, relieved when that self-protective crouch relaxed a little. Jackson extended his legs under the covers and scooted toward the middle, sighing happily when Ellery spanned his hand across Jackson's taut midsection.

Too thin, Ellery thought. But still stronger than it had been. The ribs weren't prominent. And Jackson wasn't trying to hide his scars; he wasn't self-conscious, not anymore.

For a moment, as Jackson's texting went fast and furious, Ellery closed his eyes and indulged in the soft skin and the silken hair of Jackson's happy trail, finding the scars and tracing them simply because they led interesting places.

Playfully, Ellery slid his fingers down under Jackson's navel and along the happy trail, only to be halted by Jackson seizing his fingers from over the covers.

"Patience, Counselor," Jackson hummed, and Ellery leaned forward enough to lick a pink nipple.

"Haste, Detective," he countered, and Jackson's raw chuckle was enough to make Ellery grow hard in his briefs.

Jackson's texting increased in pace, and Ellery made another foray down south, this time tracing along the join of Jackson's thigh. Barely, just barely, he brushed the satiny skin of Jackson's own thickening length, and Jackson shuddered, clearly enjoying the teasing very much.

Above him, Jackson sucked air in through his teeth before letting out a long, patient breath.

"One more minute," he begged. "I'm telling Henry what to look for when Cowboy is talking. He needs a description of this Retty nightmare and anyone with a jacket. A few more seconds, please."

Ellery hummed in response and contented himself stroking Jackson's thigh with his fingertips, knowing this was important. Jackson's fingers continued to fly on his keyboard, and then he stopped, reaching out for the lamp.

As he stretched, Ellery heard his phone vibrate one last time and grimaced as Jackson checked it.

"Heh heh heh heh…."

Oh wow. Jackson's *filthiest* laugh.

A few more urgent taps and Jackson set the phone in the charger on the bed stand of the darkened room.

Then he tangled his fingers in Ellery's hair.

"That was playing dirty," he said, his voice strong and filled with a little bit of sexy evil.

"What are you going to do about it?" Ellery asked breathlessly. He threw his leg over Jackson's and undulated against his hip, letting Jackson feel his arousal, his need.

Jackson tugged gently on his hair, which he'd wet-combed when he'd changed for dinner, leaving the strands only a little stiff as they dried. Now Jackson cradled the back of his head, turning his face up and leaving him open for a ravaging, urgent kiss.

"This," he muttered, before catching Ellery's lower lip between his teeth and nipping.

Ellery let out a breathy gasp, arching his hips harder.

"And this," Jackson promised, rolling them both so Ellery was on his back and Jackson lay between his thighs. Ellery's knees were splayed, opening him up for predation, and he was so ready to be devoured.

Jackson didn't disappoint. He moved his hungry kisses down Ellery's jaw, down the hollow of his throat, down his chest. He stopped to nip and tug and lave first one nipple, then the other, and Ellery grabbed his shoulders with hard fingers and held on with all he had.

The thing about trusting your lover with his own health, his own sanity, he thought hazily, was that you could trust him to take care of your needs too.

Ellery had powerful needs, and he'd never been shy about advocating for his own pleasure.

Jackson's firm mouth on his cock told him Jackson was up for the job.

"Ah, God, yes…." It was Ellery's turn to tangle his fingers in Jackson's dark blond hair, anchoring himself to the here and now so he didn't flail when Jackson used one hand to squeeze his base as he sucked.

Hard strokes, with playful flicks of the tongue, left Ellery moaning, thrusting into the back of Jackson's throat, widening his thighs to give Jackson access to the cleft between.

Jackson's chuckle against Ellery's cockhead drove him even higher, and then—oh hells, he'd gotten the lube from under the pillow while Ellery had been otherwise occupied. Two fingers, unapologetic and in a bit of a hurry, breached him, and he moaned, a begging sound, beseeching Jackson to raise himself up and thrust inside.

Jackson sucked hard along his shaft, squeezing Ellery's bell with his lips before pulling off with a pop. "You want something?" he asked slyly, and Ellery could feel him humping the bed with his own sense of urgency.

"Could you…?" He was beyond dignity. With Jackson, dignity was never a thing. There was wanting, needing, *pleading*, but no dignity.

Dignity was for people who could afford to lose each other, and Ellery refused to lose Jackson, even for a night in bed.

"Yeah?" Jackson blew a cool breath across Ellery's damp slit, and Ellery released his head to pound at the mattress.

"*Please!*" he begged. "Please, Jackson, *fuck me—oh God, yes*!"

Their bodies knew one another now, and Jackson drove himself up, then spent a moment testing the entrance, making sure the stretching had been enough.

Ellery groaned in welcome, even to the bite of pain, because tonight that was what he needed. A nip of darkness, a hard, heedless thrust. Jackson grunted as he seated himself completely and then bent to whisper in Ellery's ear.

"Good?"

"So good," Ellery whispered, loving that Jackson wouldn't do this if it wasn't good.

Needing him to do it.

"Now?" Jackson murmured, pulling back a little and thrusting forward.

"Now," Ellery urged, and Jackson snapped his hips forward, growling aggressively as he did.

Ellery cried out, needing, shameless, and vocal. "*Yes*—fuck me! Hard! So hard! Oh God, Jackson—*yes*!"

And then he lost his words as Jackson's body, feral, vital, hard, and hungry, battered at his in a frenzy, the two of them lost in the ecstasy of fucking, the haze of absolute lust mixed with a hint of tenderness, the comfort of desire.

Ellery's climax rushed up at him almost too soon, but he couldn't stop it. He keened, locking his heels over Jackson's ass, his own asshole bearing down as he came, shooting come between them. Jackson's roar of completion echoed in his ears. Ellery could feel the hot and thick of him, the scalding pump of come, and it twisted the last shudder of orgasm from the pit of his balls.

It was too much! It was too much! It wasn't enough, and it never would be, and he found himself sobbing for more, for less, to stop, to come, to never, ever cease—

The final wave washed through him, and he gasped, his asshole, his chamber, his groin, all of it blooming, blossoming in the final spasm of a hard, frantic climax before Jackson sank into his body and groaned in his own total surrender.

Oh God.

Ellery was breathing so hard the roar of his own heartbeat echoed in his ears, and he almost missed Jackson's helpless murmur.

"Every time," he breathed. "I want you this badly *every* time."

"Me too," Ellery panted. "Every time."

Jackson's breathy chuckle sustained him as they gulped in air, tried to regain their breath after having all their oxygen sucked from their bodies in a tide of desire.

Finally Jackson slid to the side, and Ellery thought he could hear his own thoughts again over his heartbeat and a buzzing sound that kept pounding insistently against his brain.

"Oh shit," Jackson muttered, reaching for the phone that was vibrating in the charger.

"You're talking to Henry after *that*?" Ellery protested, not sure if Jackson had *ever* put texting over sex before.

"I gave him an emergency code if he needed me," Jackson muttered, scrambling into a sitting position. "This sounds pretty damned urgent."

He paused for a moment, hair disheveled, magnificent body naked and flushed in the moonlight seeping in over the blinds.

"Oh fuck," Jackson muttered, and Ellery stared at him in alarm.

"What?"

"Oh *fuck*!" Jackson tumbled out of bed and started throwing on the clothes he'd been wearing before getting in. "Ellery, call the cops. Send them to Isabelle's apartment." Jackson rattled off the number as he hit Call. "I'm coming, Henry! I'm coming!"

"Find them!" Henry cried, voice tinny and hollow through the phone. Then to somebody else, "Go! Go! Go!"

"Henry, I'm on my way!" Jackson was shoving his feet into still-laced tennis shoes without benefit of socks.

Ellery had grabbed his own phone from the charger and was responding to the panic in Jackson's voice, in Henry's, and he hit 911 as he grabbed for the clothes he'd left on top of his dresser.

"Nine-one-one, what's your emergency?" the calm voice asked on the other end of his phone line.

Just as gunshots echoed from Jackson's phone on speaker and into the sex-saturated dark of their once-safe bedroom.

There came the sound of something hitting flesh and Henry's scream of, "Die, bitch, *die*!" And then three more shots, and Ellery was screaming the address into his telephone as he and Jackson went sprinting for the car in the garage.

Damage Done

LATER, WHEN he could think beyond the panic, Jackson would remember to thank Ellery for driving like a bat out of hell.

During the trip itself, through thankfully empty streets on the rainy late evening weeknight, he spent his entire time focused on Henry's voice through the phone, starting with "Die, bitch, die!"

"Yeah," Henry gasped, his voice falling to a ragged whisper. "You run away, you fucking cow—keep bleeding as you go!"

"Henry!" Jackson spoke into the phone. "Henry, who's there?"

"She's gone," Henry breathed, but it sounded weak, like he wasn't quite present anymore. "She's there. They got away. The boy, Bobby's mom, they got away. Told them…."

He trailed off as Ellery made a hard turn that left Jackson's eyebrows and his last bowel movement somewhere at a red-light violation that would cost Ellery a fortune to pay.

The moment to gasp and grab the Holy Shit bar gave Jackson a braincell with which to think. The boy and Isabelle Roberts—Henry had put himself in harm's way to give them a chance to escape.

A female shooter. Henry had worked hard not to be all the bad things— racist, misogynist, homophobe—but Jackson supposed when somebody shot at you trying to get to a sweet middle-aged woman and a teenager, you had the right to slip.

"Where'd they go?" Jackson asked. God. Henry—Henry, his "padawan," his assistant, his *friend,* one of the best friends in a life blessed with great ones—and Jackson could hear him growing foggy and faint on the phone. Henry had risked his life for someone because Henry was, in his heart, a hero. Jackson had to think beyond the pugnacious young redneck who had become a part of Jackson and Ellery's life and think to what they were *all* doing with their lives, which was protecting people who couldn't protect themselves.

"Fire escape," Henry mumbled. "Out the back. Told Cowboy to help her…." For a moment his voice drifted off, and then he started to… to sing? "Da-da-dun da-da-dun da-da-dun da-da-dun dun da-da…."

Jackson frowned, and for a moment they were sitting on the couch talking about everything and nothing and killing aliens again.

"What in the hell is that?" he asked, almost indignantly.

"Cowboy music," Henry murmured. "Get it? Cowboy?"

For a moment, Jackson was incensed, his worry knotting his stomach, his adrenaline roaring through his ears. "How dare you," he snapped. "I'm gonna kill you myself!"

"You love me," Henry murmured, sounding more and more out of it, and Jackson's irritation faded as though wiped clean. "Now *Lance* is gonna be pissed," he said, his voice growing fainter. "I love Lance. Do you love Lance?"

"Not like you do," Jackson told him, voice gentling. "Tell me more about Lance."

"Pretty…," Henry mumbled, his voice fading even more. "So pretty… make sure he knows…."

Oh God. "Knows what?" Jackson snapped into the phone. "Henry, make sure he knows what?"

But there was no response save tortured breathing and a faint unconscious moan of pain.

Jackson had heard this sound before, too many times to count. Oh God.

"*Henry!*" he barked, peering frantically to the street as Ellery made another surprise left, this one knocking Jackson against the window. Ellery had *flown*, Jackson realized, because they were *there*. They were half a block from Isabelle Roberts's apartment, and while Jackson kept the phone pressed to his ear, his eyes darted around the unlit block, hoping for two figures dashing through the rain. "Do you see them?" he asked Ellery.

"I barely see the street," Ellery snapped tersely. "I'll let you out in front of the building so I can circle the block to look. Hurry! I hear sirens!"

First responders were on their way; Jackson knew that sound. He needed to get to Henry to get any more information Henry could give him.

And, oh God, to make sure Henry was okay.

Please let him be okay.

He didn't remember shutting the door of Ellery's Lexus when Ellery pulled up to the curb, but he must have. The apartment was on the second floor of an old, graceful two-story stucco building, and he raced up one set of stairs, hearing in the back of his mind the clatter of footsteps down the set of stairs on the other side of the building. But first… 2B, 3B, 7B—the door to 8B was wide open, and the nonstick stucco surface of the stairs was a mottled, rain-washed red.

Jackson ignored it and burst in, following the blood drops past the small kitchen on the left to a closed door shattered with bullet holes, splintered wood still falling like snow.

Jackson pushed the door open gingerly and took in a master bedroom, decidedly female, with a bloodstained white eyelet comforter and billowing eyelet curtains in front of the wide-open window in the back.

Henry was sprawled between the bed and the wall, bullet holes penetrating the wall chest-high above him, two of them.

Unlike the holes in the door, in which the wood splintered outward toward the hall, the holes above the bed were splintered in.

Henry had gotten some shots in through the door—that much was easy to see—but someone had gotten their own shots in through the short section of wall that outlined the bedroom, and taken Henry out.

"Henry!" Jackson fell to his knees on the floor, aware of the blood soaking through his jeans. "Man, how you doing?"

"Jackson," Henry croaked. "They went out the back. She went out the front. You gotta find 'em."

"I will, brother," Jackson murmured, smoothing Henry's lank blond hair back from his forehead. "But first you gotta get help."

"All alone," Henry mumbled. "Outside, all alone."

"We'll get them," Jackson promised. "Did you see who it was?"

"Woman," Henry mumbled. "Logo on the jacket. Good call. Sent them back."

Jackson could see it, see Henry checking the door, straight from getting Jackson's hurried texts about the danger Cowboy was in. He'd sent pictures of the Moms for Clean Living—the woman had obviously worn the logo on the jacket, but how? How? How did she know where Cowboy had been taken? Who had she followed? How had she known?

"You did good," Jackson told him, scanning his body. Henry's front had two spreading splotches of red, but most of the blood seemed to be coming from the back. Shit. Hollow points? But the holes in the wall were small, and they would have spread. Maybe .22s that had shattered on impact. Bad at close range, but not a .45 or 9mm. Hell, what did Jackson know? He *survived* gunshots, he didn't treat them.

He'd grabbed Henry's hand and was squeezing it, trying to still his racing mind, trying to *think*, when he heard a clatter on the stairs.

"Medics!" he cried out. "EMTs! In here!"

"Don't let Lance yell," Henry whispered, and the last time Jackson had knelt before a fallen friend, he hadn't been able to talk because of a punctured lung. Henry was hurt, he was bleeding, but he could move his arms, his toes.

"Course he'll yell," Jackson told him. "He'll yell at me. *Can you fuckin' hurry?*"

"Of course we can," murmured a squat man with thinning hair and a usually genial smile, who was hunkering down next to Jackson. "But we're gonna need you to move, okay? I mean, I know it's usually you who's bleeding, Rivers, but you do know this goes differently when you're not the one hurt, right?"

"Yeah," Jackson said.

"Find them," Henry mumbled, obviously losing consciousness again. "Can't let them get lost."

"Where they heading?" Jackson asked urgently, pushing to a squat but keeping his grip on Henry's square-palmed hand.

"Flophouse," Henry mumbled. "My apartment. Don't let them upstairs. Warp the kid for life."

Jackson let out a startled "Ha!" before he was elbowed aside, and he stood disoriented, trying to decide what to do next.

At that moment Ellery came storming in and the friendly EMT who knew Jackson on a first-name basis, started talking. "Hello, Henry, I see you got shot here. Is there anything we should know about you?"

"Blood type B-pos," he mumbled. "On PrEP protocol. Jackson can call my people."

Jackson looked at Ellery, who said, "I'll call his people. What do you need to do?"

Jackson scanned the billowing curtains and glanced again at Ellery, who swallowed and nodded.

"Go," Ellery said. "Go. You got your phone, be safe as you can. Find them."

In the silence after he spoke, they both heard an indignant "Mew!" and Jackson grimaced. Under the bed he could see two sets of paws, one gray, one black, barely peeking out from under the bed skirt, and he gave a startled little laugh.

"Shit," he said, indicating the paws. "Uhm, Ellery—"

Ellery grunted. "I'll get them," he muttered. "I can see the carriers in the closet from here. We'll find a place for them until Isabelle gets home."

Jackson nodded, and feeling oddly fortified by knowing that Isabelle's kittens would be safe, took two steps forward and kissed him hard on the mouth before turning to slide out the window and onto the fire escape.

It smelled like wet metal and piss, and Jackson put his feet on the outside rails of the ladder, holding himself steady as his running boots let him slide right down.

The rain had picked up velocity, and the temperature had dropped. Sacramento never did snow and rarely did ice, but Jackson felt a distinctly unfriendly cold as he squelched his way across the ragged grass/dirt patch that hugged the outside of the complex. The good news was, he could follow the smallish-sized prints—most likely Isabelle's—of basic tennis shoes like Jackson's, and the size tens of a growing boy.

Jackson could almost *see* the gangly lines of the kid as he ran a little to the side and behind Isabelle, hugging her hip like she was his last best hope.

Because she was.

Jackson pulled out his phone and called Ellery.

"Have you found them?" Ellery asked.

"No," Jackson told him. "But look around the room. See if you can spot Isabelle's cell phone. Let's see if she's got it. Call John and have *him* call her. Tell her I'm trying to find her. But…."

"But what?" Ellery asked.

"Do me a favor and find someplace *not* in the apartment. Ellery, how'd somebody find this kid? I am at my wit's end. Somebody *found this kid*. Tracked him to Isabelle's place. When did that happen? I'm thinking anything—bugs, previous surveillance, phone cloning, *something*. Find a landline, get hold of Crystal and AJ, and ask them what they can do to find out how this kid was tracked. And *then* go to John and Galen's and tell them *in person*. I'm starting to think that being lost in the rain could be the best thing to happen to these two people, but that doesn't mean I want to leave them out in the cold."

"I hear you," Ellery said. "What are you going to do?"

Jackson saw the place where Isabelle and Cowboy had found the sidewalk, marked by dissolving puddles of mud and dirt in roughly shoe-sized globs. He shone his phone light along the sidewalk, taking note of where the footsteps turned. Glancing around, he realized they'd gone in the mud for a good quarter of a mile, skirting yards, sticking to the alleyway where the trash was collected when they had to walk on concrete. What made them decide to hit the sidewalk now?

And then he heard the squeal of air brakes, the choking scent of diesel, and he saw the square giant's head of a city bus. It squeaked to a halt in front of the small bench and overhang, but as the doors opened—and Jackson sprinted through the rain toward the bus—nobody was eagerly getting on.

But a lone figure *hopped off*, holding an umbrella and leaning against the open door as a sputtering flame revealed the driver, trying to light a cigarette in the rain.

Jackson got there in time to hold the umbrella and shelter the older Black man from the wind.

"Thanks," the man breathed, exhaling a cloud of smoke. "If I'd missed my smoke break, I might have killed someone."

Jackson laughed. "Hey," he said, thinking hard, "you're running a little early, right?"

The man had tightly napped gray hair, painstakingly smoothed back from his forehead with pomade. That and the cigarette under the umbrella struck Jackson as charmingly old-fashioned. This man probably shined his shoes and pressed his uniform, and Jackson respected that kind of ethic.

"Yup," the driver said before another blissful drag. "Every night. I time myself two minutes after the bus heading down J. This one's heading for the train station, you know."

Jackson nodded. He'd seen the destination in the LED banner above the window.

"So there's a bus heading down J," he murmured. He'd ridden these buses a thousand years ago—and one awful, memorable night nearly a year and a half ago. He knew that bus headed down J Street and knew it had three or four stops to go.

God. He couldn't call John or Galen; their destination and their phones had been bugged or tracked. Who did he know in this part of town—

Oh God.

Jackson swallowed, knowing what he had to do.

But first, "Thanks," he said to the older man. "Stay warm and dry tonight, it's nasty."

And then he broke into a jog toward J Street, where the 5-F was about to head close to two blocks from Henry's brother's house, and where, hopefully, Jackson would be able to find somebody who could pluck their two fugitives from the rain.

"MY BROTHER'S *what*?"

David Worrall—known as Dex from his adult film days—sounded really rattled on the phone, and Jackson didn't blame him.

"He's being taken to the hospital now," Jackson told him, feeling cold and desperate and wretched. "I'm sorry, Dex, this isn't how I wanted to tell you. But he put himself in harm's way protecting Isabelle Roberts—"

"Mrs. Bobby's Mom?" Dex blurted, and there was a note of… of wonder in his voice when he called her this childish name. Jackson, whose own mother had betrayed him with bad drugs and bad boyfriends pretty much from the day he was born, knew that sound—he heard it in his own voice when he spoke of good mothers, and he'd met Isabelle and knew her for one.

"John and Galen brought her a kid to take care of," Jackson told him. "We're pretty sure Henry put himself between the shooter and the kid and told her to get to the flophouse. I've been to the bus stop, Dex. The only bus that'll get her there is—"

"The 5-F," Dex said, and Jackson recognized the sound of somebody sprinting for shoes, keys, a jacket.

"Send Kane and the kid to a friend's," Jackson blurted. "Don't tell me who. We have no idea how the shooter knew where to find the kid—phones are suspect."

Dex made a low moan in his throat. "Can do," he rasped. "Which way should I turn when I come out of my street?"

It was a good question—a *great* question. Two blocks ahead, Jackson could see the lights of the bus brighten as it came to a halt in front of a covered bench. If Dex turned right and was in front of the bus, he'd be looking in the wrong place. If he turned left and the bus had passed him… well, he'd at least find Jackson, and they could look together.

"Call me when you're there," Jackson huffed. "I'm about two blocks behind. I should be able to see where it is."

"Gotcha. *Kane!*" Dex rasped before he hung up. "Baby, you need to listen and do what I say, okay? Grab Frances, throw on her jacket, and—" The phone went dead, and Jackson breathed a sigh of relief.

Dex had remembered not to use the phone.

Jackson sighted the bus, which had just started moving again. Checking both ways as he came to a darkened intersection, he jogged grimly on.

Dex called to ask which way to turn—left, Jackson told him, hoping—and after that he didn't remember much. He lost sight of the bus, because it was *supposed* to be faster than he was, and was startled almost out of his shoes when a glaring set of headlights coming in the opposite direction swung around, cut into the street in front of him, and pulled a dirty U-turn until it came to a halt at the stop sign of yet another darkened street. This part of Sacramento was largely residential—not a lot of streetlights, just the impression of people sleeping peacefully behind the patter of rain in the leaves.

Which was why Jackson stared uncertainly at the black SUV until the window cranked down and the inside light went on. Jackson got a glimpse of Henry's brother—truly one of the most masculinely beautiful men Jackson had ever seen, with blond hair, a rectangular face, a charming twist of a smile, and dimples—who was wearing a wet windbreaker and an expression of urgency on his face.

"I got 'em," he said, indicating two passengers in the back seat with a jerk of his chin. "Get in!"

Jackson's stomach muscles turned to jelly, and he realized how tight he'd been holding them. He hopped into the passenger seat, and as the door thunked shut and the heater hit him, he suddenly felt the cold March rain deep in his bones and started shivering.

He took a couple of deep breaths, and Henry's brother—showing an empathy that had made him one of the founding models of John's porn empire before he quit to become a family man and help run the place—idled at the empty intersection, checking for cars on the nearly deserted street until Jackson got his bearings.

"All right, Mr. Rivers," he said grimly. "They're safe, we're here. Where do we go next?"

Jackson groaned and leaned his head back against the headrest.

And that, he thought, was the million-dollar question.

"Think. Think, think, think…," he muttered to himself. Normally he would start making phone calls, but he'd already pushed his luck calling Dex. The problem was, he didn't *know* how the shooter had found their way to Isabelle's place. With a frown he thought maybe he could ask her.

"Hi, Isabelle," he said, turning in his seat. To his side he said, "Dex, go down J Street and head toward the Carmichael/Fair Oaks area. I'll give you directions as we get closer—"

"Is this K-Ski and Billy?" Dex asked, and Jackson gave a sigh of relief because he and Dex knew some of the same people.

"Yeah. We need people who can make Cowboy feel safe and who know who Isabelle knows." Billy used to model for John and Dex's company. He'd moved on to working in one of their subsidiary companies, but like most of the kids who worked at Johnnies, he remembered Isabelle Roberts fondly.

"I still see Billy," Isabelle said softly from the back. "He brought me a bag of romance books for Christmas."

Jackson turned in his seat again and really looked at the woman. She was shivering in Henry's hooded sweatshirt and a pair of pajama bottoms that were muddy at the cuffs. She'd been wearing slippers with rubber soles when she'd fled out the fire escape, not sneakers as he'd thought, and they were coated in mud and plastered to her feet. He saw a faint glimmer of pink peeking out at the ends and thought fondly that the woman had probably gotten a pedicure recently, and the graying hair plastered to her head had been cut and streaked. Bobby told him once that his mom had grown old quick in their small town, but once Bobby was able to move her to Sacramento and give her a job she enjoyed, she'd gotten young and happy again.

Jackson hoped Isabelle Roberts could recover from the events of this night, because she deserved to be young and happy some more.

"Well, somebody raised him right," Jackson said with a small smile. "And yeah. I think Detective Kryzynski and Billy might be the two perfect people to look after you." His smile slipped a little. "Isabelle, can you and your friend tell me what happened? I want to make sure it doesn't happen again."

Isabelle nodded and, Jackson noted, tightened her grip on the hand of the young man sitting, silent and big-eyed, next to her. "But first," she said, "my kittens—Lizzie and Janette? Did you—"

"Ellery got them," Jackson said, hoping that was true. "I'm sure we'll find somebody to look after them."

"Oh thank you," she said, all gratitude, and then, soberly, she added, "So about tonight." She gave the boy a reassuring smile. "John and Galen had already gotten young Cowboy something to eat, but he agreed to come to my apartment to clean up a little, get some clean clothes, and maybe eat a little more."

"She made me soup," Cowboy blurted before giving Isabelle a shy glance. "My mom only ever made soup from a can. And got bread from a bag. This was… real," he whispered, glancing away.

"What kind of soup?" Jackson asked, hoping to ease the boy's mind.

"Potato and onion," came the prompt reply. "Which sounds sort of boring, but it wasn't."

Jackson grinned, taking in the recently buzzed hair and the freshly scrubbed appearance—as well as the solid grained-in tan and dirt that could only come from being exposed to the elements for too long. "Surprise food," he said. "Promising."

He got a smile—and the teeth, too, looked freshly scrubbed. "For me, it was like, 'Surprise! There's more food!'"

Jackson chuckled softly. "Did Henry eat with you?" he asked, and before the kid could shrink in on himself, he added, "because *I* made him soup before he went to sit down with you, but he can pack away a *lot* of food."

That earned him a wistful smile. "He said he was keeping us company," Cowboy confided, "but he had a whole bowl."

"Good," Jackson told him soberly. "He'll have lots of energy. He'll need it."

Cowboy's eyes glossed over. "Is he okay?" he asked, nakedly pleading. "He was so nice to me, helped me cut my hair, helped me wash, and put stuff on my skin so it didn't hurt." The boy held out wrists with gauze wrapped loosely around them, and Jackson figured Henry had helped treat the chafing sores that came from wearing grime-stiff clothing for too long.

"He got hurt," Jackson said carefully, aware Dex was holding on to every word. "Dex and I are going to check on him once we get you two someplace safe. Then I'm going to go out and figure out who hurt him, but first I need your help. I know you ate, and I know everybody changed into their jammies." Henry had been wearing flannel PJ's much like Cowboy's— Jackson figured Isabelle kept a pair for him from the nights he'd gone over to her place to help keep an eye on a new charge. Sometimes kids got kicked out on the street because their parents were assholes, but sometimes there just wasn't enough mental health access out there, particularly for juveniles coming into things like schizophrenia. Henry had brought more than one kid in from the cold to a severe care facility after John and Galen had brought them to Isabelle's.

"Isabelle went to change too," Cowboy said softly. "Henry and I sat on the special couch mats… you know, to keep the creepers off."

Jackson had noted those, too, as he'd run into the snug little apartment. "Red plaid?" he asked, not because it mattered, but because getting a detail right would make Cowboy more confident in his own judgment.

"Yeah," Cowboy murmured. "Henry said they were just until we knew I was all cleaned up." He sighed. "I like being clean. You don't think about that when you're little. How nice it is to not be dirty."

"Well, you're in the right place," Jackson said. "Because we're all partial to showers ourselves."

Cowboy gave him a little smile then, a hopeful one, and Jackson's stomach roiled. God, he'd been in this position before, but he would always, always be afraid of letting that trust down. He had a terrible need to call his brother then, to check on the kid not too much younger than this one that had become more than a rescue or a victim—had become family.

This kid had a better place waiting for him. It was up to Jackson and his friends to get him there.

"So there you were," Jackson said, aware that Dex was making good time on the nearly deserted, rainy streets. He reckoned they had about twenty minutes before he was banging down K-Ski's door, begging for asylum, and it was time to get a move on. "You were clean, you were dry and fed, settling down to watch some tube—"

"And talk to Henry," Cowboy said. "He said it was important we talk."

"About what?" Jackson asked casually. But he was fooling nobody, and he knew it when Cowboy shrank into himself, like a marshmallow in hot butter.

"About the bad lady," Cowboy whispered.

Jackson nodded. "Were you ready to be brave then?" he asked soberly.

Cowboy nodded, and Jackson felt a moment's vertigo from staying turned around in his seat for so long. He fought it and wondered if he could give Henry's brother some sort of good-driving award for not killing him like this.

"Good boy. So how about you be brave for me now?"

Cowboy swallowed. "When I escaped from the place—the Clean Living place," he whispered. "That's when I saw her. She… she's fast. Like that soccer lady? Megan?"

"Rapinoe?" Jackson asked. "So she's fast and fit?"

Cowboy nodded vigorously. "Like she trained to catch boys," he whispered, and part of Jackson wanted to smile, because that sounded like some Roald Dahl villain shit, but part of him was horrified, because the boy was *afraid*.

"Did she almost catch you?" Jackson asked.

Cowboy swallowed. "I think she caught Caleb," he whispered. "Caleb went back inside the Clean Living place, to make sure the other boys were okay and maybe see if they could get away. And the lady…." He swallowed.

"Did she have a name?" Jackson asked.

"Retty," Cowboy said promptly. "They… they called her Retty." He glanced down. "She put me in the back of the van after my mom gave me to the people."

Jackson nodded. "Your mom shouldn't have done that," he said softly. "Maybe she got scared. Raising a boy is a big job. Sometimes people like this promise they can help."

Cowboy whispered, "It's because I was bad."

Jackson swallowed, and part of him wanted to shove this away and not talk about it, but part of him needed the boy to get it out now so he knew he'd be okay.

"How bad?" he asked. "Like, muddy shoes in the living room bad? Forget to do your chores bad?"

"I kissed a boy," Cowboy whispered. "I'm a fag."

Jackson breathed in carefully. "That's not bad," he said. "Except the name-calling. That's bad. But the kissing a boy? Everybody in the car's done it, kid. You're in good company."

Cowboy batted clotted eyelashes at him. "You've kissed a boy?" he asked, almost desperate.

"I kissed my fiancé tonight, before I ran into the darkness to find you," Jackson told him. "Did this Retty person say you were bad?"

Cowboy nodded, his face streaked with tears. "She said we were all bad. It was her job to train us up so we didn't all go to hell."

Jackson blew out a breath. "Train you how?" he asked.

A shake of the head. "Don't know. She scared me. I escaped before I could find out."

"That's not *bad*," Jackson told him with feeling. "That's *smart*. Good for you, getting away like that."

Cowboy swallowed. "I met the two men in front of the church," he said. "And… and at first I thought they were just a trick."

For a moment Jackson was thrown off, but he found his footing again. "They're not like that," he said kindly. "You're so very young."

The boy nodded. "But they took me to go get a burger. And I was so happy. They got me a burger and a shake and took me back to the car and…." He caught his breath. "That's when I saw her. She… she'd been watching us from her car. Like she was there for food too and… and she just *saw* us. And she was playing on her phone and… and she *saw me*." His voice actually squeaked.

Jackson frowned. "Did you tell John and Galen—the two men who brought you burgers—that you saw her?"

"I said we had to go," Cowboy said. "I… I was so scared. She stared at us and played on her phone and stared some more. And they asked me why I was so scared, and I… I couldn't tell them about Caleb, how he screamed when he went back. I tried, but I… I cried a lot. And I thought we left her at the hamburger place, but Henry and I were all clean and dry on the couch, and there was a knock at the door, and it was *her*, and she said her name was…." He frowned, like he was going to try to reason it out, but the words took over his mouth instead. "I don't remember!" he almost sobbed. "It was something else I don't remember! And I told Henry it was *her*, the *bad lady*, and Henry told me and Isabelle to run, to escape out the window."

Isabelle released the boy's hand and wrapped her arm around his shoulders instead. "It's okay," she murmured.

"He… he made sure we were gone," Cowboy said. "And then he let her in, and we were on the ground running, and we heard shots, and…." He tried to catch himself, but he was too far gone. "And I don't know if Henry's *okay*!" he wailed.

Isabelle wrapped her arm around the boy's head protectively and gave Jackson a speaking glance.

Jackson nodded at her and turned around gratefully, his head spinning from the story and the enforced time staring backward. His stomach, which had spent the evening being gently catered to with the brothy wonton soup and the fresh bread, was suddenly pitching and weaving like a drunken sailor on a stormy deck.

But most of that, he knew, was the kid's story.

"Okay," he murmured. "All right, then. We know what we're dealing with."

"You know who hurt my brother?" Dex asked.

Jackson shook his head. "Only kind of," he replied. "But we know how she found them. He said she kept playing with her phone. I'm going to bet that the meetup was random. She was out for a burger. Maybe she was hunting kids like Cowboy—hell, maybe she was even hunting *him* since he escaped a couple weeks ago, but suddenly he's delivered into her lap."

"But he's with two men," Dex said, like suddenly he understood the significance.

"Exactly. So I'm not great with phones and clones, but if she saw John and Galen *in* the burger place and then did the phone thing—"

"How do you know she didn't simply follow them?" Dex asked.

"Because it took her a while," Jackson said. "It would have been easier to just grab him before they entered Isabelle's apartment. She was armed. She could have taken them out easily—hell, all three of them. But she had to *find* them first. I need…." He sighed. "God, I need for your brother to be okay."

Next to him, he heard Dex swallow. "You know, he served for *nine* years, and the only times he's been hurt have been here in Sacramento."

"That you know of," Jackson told him gently. "Dex, your brother's tougher than you might ever know. What he did? Making sure Isabelle and Cowboy were out of the apartment building and stalling before he opened the door for this… this *monster*? That was smart. He was keeping that woman engaged for as long as possible. She shot him *in* Isabelle's room. He led her down the hall before slamming the door in her face and having a shootout through a wall. And he *tagged* her. He got her. She was bleeding when she left. It's the only reason she didn't go after them. He's smart and strong and tough enough." Jackson's head of steam escaped. "And God…. *God*, I hope he's okay."

To his horror he heard his voice shake, and he glanced down at his hands as he pulled his phone from the pocket of his hooded sweatshirt.

Still stained a mottled, rain-washed pink.

Henry's blood.

He fought back a hard shudder and dried his cold fingers on the merely-damp T-shirt under the hoodie so he could call Ellery.

"Jackson—"

"Safe," he said, hoping Ellery would take that to mean him *and* Isabelle and Cowboy. "Will call in ten."

There was a pause then, as though Ellery was trying to digest this and figure out why the code-speak, but it didn't last long. "Thanks for calling. See you where Lance works."

"ASAP," Jackson said, letting out a breath, and then before he could hang up, Ellery spoke again.

"Thanks," he said softly, "for calling."

Jackson closed his eyes, grateful for Ellery, as he so often was. "Course," he said. "Later."

He hung up and took a deep breath.

"That's all you're going to say?" Dex asked.

Jackson opened up his phone and started playing with the settings, holding his finger to his lips and letting out a sigh when he saw that nothing—recording, visual surveillance, proximity alerts—had been activated without his knowledge.

"Ellery and I had dinner with John and Galen tonight," Jackson said when he was satisfied. "So they left their meeting, saw this Retty shitbag without knowing it, then took Cowboy to Isabelle's house. She saw them— I'm betting it was sheer accident, but she was *tracking* them. I've been to the burger joint John took the kid to. It's not that big, and the parking lot is even smaller. Cowboy saw her, was too scared to say anything, and she got close enough to clone John or Galen's phone. *That's* how she knew where the kid was. She waited until they left, but she didn't realize Henry was there too. Maybe she was circling the block trying to find parking when he arrived—Ellery had difficulty doing that. What I *do* know is that John and Galen left Cowboy in Henry and Isabelle's care, then came to *our* place to talk about what Cowboy had seen."

Dex sucked in a breath. "And Retty-the-shitbag waited until she saw things calming down in Isabelle's place." He paused and said something that had been bothering Jackson too. "She knocked on the door first—I heard that. She knocked on the door, asked to see Cowboy, and Henry shined her on until they were clear out the back."

"Yeah," Jackson said. "Zero law enforcement experience. Any cop knows to set a watch on the back, but she was there by herself, and it didn't occur to her. Also instead of running around to find them, she engaged in a gunfight, which is panicky and stupid."

"Apparently she's not so tough when she's not beating the gay out of terrified teenagers," Dex said bitterly.

"Or stripping schools of their libraries," Jackson added, but while his mouth was going, he was still thinking. "But there's more to Shitbag Retty than ignorance and homophobia," he muttered.

"What?" Dex asked.

Jackson grunted. "Don't worry about it. Let's get Isabelle and Cowboy safe, and then we can get to Med Center and check on your brother." He shuddered. "God… Ellery's got to tell Lance—"

"I'll talk to Lance," Dex said grimly. "You had it right. Henry's not the kind of guy to sit and do nothing. He was being a hero tonight. Lance will see that."

Jackson didn't want to correct him, but he was pretty sure Henry's boyfriend was going to be much more upset that Henry got wounded on Jackson and Ellery's watch than that.

"Sure," he murmured, still thinking about Shitbag Retty's motives. "Isabelle?" he asked, pitching his voice just over the quiet engine and the sound of tires on rainy streets.

"Yes, Mr. Rivers?"

"Is he asleep yet?"

"No," came a rusty *young* voice. Fourteen—had his voice changed yet? Jackson didn't think so. "What do you need, sir?"

"Sh… uhm, Retty. She worked for the, uhm, Clean Living people, right?"

"Yessir."

"Did she have a boss? Did you see one? I mean, yeah, she gave you a ride, and she chased after you and your friends, but that's sort of flunky work. Did she ever talk about somebody? Give you the impression that she answered to someone? She's bad and she's scary, Cowboy, but we need to find out who she works for."

"So you can get her fired?" Cowboy asked uncertainly.

"So I can get them *arrested*," Jackson said firmly. Inside he was thinking violent, bloody thoughts. He knew people. Oh boy, did he and Ellery know people. There was a tiny corner of the desert that was hip deep in disappeared bodies and mysterious deaths, and nobody would ever need to be the wiser. These women could just… disappear. He took a deep breath and shook away that idea. No. *No*. It went against everything that Ellery stood for, and while Jackson had no qualms with moral ambiguity, he couldn't, *wouldn't* betray Ellery's convictions that way.

Besides….

"If they're arrested, what they stand for will be rendered… tainted. Evil. People might think twice before they hurt people like you or Henry or me or Dex because they don't like who we are. So yeah. Arrested. Not fired. Put in prison. Where they belong."

He could say that now because Henry was going to be okay. Henry *had* to be okay.

God help them all if Henry wasn't okay.

"So," Jackson asked on a shaky breath, as Dex followed what was now Fair Oaks Boulevard down into Carmichael. "Can you remember any names?"

"Someone…," Cowboy whispered. "Someone called Mrs. Twitty?"

Jackson's eyebrows went up. "Mrs. Tweety?"

"No… that's what Retty called her. Twitty. But it wasn't her real name. She… she welcomed us. Was dressed real pretty. In pink and cream with a necklace."

"Classy," Jackson said, and he wasn't being sarcastic—he got how sometimes a woman who was put together could frighten a kid who was dressed in hand-me-downs and needed a bath.

"Yeah," Cowboy said, nodding. "She gave directions. Said, 'Put him upstairs in the room with the four. We'll have our first meeting tonight.' And Retty sort of laughed." His voice fell. "It was a mean laugh," he murmured. "I didn't like that laugh."

And hence, Jackson thought, that organized escape. "You got good instincts, kid," he said, and at that moment, Dex took a left, which gave Jackson a block to finish this interrogation. "One more thing," he said. "You ran away a couple of weeks ago, right?"

"Yessir," the kid said, and it was the "sir" that tugged at Jackson's heart.

"Have you met any other escapees, any other kids that started out at the Clean Living place?"

Cowboy's voice dropped. "We don't talk about it," he whispered. "Nobody talks about it. You talk about your tricks or who's giving away food or where you can get a bath. Nobody talks about that place. Nobody."

"Okay, then," Jackson said, his voice going soft. "No more of that tonight. We're going to find you a place to sleep and some folks to keep an eye out for you—and maybe to take you on a trip or something, somewhere you don't have to worry about these people, and you and Isabelle can get some rest. How's that sound?"

"Okay…." The boy's voice wobbled. "You don't suppose… my mom? Would she want me back?"

Jackson wanted to claw at his chest and rip his heart out so it didn't have to feel like this. "I don't know," he said at last. "But we can't find out until this mess is over, okay? If she *does* want you back, this will put her in danger. If… well, if she doesn't…."

"She's the one who gave me to Retty in the first place," Cowboy said, sounding destroyed and proving once again that kids were smart and illusions were a luxury someone like Cowboy had never been able to afford.

"Jackson," Isabelle said, "I have some money. I could take him—"

"John and I will pay," Dex said. "And we'll discuss particulars later. I've got an idea, but I gotta run it by Kane first. But yeah, we're calling this a company team-building exercise, Isabelle, and you're not worrying about a penny." He sighed. "And you let us know if you need out," he finished, but Jackson got a look at Mrs. Bobby's Mom, her arms around Cowboy, holding him to her chest and rocking him back and forth.

She wiped her face with the back of her hand and shook her head. "Not going anywhere," she whispered. "Don't worry, sweetheart. I'll want you. I'm not going anywhere."

Next to him, Dex took an uneven breath, and Jackson did the same.

"Here we are," Dex muttered. "A block from K-Ski's house. It's still pissing down rain. Jackson, there's an umbrella under the seat."

Jackson stared at him, soaking wet from his run down J Street. "Sure, Dad," he said, some of his natural sarcasm slipping through.

Dex gave him a flat look. "Shut up and take the umbrella," he snapped. "I can control very little about this situation, but you can take the goddamned umbrella."

And Jackson remembered that Dex *was*, for all intents and purposes, a dad. He and his husband had been caring for Kane's niece, Frances, for the last four years. They'd been doing teachers' meetings and school presentations and juggling schedules to make sure that kid was the most beloved child in the state. And no, watching this kid, who had been so much like *all* of them at one point or another, be terrified for his life was *not* okay.

"Fine," Jackson said, taking it, and then glaring at Henry's brother. "It's pink. It's got pink fucking flamingos all over it. I'll take it, but by God, I will find a way to make you pay for this."

"I can live with that," Dex muttered, and then Jackson took the umbrella and went trotting down the sidewalk.

Both Detective Sean Kryzynski and his boyfriend, Billy, answered the door in sweats and T-shirts, hair askew, eyes squinted against the light, after being awakened out of what Jackson hoped was a sound sleep. He assumed so—Billy was going to school and working as a manager at one of the retail places John and Dex owned, where they could funnel kids who'd made their movies and were ready to move on, and Sean was a police officer who, by definition, worked fifty or so hour workweeks.

At their feet, a small dachshund yipped until Billy bent down and scooped him up with an "Enough," and then a spate of what might have been fearsome Spanish, but the dog kept staring at him with adoring eyes.

"Sorry," Billy mumbled, smoothing the little dog's fur. "Rivers, the fuck you doing here?"

Jackson swallowed, and Kryzynski's cop sense kicked in. "What's wrong?"

Jackson kept the explanation quick and to the point and watched as both men grew sober and attentive.

"I'll call in for the week," Sean said. "Can I tell Andre?"

Andre was Sean's partner on the force, and Jackson nodded. "Yeah, that's fine. But...." He paused and hoped Sean would fill in the rest.

"Nobody else on the force," Sean said, understanding. "These women—they've got an ungodly amount of pull."

"Nobody wants to piss off the big *Papi*," Billy said sourly. "I'm pretty sure he doesn't give a shit if people are gay—enough of them buy John's porn."

Well, yes, sexual repression *did* breed hypocrisy, but they had to get past that tonight.

"Here's the thing," Jackson said softly. "If law enforcement gets their hands on this boy, the DA is going to need him to testify, and they're going to keep him in custody, and guys... he's terrified. I want to get to the bottom of this, and I *really* want to get the fucker who got Henry, but...." He swallowed. Kryzynski used to be a law-and-order man, down to his toes. But a year and a half in Jackson and Ellery's circle had made him an ally—and the kind of man who could fall in love with Billy with his eyes wide open about Billy's time as a sex worker. He'd grown a lot—and he had law enforcement ties and knew how to handle a weapon and defend people.

Had he grown enough?

"You want him to be safe first," Sean said slowly. "I hear you. You're right, Jackson—he probably *will* have to testify at some point, but until the police know who they're looking for and what they'll find, it will be best to keep him hidden."

"I'll do anything," Billy said unhappily, "but are we just going to shove them in the house and tell them not to stick their faces out?"

Then Jackson gave them both a ragged grin and suggested what he'd been thinking ever since Dex said he and John would pay the tab.

Not Disneyland

"Disneyland?" Ellery asked as Jackson and Dex made their way into the small surgery waiting room they'd been shown to after giving Henry's name. Crystal and AJ were sitting behind him, appearing tired and worried, as did Jackson's sister—and Ellery's paralegal—Jade and her boyfriend, Mike, sitting kitty corner to them, and Galen, who was obviously stoic and in pain and exhausted in the bank of chairs to the rear of the tiny room. John had moved a stack of newspapers under Galen's injured leg and was pacing back and forth out of everybody's line of sight, pausing every time he drew near Galen to brush his shoulder with anxious fingers.

Ellery knew there were more people coming. As soon as Crystal had deactivated the tracking app that had been remotely opened on his phone after it had been cloned, John had been texting the boys Henry and Lance mentored almost nonstop, *as* he was pacing. Part of that had involved finding a friend to get Isabelle's kittens out of Ellery's car and take them safely home, but most of it had been for Henry.

Henry had come to Sacramento nearly a year ago, and he'd been surly and angry and deeply disappointed by life.

Once he'd come to accept himself, though, and both the good and the bad in his own heart, he'd blossomed. Ellery hadn't been the only one to see it. Henry was now not just worried about—he was *beloved*.

Which was why Ellery had understood Jackson's need to haul out into the rainy dark to find Isabelle and Cowboy and get them to safety. But that didn't mean he'd been okay with it, even knowing Jackson had no choice in the matter.

"Shh!" Jackson held his finger to his lips. "Nobody but us knows. I'm, uhm, calling Cotton and his friends to see if they can, you know, escort them for a couple days. After a week, at the very least, we should know what we're working with." Jackson let out a breath, and Ellery filled in the blanks.

"And if we need to contact the federal marshals or not," he said grimly.

Jackson was sopping wet and probably not aware he was shivering hard enough for his teeth to chatter. "I swear to God, Ellery, if I thought they'd be safer in the hands of the authorities, I'd call them."

Ellery nodded grimly. "I hear you," he said. "And I know they're in good hands. I just… do we know what our next move is?"

Jackson opened his mouth, his shoulders and feet already turning toward the door, and Ellery felt a shaft of fear. This was not the first time Jackson had gone haring off into a dark night, angry and hurt and dangerous. The first time, he had almost not returned. Ellery didn't have nightmares often—certainly not on the scale of Jackson's demons—but when he did, he would dream about the day he came home to find Jackson asleep and feverish in their bed, except… Jackson wasn't there.

And Billy Bob was gone too.

"Stay," he blurted, reaching out to catch Jackson's hand. "Just… stay until we know if he's stable. Stay and plan with me and John and Galen. If nothing else it will give them something to do. Stay and see how your friend is doing. Please."

Stay, so if the worst happens, you're not alone. Please, baby, just for a moment, just for a heartbeat, stay and comfort me.

Because Ellery loved Henry too.

Jackson's half-out-the-door position shifted, and he turned his shoulders toward Ellery and squeezed his hand. "I was going to get the flophouse guys," Jackson murmured. "Dex said they're all gathered in the entrance to the ER. They won't know to come in here."

He leaned forward then, as if to kiss Ellery's cheek, and Dex, who had been at his shoulder, said, "I'll get them, Jackson. I think Kane's here too, with Frances."

Ellery took in David Worrall's strained expression. "Go," he said. "Bring them back here. Worrying in a big group is a lot easier than worrying alone."

Dex nodded, and Jackson watched him go. Ellery could feel his muscles straining to follow him, but after a brief squeeze of the hand, Jackson focused his attention on Ellery and gave a brief acknowledging smile.

And a shudder.

God, Ellery knew how much Jackson hated hospitals.

"We need to talk to John and Galen," he said after a moment, before peering around. "Where's Lance?"

Ellery grimaced. "Trying to find somebody to come in for him and work his shift," he said, not wanting to tell Jackson about Lance's real state of mind. "And probably—"

"Freaking the fuck out," Jackson muttered.

Ellery gave a little laugh. "Never stopped you from doing your job." He took a deep breath and gave one last hand squeeze. "Come on. Let's update."

John had stopped his manic pacing, and Galen was standing, going through a set of stretches that appeared to be a familiar regimen. Both men were wearing sweats and hoodies, and Ellery was surprised to see Jackson pull out his phone and snap a picture.

"What in the *hell*?" Galen demanded, honestly surprised.

"It's for Henry," Jackson said, only a muscle in his cheek betraying his worry. "Because if I tell him you were wearing *sweats* and not a suit, he'll think I'm lying. He told me once he was pretty sure you had cotton suits made, complete with vests and jackets, to sleep in."

Galen's surprised snort of laughter was followed by an immediate panicked expression of horror.

"It's okay if you laugh," John said dryly, coming up behind him and putting a gentle hand on his hip. "He wouldn't have told you that if he wasn't trying to lighten the mood."

Galen swallowed and then nodded. "I… I am most upset," he said, obviously tamping down on a great deal more than "upset." "To take a simple job of babysitting and use it to become a hero? Rude." Galen faked a disgusted sniff. "Had to make it all about saving the nice lady and the kid. Not a thought for the rest of us. How could he?"

"That's my boy," John murmured quietly, and Galen nodded, obviously calmed down enough to assume his favorite mantle of disdain.

"Good," Jackson said. "I need you both here in mind *and* spirit. I assume Crystal has taken care of your phones?"

"Yes," Galen said, disgruntled. "Apparently mine was the culprit—it had been cloned, I assume, when I was sitting at one of the tables under the eaves while John and Cowboy went in to get food."

"So she must have seen you all go in," Jackson said, nodding. "Okay. Good. I think it was a really shitty accident that had Retty there—"

"Cowboy confirmed her name?" Ellery asked, and Jackson made a face.

"And gave me another one—sort of," he said. "And an idea about power structure. I'm going tomorrow to talk to them again, after the kid's had a good night's sleep and feels safe, and then they're all vamoosing."

"Wait—who all?" John asked.

When Jackson spoke next, Ellery could tell he still didn't entirely trust that they weren't being bugged. "K-Ski and his boyfriend."

John and Galen glanced at each other. "Oh," John said carefully, his eyes darting around. "I think it's safe to talk, Jackson. Are they okay with the situation?"

This time Ellery actually saw his shoulders twitch. "You're right," Jackson muttered. "Dammit. It's me and hospitals. Ramps up my paranoia. You wouldn't be*lieve* how bad. Anyway, yeah. Dex'll tell you the details, though. He offered to pony up the money." Jackson had spent, quite literally, years of his life recovering from injuries he'd incurred on the job. The more he came in, the worse his fear of hospitals got. He hadn't said a word until now, but he was sure John knew how much Jackson hated it here.

He loved Ellery—and Henry—more.

"Course," John said with a shrug. "Whatever they need." Then he asked the obvious question. "We're not trusting them in protective custody?"

Jackson and Ellery both shook their heads. "Not until we get a better idea of what's going on," Jackson said. "I can tell you what I know, and then tomorrow, when we're doing research and running down leads, you'll have an idea of where to go with this."

"These women wield a lot of power," Ellery said quietly. "Still. You know that. And for better or worse, if Cowboy comes forward to testify, he's not the one who's going to be exposed."

"I can handle it," John said staunchly, but Ellery found himself, surprisingly enough, shaking his head.

"You and Galen do far too much good," he said. "And if you ever tell my mother I said that, I'll deny it. But you protect a lot of vulnerable young men with your businesses, and they would be exposed too. No. Let's see if we can run down some information that will allow the DA to build a case without exposing Cowboy or Henry to having to testify." He glanced at Galen, who, he had to admit, had become to him what Henry had become to Jackson in the last year. "You know how these things work, Galen. You know that the people who end up hurt are very often the ones in the spotlight, not the ones who committed the crime."

Galen grunted and nodded. "I find your keenness of intellect quite disturbing sometimes," he said at last.

"I've heard worse," Ellery returned, in what Jackson liked to call his "prissy" voice. "Jackson, give us some details before this room gets very crowded and Lance gets here."

His voice might have wobbled on the part about Lance getting there, and Jackson shot him a sharp glance that said he knew more about Lance's fury that Henry had gotten hurt on their watch than Ellery had first let on.

Jackson outlined what they knew, his twitchiness easing as he got deeper into the case.

"So this 'Retty' carries out the commands and 'Mrs. Twitty' calls the shots," John said thoughtfully, and Galen made a face.

"The names are unfortunate," he pronounced, but John shook his head.

"No, I get it—it's like Johnnies. Some of the kids keep their names long after they've quit the business. That was their identity, and they hold on to it. Retty and Twitty, no matter who they are *now*, have a history where these names meant something." His murky green eyes sought out Jackson's. "That's what you meant by us having to run down leads," he said.

Jackson nodded. "Yes, exactly. Also, John, you have contact with the kids who have recently come off the streets. Usually Henry is our contact—"

"Or Isabelle," John murmured glumly.

"But you need to do this for us," Jackson urged. "Ask them if they've heard of anything like this. As old as it makes us all feel, these women have been here for, what? Two years? They've come after school libraries, and some of your kids might have been affected. Tell them it's for Isabelle and I'm sure they'll do it."

John grunted. "And now that *we* all feel ancient, yes, I'll do that. I haven't visited that side of the business in a few days. Dex and I promised to keep our noses in." He shrugged. "It's an easy business to exploit the models in. We made promises that we wouldn't let that happen. Just because we're working the other sides of the business now, the ones where everybody keeps their clothes on, there's no reason to break that promise, right?"

"Right," Ellery said, wondering if he *should* tell his mother about John and Dex's involvement, because if anybody could help keep them separate and safe, *she* could.

"Good," Jackson said. "I'll run down the—"

And before he could finish his plan, the waiting room grew *very* loud and *very* excited.

Dex and the flophouse boys had arrived.

WHEN ELLERY had been a teenager focused on academic success—and filled with moral rectitude and sexual frustration—he used to dream of being

in a room with affable, well-muscled young men who thought nothing of draping their arms over his shoulders and telling him how glad they were to see him.

As a man in his thirties, with a fiancé he loved more than he had ever imagined loving *anybody*, he found the experience… unnerving.

"Dear God," he said to Jackson as the fifth kid from the flophouse left off hugging him and went to hug John, "are *any* of them wearing sweatshirts?"

Jackson—who often spent his weekends playing basketball with the guys or assisting Henry with their mentoring, shook his head.

"It's March, Ellery—we're lucky they're wearing *shirts*."

Ellery shot him a disbelieving glance, but Jackson nodded soberly, and Ellery thanked his lucky stars until a *really* big kid, in his early twenties, with the grave, sober look of somebody much older, approached. This one *did* have a jacket on—denim, but it still counted—and so did his boyfriend, a smaller, almost bandy-legged man who was close to Ellery's age but who had the open, trusting expression of a child.

"My mom," said the taller of the two. "Jackson, Ellery, is my mom all right?"

Jackson turned to Bobby—Isabelle Roberts still called him Vern but nobody else did—and gave him a tight smile.

"Yeah, kid. We've got your mom stashed someplace safe, and the boy they were protecting too. Henry, he was working really hard to make sure they got away."

"But who?" Reg, his boyfriend, asked plaintively. "Who would want to hurt his mom? She's such a nice lady and—"

"Rivers?"

The hard, angry voice from the doorway made Ellery's heart sink. Jackson turned toward the door with a mask of careful neutrality. He wasn't going to get angry back at Lance, Ellery realized. No matter how mad Lance Luna was, Jackson was going to take it.

"Hey, Lance," Jackson said, softly but loud enough to carry. "I'm glad you could get off your shift. The guys have missed you."

That set Lance back a moment, Ellery could tell. It pulled his focus to the mass of bodies in the room, the kids from the flophouse that Lance helped Henry mentor, and Ellery saw the exact moment Lance swallowed down enough of his fury to deal with Jackson in an adult way and not with the misplaced anger of a child.

Ellery tried to remember the moment *he'd* faced adulthood like that, and what he came up with was when he'd walked into a witness interrogation room to interview Jackson's brother—and met a large, well-muscled Black man with two children and a deep distrust of lawyers who *was* Jackson's brother in all the ways that counted.

Letting go of your preconceptions and your prejudices was always the most adult moment of your life, Ellery thought ruefully—and it *should* hurt.

He just really didn't want Jackson to be the one in the fallout.

"Can I speak to you out here, please?" Lance asked from between his teeth, and Jackson gave Ellery an absent pat, as though Ellery—and John and Galen and Bobby—weren't following him out to the corridor.

Jackson went through the door first, though, and he caught the solid left to his jaw.

"What in the *hell*!" Bobby was the one who caught Lance's flailing arms, and John—smaller, not nearly as built—thrust himself between Lance and Jackson while Ellery bent to help him up.

"I'm fine," Jackson muttered, shaking his shoulders and spitting blood. "C'mon, Lance, you gonna hit me again? Get it out. Go ahead and let him, John. He's been dying to say this since Henry started working for us."

"*How could you*!" Lance howled, obviously taking Jackson at his word even while Bobby pinned his shoulders. "How could you? He *trusted* you! What did you have him doing? He went over to your house to play video games and then, what? You took him on a run? One more fucking run when you felt like hell? Is that what happened? You took him on a run and got him *shot*, you fucker! *Shot*!"

"*That's not what happened*!" Bobby shouted, and he must have wrenched on Lance as he hollered because Lance let out a sudden bark of pain.

"Bobby," John said, his voice level and almost kind, "you are still officially on probation, remember? If security runs in here, we can't fix that. Reg, you grab Lance."

Reg, who was built like an average guy who worked out regularly, and not like a brick shithouse like the rest of the Johnnies boys, stepped forward gamely, but Dex was the one who took over for Bobby. Lance, aware suddenly that two men he admired and probably owed, if Dex and John's history of helping their models out meant anything, were physically restraining him, sagged in Dex's grip.

"What happened?" he gasped, his voice warbling but not broken, not yet.

"Lance," Bobby said, bending down to make sure Lance saw his eyes. "It was my mom, dude. Henry was shot at my mom's place. She was taking care of a kid, and Henry went there after he left Jackson's. Jackson just ran through the rain and helped Dex find my mom and the kid. He didn't get Henry shot, he saved my *mom*."

"Your mom?" Lance shook his head like an awakening sleeper. "Bobby, man, why would somebody try to shoot your mom?"

"It was the kid she was guarding," John said softly. "And Bobby, I'm sorry. The kid was scared, so we called Jackson and Ellery to tell them the story, but in a million years, we had no idea what kind of danger this kid was in. He… he was another street kid who hit on us, you know?"

"Like Cotton," Bobby said. "And Randy. I know. Mom's been…." He took his own deep breath. "She's really proud of what you and her and Galen do. Getting the kids off the street. Getting them help. You take care of us. You always have." He turned that prematurely wise face toward Lance. "I don't know what you've got against Rivers, man, but you have got to let it go. This wasn't his fault. This was the fucker who shot Henry's fault, and that's all there was to it."

Lance turned stricken eyes toward Jackson, who was glaring at him and spitting blood like he was ready to take another blow, and said, "Then why were you there? Why were you even at the apartment when Henry got shot?"

"He called me," Jackson told him. "He called me when the assailant got to the apartment. We hauled ass over there while we were calling the cops." He paused and glanced at Ellery. "Where the fuck are they, by the way?"

"Oh, we got your buddies," John said. "Fetzer and Hardison. They took one glance at Ellery and told us they'd meet us here."

"Oh shit," Jackson muttered. "I've got to talk to cops tonight." He gave Lance a sour look, his mouth puffy and a bruise already swelling under his eye. "Can somebody let him go so he can get me some fuckin' ice?"

"I'll get you ice, baby," said a familiar voice. Ellery glanced over Lance's shoulder to see a tall, whisper-thin Black man in nurse's scrubs swanning down the corridor behind Lance. "And you"—he glared at Lance—"you go in that room with all your friends and try to remember your fucking manners before the security officers get here. I'd lie to them personally, but they're nice men and I don't wanna, so get gone."

"Fuck," Lance muttered, and it wasn't Ellery's imagination—apparently the fight and then getting the wind taken out of his sails had been what was needed to break him. Good. When Ellery had seen him last the man had been wound so tight he'd been going to shatter. Maybe a solid one-two punch of fury and guilt had softened him up enough to simply fracture, because that was easier to heal.

"Yes, fuck," Dave retorted. He gave Bobby an assessing once-over. "If you promise not to kill him, you can go now."

"I'll go too," John said, pausing to let Galen take his arm.

"You were going to let that gigantic teenager kill you," Galen said accusingly.

"He's a grown-assed man," John said. "He's a doctor, even."

"I don't care." Galen grunted. "You and the letting people beat up on you. You suck. I can't believe you talked me into bed the first time."

John let out his goofy little laugh. "You *begged* me the first time. It was the tenth or the fifteenth that were surprises to me. All the rest could be ascribed to a lapse in judgment."

"Junkies are known to have them," Galen retorted, and Ellery watched fondly as the porn mogul and the lawyer made their slow way back into the waiting room.

Lance was still there, and in spite of Dave's obvious dismissal, so were Bobby, Reg, and Dex—and Dex hadn't released Lance's arms.

"I'm okay," Lance said softly. "Dex, you can let me go now."

"Can I?" Dex asked softly. "Because Kane's coming down the hall with Frances in a few minutes, and it would really put a crimp in her day to wonder why her uncle Lance is being mean to Uncle Henry's friend."

Lance closed his eyes, like that last one was the worst blow that could have landed. "I promise," he said, his voice throbbing with hurt. "I'm under control now."

"God, I hope so," Dex muttered in disgust before dropping his arms. "For the record? So you know? Rivers is sopping wet because he chased down two buses in the rain making sure Bobby's mom and the boy she's caring for are safe, because that's what my brother *begged* him to do before the EMTs got there. So whatever bug is up your ass about what Henry does for a living, shit it out right now, because you just hit the wrong fucking guy." He glanced at Bobby and Reg, pulling them with him with a jerk of his chin. "C'mon, guys. Let's let them talk."

"I'll be back with ice," Dave said, and Jackson stilled him with a hand on his arm.

"Is there, you know," he murmured, "any news?"

Dave shook his head. "Our boy's with one of the best surgeons in the place. Don't worry, we love Dr. Luna around here, although I couldn't tell you why right now. But we made sure Henry was well taken care of."

"Thanks," Jackson said, and then it was Ellery, Jackson, and Lance.

Ellery was still standing between them.

"I said I'm fine," Lance said like a penitent schoolboy.

"Don't touch him again," Ellery said, his voice like ice. "I know I'm not the violent one, but I have other ways of doing damage—"

"Ellery, it's fine," Jackson said.

Ellery turned toward him, his heart suddenly pounding in his chest. "No, it's not," he said. "You'd die for Henry—I know that, Jackson. *I've* accepted it. The fact that Lance doesn't makes him worse than a bad friend. It makes him a bad *partner*, because he doesn't know what Henry would die for, and worse? He doesn't care. So he doesn't get to take it out on you. We love Henry too, and he just disrespected everything Henry stands for." Ellery's jaw was clenched so tight his head hurt as he whirled on Lance. "You make your peace with us, with Henry, *now*. He thinks you love him. I would hate to be there when he finds out you only *think* you do."

Jackson sucked air in through his teeth, and Lance Luna's eyes went wide and shiny.

"Ou. Ch." Jackson took Ellery's arm and moved him gently, but Ellery wasn't leaving that hallway.

"He can say his piece to me, Jackson."

"Sure he can," Jackson murmured. "When you stop breathing fire, okay?"

Ellery scowled, and unexpectedly, Jackson grinned at him, his face still a little swollen from a punch he hadn't had to take.

"You're sexy when you're all het up," he said, and Ellery recognized the same energy as when he'd taken the picture of Galen.

"Fine," he muttered, his face heating. "Talk."

He finally stepped aside and cast Lance an unfriendly look. Jackson stepped forward and said softly, "How is he? The EMTs booty bumped me, and I didn't get a full assessment of his injuries."

Lance swallowed and glanced involuntarily to Jackson's hands. Ellery hadn't noticed before, but although Jackson had obviously washed since then, there was still blood on the cuffs and pocket of his hooded sweatshirt. Jackson glanced down at the same time, and an absolute silence fell.

"Shoulder and stomach," Lance said after an audible breath. "Small caliber bullets, fired through plaster at close range. They didn't fragment, and their velocity was significantly slowed, so it's only the two wounds, but the slow bullets left big holes. There was organ damage." He let out a breath. "They're going to be stitching up a lot of that. When he's recovering, infection is going to be a real problem."

"When," Jackson whispered, and Ellery heard it, the desperation to know there would be a "when."

"Prognosis sixty percent," Lance said, his voice as quavery as a bad flute.

"He can…." Jackson took a breath. "This is Henry," he said at last. "He's… he's really strong."

"But he's *my* Henry," Lance almost wailed. "And he's all I've got—"

"No," Jackson said, and Ellery *willed* Lance to break. *Willed* him to let go. "You've got a whole room of brothers in there. Why would they desert you now?"

"Because they love Henry best," Lance said with a little shake of his shoulders. "How could they *not*—"

Jackson moved first, bridging the gap between the two of them, wrapping his arms around Lance's big shoulders. "Course they do," Ellery heard him whisper. "He's our Henry. That's what he does. Make a difference in our lives, right?"

But Lance was too busy sobbing to answer.

AN HOUR later, Lance was huddled with the rest of the Johnnies guys, and Bobby, Galen, and John were huddling with Jackson, Ellery, Jade, Mike, AJ, and Crystal.

"You sent my mom to Disneyland?" Bobby was saying for maybe the thousandth time. Once Jackson had a chance to confer with Crystal, who was even more ethereal in a one-piece catsuit pajama with AJ's hooded sweatshirt over her thin shoulders and her brown hair waving around her face like plant fronds, Jackson was much more forthcoming about the state of things.

"Yeah, Bobby," Jackson told him. "I'd say go join her, but…." He let out a breath.

"We don't know how much these people have figured out about the place she shot up," Ellery finished for him. "This Retty person took off, and as Jackson said, she reports to somebody. They're *going* to be searching for Isabelle and Cowboy, but I don't think they'll expect either one of them to have the resources to go so far away."

"But why Disneyland?" Bobby asked, legitimately puzzled. "She… we never got a chance to go when I was a kid."

"Couple of reasons," Jackson said, smiling a little. "One, the boy she had with her hasn't had a chance to be a kid in a while. I thought sending him someplace where he could, you know, be fourteen—that would be beneficial. And it's far away. K-Ski is in law enforcement. He'll be prepared to keep track of both of them. Billy's done sex work—voluntarily, but he's still worked with guys who were on the streets and had to learn how to function when they landed. Which is why I sent Cotton down there, with a few of Jason's friends from down south."

"Ernie loves Disneyland," Crystal said dreamily, and everybody's heads swiveled toward her—not least because she'd never *met* Ernie, and she definitely hadn't been there for the conversation. "The other guys were sort of involved, so they sent him and Sonny with Cotton." She closed her large eyes as though she was falling asleep. "They'll have adventures and be fine," she murmured.

"Do we even—" Ellery began, but Jackson shook his head.

"Don't ask, don't ask, don't ask, don't ask…," he muttered, and given how comfortable with Crystal's clairvoyance Ellery was *not*, he left it at that.

"So you sent them there so they could be protected," Bobby said, and for the first time *his* composure slipped. "Thanks, Jackson. That means a lot." He swallowed. "She's my *mom*, man."

"Have you been paying attention?" Jackson asked, glancing around the room. "Dude, everybody here has asked to make sure she's okay. She's *everybody's* mom. You don't let the team mom get hurt on your watch." He gave a crooked smile. "I think Henry's proved that already."

Bobby nodded, and Jackson turned toward the people from their office. Ellery knew that the numbness of waiting had set in, and now that everybody's fears about the phones had well and truly been put to rest, it was time for them to get to doing what they did best.

"We need to know," Jackson said, glancing at Ellery, "how much pull the Stepford Dragons have. That's you and Galen. You need to look into their contacts, who they're in bed with, and what sorts of things they're permitted for. If Cowboy and his friends were taken into that big house off W Street— that's where it is, right?" He turned to John and Galen, who nodded. "If he was taken in there, and there were other kids, we need to see if they're permitted to have kids there. Are they a school? Are they a shelter? What rights do they have in terms of keeping kids there against their wills?"

"Conversion therapy is illegal in California," Ellery said quickly. "But it's not banned in places in the south and the Midwest."

"Do we know where this group was spawned?" Jackson asked. "Because we need to contact their headquarters in other places to see."

"That sounds like a job for me and AJ," Jade said. "Ellery and Galen can do the calling because they're all lawyerfied and shit, but AJ and I will be doing the research in the morning, right, AJ?"

She held out her hand, and AJ, their general dogsbody and secondary tech guy, gave her five because you didn't leave your good friend hanging. AJ's pale brown skin was even paler under the fluorescent lights, but he'd been keeping his orange curls cut tight to his head to look "professional." The lost junkie Jackson had pulled out of hell was gone now, and the young man who was left looked ready to take on any task he was given.

"Fair," Galen said, and then peered perceptively at Jackson. "And what will you be doing?" he asked.

Jackson grimaced. "Well, I'm starting with the boy's mother, to see how the kid ended up there. He said she had the Stepford Dragons come to his apartment to take him away. I want to know what made her think that was a good idea."

They all nodded, but Ellery got a low bubbling in his stomach because he knew that wasn't all. "And?" he prompted.

"Well, I was going to follow down what she tells me, and then tomorrow evening go explore the grounds."

Ellery nodded, and before Jade could go off—Jackson's hot-blooded sister had her hackles up for good reason—he said, "You and who else?"

Jackson blinked bleary, bloodshot eyes at him, and Ellery felt every second of every minute of every hour that neither of them had slept that night. "Ellery," he said, as though Ellery had committed an unforgivable faux pas in public, "Henry's *injured*!"

"I know he is," Ellery confirmed. "We're all here for exactly that reason. He's injured because he didn't think he needed backup. Sadly, he did, and none of us knew it, but we know it *now*. Jackson, who's your backup?"

Jackson opened his mouth and closed it and glanced around, almost like he was looking for volunteers.

"Mike would kill me," Jade said calmly. "And I'll be needed in the office. Sorry, sweetheart, but this gun-toting badass has to go administrate for the greater good."

Jackson rolled his eyes, and then, with the jerky movements of a drowning man, glanced around the room.

Ellery saw the moment his eyes landed on Dex and lit up, and then fell on Kane, next to him, rocking his sleeping niece over his shoulder. Once Frances had learned she'd been shuttled out of bed and down to her uncle Evan's house because Uncle Henry had been hurt, she'd apparently harangued Kane into turning around and going back to the hospital so she could wait to see if Uncle Henry would be okay.

Kane and Dex would be *okay* backup, Ellery thought critically. Good in a fight—they were both stacked—and they'd be loyal to a fault. But they had no law enforcement background, no weapons training, and they both had the appearance of men who had enjoyed settling down and found being comfortable everything it was cracked up to be.

Jackson saw it too.

He'd sent Sean Kryzynski to Disneyland with their witnesses. Sean's partner, Andre, was going to be absolutely vital to feed them information from the SACPD precinct, and he couldn't be spending his time helping Jackson.

Jackson was opening his mouth, obstinate look in his eyes, probably to say he didn't need no stinking backup, when there was a quiet commotion at the door to the waiting room. Ellery glanced up, hoping for Henry's surgeon, and he heard Jackson's weary sigh in his bones.

The cops had arrived.

Unexpected Backup

JACKSON HAD known some good officers and some really, really bad ones, and when all was said and done, going to the wall for Adele Fetzer and Jimmy Hardison had been one of the smartest—and best—things he'd ever done.

Officer Fetzer was a thirty-year veteran of the force, a Black woman in her fifties with a few gray hairs clubbed into submission with the weight of the midnight black wealth of them into a tight, single braid down the back of her head. Jackson had been with this woman in a firefight, and he'd never seen that braid—or Fetzer's composure—waver. Not once.

Hardison—or Jimmy, as he was known to his friends—was the kind of paunchy white guy who had probably needed to work his balls off to pass his fitness exams year after year, but he kept doing it because he didn't trust anybody to have Fetzer's back but him. They were both married to other people—thank fuck, because they'd kill each other otherwise—but they had the kind of partnership that brought out the best in them.

It was what partners were supposed to do for each other, and Jackson felt the pang of Henry's absence so strongly he had to suck in a breath.

"Rivers," Fetzer said as they neared, "I understand you were first on the scene. Would you like to sit down?"

Jackson nodded and glanced at Galen and John, asking them to move away with a flick of his lashes.

They exchanged glances, and while John shook his head, Galen made shooing motions and proceeded to move aside so Fetzer could take a seat near him. Jade and AJ stood and quietly made their way to the other end of the room, and Crystal whispered, "I'll get you a soda, Jackson," before fleeing down the hospital corridors.

"Sorry," Ellery said, not moving from his elbow. "I should have thought of that."

Jackson winked at him, suddenly grateful for Ellery's constant manners, the sanity he tried to inject into every situation.

"I can tell you what I know," Jackson said, and then with a careful emphasis, he said, "or I can tell you what I *know*."

The two police officers understood what that meant.

"Start off telling us what you know," Adele said, pulling out her notebook. "Jimmy and I are trying to make our paperwork look good. Then tell us what doesn't need to go into the paperwork."

Galen raised his eyebrows. "I am impressed," he said dryly. "That is a lot of loyalty."

Hardison shrugged. "Not sure if you saw this guy bail our asses out of a firefight about six months ago, but we were *very* grateful." He glanced around the room, and for a big guy with a jowly face and pouches around his eyes, that visual catalog missed nothing. "Are you gonna tell me these guys are hand models?" he asked.

It was close, but Jackson managed to contain his snicker behind his own hand. Ellery's mouth had a little war with itself, but he kept his face straight. Galen, on the other hand, almost whooped with laughter, and only burying his face in his shoulder kept him from alerting the entire room.

"So no?" Fetzer asked dryly. "Not hand models?"

"No," Jackson said on a barely contained chuckle, and the moment he thought, *Wait until I tell Henry*, the mirth drained out of him. "No," he repeated again, feeling the strain back on his shoulders. "So like I said, let me tell you what we know."

He told the two officers about their friend's mother and her propensity for taking in strays, feeding them, clothing them, helping them find shelter. Henry had been on call to make sure this nice woman was safe, and he'd called Jackson with gunshots in the background. Jackson had shown up on scene, ministered to Henry, gotten the details about the two people running away from violence, and had gone after them to protect them.

And had then come here to see if Henry was okay.

Fetzer put her notebook away first. "Okay, then," she said. "Now tell me everything you left out."

And Jackson, who ten years ago had sworn he'd never trust his former boys in blue again, did.

WHEN HE was done, Hardison took another glance around at the "hand models," and then cast Galen a gimlet eye.

"He said you were walking from the church with your boyfriend," he noted, "and a kid tried to solicit you both, as a couple. Why?"

Galen grunted. "I think because we were nice to each other. I think he figured he'd rather be with two safe old perverts than with someone a little less old."

"Yeah," Hardison said, "but you guys—you got a… I don't want to say operation going, but you've got a system here. This kid was young. You wanted to make sure he was taken care of. Where would you have sent him if he'd been legal?"

Galen glanced at Jackson and then shook his head. "Well, probably to Isabelle's house first, anyway. But yes—you guessed that we've got a connection to adult industries. In this case, film. My boyfriend doesn't put anybody underage in front of the cameras—besides it being a felony, he hates the thought of kids feeling coerced. But sometimes the over-eighteen-year-olds know who he is, and they want a job. Three-quarters of the time, he talks them into working for a gas station or a pet store—that's a lot of his business right now, if you must know the truth. Places where someone young and unskilled can start out in retail and then earn a living wage. But some kids want to make a living with their bodies still—they're good at it, they've had practice, and they can make *more* than a living wage, and my boyfriend gives them that chance."

Fetzer and Hardison met eyes, and Hardison said, "Johnnies."

Galen inclined his head. "Guilty as charged."

"We've just seen a lot of your clientele mixed up with this guy," Adele said, indicating Jackson. "And you know what? I'm not going to judge. Nobody else was giving that kid soup and a place to sleep and not making demands on him. Your boy stays on the right side of the line, we won't give him crap, are we understood?"

Galen nodded. "We are. But I'm still not going to point out which guy he is."

Fetzer laughed a little. "You *are* a good partner. Understood. So this kid hit on you, and you took him someplace safe. What happened to make it not so safe?"

And it was Jackson's turn to talk again. This time he told them about what Cowboy had seen in the night and the mostly untold story of Shitbag Retty and the Twitty woman.

"Oh…." Fetzer let out enough of a breath to sound scared, and Hardison glanced at her.

"What? These Moms for Clean Living people—nobody takes them seriously, right?"

"Jimmy, does your wife *ever* get you to go to church with her?" Fetzer asked sharply.

Jimmy managed to look abashed. "You know, Adele, with the kids out of the house, we don't really… you know. We got better things to do on Sunday besides go to church."

Fetzer—and Jackson—stared at him in surprise, and Hardison's ears turned red.

"See," Galen pointed out dryly, "sex really can save the world."

Jackson and Ellery stared at him in horror, but Galen's night had been as awful as theirs, and he refused to back down.

"Conceded," Jackson finally said, and dammit, something in his soul lightened saying the word. "Jimmy, they might not have a lot of pull on you and your wife, but there's a lot of…." He wanted to say "good." Oh, he really did. But "good" people shouldn't be swayed so easily to hate other people, should they? "Gullible," he said after a noticeable pause. "There's a lot of *gullible* people who really do think that reading a book about a gay kid or a kid who's Asian or Latino or Black will make them *less* White and *less* Christian. These organizations prey on that *gullibility*—"

"Ignorance," Ellery and Galen spat together.

Jackson gave them a look and then again *conceded*. And felt better for it.

"Ignorance," he said. "And they use people's fears against them. Our young friend wasn't talking about a safe place for LGBTQ youth—he was talking about the kind of place where they pray it away."

A whole treatise on fatherhood and acceptance could have been written on Jimmy Hardison's glance around the room this time. "This is a safe space now," he said, glancing at Fetzer. "And you trusted us in it. So you trust us not to fuck up dealing with these yoyos. What do you have in mind?"

Jackson let out a breath and outlined his plan to interview the kid's mother before skulking around the Stepford Dragon compound to see "what could be seen."

Fetzer wrinkled her nose. "That's it? That's your plan?"

Jackson scowled at her. "I may have to improvise," he told her, wounded. "Not even Ellery knows everything I'm gonna do, you know."

She humphed. "Listen," she said after a moment. "You know we can only do so much. We can pursue this Retty person—and the boy's description was pretty thin—and we can look for someone called 'Twitty' who likes to dress like June Cleaver in slacks, but until we interview your boy, we've got nothing on them. Jimmy and I can't stop you from looking, but we can't help you either. But I *can* tell you what constitutes a reason to intervene. If you get a chance to talk to the kids in the compound—and no, I won't ask you how—ask why they stay and if they're afraid of punishment if they leave. Ask if they get fed, what their daily regimen is. There's no laws against making kids pray if the place is billed as a religious school." She turned to Ellery. "Is it?"

"On my to-do list," Ellery told her promptly.

She nodded. "No laws against making kids pray, but there's laws about not feeding them, not letting them sleep, not letting them pee—anything that reeks of kidnapping, that will get our toe in the door, and Jimmy and me can ask for a warrant."

"Or fraud," Ellery said, and Jackson saw his sharkiest, most toothy smile, the kind that made bad guys shiver.

Fetzer nodded. "Hard to do with a church, but as far as I know, this is just a 'special interest group,' so we might make it stick. But yeah. Your instincts are good as always. I'd say that's a place to investigate."

Ellery nodded, looking suddenly thoughtful, and he glanced at the clock. "Actually, that gives me an idea. If you will all excuse me?" He was pulling his phone out as he walked away, and given that it was almost human time on the east coast, Jackson figured he was calling his mother.

Fetzer broke into Jackson's thoughts by saying, "Okay, that's my good deed for the night. But how about you? You got anybody to go as backup?"

Jackson liked the woman, but he thought seriously about kicking her.

But before he could crank himself up to do it, she dropped a gift from heaven in his lap. "What about that Gabriel kid?" she asked. "You know, the one who testified back in November? I always thought he got a raw deal. What's he doing these days?"

Jackson blinked. "He's managing a trailer park and keeping his nose clean," he said, but inside, a part of him was doing a touchdown dance.

"He miss being on the job?" Hardison asked. "He was a big deal UC, you know. I mean, yeah, he tasted the candy, but that happens undercover. Forced retirement—that was rough."

Cody Gabriel had been on the verge to confessing his habit to his CO when some of the bad cops that made Jackson distrust the breed as a whole had fucked him over and forced him to make a bad choice out of a hand of worse ones. What had been a worrisome habit, picked up to make his cover viable, turned into his entire life in one terrible day. Jackson and Henry had pulled him out of that, and he'd absolved himself with his testimony—and hopefully found some redemption as well. Jackson had promised not to cut the guy loose, and he'd lived up to that. A couple phone calls a week, and he stopped by on the weekends or when he was in the area.

He knew Cody's nagging little secret.

"He's bored shitless," Jackson said, and it was hard not to do a cartwheel as he said it.

"Bet he'd love to ride some shotgun," Hardison told him.

"Oh no," Galen muttered, correctly sensing that Ellery would probably have objections.

"Oh yes," Jackson agreed, and he felt some hope thrumming through his veins, some excitement. Henry would pull through, and Jackson *would* find out who'd done this to his friend.

"Oh fuck," Galen said.

FETZER AND Hardison left shortly after that to go file, Fetzer promised, just enough of a report to make sure their bosses could keep an eye out on the Stepford Dragons and to be alert for kids in the compound where no kids should be, but not enough to make anybody look twice at Galen Henderson.

He'd never pointed out who John was, and Jackson and Ellery were fine with keeping it that way.

For a moment the waiting room was quiet; many of the kids were sleeping, Dex and John were busy on their phones, making sure everybody knew the office could expect a late start the next day and securing their old receptionist, Kelsey, to come sub for Isabelle for a week or so.

Galen had brought his own tablet, but it was currently using the one outlet in the room to charge. Jade's boyfriend—and Jackson's good friend— Mike had gone to pick up coffee and breakfast sandwiches for everybody, with careful instructions from Vinnie, one of the flophouse kids, detailing what they would and would not eat. (Mostly, Jackson figured, they'd eat eggs and dry toast. The thought made him shudder. It was no way to live.)

Jackson was restlessly playing a game on his phone when Bobby approached him.

"Heya," Jackson murmured, glancing over his shoulder to make sure Reg was asleep. There was probably a name for what Reg had suffered from most of his life—his short-term memory wasn't great, and he had difficulty with words and reading in general, although he tried to read every day. He'd always wanted to be smart, and Bobby, who had come to Sacramento to work right out of high school, had helped him better his education as best he could.

But there was no magic cure for whatever short-circuited in Reg's brain on a daily basis, and part of the job Bobby had taken on as his lover was to make sure Reg was cared for. Simple things—Bobby's coat over his shoulders and a borrowed pillow so he could sleep in the chair—kept Reg from losing his composure. If he woke up and Bobby wasn't where he was expected to be, and he was in a hospital to boot, because those places had bad memories for the two of them, Reg could have a *very* bad night.

"He should be okay," Bobby said softly. "But… but what can you tell me about my mom? Besides the Disneyland thing?"

Jackson gave the young man a quick smile. "She was scared," he said bluntly. "But brave. Cowboy was clinging to her. I don't think she would have agreed to go down south with him otherwise, but you know. The kid had been let down so badly by the women in his life, I guess. She refused to be one more."

Bobby gave a short nod. "You know my mom's the best, right? I mean, I didn't take it easy on her, really. I left fuckin' Dogpatch, and then, as far as she knows, the next minute I'm gay, and I've got a boyfriend, and hey, hello, *porn*. But she… she never tried to yank that whole 'You're my son and I love you,' thing away from me."

Jackson grinned at him. "Did she tell you she was disappointed in your life choices?"

Bobby had a wicked grin himself, and a strongly handsome face that had made him a favorite on the website. He was still, as far as Jackson knew, making the occasional video. Reg was proud of him. It wasn't how Jackson worked—but God, if it worked for these guys, he was all for it. They were solid people.

"She told me I'd never be a teacher," he said with a shrug. "But I was never smart enough for school as it was. I sort of figured that ship had sailed."

Jackson doubted that he wasn't smart enough, but he *was* an amazing carpenter, which was how he made his real living. "You were lucky," he said, meaning it. "And she loved being a mom, I think."

Bobby nodded soberly. "I knew she was helping John place the kids that he ran into on the street. I just, you know, never thought…."

"Nobody did," Jackson said, thinking about Henry. "There was no reason for it to be dangerous like that."

Bobby nodded. "Which is why you shouldn't blame yourself too much for Henry," he said, and Jackson felt as though the boy had punched him in the chest—but lovingly so.

"I don't—"

Bobby shook his head. "Course you do. But don't. You and Henry, you both do what you can to back people up. If he called you when it was going down, he knew you'd get there. I mean, when I was a kid, I always wished I could fly. Still hasn't happened. Pretty sure you don't got wings either. Thanks for what you did for my mom."

And with that, he stood and made his way back to Reg, and finally, finally, a woman walked in with a bloodstained smock and a set of magnifying specs balanced on the top of her head, and Jackson thought they just might have some news.

Dex and Lance got there first, but Dex grabbed Jackson's shoulder when he tried to hover in the background, and Jackson was grateful.

"Surgery was a success, mostly," the surgeon said soberly. "He had some intestinal perforations, which are always tricky, and we had to patch up the leaky parts and clean out the contaminated ones. His shoulder was a through-and-through, so thankfully no shattered bones to contend with. But he's going to need to be monitored constantly for internal bleeding and infection. We're looking at a week in the critical-care unit at a minimum, and there's the possibility of more surgeries in his future. But you can tell his friends—" Her eyes scanned the waiting room and widened slightly. "—all of them," she said, "that for the moment, he's stable. He should be coming out of the anesthesia within the hour. We checked his paperwork, and David Worrall?"

Dex nodded.

"You're his only blood relative. Is there anybody else you'd like to clear to be in the room with him at any given time?"

"Lance," Dex said promptly. "I mean, Dr. Luna—he gets visiting privileges. My husband, Carlos, for the times I can't be. And he's gonna need to talk to Mr. Rivers here sometime tomorrow."

Jackson wanted to cry with gratitude. He also wanted to run the other way.

"Okay, then," the doctor said. "I'll put him on the list too. Anybody else?"

"Jackson?" Galen Henderson was a lot of things—dry, snarky, self-assured, disdainful—but this was the only time Jackson could remember him sounding as though he were pleading.

"Galen Henderson," Jackson said. "His boss—and his friend. Trust me, if Henry needs diverting, sniping at Galen will punch the ticket."

"Yeah," Dex said, nodding. "Galen's fine."

"Good." The doctor nodded. "So, who's first?"

"Lance," Dex said softly, nudging Lance with his shoulder. "But please tell him the rest of us were here, and we love him, okay?"

And Jackson saw the tears that Lance Luna had kept at bay during the entire awful night, finally slipping down his cheeks.

"You gotta come with me," Lance almost begged. "God, Dex, I don't think I can do it without you."

Jackson watched Henry's brother wrap his arms around Henry's lover's shoulders and soothe him enough to function, and suddenly he hungered for Ellery in his own arms so he could cling to somebody too.

It had been a long goddamned night.

Dex turned to Jackson just before he and Lance followed the surgeon down the hall and held his fingers up to his ear in the universal "We'll talk" gesture, and Jackson nodded.

Then he turned wearily to John, who stood and spoke. "For those who didn't hear—he's stable. Not out of the woods completely, but Lance and Dex are going to go sit with him as he comes out of the anesthesia. You guys should all go back and get some sleep, and while I might hit the office around noon, tomorrow wasn't a scene day, so pretty much Kelsey's going to be answering phones for a few hours and that's it." He gave a little smile. "You guys were great tonight. You really showed up for your brother, and me and Galen and Dex and Lance—we'll make sure Henry knows how much he means to y'all."

Jackson blinked, and he felt Ellery's almost comic surprise next to him.

John had to be tired if he was letting his southern roots show.

The waiting room started to empty out, the kids holding hands or draping arms over shoulders, seeking comfort in physical closeness, Jackson thought, which probably said a lot about why they'd ended up at Johnnies in the first place. Sometimes sex was just expression—and sometimes when you were young and fit, it was the expression you craved.

"I'm going to take Galen home," John said, offering his arm to Galen on one side as Galen leaned heavily on his cane on the other. "I already texted Dex to tag me after Henry wakes up, and Galen can come take a shift after he's had some rest."

Jade drew up alongside them, Crystal and AJ at her side. Jackson had taken a few moments to talk to them quietly as they'd waited and update them on the game plan.

"We'll text you about any new developments," Jade promised. Jackson's sister-of-the-heart looked rumpled—she still wore a cap over her magenta-tinted hair to keep the style neat, and her usually impeccable makeup hadn't been applied. The crackling intelligence that characterized her sharp brown eyes and curvy body had been dimmed a little by sleep deprivation, but Jackson could feel it—will and vitality and a pure lack of bullshit—thrumming under her frowzy demeanor. Jade yawned in the middle of saying something else and then picked up the thread again. "And don't worry. Jackson's not going anywhere until he's got backup." She gave him a mutinous look then, and he held up his hands.

"I've got backup," he said placidly. "Or I will before I really go at it tomorrow."

"Who's backup?" Jade asked, narrowing her eyes.

"Yes, Jackson," Ellery said smoothly. "Who's backup?"

"I'll tell you when he says yes," Jackson returned, just to be contrary. Ha! Think they were going to keep *him* down because his partner was laid up. Nope nope nope nope nope.

Jackson Rivers was done being a grown-up for this long, awful night. Peace fucking out.

THE DRIVE back was about a thousand years long, but part of that was that Ellery had to take him to Isabelle's apartment building to pick up Jennifer. Thank God the haunted minivan cooperated, because by the time Jackson pulled up alongside Ellery's Lexus in the garage, his legs and arms felt leaden, and his throat was doing that awful tickle dance that said he'd gone out in the rain and dried in the air-conditioned hospital and wouldn't that be a nice way to get sick?

But Ellery had arrived first, and he shoved a hot tea and Theraflu concoction into his hands pretty much the minute he got undressed.

A year ago he might have chafed at the nurse-maiding, but now? He just grunted, "Thanks," before he tossed that shit back, let out a belch, and took his glass to the dishwasher while Ellery eyed him suspiciously.

"What?" he asked as he returned to their bedroom. There were two bedrooms in this house, and each one had an absurd amount of floor and closet space. Jackson had noted this before, but he didn't really appreciate it until he climbed into the king-size bed and realized it *felt* as though he and Ellery slept in a corner, almost like their bed alone was a loft and the rest of the house belonged to somebody else. Sometimes being able to curl up in a ball in the corner was way more comforting than being in freefall with every step through the atmosphere.

"That was way too easy," Ellery said as they climbed into bed. "Why didn't you fight me on that?"

Jackson grunted. "We're getting married in June—I assume we'll discover more, better things to fight about by then. In the meantime, the person who shot Henry is running around free like a Tweety bird, and I don't have time to be sick."

Ellery scowled, only appearing partially mollified. "That's very mature," he said, snuggling up to Jackson like a magnet to a refrigerator. "Why has it taken you this long to figure that out?"

Jackson managed a reluctant smile in the dark, and he rolled to his back again, the skin only a little tender from a long, nasty wound inflicted before Thanksgiving.

"I'm stupid," he said, letting Ellery rest his head on his shoulder, "but I'm not *that* stupid. Thanks for the nurse-maiding, Counselor. It was kind, and I should have said something coherent."

It was Ellery's turn to grunt. "Given that you didn't fight me too hard on backup, you're completely forgiven. You're, uhm, not planning to go back on your word, are you?"

Jackson recoiled as though slapped. "No. *No!* Geez, Ellery, has it occurred to you I have somebody suitable in mind?"

"Well, yeah, but you sent them to Disneyland," Ellery snapped, probably irritated because he'd rather been counting on Sean Kryzynski himself.

Jackson chuckled, remembering the look on the young detective's face when Jackson had, with Dex's blessing, consigned the little party to the unexpected trip. Well, it wasn't every night your once sworn enemy got you out of bed, shoved two fugitive witnesses into your hands, and said, "Hey, everybody, I've got an idea!"

But the timing would be perfect. By the time Shitbag Retty or whoever could track down exactly *who* had been shot that night and then looked up friends and contacts, Sean and Billy could be most of the way to the Grapevine. It would take some fancy computer skills—and a psychic, which Jackson understood did not come standard to most outfits, which was why he bought Crystal yarn and catnip tea and pastries as often as possible—to figure out where Isabelle and Cowboy had been placed and where they might have gone at the drop of a hat. And even then, tracking a group of people you didn't know—and Jackson knew for certain Billy's ID was problematic because he'd never legally changed his name from Guillermo Morales to Billy Carey, like many of the kids did when they wanted to reinvent themselves via Johnnies, although much of his ID was in that name.

Frankly, Jackson didn't think Shitbag Retty had the master-criminal skills to navigate that wrinkle.

No, the more he'd pondered it—and questioned Cowboy and Isabelle and John and Galen—the more certain he'd become that their Retty had *stumbled* upon Cowboy, and every move thereafter had been a decision of impulse. She didn't know *who* she'd shot through that wall in Isabelle Roberts's apartment, and she had no idea who she was dealing with.

Jackson smiled into the dark and knew the expression was unpleasant.

"What?" Ellery asked. "What are you thinking?"

"I'm thinking she has no idea what she's unleashed," Jackson said, his voice hard and angry. Henry Worrall wasn't just liked—he was *beloved*. He was *necessary*. And Shitbag Retty, whoever she may be, had tried to take him out of the world.

"Be careful," Ellery murmured, stroking Jackson's bare chest. "I've been where Lance is tonight. It's… rather awful, knowing *exactly* how he feels."

And Jackson had a very clear memory of waking from a bare doze at Ellery's hospital bed and seeing an assassin preparing to take Ellery out.

His blood froze all over again.

"Same, babe," he whispered, smoothing Ellery's hair back from his brow. Any product had long since flaked away, and it was limp and smooth and soft. "Same."

"Which is why…."

Jackson wanted to laugh, but outside the sky was lightening up just the tiniest degree, and the rain had all but stopped. He felt sleep weighing on him like a wet bag of wool, and what he managed was a mumble.

"He'll be fine, baby. He'll be fine."

As his eyes closed and consciousness whispered out, he couldn't decide if he meant his choice for backup or Henry.

In the end, he decided it was both, and for once his sleep went untouched by dreams.

Mama Said

JACKSON TOOK off into the wild blue yonder in the haunted minivan shortly after breakfast. Ellery did some computer work at home and then left as well to be at the office by eleven thirty, still tired and irritable, not least because Jackson was spending all his immaturity points on not telling him who his backup would be.

It didn't help that Jade and AJ seemed to know, and they wouldn't share the secret.

"It was right there," Jade said. "His name was even mentioned last night—don't know why you don't remember."

Ellery stared at her. He couldn't for the life of him think of who she was talking about. "Is it somebody I'd approve of?" he asked hesitantly, and now she was staring back.

"Who are you, his agent?" she asked, and he had a flashback to the days when he and Jade had loathed each other, before they'd bonded over the care and feeding of Jackson.

"I'm his boyfriend. Fiancé. Husband to be." Ellery paused before he added "soulmate" to that list. "Jesus God, I'm a man sorely in need of coffee," he finished pitifully, and since he was normally a tea drinker, that spoke to his desperation. Jade *did* have pity on him then and pointed to the giant pot on the counter behind her perch at the reception window, where everybody's mugs sat next to the sink.

"Thank the gods," he muttered, moving forward to pour his coffee into the "World's Most Uptight Boss" mug Jade and Mike had gotten him for Christmas. He liked to think it was a term of endearment, but if he kept harping on Jackson's mystery partner, he suspected it might not be tongue-in-cheek anymore. After a grateful sip—cream, no sugar—he turned toward Jade and tried to start their conversation again. "Do we have any news on Henry?"

She nodded and took a sip of her own coffee. *Her* mug had been a gift from Jackson and Ellery, and Jackson had found it at a craft fair in Colton. It was of solid ceramic construction with a weighty base and a fiery black glaze with a magenta finish. Ellery remembered the conversation surrounding it.

He'd been worried about it being dishwasher safe, and Jackson had pointed out that it would probably be used in the office—no dishwasher, just a sink. The point was, the object was beautiful, it was well suited for Jade, she was using it, and Jackson's propensity for being thoughtful was one more reason Ellery was going to worry about him when he was out there on his own.

Gah!

"Dex texted me and Jackson this morning right before you got in," Jade said, oblivious to Ellery's rabbit hole. "He said Henry woke up for a few, got all cryey and slobbery because Dex was there, mooned at Lance, and said Jackson needed to get his ass in there the next time he's awake. I suspect that might be Jackson's final stop before backup."

Ellery tried not to gulp coffee—even with cream it was rather hot. "Wait… where's he going first?" Jackson may have told him, but honestly, Ellery's memory of the night before was a little fractured. Worry, he knew, and sleep deprivation. And worry.

Jade scowled. "First he was going to visit K-Ski's house and get Cowboy's address and pick his brains a little more. Then he's going to go visit Cowboy's mother. We need to see if the kid was taken on false pretenses or kidnapped or what. C'mon, Ellery, I thought you were a lawyer!"

Ellery scowled at her. "I am," he said. "I'm even a lawyer who was in the room last night." He let out a breath and conceded defeat. "But I have to admit, I was really worried about Henry, and I may not have been on the top of my game."

Jade gave him a measured once-over. "Wow—look at you. A year and a half ago, you would *not* have admitted that."

Ellery decided to give her a gift. "Well, a year and a half ago, Jackson wouldn't have let me pump him with Airborne and Theraflu after a night in the rain, and *you* might have insisted on going out with him packing a weapon. We've all grown wiser."

She cracked a smile then, a radiant one, and Ellery felt his fondness for Jackson's sister steal back. "Yeah, we have." She sobered. "And so has Henry. I will *not* be okay about that boy until they let him come home. This is like when you and Jackson were in the hospital for what? Three weeks? God, I can see why Jackson hates the place so much."

Ellery could only nod. Jackson had hidden his discomfort well—and part of it had probably been fatigue—but he'd managed his phobia like a champ the night before. Now that Henry was better, though, and everybody's fear wasn't such an overriding stabilizer, Ellery hoped he could continue to manage today.

Also, "God, I wish I could see Henry with him," he added, not even sure the words were going to come out.

Jade raised her eyebrows. "That was good, Ellery. Like a real person with friends and everything. What prompted that?"

Ellery didn't even bother to scowl at her. He simply shook his head. Henry had carried *such* a chip on his shoulder when he'd first come to Jackson and Ellery—their first client, actually, with Galen by his side, forcing him to contain what they'd all thought was raging homophobia and chronic ingratitude.

It had turned out to be chronic self-hatred and raging embarrassment. Henry had spent his life parroting his father while at the same time knowing he was everything his father hated. Once he'd come to Sacramento, come out to his brother, and realized he had people here—and not just people, *family*— he'd turned not only into Dex's little brother, but *everybody's* little brother.

Even Ellery's.

Ellery had seen how frantic Jackson had been as he'd driven them both to the crime scene the night before, but he hadn't, until right now, told anybody—even Jackson—how worried he'd been for somebody he'd come to care for very much.

"It's so easy for Jackson to care," he said weakly, and then he *did* take a gulp of coffee because his voice sounded wobbly, and he was *supposed* to be here to work on Henry's behalf, dammit.

He was surprised to see Jade's dark fingers, tipped with magenta polish, wrapping around his own as he cradled his mug.

"It's not," she said throatily. "But he does it anyway. Just like you. Who do you think you're fooling, Ellery? You let the boy use your cabin on New Year's so he could take Lance on a vacation. You asked your mother for a loan to pay him before we got up to speed so Galen could have him as an assistant and Jackson could have him as backup. Yeah, I do the bills. I know how much we make and how much we don't. You've gone to the wall for him a thousand times since he and Galen walked in here last June—and not just because Jackson loves him. And not only because Galen loves him too. It's okay to have friends, Ellery. In fact it makes you a better human."

Ellery shrugged and lowered his hands so she didn't have to reach so far to keep holding them. He liked it—it reminded him of his mother's careful comforts. "I thought you and Mike were my hard limit," he said, trying to be flippant, and he did manage to make her smile.

"Too bad, we're family," she said, practically singing. "And I know Galen is like your work wife. It's almost sickening how good you two are as partners in this firm. And I know it's not something you expected, but, you know, it's not a bad thing."

"It is for *them*," Ellery said, almost grumpily. "As thrilled as I am that it wasn't Jackson this time, I was *not* happy to be in the hospital for Henry either. People aren't going to be our friends for long if they find out taking a bullet is the cost of it."

She dropped her hands and rolled her expressive eyes. Even after their late night, she'd come to the office in full makeup, and her hair—lately allowed to curl naturally into tight spirals but still tipped with magenta—looked "done" as his mother would say.

"I know you're dumb," she said, obviously out of patience, "but last night's bullet was taken for Isabelle and a fourteen-year-old kid John and Galen saved from the streets. I mean, yeah, Henry *would* take a bullet for you, but you need to keep track in case that's what happens next time."

"There won't *be* a next time," Ellery snapped, stung.

"Tell that to Jackson," she retorted. "For guys like that, there's always the possibility of a next time. And every next time, the people like us have to deal with it. C'mon, Ellery—you and I have dealt with it as partners for a year and a half now. Are you bailing already?"

He shook his head. "No," he said on a sigh, and with that resolution, it felt like some of the fuzz had cleared out of his head—even without coffee. "But thank you. Like you said, we're family, but you're really good at it."

She grinned again—blinding, but still a little softer than it might have been before they'd gotten to know each other. "Thank you," she said. "So AJ and I have started background on the Wonderbread Wagon Stepford Dragons—"

Ellery surprised himself by almost snorting coffee.

"It was either that or the Killer Karen Klub," she admitted, "you know, KKK? But"—her expression grew grim—"one of my favorite people is actually *named* Karen, and I just can't use her name like that. Makes me feel dirty. So anyway I sent you a link, and AJ and I have more to scroll through. I was going to try to do a dossier on all the leaders of the chapter out here but…." She grimaced.

"What?" Jade was more than capable of that kind of research. In fact between her and Jackson, Ellery and Galen almost never walked into a case without knowing *exactly* who they were defending and whether or not they had a chance at a defense.

"None of these people are who they say they are," she said. "I mean, most of it is superficial—a name change in another state, a move, an altered employment record—but that's even on the lower levels. So far. You'll see what I mean when you start to look through it. I've gotten through two of their top five officers—they've got a chapter system, and this is the Sacramento chapter. It's one of six across the country. However… fun fact. You're gonna love this…."

She made the "gimme-gimme" motion with her hands, and he blinked and tried to remember he was supposed to be intelligent.

"None of them are from Sacramento?" he hazarded.

"Give the man another cup of coffee!" she crowed before quickly sobering. "None of them. Not one of these uptight, 'let's fuck shit up for anybody not straight, rich, and white' bitches is actually *from this state*. I mean, it's sort of weird. It's not like California doesn't have its own supply of shitheads, right? In fact, I *assumed* this chapter was from here. We've all met homegrown shitheads out in public, showing their asses. But this *particular* chapter of Sacramento Shitheads does not appear to be from Sacramento." She shrugged and held her hands out. "Maybe I missed something. I could be wrong. Like I said, I only got to the first layer of changes. I'll continue to data mine, and so will AJ, but that is something you may want to take a look at when you go all lawyerly and shit, right?"

Ellery smiled in bemusement. He remembered how Jackson had assumed Jade would eventually go on to law school and how Jade had laughed at that, saying she didn't want the responsibility.

"You know," he said thoughtfully, "you really would make a great lawyer. Are you sure you wouldn't—"

Her expression of horror was eloquent. "No. No. We've lost our chance to have a Black woman president with a law degree. I'm going to just mind the shit in my own backyard, thank you. Now go do official stuff with what I gave you. Go! Before you finish your coffee and we have to start the coffee/bullshit cycle all over again."

Ellery held up a hand, balanced his coffee, and went, more eager to see the information she'd sent him now that she'd given him an angle.

He wished rather wistfully that she'd take him and Jackson up on the offer to put her through school, though. She'd make an awesome Madame President someday.

An hour later, after scanning the data updates that Jade and AJ sent him periodically, he wasn't thinking about anything but the mess of identities on his computer. There were maybe twenty people employed by Moms for

Clean Living—fifteen of them locals, male and female—who had been hired through nearby churches. But as Jade had noted, the five most prominent women, the ones with titles—president, vice president, treasurer, activities director, public relations director—had, well, *diverse* histories, to say the least.

Ellery could see how tracking their info could have been difficult. Valerie Trainor, president, had been Valerie Schmitt in Nevada before a divorce, but she'd been *Melanie* Schnarf in Arkansas before she'd gotten married to Conway Schmitt after she'd gone to school in Florida.

Conway Schmitt was a preacher, until he'd been arrested for—Ellery had to suppress his gag reflex here—molesting the preteen boys in his choir, which had happened shortly before Valerie had changed her name—and her identity—for the final time.

Okay, then. Valerie Trainor, *originally* from Arkansas, and originally Melanie Schnarf.

One down.

Ellery moved on to the vice president of the chapter, Ellie Medlar, who used to be Elinor Carpenter before she got married in Tennessee, and before that had been Selena Chalmers in Alabama. Before she'd gone to school at—oh, hey.

Florida State.

Ellery took a deep breath then, checked the time, and realized that an hour had gone by already and he hadn't heard a thing from Jackson.

Which was too bad. He finally had the barest hint of a pattern.

At that moment Jade slipped into his office and glanced over his shoulder.

"What's up?" he asked, rubbing his temples gingerly. Low on sleep, high on coffee, and now buzzing on information overload, he wasn't sure he could open a folder on another ladder-pulling white woman. It was incomprehensible to him. These women had, so far, been born poor, worked hard for an education with their MRS on the side, and then had set about making the same support systems that had given them food, clothing, and education when they'd been children absolutely *unavailable* to anybody else. Valerie Trainor and Ellie Medlar had been given access to libraries and free books as children, as well as free lunches and after-school programs, and then had spent the last three years trying to kill those programs in California. It wasn't even their state!

He tried to breathe through the indignation and focus on what Jade was doing, but it was hard. Jackson didn't have a corner on retribution and vengeance, he thought crossly. Ellery had been hoping his big brain could kick some ass, but it didn't feel like that was happening right now.

"I'm sorry, Jade," he murmured. "What did you say?"

"I asked if you were ready for some fucked-up bullshit and a break," she said, and he finally caught on to the unholy smile on her face.

He cocked his head. "Yes and… uhm, yes?"

"So you would not believe who is canvassing our neighborhood today. Want to guess? C'mon, Ellery," she said, practically dancing. "Guess."

Ellery knew his eyes rounded. "No," he said, not sure if he'd heard right.

"Oh yes," she said, nodding. "Yes. If you guessed the Stepford Dragons, you would be *right*. How far have you gotten on the information I gave you?"

He grimaced. "The grand poobah and vice grand poobah. Don't tell me either of *them* are in our reception room."

Jade shook her head. "No. This one claims to be one of the local folks. I forget the designation—volunteer, minion, whatever—"

"Flunky," Ellery said, and she nodded.

"Yeah, that. Anyway she was going to leave some pamphlets here, and I told her I'd have to ask my boss."

Ellery snorted, because if Jade had wanted to set those pamphlets on fire, nobody in the office would have much more to say than "The fire extinguisher is in the corner by the shelves." But they wouldn't *have* to do that because Jade herself had been the one to install it.

"Yeah, I know," she said, as though he'd stated the observation out loud. "But keep it to yourself. I'm saying, we've got *a flunky* in here, and we have a chance to—"

"Pick her brains," Ellery finished, because he wasn't stupid. "Did you get her name?"

"Piper Lutz," Jade said. "She's in your list of people to check out, but way at the bottom."

Ellery nodded, suddenly much more awake—and much more excited about his day. "Well by all means, offer the young—"

"Forty-five if she's a day," Jade said.

"—ish woman some coffee," Ellery continued smoothly. Then, "Are we her first stop in this complex?"

Jade frowned. "I'll have to see. Why?"

"Because you may want to warn the other businesses. Just… you know. Have them play along. Or, you know, in the case of the teacher's union, have them not be there when she comes knocking." There were three businesses in the upstairs part of the converted Victorian house/office building strip where Ellery leased office space. His own corner suite was big enough to fit three lawyers comfortably—he and Galen had decided to be particularly picky about their third since so far their chemistry was pretty solid—and a teacher's union was next door. Next door to *those* people—who had all proven to be lovely and kind and a cross between cynical as hell and too innocent for this world—was a headhunting/temp agency run by a couple—men—who specialized in niche markets and queer-friendly businesses. Often their workers used the office space Derek Huston and Rico Gonzales-Macias provided to deliver contract work Rico and Derek had procured for them, and the office culture was practically sparkling with optimism, good will, and genuine friendliness.

And rainbow flags of every variation.

Ellery wouldn't sic this woman on them for all the gold in the world.

"On second thought," he murmured, "maybe you and I should... discourage this woman before she leaves."

Jade's manic gremlin grin cranked up a notch. "Oh please, oh please, oh please," she muttered, holding her hands together like the praying angel he knew for a fact she'd never been.

"Yeah," Ellery said, a shaft of pettiness brightening his heart from the inside out. "Let's do that."

"Excellent," she said. "Excuse me, Mr. Cramer, I need to go fetch some coffee."

"That will be all, Miss Cameron," Ellery said primly, and they exchanged grim glances of the same evil joy.

Fifteen minutes later—and Ellery had to applaud Jade for keeping the woman waiting that long—Jade escorted a brittle blond woman in. She was a well-preserved forty-five, he thought critically, with ropy muscles in her thin wrists indicating a dedication to the gym, and an impeccable outfit of blue slacks and cream-colored Chanel jacket over a gray blouse. Understated and classy, right down to the little touches of pearls in the ears and a thin gold chain with a cross at her throat.

Jade gestured to the seats across from Ellery, and she turned and said, "Thank you, Jade, that will be all," as though she owned the place, and Ellery widened his eyes at Jackson's sister because he honestly thought she was going to set the bitch on fire.

"Ms. Cameron," Ellery said mildly, emphasizing the title. "Thank you so much for keeping Ms. Dunkel company while I finished up in here."

Piper Lutz's face, which had been schooled and pleasant—and mostly unmoving thanks to healthy injections of Botox in the cheeks and forehead—froze, and her large, heavily kohled and mascara-enhanced blue eyes turned into ice chips.

"Lutz," she said coldly. "My last name is Lutz."

"Oh, my bad," Ellery said, smiling at her. He'd been told by everyone in the office to stop trying to charm people with his smile—charm was not his strength. He believed them today as he watched the woman recoil with what looked like uneasiness. "I was studying a file, and I must have confused you with someone else. My apologies. By all means take a seat. I understand you were asking to solicit your political group here?"

Ellery wondered if shifting gears was more or less painful with that much of her face frozen. More painful because her muscles had to work twice as hard to present any sort of emotion, or less painful because humanity had been frozen with her face and everything was numb.

It was an uncharitable thought, but then, since her organization didn't pay taxes, he figured she didn't really need his charity.

"It's a mother's group," she said, obviously trying to force the mask in place. "I'm sorry if you were misled by your receptionist—"

"My paralegal assistant," he corrected. "And what do *you* do for a living?"

Watching somebody flush after having as much work done as Bertha Dunkel, now known as Piper Lutz, was pretty entertaining. The parts of her face recently injected didn't actually *turn* red—but the rest of her face blotched up nicely.

"I'm a stay-at-home mother," she said. "My children take up most of my time, but I do try to dedicate a few hours a week toward Moms for Clean Living." Her smile was back in place, and Ellery remembered his mother and sister fiercely advocating for stay-at-home moms. "It's not something *I* could do, Ellery," his mother had said often enough, and Ellery tried to give this woman the benefit of the doubt.

It was harder, though, now that he'd read her dossier.

"Oh really," he said, giving his scary smile again. "How old are your children?"

Piper's hair formed two graceful wings framing what was probably a round face in an effort to create the "perfect oval" women seemed to chase. She carefully ran her third finger from her part, down her hairline, to her ear, where she flipped her wing of hair back—a tell of discomfort if Ellery had ever seen one.

"Oh, my youngest is a sophomore in UCLA," she said, trying for an indulgent smile. "Which is why I have time to volunteer in this worthy cause."

"And what is it, exactly, your organization does?" Ellery asked.

"We like to think of ourselves as public education's watchdogs," she said, with a slow bat of her eyelashes. "We're a grassroots movement that sees the gaps of oversight in our public schools, and we try to add that extra layer of monitoring to protect our children."

"So you help in the classroom?" he asked, pretty sure that was not the case.

"Oh no, our focus is more generalized than that."

"So you raise money for school activities and enrichment?"

"Oh no—going outside the classroom to see the larger world is something that should be between students and parents only. We don't believe in enrichment."

Ellery knew his head tilt of disbelief had increased a few degrees, but God help him, that was a rough one to swallow.

"You help purchase materials?" Ellery asked. "Because it's well known schoolteachers are already putting a great deal of their own money into classrooms, so I'm sure that sort of thing would be helpful."

"But that's their job!" Piper laughed, and Ellery fought the urge to lean over the table and grab her by the throat. "They sign on knowing that they're responsible for what the government won't provide."

Behind the door he heard a strangled sound of what might have been fury, and he politely coughed to cover Jade's grunt of disbelief.

"So," Ellery said carefully, "you don't help the schools obtain resources, you don't volunteer time to assist their personnel, and you don't seem to be rallying for them to have more materials or to enrich their curriculum, have I got that right?"

The weird, uneven blotch had bled from her overplumped features, and what remained was an almost corpse white. "Well, we leave those things to the powers that be," she said.

"So what exactly do you do?" Ellery kept his "pleasant" smile in place, and she did that smoothing the hair back thing again, so he knew it was working.

"I beg your pardon?"

"You say you're a school monitoring system—what exactly do you monitor?"

"Well, we are particularly interested that teachers stick exclusively to the curriculum—"

"That you expect the government to buy materials for—"

"And in no way deviate from what is the acceptable list of standards and concepts that children should be learning."

"But you're not willing to help in the classroom," Ellery summarized.

"We mostly look to make sure no foreign concepts enter the school system that parents don't approve of," she finished in a rush, as though she and Ellery had been racing to a conclusion.

"You ban books," he said shortly, and that flush returned, this time with more force and intensity.

"Only the ones we feel—"

"Who feels?" he asked.

"What?"

"Who's we?" he asked.

"Our coalition," she said, almost eagerly. "Moms for Clean Living."

"So your little group"—he waved his hand dismissively—"has suddenly decided that they get a say in what kids get to read?"

"We don't want children exposed to foreign ideas," she said, her mouth setting mutinously.

"Foreign to whom?" he asked. "Explain this?"

"Well, to regular, law-abiding—"

Ellery pulled up a list of books that Jade had printed out for him while they'd put Piper Lutz on hold. "So a book about Rosa Parks as a child is foreign?" he asked.

"It makes white children feel bad about a specific time in history," she said stonily.

"They should," Ellery retorted. "We *all* should, so it doesn't happen again. This book about the kitten bringing sushi to school—that's bad?"

"*Americans*," Piper enunciated, "eat sandwiches."

"Not in this law office," Ellery said promptly. "And what's your problem with purple crayons?"

"We feel that six is too young to learn about the LGBTQ world," Piper said, her voice getting shriller. "That book encourages sexual deviancy."

"That book encourages children to be purple," Ellery said. "Whatever purple means to them. And it tells them to be kind to children who *don't* fit into the already established modes. I notice your group doesn't promote any sort of antibullying campaigns, and it has, in fact, defended bullies from school administrations all across the country. Do I have that right?

You would rather have the bigger kids pick on the smaller kids than have the smaller kids be safe?"

"We think of it as peer reinforcement of societal norms," she said without a trace of shame.

"That's amazing," Ellery said. "You can justify shoving queer kids in lockers and driving them to suicide. I'm in awe." He picked up the fliers she'd placed on his desk, yanking them from her hand before she could reclaim them. "Ma'am, do you have any idea who's in this office complex where you've chosen to peddle your ideas?"

For a moment there was silence, and Ellery watched as the slow realization seeped in.

"Your law office, a union office next door, and a temp agency?" she said, and he realized she—or somebody else—must have briefed her without truly comprehending the thumbnails provided by the internet.

He nodded slowly. "Ms. Lutz, are you a Sacramento native?" The first level of her dossier had claimed that, but the lower levels—the Bertha Dunkel levels—had proven that claim false.

A look of puzzlement crossed her features. "Nossir. We came to California about five years ago." Her accent slipped, and for a moment, the entire façade of elegant, wealthy woman seemed to slide, like her plasticized features, off her face.

"Was that when you changed your name from Bertha to Piper?" he asked.

"No," she said, more and more baffled. "That was back in college."

"Florida State," he clarified.

"Yes," she said, "How did you—"

"Are *any* of the people in your organization actually from Sacramento?"

"Well, most of us followed Twitty from school—"

"Wait," Ellery said. "You followed *who*?"

Piper Lutz—once Bertha Dunkel—had fully abandoned her wealthy socialite on a mission guise and was now a cornered wolverine. "I don't know who in the hell you are," she hissed, "or how you know so goddamned much, but I will just take my fliers and go on my way—"

"Who's Twitty?" Ellery asked, his voice hard. "You tell me who Twitty is and I'll tell you a little secret that will make your entire day much easier."

"It's our little nickname for Mel… I mean Val… I mean—"

"Valerie Trainor," Ellery said, his heart thudding in his ears. "Okay, why do you call her that?"

"It was an old joke. Her ex-husband's last name was Schmitt, but his first name was Conway, so, you know, Conway Twitty, but Schmitty? But we just called her Twitty—"

"What about Retty?" Ellery asked, suddenly so eager for this windfall of information that he could almost jump over the desk and *sit* on this woman for intel. "Do you have any background on her?"

"You can't make me say anything!" Piper Lutz screamed. "You can't make me say *anything*! Now tell me your filthy little secret!"

Ellery blinked and had to scramble before he remembered what he'd meant by that.

"Oh," he said, rocking backward. "Absolutely everybody in this business complex thinks of your organization as the Ku Klux Krazies. There is a *plethora* of lawyers in this immediate vicinity that would love to sue you for inflicting unnecessary trauma with your little spiel. I'm a criminal attorney, so you don't have to worry about that coming from *me*, but my partner in the firm is dying for a shot at you. You're lucky he's not here—he would have stripped the skin off your body with his acid tongue. But seriously, nobody here likes you. By all means, take your shit and go."

He threw all but one flier at her, and she gathered them up, stuffing them into her Coach bag before fleeing out the door Jade was holding open for her. They both heard the ring of the glass door to the walkway outside the office, and before the hydraulics would let it close, the clatter of her pumps as she hauled ass down the concrete-and-iron staircase next to the elevator.

The door rang closed, and they both heaved a little sigh of relief while Jade slumped against the door.

"Holy God," she murmured. "Ellery, I haven't seen a takedown like that since you had Jackson on the stand bleeding."

Ellery shuddered, remembering that moment. Jackson had testified willingly, shown the wound on his back from the plaintiffs without judgment, but Ellery had never forgotten the fury that had coursed through his veins and how hard it had been to control.

This had felt worse somehow.

Maybe because Henry wasn't able to defend himself. Maybe because Jackson was out there suffering, on a mission of vengeance, hurting inside while missing his friend, his partner, and needing so badly to get the people who'd hurt him.

It was the helplessness, Ellery realized wretchedly. The helplessness bred the fury, and the fury… he took a deep breath.

The fury bred mistakes.

"Oh, I shouldn't have done that," he murmured.

"I don't know why not," Jade said with a snort. "That was really impressive."

Ellery shook his head. "I tipped our hand," he said. "I just made things harder for Jackson. I just made things harder for *us*." He swallowed sickly, thinking about all the things a group like this could do to the people in their office complex. "I made our entire office complex into a target for these assholes." Oh hell. "Oh, this is bad."

"No," she said soberly. "I mean, yes. It's possible they'll take some shit out on us. But I'll go talk to Nate, the receptionist next door, and to Rico and Derek next to them, and warn everybody. Nobody has the right to make you eat shit, Ellery. Everything that woman said was abhorrent. I've rescheduled everybody for today, and AJ and Crystal are still on research and backgrounds. As you can tell, it's a slog. You call Jackson, because we're both dying to check in with him, and then we'll get back to work. Tomorrow we'll make the firm run. Today we're hunting down whoever did this to Henry. But what you just did? That was part of who we *are*. Like you told her—Galen would have left her in tatters. Neither one of you has it in you to lie down and take it, even if it would make it easier."

"None of us does," he said with a sigh. "Maybe we should have AJ take some time off research to beef up security around our building. I… I've got a bad feeling about these people, Jade. I just pissed them off and made it personal. You make sure the other offices know this, okay?"

"Will do," she said. "I'll order lunch when I get back." She gave a little smile. "Sushi."

Against his will, Ellery found himself chuckling. "Chopsticks only," he said primly, and she winked before grabbing her coat and venturing into the windy bright sunshine of the post-rainy day.

Ellery sat thoughtfully down at his desk and checked his phone for a text from Jackson, pleased to see that he had one.

Just saw Cowboy's mother. Ugh. OMW to see Henry. Talk when done.

Part of him was disappointed. He wanted to talk *now*, and he was not ashamed to say he wanted comfort. Dammit, the office was unnervingly silent without Henry and Galen, and Ellery's heart hurt because he was missing *friends*, not merely coworkers, and Jackson's voice would take some of that loneliness away.

But part of him *was* comforted, because Jackson *had* texted. Ellery knew he was on task and where he was heading.

It hadn't always been like that. Ellery could take the win.

But he couldn't go back to reading those dossiers with all those fake identities sliding from one picture of a smiling white woman with botoxed cheeks and streaked blond hair to another. After his confrontation with Piper Lutz, the thought made him nauseous—but also curious. Where had all these women come from? Florida State University seemed to be the epicenter, but what had happened there, and who had been involved, to send them all on a quest to ban books and bully anybody who wasn't exactly like them?

Ellery had one major resource in this matter, and he wasn't afraid to tap it.

Besides, his mother had a soft spot for Henry, and she'd never forgive Ellery if he didn't update her on his injury. If nothing else, she'd already asked for his hospital room number to make sure his room was overflowing with flowers.

And she'd be really hurt if she wasn't asked to assist with the vengeance part too.

Undiscovered Talent

JACKSON TOOK a look at the apartment complex Cowboy's address had led him to and swallowed.

Oh God. Not one of these.

Cowboy and Isabelle had been sitting to breakfast when Jackson had driven by K-Ski's, a box full of doughnuts as a peace offering for the hour of the visit after the late night. Billy—a health food nut with a capital *nut*—had scowled until Jackson pointed to the three red-bean pastries he'd gotten so Billy could have some and not worry about processed sugar.

Sean had given Jackson a grateful look and snagged one of the cream-filled maple bars, the expression on his blue-eyed, Polish-handsome face that of a man about to indulge in a favorite vice.

Cowboy appeared different in the light—less scared, more street savvy. But he kept hold of the little yappy dog, and Billy confided that he was going to have a hard time ripping "puppy" out of the kid's arms.

"I swear to God, if they took dogs in Disneyland, we'd bring him," Billy muttered.

"Well, promise him he can see the dog when he comes back," Jackson said. He paused. "And then *keep* that promise."

Billy—a consummate smartass—rolled his eyes. "You think I don't know that? You don't make promises to that kid and not keep them." His face softened. "Besides, my little brothers would be happy to be his friend. They can bond over little dogs. We'll make him an honorary stereotype."

Billy was proud of his Mexican heritage, and of his family, sans a father, who, Jackson understood, was a piece of work.

"The more family for this kid the better," Jackson told him. He eyed the kid critically, knowing that a month on the streets could leave a lifetime of damage, some of it purely physical. "Make sure you and Sean take him to get tested," he said softly. "And when you get back, he's going to need a thorough physical."

"And psych workup," Billy agreed with a sigh. "Yeah. Three days at Disneyland isn't going to wipe away all the bullshit like a magic diaper rag."

"No," Jackson said thoughtfully, eyeballing the way Cowboy took furtive bites of his doughnut as though somebody was going to steal it from him, "but you'd be amazed at how one great memory can help you hold on when shit gets bad. Don't underestimate what this can mean to him, Billy. But don't take your eyes off him either—not even in the bathroom. *Especially* in the bathroom. Make sure he knows he can have anything he asks for, even silly things like stuffed animals and toys and sweatshirts, and offer to buy him food or candy every hour. Don't be surprised if he starts grifting for sugar daddies, thinking he's got to pay his way, and make sure he doesn't steal anything. Don't take it personally if you have to teach him more than once that he's cared for on this trip."

Billy made a helpless gut-shot sound. "Yeah. Yeah. I hear you. My brother Roberto, after my dad left—he… he did bad shit because he thought he had to be the man of the house. Kids. They take on all this weight when the grown-ups around them fall down on the job."

"You, Sean, and Isabelle can help him give a little of that up," Jackson told him. Then he grinned. "Of course he'll have to compete with Sean for the biggest kid at the park, you know that, right?"

Billy's return smile was a little bit bashful. "I can't wait to see," he said, his ears turning a warm magenta. "My cop, man—he's always so serious. I think he's gonna be fun."

And that alone sort of made Jackson's morning brighter. "Pictures," he said, sobering. "Your job is to take pictures of all of them. When you come back, Henry is going to need pictures to show him what the outside is like. You know him. He's always so busy. He's going to need something to help him make plans."

"Like he and Lance needing their own trip to Disneyland," Billy said excitedly.

"Yeah. Like that. I mean, he hasn't seen a lot of great stuff about California. Show him what he's missing."

Billy let out a long breath. "Thanks," he said softly. "Me and Sean, we felt so helpless last night. It's good to have a plan so we don't feel that way anymore."

"Straight up," Jackson said, and then, conscious that the morning was moving on, he turned toward Cowboy. "Hey, kid, is it okay if I sit by you and have a doughnut?"

Cowboy smiled shyly. "It's okay, Mr. Rivers. You don't even want to know what I'd do for a doughnut."

Jackson winced. "You are absolutely right about that," he said, meaning every syllable. "But don't worry. All you gotta do now is give me a little more info, okay?"

The boy nodded and took another furtive bite of the doughnut that carved up a little more of Jackson's soul.

Jackson took out his phone and opened a notes file. "Okay, first off the easy stuff. Your old address when you lived with your mom."

Cowboy rattled off the numbers quickly, down to the apartment number and his mother's first and last name—Reba Milton—and seemed faintly surprised, as though he hadn't been aware he could do that.

"Awesome," Jackson said. "Now, can you tell me what school you went to and who your favorite teacher was."

Cowboy looked stricken. "You… you're not going to tell them where I've been, are you?" he asked, suddenly near tears.

"Oh no. No, kid, not at all." Jackson felt like a heel of the first order. "No—no. This is for later. When you come back I just want to get some books for you to read, you know? See where you are in math and stuff. You seem like a smart kid. We can catch you up in school in no time."

"Will I have to go back?" Cowboy asked, those tears still threatening. "They all know I kiss boys now, and for all I know I'll get the shit kicked out of me and—"

Jackson held his hands up. "Cowboy, I promise—*promise*—you that wherever you end up, it's not going to be until *you* are ready. Right now I don't want you to forget what school looks like, that's all. And if you've read all the books from English class, you can usually pass all the tests so you don't get too far behind. Okay?"

Cowboy relaxed a little. "Okay," he whispered. Then, a little less frightened, he said, "Thank you, Mr. Rivers. I liked school. You're right, I've been sort of bored, in my head, you know?"

"Smart kid like you," Jackson said, "I bet you were. Don't worry. It will make Isabelle feel more like a mom if she sees you reading some schoolbooks." He was also thinking about Randy, who was *amazingly* smart with books but not great with almost anything else. That kid would have come in *so* handy right now, and Jackson hoped for the thousandth time that Randy was safe and cared for. "So that's one thing—you write down your teacher's name, and I'll get you some books and stuff, and we're good."

"Okay, then, what's the other thing?"

Jackson slid his phone over, and Cowboy started typing in his teacher and school. While he was doing that, Jackson started with the hard stuff.

"Okay, so you said four other boys, right? Caleb was the one who went back. Do you remember the others?"

Cowboy frowned and, unconsciously, took a big healthy bite of what was left of the doughnut. His eyes widened comically and then closed, and Jackson watched in fascination as the hit of sweetness hit the kid's bloodstream like heroin.

He smiled slightly and said, "Caleb, Jacob Cornell, Danny, and Otto." He opened his eyes again, and the most bemused smile crossed his face. "Otto Karekes," he said in sudden memory. "It was a *really* odd name, and he said he was German." His face fell. "And then he said this was better than he could expect to see in some other countries, where he might have been killed outright. I…." He turned troubled eyes to Jackson. "Do you think he was okay? Jacob too? Otto was the one who hurt his leg."

"I'll do my best to find out," Jackson promised soberly. "And now one more thing. Sh… erm, Retty. She's the employee you had the most contact with. Can I get a description of her? And Twitty too? Tall, short, dark hair, light hair, that sort of thing. Let's go with Retty first."

Cowboy was much more lucid—and much braver—now that he had some sleep in him. He described Retty as having long, wildly curly black hair, a square jaw, and—in Cowboy's words, "Rough skin. Her cheeks were red. She was wearing, like, work clothes and that jacket—green with the logo in white. She looked, you know. Regular. Like a waitress or a lunch lady or someone who works at a pizza place. Like, no makeup or anything, and her shoulders were… sort of forward."

The boy hunched his shoulders and, apparently unconsciously, assumed a grim expression, but also one that was almost… slack.

Retty really *was* hired muscle, Jackson thought. She was the attack dog. And Twitty—who was blond and thin and looked "like she should be on a magazine"—was the face of the operation.

Interesting.

Jackson winked at the boy when he was done and told him he was so smart and told him that they would probably leave on the trip that afternoon. He said this exchanging glances with Sean, who nodded, the unspoken order passing between them that Cowboy needed to be out of town by then.

And then Jackson turned toward Isabelle Roberts, who was wearing a set of Sean's sweats and a clean pair of crew socks. She wasn't a wispy woman—she filled out the sweats with middle-aged curves and comfortable hips—but she wasn't self-conscious about it either.

"Ms. Roberts?" he said, pulling up near her to give her the illusion of privacy, "I saw Bobby last night. He can't come—"

"He'd be easy to follow," she said promptly, and he nodded.

"Exactly. But he wanted you to know that he's really proud of you. And he and Reg are *so* glad you're safe."

Her wide green eyes sheened. "Thank you," she whispered before shaking herself. "Are you sure there's no way I can go to my apartment? I would *really* love my own clothes."

Jackson laughed a little and pulled out a wad of cash Bobby had shoved into his hands before they'd all left the hospital.

"He gave me this to give to you," Jackson said. "For clothes. Apparently he got tipped *really* well under the table on his last carpentry job. He was going to buy you cross-stitch patterns, but he said there was probably enough here for clothes too."

Ms. Roberts gaped in surprise at the wad of cash before counting it. She gave Jackson a droll look. "You would think after three years on his own, he would know what things cost," she said, her voice ringing with such amazing momness that Jackson's mouth twisted. "Dear God. Well, me and Cowboy are going to have a *field* day at a Target somewhere out of town. Did you hear that, Cowboy? New clothes for the both of us. And then T-shirts at Disneyland."

Cowboy gave her an unfettered smile, hugging Charming the dachshund close and seeming, for the first time, like a fourteen-year-old boy. "Awesome," he said, and Jackson had some hope for the lot of them.

He and Ellery would make Sacramento safe for these two people if they had to dig a trench under all of Moms for Clean Living and its environs and let the building collapse into dust. There was no other way.

As soon as he got into Jennifer, his phone buzzed with Dex's message that Henry had woken up, and Jackson should be by around lunch. He closed his eyes for a moment and sent up a prayer to Gru—or the spaghetti monster or the sky daddy or whoever was in charge of making sure smartass ex-soldiers with hero complexes could survive—and took off for Reba Milton's apartment complex.

When he'd found a spot to park on the cracked, crumbling asphalt, he got out of Jennifer and paused, scoping out his enemy. He spent a moment staring at the two-story structure, old, with peeling paint on the warped eaves, cracked yellow stucco, and concrete stairs that didn't look like they'd take a grown man's weight.

The place was located on Watt near Whitney, and there was such a spotty vibe in this area. This particular complex was shoved between two brand-new strip malls, for instance, and while the strip malls appeared busy and prosperous, the complex, with the full concrete apron and the single row of apartments on the ground and on the top floor, was so damned....

Sad.

Jackson, Kaden, and Jade had grown up in a place much like this, not too far away from this one, but their complex had been surrounded by houses with trash in the yard and other complexes with the same concrete floor. No green *anywhere*, not even a tree in the back. But the difference, Jackson tried to remember. The difference in the apartment Jackson had shared with his mother versus the apartment Jade and Kaden had shared with their mother, Toni....

Jackson shuddered, remembering the bare, scarred walls in his mother's apartment. The one couch, stained, the battered kitchen table and chairs that wobbled. He'd slept on a mattress on the awful brown carpet in the living room, and she'd had the one bedroom, with the bed that squeaked and howled whenever his mother was putting out for drugs, cash, or food.

Not often for food.

And one floor above, up the rickety stairs—don't lean on the wrought iron railing because it wouldn't even support the scrawny fifth grader he'd been—there'd been the Camerons' apartment. Same icky brown rug, but it had been vacuumed, and any stains had been scrubbed out. A couch and a stuffed chair and a—oh joy!—television set, but also curtains and valences that were bright and cheery. The couch was frayed at the corners but clean, and the table was battered but sound. The chairs might have been a little wobbly, but they were shored up with sugar packets, and nobody got scratched on metal edges that had been torn from the sides.

There were pictures on the walls—discounted art, but matted and framed—and Kaden and Jade always, *always*, had a test or a project on the refrigerator. There had been two bedrooms, one for the twins and one for Toni, and Kaden and Jade had homemade blankets, from on-sale fabrics, but still *homemade*, that were in their favorite colors with action figures on Kaden's blanket and, well, *female* heroines on Jade's blanket, because even then she'd been a fighter.

And art. And color. And clean clothes in battered dressers. And schoolbooks.

And care.

But all of that had been behind the same door of peeling paint that had hidden Celia's squalor.

Jackson checked out the apartment number—#4—saw that it was a downstairs unit, and stopped leaning against Jennifer the minivan to go see what was behind door number four.

He gave the door an authoritative rap, and then, true to his history in law enforcement, he moved to the side. Doors were thinner and easier to shoot through. After a few moments, during which he could hear footsteps and swearing and then the chain being put in the slot, the door creaked open and he was eye to eye with a woman who was doing her thirties the hard way. She was thin, with about four inches of roots showing and a lot of brassy, teased hair below that. Once upon a time she'd had delicate features, Jackson thought, but her face showed fatigue now, poor diet choices, and the ravages of nicotine, which issued from the apartment in a cloud. She was wearing black yoga pants, pilled almost into transparency, and a tight once-white tank, and was clutching a battered plaid blanket around her shoulders in deference to the weather.

She regarded Jackson with unfriendly eyes through the crack between the door and the frame, and he watched the slow computer in her head as she tried to figure out who he was and what he wanted.

"Kenny's next door," she muttered, "but he doesn't got anything until tomorrow."

He rolled his eyes. "I don't want your dealer," he said, and her grimace proved him right.

"What do you want?" she asked.

"Where's your kid?" He said it bluntly because he hated this place already, and he hated that Cowboy had lived here, and he really, really hated *her*.

Her eyes darted back and forth, and he wondered how badly she hated that Kenny was out of product. "He's not here," she said. "Kid's in school."

"No, he's not," Jackson said. "Guess again."

Her lower lip trembled. "He's supposed to be in school," she whispered. "Someplace to teach him, you know?"

"Do you remember the place's name?" he asked.

She closed her eyes. "Moms for Clean Living," she whispered. "They were at the place, the rehab place. I was talking in group about how my kid was a fag, and this woman came up to me, all official and everything, and said they had a school that would fix it."

She met his eyes for the first time, hers a bruised and battered brown with an element of childish hurt in there. *Not in her thirties*, he thought. *Barely thirty. Had him too young. Didn't know what to do with him. All the places she went to for help only fixed one side of things, like paint on five pieces of a thousand-piece puzzle.*

He gasped and tried to jerk his gaze away, but she went first.

"Is my boy all right?" she asked, her voice a husky rasp. "They said he'd write, but… but he ain't written." She studied her bare toes with not even a hint of polish and swallowed hard. "I miss him. But they said he had to get the devil out of him because he was a fag."

"That," he said, not sure where his emotions were going, "is a terrible word. Your son is kind, and he's funny, and he's brave. You had no right— *no right*—to throw him away because of who he wants to kiss."

She tilted her head and gestured with her chin. "Mister, I don't know if you seen their place in midtown, but it was like throwing him from a trash heap to a castle, you know?"

"Not if they were going to beat him into submission, Reba," he said, and part of him was screaming that he needed to get information from this woman before he went off, and part of him wanted to turn around and run, not walk, back to Sean and Billy's and beg them, beg Isabelle, to take this woman's child and raise him in a circle of love he would never want to escape.

And part of him wished somebody would do the same for Reba Milton, because even he could see that this woman had once been a girl badly in need of help, and nobody had stepped up.

"They wouldn't beat him," she said, with so much certainty he had to remind himself that Cowboy had run away because the other kids had told him they were scared there.

"Whatever they'd do," he said, "it had them all terrified enough to run away. Your boy's been living on the streets for a *month*, Reba. I mean, are you going to kick him out for kissing a boy when he's sleeping on the sidewalk eating garbage?"

She squeezed her eyes tight. "Don't lie to me, mister. I know what you do when you're on the street. I did it so I could afford an apartment. My boy was staying in the family business, that's all."

Oh hell. Jackson needed caffeine, and sleep, and for Jade to remind him that he'd gotten clear of this apartment a long time ago. And he needed Ellery to ask him if he needed help so he could kick his feet and say no, he'd do it fine on his own, thank you, and he needed Henry to ask him what in the fuck he was doing there, and he needed *Henry to be all right.*

That last thought was what straightened his backbone.

"Reba, I'm not here to shit on you," he said. "And I'm not going to report you to the cops. I need two things from you, and then I'll leave you alone."

She sniffled in response, and he wondered how much more he could hate himself.

"One, I need you to tell me about the woman in the rehab center, the one who told you she could 'fix' Cowboy. What was her function there? Was she an addict as well?"

Reba shook her head. "No—but all the people who worked at the center knew her. Some didn't like her, but she had sort of... you know. A pass. The lady who ran the center, Cora, hated her, but it was like Retty had something on her. You could tell. Cora would scowl and look like she swallowed a bug whenever Retty was walking the halls."

Jackson nodded. Blackmail or threats—something had forced the rehab's director to violate confidentiality and allow an interloper.

"Sacramento Recovery?" Jackson asked. It was a few buses from this apartment complex, but he figured Reba must have worked nearby.

"I've got a job waitressing down the block from there," she confirmed. Her face screwed up in pain. "It's been hard to go," she admitted, "without Cowboy to come home to."

Jackson let out a breath. "Reba, you need to be not a mess to take care of him. You understand that, right? Giving him away to the Moms for Clean Living people—that wasn't something you should do if you weren't using, do you understand?"

"But he's... he's gay, and how am I supposed to deal with that?" she asked, and he heard the genuine question in her voice.

"Look," he said, taking a breath. "My mother was a junkie and a whore, and yeah, she sold me to a john once for drugs, and I almost went to juvie for a year when I clocked the guy in the throat defending my virtue. But you know what she never, ever fucking did?"

"What?" Reba asked, voice shaking along with her hands. Jackson bet she was dying for a smoke right now, but she seemed to be glued to the crack between the door and the doorframe the same way he was.

"She didn't give a *damn* who I kissed," he said. "And she didn't judge. Now if the sex work keeps you in your apartment, that's something you can make your peace with, but I think you and I both know your waitressing money will go a lot farther if you're not spending it on junk, amirite?"

She nodded. "Cigarettes are almost more expensive than meth," she whispered.

"Right? So priorities. So if you want to see your son again, you get yourself straight. And if the Moms for Clean Living come by, you never fucking saw me."

She nodded and wiped her face with the back of her hand. "Was that the other thing you wanted from me? Before you leave me alone? Because I sure could use to be left alone."

"Yeah," Jackson said, swallowing hard. "I'll be back in a month. If you've got your shit sorted, and you think you can not be shitty to your kid, maybe you could see him again for a little bit. But in the meantime, don't fight where he is right now. He's got people right now who will take care of him. I can make sure your kid lands soft. But you—you've got to not fuck with his head. No coming back and telling him that all is forgiven if only he's straight again. None of that shit. Let him be a kid. Let him have some safety and some steady food. Take care of yourself, and remember how to be a mom." His voice, which had assumed the hard edge of somebody reprimanding a teenager, softened. "He's a great kid no matter who he kisses. If you can't see that, you need to leave him alone."

She swallowed and nodded. "You'll be back in a month?" she asked.

"Yeah," he said.

"If I'm not here, don't look," she said, and his heart fell. "But I'll try to be here. I'll try to be better."

Jackson nodded, thinking that was about as good as he was going to get, and he reached into his wallet and pulled out another card. "This is for Marconi rehab. It's a lot closer. It might be easier if you've got someplace for meetings that's only a couple blocks over, and this way you won't see Retty again."

She snatched the card from him with nicotine-yellowed fingertips. "Yes," she said, sounding almost greedy. "Yes. Someplace else. Someplace they tell me how to love my boy."

"You just love him," Jackson said, feeling overwhelmed. "You just… just fix yourself and love them."

"But nobody shows you how," Reba Milton said. "Nobody."

She shut the door then, slowly, like she'd lost all the energy to do anything else, and Jackson closed his eyes for a moment, grateful for the fresh air once the apartment was closed up. He walked away, reluctantly at first, and then with increasing resolve.

He'd done what he could. He'd be back in a month—he'd promised. And in the meantime, he and his friends would keep her son safe.

And someday, Jackson thought, he'd have a talk with Cowboy about how sometimes it wasn't that the person who let you down was bad. Humans didn't always have the strength to win with the hand they'd been given. Not all love was perfect love. And sometimes wanting to be better wasn't enough.

When he got to the car, he wanted to talk to Ellery so badly his hands almost shook with it. But he had to head to the hospital to see Henry, and then go to Richards Boulevard to get backup, and then he really did have one hell of a day planned out.

But he missed Ellery, and what was all that "internal work" for if he couldn't reach out to the man who was probably fretting over Jackson's well-being during this entire anxiety-filled day.

He sent the text and smiled a little when Ellery hit the little heart key on it, and then plugged his phone into the charger on Jennifer's dash. There was no Henry here, he thought dismally. He had to keep his phone charged and his contacts live and his whereabouts known, because Henry wasn't there to have his back, and the rest of the world was worried about Henry and didn't have the wherewithal to fuss over Jackson's worthless scrawny ass in the meantime.

Being a grown-up meant taking care of his own damned business, but it was always a lot more fun when he and Henry were nagging each other to do it.

With a choice swear word, he started Jennifer and drove.

HE HATED the hospital with the fierce passion of somebody who once had the nurses schedule memorized so he knew who to hit up for things like real chocolate and paperbacks.

Dave, who had been there the night before, and his boyfriend, Alex, were frequent visitors at Jackson and Ellery's house for dinner. They were fond of saying that Jackson had been their worst patient—but he was a fairly decent friend.

Today he walked the familiar corridors of Davis Med Center with what he hoped was a relaxed posture, while he inwardly cursed himself for that damned doughnut two hours ago.

He had to keep his teeth from chattering every time he turned a corner or heard a footstep or the clatter of a gurney. The halls themselves were hushed—there weren't a lot of party people in the critical care wards—but somebody was always going somewhere, doing something, even in a darkened room.

It made it damned hard to sleep.

Maybe it was his visit to Cowboy's mom or his sudden loneliness without his backup, but a freight train of memories plowed through his head, flickering like a slideshow on speed.

The explosion of pain in his shoulder, his chest.

The numbness of shock, the confusion of people over him, touching him, shouting about him.

Darkness, so much darkness, while the inside of his body was pushed, pulled, stitched, irrigated, but in his head, just darkness.

He must be dead.

His body shattering into life, to light, to pain.

He must be in hell.

Seriously, that was the only explanation. He was in hell.

"Whoa, whoa, whoa" came a familiar voice. "Oh, sweets, you're blacking out on me, aren't you?"

Jackson took in a breath and realized he'd been holding it for too long. "Alex?" he asked, feeling a little bit of déjà vu. For all he knew, those were the exact same words Alex had used eleven years ago when Jackson had come to in critical care after he'd been nearly fatally shot.

Well, he'd died more than once on the operating table. Did that count as *fatally* shot?

"Yeah, sweetheart. You're here to see your friend, aren't you. Dr. Luna's hot boyfriend—that one."

"Yeah," Jackson said, forcibly shaking off the freight train. "Sorry—PTSD flashbacks. Fucking hospitals."

Alex had tucked his hand under Jackson's elbow and was walking with him, slowly, toward the ID-only hydraulic door into the ward.

"Yeah, I hate them myself," he agreed, and Jackson's chuckle took them both by surprise.

"Alex, you're a nurse!" he said.

"Well, yeah. But I mean, work. Who wants to be *there*?"

Another chuckle, and another step, and Jackson was taken, one breath at a time, back from that early trauma, that *first* trauma, into the here and now.

"I don't mind so much," he said. "Work, that is. I mean, I meet the nicest people."

It was Alex's turn to chuckle, but the slight, blond, practically elfin man grandly escorting him down the hall burbled more than chuckled.

"You say that, but Dave tells me that nice Dr. Luna tried to beat the shit out of you last night. Well done, by the way. I didn't think Dr. Luna was flappable, but you got him well and truly flapped."

Jackson grunted this time, suddenly too tired to chuckle. "He was mad at me because Henry got hurt," he admitted baldly, trying to pull that mantle of maturity on his shoulders. The interview with Reba Milton had stripped it away, apparently, and a lot of his thick skin with it.

"It was your fault Henry was shot by some crazy woman trying to hunt down a kid?" Alex said, sounding legitimately puzzled. "You weren't even there."

"Yeah, but, you know. I'm, like, this black hole that pulls people into my bloodbath," Jackson told him bitterly, and Alex paused in the corridor and *slugged* his arm.

"Ouch!" Jackson pulled back and rubbed his bicep. "Alex, the *fuck*!"

"You know what you did," Alex said darkly and then took his elbow again like he hadn't almost incapacitated Jackson to begin with. "You end up pissing off the bad people because you defend the innocent people. We all know Henry—he's the same way. If Lance can't handle that about Henry, he needs to get out now, because it's not fair. It's like me breaking up with Dave because he can't dance—"

"You lie," Jackson said, laughing. Dave moved with fluidity and grace. Jackson couldn't imagine him not being able to dance.

"Ballet? Yes," Alex told him sourly. "But get that man on a hip-hop floor and all the other gay men are telling me to get him *off* the floor because he's making our people look bad."

"Now I know," Jackson said, feeling bemused—but also much better. "Thanks," he told Alex seriously.

"Just doing my small part to keep your well-oiled justice machine running smoothly," Alex told him. They'd arrived at the ID station, and Alex waved his ID in front of the reader, and the hydraulic door opened. Alex pulled him in, still keeping that cheery, grounding contact until they came to Henry's room.

Dex and Lance weren't there, but Dex's husband, Kane, a handsome man with dark hair, enormous brown eyes, and a chest and shoulders as wide as a Volkswagen, had folded himself into one of the chairs next to the bed, his tiny seven-year-old niece tucked under his arm.

"Unca Kane," she whispered, "is he up yet?"

"No, bunny," Kane said patiently. "We told you, Uncle Henry's not feeling good. We don't know when he's waking up."

"But he needs to wake up so he knows we love him," Frances whispered.

Kane glanced toward the door and caught Jackson's gaze before rolling his eyes. "He knows," he replied. "Bunny, we've been over this. Uncle Dex knows you love him. Uncle Henry knows you love him. I know you love me."

"Does Uncle Lance know I love him?" Frances asked.

"Yes, he does," Kane replied.

"Does Jackson?" Frances asked, and she slipped Jackson a sly glance that let him know he wasn't invisible hovering at the door.

"No," Jackson told her, grinning into sparkling brown eyes and returning the irrepressible smile. "I have no idea. Tell me."

"I love you, Jackson!" Frances sang, and Jackson moved from the door to sit in the hellishly uncomfortable chrome-and-vinyl-cushion thing next to Kane's respectable green office chair.

"I love you too, Frances bunny," Jackson told her gravely. "How's Lizard the cat?"

"She loves me!" Frances said happily. "She likes to give me kisses by rubbing her nose up against my nose, and her breath smells like fishes, and her naked skin is all prickly, and she's wonderful."

At the doorway Jackson heard Alex chuckle, and he glanced up in time to see Alex give a brief salute. "His chart says he's getting his vitals checked in half an hour," Alex said. "If he's not up by then, they'll wake him up, but you'll have to wait a bit before you can talk. Sorry about that, Jackson. I know you need to talk."

"It's good to see him," Jackson lied, and Alex rolled his eyes before he left. Jackson had no choice but to take his courage in both hands and *look* at Henry as he lay, still and pale, on the bed, surrounded by rails, with tubes and wires connected and the senser showing his vitals bumping silently along.

He was shirtless, probably because his shoulder and torso were both heavily bandaged, and for the moment the dressing had to be changed often enough to make even a johnny a pain in the ass.

Jackson couldn't remember if he'd worn one in his early days either.

But worse than shirtless, and worse than the bandages, was the stillness.

Henry was like Jackson—he was always in motion. Always on his way to somewhere to do something for somebody. Even when he'd been sort of an asshole, he'd taken on the job as Galen's driver and had adapted to it easily, learning when to offer help when Galen was suffering and how to give back Galen's acid humor as good as he got, because Galen was brilliant, and being bored was almost as painful for him as being injured.

But Henry wasn't moving now. Even his breathing and heartbeat were slowed as his body took its time to heal. His square, handsome face appeared older—grimmer. It was easy to think of Henry as "sparky" or "kid" when he was sassing back, but now, as even in sleep he fought a grimace of pain, Jackson could see the very adult lines that years of active deployment—and toxic relationship entrapment—had left on his face.

If he was "sparky" or "kid," it was because he used all his energy to have joy and enthusiasm and excitement about life, and Jackson needed to remember that.

"He'll be fine," Frances said softly, and Jackson managed to summon a smile for her.

"I know," he lied. He didn't know. Not really.

"Then stop looking at me like I'm dead," Henry muttered.

Jackson scowled at him. "You're supposed to be asleep," he accused. "Here I was getting ready for a wasted trip because you couldn't be assed to wake up, and you pull that shit on me?"

"You told Frances you loved her, but you didn't give me the tearful soliloquy," Henry said, his eyes still barely open. "I feel slighted."

"Your brother-in-law saved me from the tearful soliloquy," Jackson retorted, but his chest was tight, and he felt like he might have been maybe a breath away. "I'll have to thank him for that when you stop slacking and get up and help."

"Admit it," Henry murmured. "You were worried about me."

"I'm a man," Jackson said, sounding stung, but inside so fucking happy he might actually cry anyway. "I can admit it. It would have pissed me off if you'd died, you…." He glanced at Frances, who was staring at him and Henry with open curiosity. "You jerk," he finished piously, mindful of Kane's snort at his delicacy around the little girl.

"Yeah. Pissed off is your default, Rivers. I'll call that a win. You catch the bi… uhm…."

Kane had apparently had enough of the two of them trying not to swear. "Frances, tell Henry you love him and we'll go get you some pudding." Kane held the little girl up to kiss Henry's cheek while Kane told him, "Listen, if one of us isn't in the room, it's because we're taking a leak or getting coffee or something, okay? I'm going to send Dexter home after he comes back in to check on you because he's so tired he's running into walls, but don't worry. After me, you got Galen, and after that, the flophouse kids. After them, we'll go kidnap people off the street. You don't have to be alone, okay?"

Henry forced his eyes open to meet his brother-in-law's steady gaze. "Thanks," he said with naked gratitude.

"Yeah, well, it was rude of you to get hurt when I was starting to sort of like you. I mean, you brought us the most frickin' ugly cat in the world for Christmas, and I can't think of another brother-in-law who'd do that for me, so, you know. Don't stop breathing."

Frances laughed, because obviously the little girl could see through her uncle's almost transparent bluster. "You're funny, Uncle Kane. You love Uncle Henry too."

"I do, bunny," Kane told her as he hoisted her out of the room, "but I don't want him to get too confident, or he'll stop bringing us hairless cats for Christmas."

They left the cubicle, and Jackson turned toward Henry, who had watched them go as well. "Great call with the cat," he said. "I wasn't sure that was going to be a good idea, but you were right. Kane wouldn't be able to resist something that ugly." The cat had been payment for a client's legal fees, and the office—all of whom had been rooting for the client, whose big crime had been to help bust a kitten mill by breaking and entering—had been called upon to place all of the kittens in the mill. Princess Leia Organa Lilith Persephone Caligula had been the last cat they'd needed to place by the morning of Christmas Eve, and Henry had said, "Hey, you know, my brother's husband likes weird-looking critters. I bet something this hideous would be right up his alley."

The cat had been unbearably sweet, but, well, hairless, and Jackson had privately thought she was amazingly beautiful.

Which was why Henry had taken it upon himself to get the thing the hell out of Dodge before Jackson ended up with three cats and no house, and possibly no fiancé either.

"Dumb cat," Henry said affectionately. "She seems to think she's a lizard or something. She loves all the fucking reptiles. Even the snake."

Jackson chuckled, although Henry had said this before. "Happy family," he said softly.

"Yeah." Henry blinked at him. "Who got you?"

Jackson blinked back, and in a rush the aching in his jaw and cheekbone hit him—much like Lance's fist the night before. "Unimportant," he said. "How bad does the hospital suck? You can be honest. A twelve? A fifteen? Out of ten?"

"A twenty," Henry said and then fought his eyes closing. "Accent," he said. "South. Alabama, Tennessee. Thick."

And Jackson knew he was talking about the assailant before he fell asleep.

"Good boy," Jackson murmured. "Anything else?"

"Lots of thick black hair pulled back," Henry said. "Curly. Some gray."

"Cowboy's description of Retty," Jackson told him. "Good."

"ID'd herself as with Moms for Clean Living," Henry murmured. "Saw through the peephole. Went for the gun in Isabelle's dresser. Isabelle handed it to me. They got away."

"They did," Jackson told him. "We got them to safety." He knew Dex had probably told him this earlier, but it never hurt to hear it again. "You did good, Henry." And now his throat was tight, and his eyes were watering. "Really good."

Henry's eyes were closed, but he wasn't done talking. "Screamed shit as she fired. Said, 'Caleb wasn't my bullet, but you will be.'"

Jackson's breath caught. "Fuck," he muttered.

"Don't know who Caleb is…." Henry was falling asleep again, and Jackson wasn't ready to leave. Imagine that—so hard to take his steps in the door, but God, he hated to leave his boy in this awful place.

"Friend of Cowboy's," Jackson told him. He'd been told once that premature babies would strain themselves to hear whispered voices around them, but if people spoke in normal tones, they were reassured, and slept when they needed to. He figured if Henry was asking, Henry would fret if nobody gave him the answers. "We think it's why that woman came after him."

Henry grunted. "I winged her," he said, and even stoned and in pain, his satisfaction came through. "Hope her ride got blood all over the car."

Jackson sat up. "Ride?"

"She shouted as she ran away," Henry murmured dreamily. "Bertha, hit the gas." He giggled. "It's almost a country western song."

"Don't try to convert me to your cult," Jackson warned, mostly to keep him smiling as he fell asleep.

"You'll listen to Dixie Chicks and love it," Henry mumbled before finally drifting off.

Jackson stood and took his hand carefully, avoiding the tubes and ports and monitors. "Get rest, kid," he murmured. "Heal up. You and me, we got shit to do."

He squeezed Henry's fingers, and his eyes grew hot when he felt Henry squeeze back. He released Henry's hand with a sigh and turned toward the door, not surprised to see Dex in the doorway with a crooked smile on his face.

"You talked?"

"Yeah," Jackson said. "I was just leaving."

"Well, I'm glad you were here when he woke up this time. He felt like he had to make a report to you. It weighed on him."

Jackson lifted a shoulder. "I figured. He doesn't like to be left behind on an op. Had to keep him informed."

Dex nodded and ventured farther into the room. "He really loves what you guys do," he confided. "I mean, we worry—all of us worry. But we can't take it away from him, you know?"

Jackson met Dex's shadowed eyes and made a guess. "Lance still mad at me?"

Dex shook his head. "No. He's got to process, though. I think…." He let out a breath. "There's that tipping point in any relationship, you know? Whether it's fooling around or screwing around or yearning—that point when you realize that 'Hey, losing this person will end my world. Am I ready to love someone that much?' And the people who answer yes? They usually have what it takes. I'm not sure Lance had that reckoning. Not up close and personal in the way that counted. This… this makes it real."

Jackson cocked his head and studied Henry's brother—who was still the most beautiful man Jackson had ever seen, although yeah, Lance came close.

Maybe it was the softness around the eyes or—ever so slightly—around the middle that made him seem so much older. Everybody had a story, Jackson knew, and he was always curious.

"Someday," Dex said, smiling slightly, "we'll get together and have a beer, and I'll tell you things. And you can tell me some shit too. Yeah, Rivers, we're friends like that. You don't have to worry about asking."

Jackson returned his smile. "I am always—*always*—pleasantly surprised to find I have friends," he said. "And I will buy you that beer." He turned to Henry again, and while the oppression of the hospital beat on his shoulders, a renewed sense of urgency, of mission, was screaming his name. "Once we get the people who did this," he promised. "Nobody does this to your brother and gets away with it."

"Vengeance," Dex said. "I like that in a friend. What's your next step?"

Jackson opened his mouth, about to say "backup," but then he closed it again and let out a sigh. "Next stop is talking to a friend downstairs in the place we don't mention in critical care."

"And then?" Dex said.

"Then, backup," Jackson said with determination. "It's not even noon, Dex. I've got some ground to cover."

Dex held up his fist to bump. "Good hunting. We'll take care of Henry. You were right—he's got way too much to do to fall asleep right now."

Jackson bumped his fist and slid out of the cubicle, reassured by his visit and more determined than ever.

Which was good, because in most hospitals "downstairs" was code for the one place patients didn't want to end up, and that took a whole other kind of strength to face.

Bricks

"No, Mother," Ellery said patiently. "I don't think you need to—"

"Nonsense," his mother said briskly. "Your father and I love it in California. In fact we're thinking of buying a summer house there."

Ellery's eyes widened in horror. "It was over a hundred and ten degrees for a *week* last summer," he said. "*Nobody* wants to come to Sacramento for the summer."

"Oh dear God," his mother said, his horror echoed in her voice, and he could tell he'd caught her off guard. "Well on the *beach*, then. I understand it's only a few hours away."

"Between two and five, depending on which beach and which traffic," he responded automatically. People always thought any part of California was "at the beach," and he'd gotten very adept at correcting that notion.

"Perfect," she said, back on her stride again. "Far enough away not to smother you, close enough to not have to *book a flight* anytime one of you is injured."

"Rebekah will be hurt if you leave the East Coast," he said patiently.

"Your sister," his mother sniffed, "is moving to Europe for three years to participate in a study on the effects of infectious diseases on the heart, and taking her husband and my grandchildren with her. And while there will still be visits at least twice a year, I think it's safe to say you and Jackson might need me more than she does."

"But Mother," Ellery said, truly scrambling, "don't you *have a job*, one that demands frequent trips to Washington?" His mother had started out as a criminal attorney, but her specialties had branched out into international law and human rights, and she did a lot of work with the Department of Justice. She'd pulled strings for Jackson and his friends more than once, and he'd always been under the impression she loved her work.

God knows, enough people in DC were terrified of her that she *should* love it.

She sighed. "Of course I would still do some work here. But your father is retiring this year, and I'm thinking of cutting my work down, and frankly, Ellery, I miss my children. Is that such a terrible thing?"

"No," Ellery said, his voice softening. "And you're right. Three to five hours away would be a vast improvement over a minimum of twelve hours travel time. And Jackson may not admit it, but he loves seeing you too."

"Don't tell me that, my boy," his mother urged dryly. "It's not as much fun if I don't think of him panicking."

Ellery chuckled. "Understood." And then, pleasantries and family business out of the way, it was time to get back to the matter at hand. "But, uhm, about our little situation...."

"Oh yes. Moms for Clean Living," she muttered. "How could I possibly forget. You're positive Henry will be okay?"

Oh God. "No," Ellery said softly. He hadn't wanted to say this to Jackson because Jackson knew the truth. "Mom, you know the statistics on infection and internal bleeding with gunshot wounds as well as I do. Jackson's wound from a year and a half ago is going to hurt him for the rest of his life—as will every other wound he's ever sustained. We *think* Henry will be okay, but we won't know until he's out of the hospital and recovering."

She let out a sigh. "I don't know how you do it, son," she said after a moment, surprising him badly. "Loving that boy when you know what he may be doing on any given day. When you *know* one day he might not come back. I raised my children to be strong and self-sufficient and so many things, but in a thousand years, I never thought you'd find this much iron will."

Ellery caught himself gaping, opening and closing his mouth like a fish. His mother loved him, but she rarely gave out compliments this generous, so he felt compelled to reply with the truth.

"The only other option was walking away from him," he said at last. "And who in their right mind would do *that*?"

She laughed softly. "I most assuredly didn't raise a fool. Okay, then. We shall *will* our young friend into health and wellness in the same way we've willed Jackson. Now on to your little problem with a whole lot of psychopaths."

Ellery frowned, opening up the files on his laptop again. "What can you tell me about them?" he asked.

"Well, they are not *yet* considered a hate group by the Southern Poverty Law Center, but I know Beatrice Campbell, the assistant director there, and I'll ask her if they're on the watch list. Like the rest of America, I've seen their operatives infiltrate small elections and literally conduct raids on elementary school libraries, then hound the local law enforcement and school authorities with lists and law measures forbidding students from reading, well, anything really that isn't straight and white. It's a way of starting the brainwashing early, and it's surprisingly effective."

"I know it is," Ellery said sourly. Every now and then Jade would bring in gossip from the teacher's union—a depressing amount of their time was spent defending teachers from charges of teaching "inappropriate content" because a student was surprised or a parent offended by things such as science, math, history, or reason. Derek and Rico, the men who ran the headhunting firm on the far end of the second floor, had similar stories but farther up the food chain. *They* had to deal with new graduates whose inability to face actual education had left them unprepared not only for Derek and Rico's commitment to diversity in their firm, but also to the jobs that they would be expected to do.

Keeping schoolchildren ignorant was costing the world so much, and yes, sometimes that cost really *was* financial.

"Well, the election didn't help," his mother was saying, "but the underlying idea has always been there. By depriving children of progressive ideas, organizations like this hope that the next generation will be more willing to turn the clock back pre-civil and -LGBTQ rights—children without libraries are like little time bombs of hatred. It's appalling." She paused in her unusual diatribe—Ellery knew that keeping children away from learning and reason offended her not only on an intellectual level but on a *maternal* one, someplace visceral and angry, but suddenly she grew thoughtful. "And while the *ideas* they're so fond of aren't far removed from the pray-the-gay-away movement, their *facilities* and *personnel* have yet to be associated with that particular abomination. Are they licensed as a church in your area?"

Ellery grimaced, wishing badly for Galen to be there. He knew his business partner had been up late and was going to take a turn sitting by Henry's bed when he woke up, but Galen's specialty was tort law, and that dealt with things like facility use and contract violations. More often than not, Ellery's branch of the law dealt with actual physical things like guns, knives, drugs, and money.

"I don't think so," Ellery said. While he was speaking, he took out his trusty legal pad and added to the list he and Jade had started. "As far as I know they're listed as a nonprofit, but their status as a religion is on our list of things to research. But it's a good thought. And what are their licenses regarding custody of minors. One of Jackson's jobs today was to see if the boy's mother had given them permission to even *have* custody, and what she thought the custody was for."

"Well, it would be worth looking into." His mother paused, and Ellery could sense she was troubled, possibly skimming through something she thought was relevant. "Son," she said softly, "the thing with these organizations is that they're usually run with Political Action Committee money—as in, they're politically funded to align with whatever highly conservative candidate wants to pick on schools this cycle. In November, as you know, their candidate probably won. I need to talk to Beatrice, but I would imagine the other chapters have expanded with that funding. If that's true—and I do need to check my facts—the big question would be does this PAC know where their money is going. Remember Law 101—it's *always* about the money."

Ellery grunted. "Until it's about the kid and the bullet and the blood," he reminded her, not even able to joke about it.

"Until then," she agreed soberly. "So let me tap my sources, and you need to keep digging. But I want to add something here, and it goes along with what I just said."

Ellery knew it was coming, but he valued his mother's opinion and wanted to hear her say it. "Go on," he told her.

"Groups like this are often as devoid of reason as their causes. But that leaves two things driving them. One is money, of course, but the other is blind loyalty. *You* said you tracked this group of women back to the same school in Florida. How long ago was that?"

"Twenty, twenty-five years," Ellery said, needing to check his timeline again.

"That's plenty of time for blind loyalty to do its damage, son. Add the religious overtones and you've got some dangerous thinking here. Somebody shot Henry through a wall because they were trying to get to a fourteen-year-old boy. That speaks to *very* goal-oriented thinking. Keep that in mind."

Ellery grunted. "And be careful," he filled in.

"And be careful," his mother added soberly. "And tell Jackson the same thing."

"*That* I can do," Ellery said, feeling overwhelmed.

"Don't worry, son," his mother said. "You've got people helping. It's not all you."

Ellery had to smile. "Thanks, Mother. Give Dad my love."

"I should be able to secure a ticket for the day after tomorrow. Give it to him when we arrive."

And with that she hung up, leaving Ellery with a revised "things to do" list and a little bit of hope it could be done.

At that moment there was a knock at the door, and Jade poked her head in. "Ellery, I brought us some lunch. Do you want me to eat with you?"

He smiled at her, and it must not have been his professional smile because she seemed to warm to him when he did. "*Yes*," he practically begged. "My God, it's quiet in here without Galen and Henry. I mean, yes, Jackson and Henry are out sometimes, but Galen is usually in his office, and there are clients here, and I'm *lonely*."

She laughed a little, and he realized how petulant he'd sounded.

"I mean, it's quiet," he said, trying to regain his dignity. "Where's AJ working?"

"His and Crystal's house," Jade said, bringing in the takeout bag and setting it down on his desk. "She's got some unregistered equipment—he can check out websites without being traced."

Crystal still worked at the law firm that had fired Ellery. She claimed she was waiting for Jackson and Ellery to make enough money to be able to afford her services, but Ellery thought she secretly enjoyed pirating the resources of the larger law firm to help the underdog. Currently AJ and Crystal were still rooming together, and AJ was enjoying his first healthy relationship with a kid Jackson couldn't stop calling Jail, but whose real name was Jael.

"Good," Ellery said. "I… my conversation with my mother was disquieting." He grimaced. "And not only because she's making noises about getting a summer house on the coast."

Jade stared at him in horror. "Why? Why? Why would she do that?"

"She claims it's to save on airfare," Ellery told her blandly, and Jade's expression softened.

"She's coming out?"

"Well, she thinks of Henry as family too."

Jade shook her head. "Your mother is a bossy-assed woman. But she's a good person too. Weird how that works."

Ellery accepted the compliment with a small smile. "Very strange," he agreed, opening the box Jade indicated with his two favorite sushi rolls inside. "Thank you," he said with a sigh of joy. "Did I do anything to deserve this?"

Jade grimaced as she opened her own box. "Actually, it's on credit. Do you remember the kid Jackson hired to write code around Christmastime?"

"Lewis?" Ellery said in surprise. "Yes, I remember him. He placed three kittens."

Jade nodded. "That's the kid. Anyway, he's got a friend who could use some legal advice, and I told him to come by around two. I hope that's okay. I've canceled all of today's appointments, but—"

"Dear God, the office is quiet," Ellery said ruefully. "No, it's fine. We'll both be ready for a break by then, and he seems like a sweet kid. What did his friend do?"

"Well," Jade said, picking up a bite of sushi with chopsticks and seamless technique, "apparently his friend is a bouncer, and he's had to bounce the same guy three times—once for socking Lewis's boyfriend in the nose. The guy went to his *own* lawyer and is trying to sue for pain and suffering, but he never went to the police, so...." She bit the piece cleanly in half—not a grain of rice fell.

Ellery scowled. "So he has no case, but he's probably hoping Lewis's friend will settle out of court because lawyers are expensive." He grunted. "This should take a phone call," he said with satisfaction.

"That's what I thought," Jade said sagely, deftly popping the rest of the bite in her mouth. After she chewed and swallowed, she added, "Like I said—"

"A welcome distraction," Ellery finished. "Excellent. Do you want to hear the bad news?"

She scowled and picked up another piece of sushi. "Thrill me," she said, gesturing with the chopsticks.

And Ellery proceeded with the grim truth about how much deeper they were going to have to dig on Moms for Clean Living.

THEY HASHED out a lot during lunch—which phone calls Ellery would make, how much data Jade could mine, what to tell AJ and Crystal. When they were done, Ellery got to work, but this time with his mother's conversation in mind.

Who was giving this group of extremists money to strip libraries, and when did they branch out into torture by religion? If they were paving the way for an extreme right-wing candidate, who was it, and what connection did he have to the members of the group? And where was the money ultimately coming from? Who would benefit from an ignorant voting population—besides the obvious candidates for "enemies of the state."

And how had this entire plan come down to one fourteen-year-old street kid who had climbed out the window with his middle-aged guardian to escape into a rainy night?

The answer was somewhere in the personnel and finances of Moms for Clean Living.

After Jade left with their takeout trash, Ellery texted Jackson with *Ate lunch with Jade, talked to Mother—have much to discuss.*

Jackson got back: *I have backup. We're doing things.* He sent a picture that surprised Ellery as much as it gratified him. Of course. *Of course* that's who Jackson'd had in mind.

But did you eat? he persisted, and the time Jackson spent trying to compose an answer told him everything he needed to know. *Eat, or I call you in.*

You're not the boss of me.

Yes I am. It's in the marriage rules, look it up.

We're not married yet.

We're common-law spouses—it still applies. Now eat.

Had a breakfast bar. Gotta run. Nag later.

Ellery checked the tracker on his app and saw Jackson was in one of the seedier sections of downtown, and he growled to himself as he set his phone down. Fine. Jackson would fill him in later—he had no doubt of that—but in the meantime, they all had to do their part.

Two hours later, as he'd begun to assemble a picture—a revolting one, but a picture nonetheless—of the finances and goals of the organization that seemed to be behind Henry's shooting, his phone rang.

"Are you done running?" Ellery asked acidly.

"Yes," Jackson replied, "and we've even eaten. My backup apparently took lessons from you."

Ellery rolled his eyes. "Well, I'm glad he's proving useful. What do you have for—"

And at that moment, glass shattered in the front of the firm, amid shouting and chaos and the smell of smoke.

"Ellery!" Jackson cried, obviously panicked. "Ellery, are you okay?"

"I've got to go," Ellery replied with as much composure as he could. Then he tucked his phone in his pocket as he ran for the front of the office to see what in the holy fuck had just happened.

Backup

Toe-Tag's offices, which sat in the basement of UCD Med Center, were always cool and quiet—as well as small, underfunded, and very, very attached to where Toby Tagliare, father and doctor of forensic science, did his actual work.

Toe-Tag wasn't the coroner or a forensic pathologist. They had their own office out on Broadway. Toby was attached to the hospital morgue—he was the gateway between the people who came into the hospital alive and the people who ended up at the coroner's office because they died of special circumstances.

Given that he spent his days in a refrigerated room stacked with corpses waiting to be sent to their destination—be it crematorium, funeral home, or the coroner's office itself—Toby was a downright cheerful little man with a plethora of curly gray hair, much of it in his ears, and a father to his furry toes, who had spent much of his and Jackson's early acquaintance trying to match Jackson up with his son.

Toby had been there during one of the grimmest days of Jackson's life, but he'd also come to Ellery's house for some much more pleasant days of celebration.

He was always happy to see Jackson but also mindful that the basement of a hospital was Jackson's least favorite place to be.

"Come on in!" Toby gestured to where he stood over a body, one of a stringy, tattooed young male who had obviously died violently. His flesh was peppered with scars, both round like bullet holes and long and jagged like knife wounds, including new holes in his flesh, presumably from whatever had killed him.

"Wow," Jackson said on a low whistle through his face mask, taking in all the damage. "He… he doesn't look like his death was a surprise," he said as diplomatically as he could. He was well aware that if it was *him* on the slab, a stranger might come to the same assessment.

"Well, given that the last young man on my slab had the same sort of wounds—delivered by this young man—I'm going to say that it probably wasn't," Toby told him mildly, stitching up the bullet hole with a sigh of sadness. He'd once told Jackson that he mourned everybody who came through his corridors because *somebody* had to. But he also lived a surprisingly happy life, Jackson often thought, probably because he was very aware how quickly it could be taken from him.

"It's a shame," Jackson said respectfully. Even if the guy had been a dirtbag in life, he didn't have any more chances now either for redemption or change, so mourning what his life *could* have been was part of the process.

"It is," Toby replied, setting his needle and thread down and turning Jackson's way. "But not why you are here, yes?"

"Yes," Jackson said with a small smile. "Good to see you, Toby."

"Me too. I'd say engagement and domestic life agrees with you, but you're looking quite tired, my boy."

Jackson let out a groan, feeling weirdly flushed. God, how was he going to convince his backup to *back him up* if he was this strung out?

"Last night was rough," he said vaguely, but Toby had known him since he'd been a prisoner, erm, patient in this very hospital. Jackson would escape his ward, erm, unit, searching for a quiet place, and the morgue qualified. It also, when his body was a constant patchwork of leaky pipes and shredded fabric, reminded him that he'd survived. He *was* alive. He needed to stay that way.

"I heard about your friend," Toby said softly. "Dave came down when his shift ended to give me the heads-up. How's he doing?"

"So far so good," Jackson said, not wanting to think about Henry, pale and still, groggy and spitting out facts because he knew he'd be sleeping again soon. "We're looking into who shot him—"

"Who's the detective assigned to the case?" Toby asked.

"No idea." Shit. One more thing on Jackson's to-do list. He and Ellery had been so rattled he'd forgotten to ask Fetzer and Hardison the night before. "It could be Christie, but I sent K-Ski out of town. The thing is, there are some… well, vulnerable parties here. People who shouldn't end up on law enforcement radar."

Toby snorted. "You mean your porn friends? Yes. I can see how that might be misinterpreted."

"John does a lot of good in his community," Jackson told him. "And he treats his models like professionals, not like meat."

"I agree," Toby said. "I've met the man, remember? How was Henry injured, may I ask?"

"John and Galen were, uhm…." Jackson felt a blush steal over him at the oddest time. Poor Cowboy. He remembered the advice he'd given Billy that morning, and his heart twisted. No fourteen-year-old should have to pin his life and his hopes on his ability to hustle. "Solicited," he said after a pause. "They were solicited by a fourteen-year-old boy. And while they were getting him to a friend's place to be cleaned up and possibly placed in foster care or in a shelter, the kid let it slip that he'd seen something awful. They called Henry, because Henry comes to watch over their friend in case the person they're helping turns out to be dangerous, and somebody tracked the boy down. Henry was shot giving the kid and his new guardian a chance to escape."

Toby—who could concentrate on his work during almost any distraction imaginable—had set his needle and thread down and, using the back of his wrist, lifted up his headband light. His homely middle-aged face was still masked, but he was staring at Jackson with rapt attention.

"Oh dear God," he said in horror. "Is the boy safe?"

Jackson nodded, his own mask reflecting the heat from his blush, making it worse. "Yes, and the guardian too. They're… well, they're not here, if you know what I mean."

"Understood," Toby said. "So I get it. This case is tricky, but so far everybody is still alive. I mean, not that I don't love your company, but…."

Jackson laughed a little, his face still hot. He put out a hand to steady himself, and Toby huffed out in exasperation. "Josh!" he called, stripping off his gloves and stepping away from the body on the table. "Josh, are you there?"

Toby's assistant, a tall, blond, beefy ball of cheer, stepped out from behind a divider where, Jackson assumed, his own preliminary autopsy was in session.

"Right here, boss. Waiting for the dieners to come help move my latest patient."

"Where's he going?" Toby asked curiously.

"Oh, definitely the funeral home. The only thing questionable about this guy's death was why it didn't happen sooner. I've never seen such a liver."

Toby's eyes went wide behind his mask, and Jackson couldn't help smiling from behind his own. Josh had his degree in medicine—what he *didn't* have was a bedside manner. But he and Toby seemed to get along well, although Josh was, sadly, devoted to his girlfriend and not a match for Toby's son.

"Okay, then," he said. "Could you please close this one up? He needs to go to the coroner—the bullets killed him, but the intestines full of product might need to be investigated."

"Oh! Another Francis." Josh pulled off his gloves by the gowning station and recovered himself in another paper gown as he spoke.

"Francis?" Jackson asked, still feeling hot and a little queasy, which was odd because with one notable exception he wasn't usually squeamish in the morgue.

"The talking mule," Josh said absently, studying him. "Doc, is he gonna topple?"

"Not usually," Toby said as he finished stripping his own gear. "I suspect he hasn't eaten today. It's sort of a thing with him."

And with that, Toby took Jackson's elbow and guided him out of the autopsy room and into his own tiny, cluttered office.

Jackson sat down on the hellishly uncomfortable guest chair with a thump, right as his head *really* began to swim, and Toby thrust a bottle of water into his hand first.

The mask came off—thank God—and the water went down blissfully cold. The protein bar was not his favorite, but he found he'd destroyed it before his taste buds had a chance to protest.

For a moment after his last swallow, he just sat, panted, and watched curiously as the spots stopped swimming in front of his eyes.

"Well," he said after a moment, "that was embarrassing."

"Skip breakfast, did we?" Toby asked critically from behind his desk.

"It's been something of a morning," Jackson confessed. "But yes." He sighed, aware that his body was no longer allowing the abuse he'd inflicted on it for so many years. "I can't tell Ellery about this," he decided. "He'll never let me live it down."

"I won't say a word," Toby promised. His voice fell. "But I am aware that being down here, being *here* at the hospital, is rough on your nerves. Ask me what you came down to ask me, and then you can get out of here and have some real food. Is that a plan?"

"An amazing one," Jackson agreed, loving Toby so much in that moment. Like Ellery's father, a gentle professor in tweeds with a thinning crop of bird-nest hair and a charmingly Yiddish accent, Toby emanated dad vibes in ways that Jackson had no idea he'd craved. He let out a breath and tried to get out of his own head long enough to make some progress.

"It must be bad," Toby murmured.

"I'm looking for bodies," Jackson told him baldly. "Unclaimed ones of teenaged boys. Cowboy heard one incident, but—and I can't explain this any more than gut instinct—I get the feeling there's more. This operation we're looking at? It's big, and it… it *dehumanizes* these kids. And it's well funded." That had occurred to him as he'd been driving around that morning, and he was pretty sure Ellery would already be walking down the money trail. "I am wondering if this was the first time something awful happened."

Toby frowned. "I haven't heard of any in Sacramento," he said at last. "Not of adolescent boys." But before Jackson could get hopeful, he said, "However… I seem to have heard about some in another nearby county." He shook his gray curls. "Our tattooed mule in there was my last case of the morning. Let me get on the phone to some of my contacts for you. My memory isn't what it used to be, and you know what the news is like these days. You're never sure what's going to hit and what's going to be buried." He grimaced. "No pun intended. But yes. Let me get on that. I'll call you when I get a hit, and…." He chewed on his lower lip again. "I know I will. I am *positive* it's out there." Some of his animation died. "It's horrible," he said bleakly, "when sometimes your worst fears about humanity prove accurate."

Jackson nodded. "Yeah," he agreed. His stomach had settled, and he was feeling a little better, but as he stood he realized how happy he was not to be going into the prelim room with Josh and the deceased again. "Thanks, Toby," he said sincerely, extending his hand.

Toby took it. "Anytime, Jackson. And I do mean that. But next time come in with more than coffee in your stomach, yes?"

He was about to say, "Henry will make sure of it," but then he remembered where Henry was. "Yes," he said, his resolve firming up in his chest. "Absolutely." He couldn't do for his friend if he couldn't do for himself—and he absolutely wouldn't let Henry down.

BUT IT wasn't until he and Jennifer were on their way from Davis Med Center to Richards Boulevard that he realized what a drive-thru desert downtown and midtown could be. He was *busy*, dammit, and driving crosstown to a trailer park under an overpass didn't give him a lot of options in terms of food. His stomach grumbled, not liking the protein bar without backup, and he thought yearningly of the Starbucks a few blocks over. The day was getting on, though—and hey, maybe if his backup needing coercing, Jackson could offer food.

The trailer park was… well, depressing, Jackson realized as he piloted the minivan through the mouth of Richards, which had become a construction site, down a street that most people didn't know was there, and into a residential area that had probably been sweet at one point, but after the cloverleafs of 50, 80, 99 and Business Loop 80 had been installed directly overhead, it was a place shaded by concrete, where traffic noise was a low hum in the consciousness.

As Jackson pulled Jennifer into the through road of the park, he saw a tanned man in his early thirties with dark brown hair and a once-white T-shirt flapping around his bone-thin frame. He wore jeans just as big on him and held around his waist with a battered leather belt, pulled to its last loop, that barely stayed up as he worked on a brick retaining wall around the outside of the limited, maybe thirty unit, trailer park.

He had an absurdly beautiful triangle-shaped face, even as gaunt as he was, and Jackson was struck once again by how unfair Cody Gabriel's life had been over the last year.

Gabriel did a double take as Jackson passed and set his cinder block carefully down before striding to where Jackson parked: A sturdy 14x35 single-wide with cheerful yellow siding and a welcome mat with a cat staring from the front.

That mat had been part of a housewarming gift Jackson and Ellery had brought after they'd secured the place for its current tenant, trying to make the best of a bad situation.

Cody Gabriel had been screwed over by his fellow cops, and while he'd been retired with a full pension for the rest of a hopefully long life, he was still a former drug addict with a chip on his shoulder, who'd lost most of his possessions when he'd had to go on the run and deep, deep under in the city's homeless population in order to stay alive.

Jackson knew from personal experience that the loss of identity after being tossed onto the other side of that toxic blue line was a terrible, terrible thing. Jackson himself had been "blessed" with a year and a half in the hospital and long-term care facilities to come to grips with the idea that he'd never be a policeman again—but he'd only been on the force for a few months when he realized his training officer was as dirty as they came and had tried to build a case against him. Cody had gotten thirty days in rehab over Thanksgiving after a twelve-year career.

Much like Henry, in spite of some significant pressure from the dark side, he'd managed to do the right thing, and this trailer park was his reward.

Jackson and Ellery made an effort to visit as often as possible, but in spite of the groceries, clothes, and furniture they'd brought in the past, this was the first time Jackson felt like he had anything tangible to offer.

"Rivers!" Cody said, drawing near as Jackson got out of the car. "Good to see you, man!"

They exchanged a bro hug, with the requisite thump on the back, and Jackson gave Gabriel a sharp-eyed once-over. In spite of the looseness of his clothes, Cody was looking stronger and more substantial this past month, and his thoughtful hazel eyes were just as clear-sighted as they had been when Cody had testified against the cops who'd tried to kill him.

"How're they hanging?" Jackson asked, and there must have been a note to his voice because Gabriel cocked his head.

"Low, inside, and tucked out of the way," he responded almost absently. "What's up?"

Jackson tried to sell this idea a little. "Nothing," he lied. "Just, you know, coming to check on you. How's the gardening going?"

Cody glanced over his shoulder at the retaining wall and grimaced. "Slow," he said. "So's the fence painting, the rent collecting, the plumbing diapers out of toilets, and all the other bullshit that goes along with managing this craphole." He glanced around quickly to make sure none of the other tenants had overheard him. "God bless it," he added weakly when he realized he'd gone unheard.

Jackson gave a wicked laugh. "Sounds dire," he said, peeking slyly upward from under his brow. "I can tell you're busy. I was going to offer you a little job, but, you know, you're swamped here—"

Gabriel shook his head, hard. "No, seriously, what do you have for me? What am I doing? Where am I going? How much does it pay?"

Jackson let the smile he'd been hiding start to bloom over his face. "You're doing some PI work with me. We're going to a couple of rehab centers, and then we're gonna crash the holy grail of fake church moms, and then we might be heading out of town. And it pays lunch, dinner, and a few days of your time." He sobered. "Plus a recommendation for the local PI school, and it will count as hours following a trainer."

Cody's breath caught in his chest, and he seemed momentarily transported. "Seriously?" he asked. "You think we could do that?"

"Yeah," Jackson said, his voice softening. "I told you I'd vouch for you when you were ready, Cody. I thought I'd give you a few more months to get your life together, that's all." He sighed and told the *whole* truth.

"And Henry's out of commission, and Ellery won't let me investigate without backup."

Gabriel frowned. "Out of commission—"

"It's a long story," Jackson said, and out of nowhere his stomach growled. "But it's a good one," he added. "You got any clothes that fit?"

"Some," Cody said, "as you well know since Ellery brought them. Would you like me to change?" He glanced down at himself. "Of course you would—"

"Bring the good ones," Jackson said. "But wear those. Our first stop is at a rehab facility. Somebody is hanging around there, trolling for… well, I'm not sure what. But I figured I'd go and be official—"

"And I'd go and be a client," Cody said, getting it immediately. "I hear you. Let me pack my knapsack and give Clive and Poppy some food."

"I know what a Poppy is," Jackson said, referring to the tiny Chihuahua mix that Cody had acquired during the adventure that had brought him and Jackson together. "What's a Clive?" At that moment, a ragged, long-haired black-and-white cat appeared on the windowsill of the trailer again, his once-handsome white whiskers ravaged and torn, and part of his twitching tail missing. "Oh." Jackson smiled at the cat's imperious batting against the glass. "*That's* a Clive. Indoor only?"

"He has to be," Cody muttered. "There are freeway onramps *everywhere*. I'm surprised he survived this long."

Jackson nodded. "Yeah—once Billy Bob got fixed, he had no urge to wander anyway. It's like he's been born to soft food on special plates, you know?"

Cody chuckled. "Come in, have a soda. I'll pack, and you can fill me in on the job." He paused before he opened the sliding glass door. "I hope Henry's okay," he said seriously. "You all were so kind to me, not just during the trial but afterward. Henry brought me Poppy when the rehab center would let me have him." As Cody stepped into the foyer of the trailer, he kicked off his work boots and then bent to greet the tiny black dog who had run up to him, tail wagging fiercely.

"Hello, fella," Cody said gently, scooping him up in his arms. The wild little tongue went crazy on Cody's chin, and Cody laughed a bit and allowed the doggy kisses before he handed the creature to Jackson.

Jackson and Poppy regarded each other soberly before Poppy curled up in the crook of Jackson's arm and started to clean his wrist with singular dedication.

"Alrighty then," Jackson said, soothed by the little dog as he didn't think much *could* soothe him right now. "I guess he remembers me?"

The trailer was laid out with the kitchen to the left and a small living room to the right. Jackson knew there were a bathroom and two bedrooms past the kitchen, all the rooms and necessities fitted together like tiny puzzle pieces, but he still felt like a deep breath would cause the whole place to explode like the Hulk's clothes.

Carefully, trying not to make his shoes thump on the hollow floor beneath his feet, he settled into the surprisingly comfortable tweed sofa, Poppy still tucked against his ribs.

Cody reached into the fridge and came out with a couple of sodas, and Jackson accepted one gratefully. He realized he had a low-level caffeine headache working and wanted to kick himself for not even remembering coffee.

Jackson took a healthy swallow as Cody grabbed a chair from the tiny kitchen table and swung it around, straddling it while he chugged his own soda.

"Okay, so talk," he said after his first gulp.

"Well, I was going to take you to lunch first," Jackson told him, sighing when the sugar hit his bloodstream. "Seriously—I'm starving, and we've got a lot of ground to cover."

Gabriel shook his head. "Nope. You had me at 'I've got a job,' son. I am losing my mind with boredom here if you haven't noticed. I've got sandwich fixin's and more soda where that came from. You sit there and pet my creatures and we can hash this out right now." He took another gulp of soda, killing it in a couple of chugs.

"You're harshing my 'Jackson's got his shit together' vibe," Jackson admitted, but the dog really was a magic talisman against stress. "But since I almost passed out in autopsy thirty minutes ago, I'll take it."

"Ugh—not my favorite place, the morgue," Cody said, swinging his leg around the sturdy wooden chair and replacing it at the table. "What brought you there—" He paused his stride to the refrigerator. "Not Hen—"

"No!" Jackson blurted. "No—no, don't say that. But he *is* in the hospital, so's you knows."

"Well, shit." Gabriel swung the fridge door open and started pulling out mayo, mustard, lunch meat, tomatoes, onions, and pickles, and Jackson's mouth started to water. He was going to get up and make those vague motions people did about helping, but the cat chose that moment to leap out of the windowsill and onto his lap, unashamedly purring and rubbing up against Jackson's chest.

"This is fun," Jackson said in surprise, and Gabriel glanced over at him, a smile making his foxlike features almost angelic.

"Yeah, Clive's a slutbag. I woke up one morning and he was on my step, his paw all bloody. I brought him inside, and you know Poppy—that little goober is bomb proof, but he's also sort of a nurse. Checks on Clive, checks on me, makes sure we're okay. Anyway, I bandaged the foot, bought some kibble, and risked giving him a bath—he was fine. Got him to the vets and got him fixed, and we've been roommates ever since." Cody sobered. "Perfect friends for a recovering junkie. Can't run off and score because you gotta pay the vet bills. And who could betray those little faces, right?"

Jackson rubbed Clive's ears, and the cat collapsed onto his lap in ecstasy while Poppy continued her cleansing of his other arm. "Your creatures seem more… uhm, affectionate than the ones I'm used to dealing with."

"Hee!"

It was an unexpected sound from such a hard man, and Jackson glanced at him quickly as he pressed a free hand to his mouth, his eyes dancing over it. So pretty, Jackson thought a little wistfully. So broken. It's a good thing he was in love with Ellery, because otherwise he'd be happily engaged in a trainwreck of brokenness with this man, he had no doubt.

Cody schooled his features. "I've met your cats," he said, shoulders still shaking a little. "Trust me, I'm aware." He gave Jackson a wistful glance of his own. "But then, I'm not sure you'd trust all that open affection on tap."

"Probably not," Jackson said, now rubbing noses with Clive. "Remind me to wash up after this by the way, because Billy Bob knows when I'm cheating on him."

Cody made that unexpected sound again, and Jackson found himself relaxing as well as making out with the cat. Without warning, some of the awfulness slipped from his day, some of the worry, the anxiety, the film that covered his body from treading backward in the waters of time. He found himself melting into Cody Gabriel's couch and enjoying the sun through the bright yellow curtains.

"Nice digs," he said, meaning it. While space was at a premium, the two couches were only gently used, and the curtains and valances were cheerful. There were pictures on the walls—sports shots of the Giants baseball team and the Kings—and his lamps were graceful ceramic columns of pale blue.

"I had a friend help me pick stuff out," Cody admitted, coming to Jackson with a bowl of chips and a fresh soda, which he deposited on a sturdy coffee table since Jackson was still otherwise engaged. He returned to his counter with two steps. "I'm sorry—I didn't ask. Is there anything you didn't want on this?"

"Not a thing," Jackson told him, as his stomach growled again. He reached out to grab a chip, but Clive clung to his arm and shoved him back against the couch with a forceful headbutt. "Although I think it's cute that you assume they'll let me eat."

"They'll move when it's time," Cody said, laughing a little.

"Which friend?" Jackson asked. He'd seen a telltale twitch to Cody's eyes, and now, at the question, he refused to look up from his counter.

"You, uhm, remember North Albright? The, uhm, marshal who took care, erm, kept watch over me when I was testifying?"

Jackson's eyebrows went up. "I do," he said, surprised. "I, well, I thought there was something about, you know, waiting a year…." Oh, he hated to bring up recovery rules when it seemed like Cody was doing so well.

"Not that kind of friend," Cody retorted, way too defensively.

Not yet. Jackson would put money on it—but he wouldn't put Cody through any embarrassing discussion. "Either kind is fine," Jackson said softly. "Don't mind me. Being nosy."

Cody shrugged and finished up with the two sandwiches as he spoke. "Isn't that what friends do?" he asked. "Speaking of which, are you going to tell me what happened to Henry?"

Clive had tucked his entire head obtrusively in the hollow of Jackson's neck and shoulder, and was purring so loud Jackson could feel it in his stomach. Poppy had moved the cleaning session back to the crook of his elbow, and he had to work at not giggling.

He was never going to be more comfortable and cared for than this.

With a deep breath, he started to tell the story.

By the time he was done, both of them had finished their sandwiches, and Cody had cleaned up, insisting the whole time that Jackson stay right where he was. Clive had managed to drape himself around Jackson's neck like a stole, and Poppy had burrowed back behind Jackson's ass in the fold of the couch, but he still felt as though he'd be betraying friends to get up.

Cody had listened to every detail with what Jackson thought of as "cop's ears," asking questions that mattered and weeding out the less important details, mostly about the shooting and how certain they were about Moms for Clean Living.

"We've got three witnesses," Jackson said. "We've got Cowboy's mom, who was pressured into giving her son into their custody, Cowboy, who spent a whole two hours at their compound and pointed it out to John and Galen, as well as identified this Retty humanoid as being their chief enforcer, and Henry, who *also* identified her windbreaker and gave the same description as Cowboy. We're pretty secure there, and Ellery and the office staff have been researching their eyeballs out all morning."

Cody nodded, coming to sit in the chair kitty corner to Jackson. "Okay, then. Do you have a plan?"

Jackson filled him in on his thoughts about the rehab center as well as scouting out the compound itself, although he hadn't decided how he wanted to do that.

And then, because Cody understood theories and how they could be pure speculation and not based in fact, he tentatively talked about his fears for Caleb, the lost soul Cowboy had been so upset about.

"Do you really think the boy witnessed a murder?" Cody asked, disturbed.

"Think about it," Jackson said. "If it was any other crime—including a sex crime, torture, or bullying—these women could take their chances in court. With a savvy lawyer and some fast talking, all they've got is their word against a fourteen-year-old sex worker. Doesn't look good for him, right?"

Cody grimaced. "Yeah. Yeah. I know all about credibility." He'd run because he'd been blackmailed with his drug use into doing something he hadn't wanted to do.

Jackson nodded. "So why risk *everything* to bust into a stranger's apartment, guns blazing, to try to get to this kid? Why start a shootout through a wall if you weren't hoping to hit a witness?"

"Ugh," Cody said, shuddering. "That's so dangerous—and not very bright. Nothing worse than somebody scared, desperate, and *stupid*."

"And armed," Jackson said grimly. "Do not forget armed." He paused, enjoying one last purr from Clive and Poppy's warm presence below his left-hind-yab. "So. You want in?"

Cody gave an almost evil smile. "Does my cat want to hump your face?"

"Disturbingly enough, yes," Jackson told him. "My God, Ellery and I need a cabin up in Tahoe to get this much action."

Cody laughed. "Wait here while I go pack some extra clothes. You were right—the visit to the rehab center should be done while I'm at my worst."

"But you're gonna help me with the creatures," Jackson called as Cody disappeared down the narrow hallway to one of the bedrooms. "Gabriel? Cody?"

Cody's insanely innocent laughter trailed down the hall, and Jackson was pulled forcibly back against the couch by Clive, who had not yet violated Jackson's left ear with his bewhiskered muzzle but obviously had plans.

THE REHAB clinic was downtown, on W, about three blocks from the YMCA. Jackson was surprised to find a shaded spot on the street near a series of large houses with manicured grounds.

"This always struck me as such an odd spot," Cody said from the passenger seat. "You forget—everybody's susceptible, you know?"

Jackson had spotted Reba Milton's restaurant enroute, about half a mile away near N Street, but otherwise he was in agreement.

"You were in the one off Marconi, weren't you?" Cody's had vibed like a golf club, set off the road on an unexpected burst of property seemingly plunked in the middle of the city.

"Yeah. Nice grounds. Someone told me they used to have weddings there."

Jackson stared at him, and Cody shrugged. "Don't look at me. My dog, the one I wasn't supposed to have, crapped under every shrub in the place, and I gotta tell you, I wasn't the greatest with the poop bag."

"You need to stop talking now," Jackson told him. "I'm not sure I can trust somebody who wouldn't pick up their dog's crap on the lawn."

Cody shrugged. "Sometimes I'd take an air gun and use the turds as target practice. It was a crapshoot," he said with a straight face, and Jackson shook his head.

"Just so you know, when Henry's back, the first thing I'm having him do is kill you. He can make it look like an accident."

"You do what you gotta. If you think Ellery can get you off for it, do your worst."

"If they heard that joke, no jury on earth would convict me."

As they spoke, both of them were staring at the rehab center, making note of ingress, egress, and escape routes.

"I'll go in asking for a meeting," Cody said. "You want me to keep my eyes peeled for this Retty woman?"

"Keep for recovery rooms," Jackson said thoughtfully. "Cowboy's mom said she had something over the woman in charge. Henry tagged her last night—they've got medical supplies in there, right?" It was an educated guess. Recovery wasn't always a pretty process, and spouses in relationships built on substance abuse often came in with injuries.

"Mine did," Cody said. "Let's just call it an unusually well-stocked nurses station."

"Okay, so you search for that. I'm going to hunt for the leader of the center, be all official, and ask some questions. Meet back here in half an hour?"

"Fair," Cody said, his eyes roaming the terrain again. "Look, if I get rousted, I'm going out the side door—you see it there?" Jackson marked a small door on the east side of the building. "I'll go around the block and head for the car—"

"Jennifer," Jackson said, feeling both guilty and a little embarrassed.

"What?" Cody sounded legitimately flummoxed.

"The minivan. Her name is Jennifer." Jackson held his finger to his lips. "We need to be very considerate of her feelings. She's an important part of the team."

Cody slow blinked. "Oooookay—"

Jackson shook his head. "This is nonnegotiable." Very deliberately he mouthed, "She will refuse to start if we are not kind to her."

Cody blinked again and tentatively stroked the glove compartment. "Jennifer," he said, nodding slowly, as though Jackson was insane and Cody was trying not to upset him.

"That's right," Jackson said. "We'll meet at Jennifer. She'll be open, so hop in and hide if you need to." Jackson patted the steering wheel. "Did you hear that, girl? Be ready for us."

The blinker clicked once, without a touch to the turn signal, and Cody's eyes bugged out before they hopped out of the vehicle together.

And no, Jackson didn't lock the doors. He and Henry had never put voice to it, but Jennifer was a 2008 Dodge Caravan, by far one of the shittiest years of one of the shittiest vehicles ever put out. Henry had once *written a note* to Jackson, stating that the only thing holding that piece of crap vehicle together was Jennifer's sour disposition.

Then he'd burned the note.

Nobody was going to steal this car, and Jackson firmly believed that if anybody tried, Jennifer would eject them out of their seats and into the windshield.

It would not be the worst or the weirdest thing she'd ever done.

After the first few steps, Cody's shoulders slumped, and he pulled his head down, eyes toward his feet, gaze shifting restlessly from right to left.

Jackson was pulled immediately to the first night they'd met, when this had been Cody's habitual walk, his junkie's shuffle, and he was both startled by how far the laughing young man had come and saddened by the things he'd been through.

And really grateful that Cody had been so eager to use his painful experience to help Jackson's mission. With a brief nod, Jackson passed Cody up and strode purposefully toward the main entrance of the place, full of "official business" so he could question Cora, the surprisingly compliant facilities director.

The smell hit Jackson first—stale cigarette smoke, Lysol, and urine. He glanced around and realized that the bright stucco exterior of the place had been the best kept area of the building. The interior had once been just as bright, with laminate floors that were now warping from too much moisture at the seams, and water stains creeping up the yellowing walls. The podium in the front was battered, and the Plexiglas barrier had divots in it that served as old scars of violence. Down the hall to Jackson's left, he was aware of the door opening, and he heard Cody's voice at its most defeated, asking if there was a meeting he could go to, a person he could see. He was directed to a meeting in session right as the tired young woman at the reception desk was able to set her phone in its cradle and give Jackson her attention.

Tiny and Black, she had an entire swing of heavy braids, threaded with bright white and tipped with beads, and from watching Jade's attention to her own beauty regimen, Jackson knew what a big deal that was in time, money, and maintenance. Her round dark eyes were playfully made up, with sparkles in the corner on bold gold shadow, and her nails, while cut practically short, were tipped with sparkly acrylics. Her full lips summoned a smile from what looked to be the depths of the woman's toes and the bottom of a long day, and Jackson felt himself lifted.

"Can I help you?"

"First," he told her, "can I just say you are absolutely stunning? I'm not hitting on you, but that much beauty needs to be appreciated. Thank you so much for your smile *and* your style."

The smile blossomed. "It's a good thing you're not hitting on me," she said coquettishly, "because my girlfriend would object, but boy, did I need a compliment about now."

"Long day and hard job?" he asked sympathetically.

"Yeah." She sighed. "It's… it's a tough gig, you know? You get the degree in social work to help, but you get paid about enough to feed your cat and keep your phone so you can mooch off your mom."

"And the job's hard," he said, confirming what he knew to be true.

"And the job's hard," she agreed. Her eyes darted left and right. "And this place is falling apart. But I bet that's not a surprise."

"I did notice some things," Jackson said softly. "I thought the state just gave you guys money."

She nodded. "They *did*, and our director has been filing the paperwork to get some. But…." She scowled. "There's some people in the way. Something about permits and such, but they're not in the neighborhood— they just blocked our shit up, and I swear, Cora's getting desperate. One of them fucking people's here every goddamned day, poking her nose where it doesn't belong, and Cora bows down and kisses the ring so she can get money for internal repairs, supplies, hell, for two more counselors and someone to help me out. And that bitch—"

Jackson saw the moment it occurred to his new friend that she was talking out of school and gave her a gentle nudge. "What's she done now?" he asked.

"She showed up this morning, looking like death," the woman hissed. "I'd say she was jonesing, but there was blood *everywhere*. Anyway, Cora took her in and is dressing her wound and shit, and this woman's *horrible*. I've heard addicts in full withdrawals not vomit this much bullshit. No Black people, no gay people—I heard her screaming down the fucking hall about how we better not let no 'dykes or fags' touch her. And every other thing. I told Cora my gay Black ass was fucking *out* of there, but"—her eyes watered—"Cora let me go. Told me I should keep everybody else away too. She loves this place. I think she made a deal with the devil to keep it from falling completely apart, and I don't know what to do."

"Oh, honey," Jackson told her, hating the Plexiglas partition. It was obvious his new friend had been on the edge of venting and crying all day, and Jackson had given her the opening she needed. "Don't cry, baby—your eye sparkles will get in your eyes, and my sister tells me that's the fucking worst."

"You've got a sister who wears falsies?" she sniffled, carefully wiping under her eyeliner with a tissue.

"Well," Jackson said with a wink, "she looks a little more like your sister than mine, but we'd die for each other. Her twin brother too. We stopped explaining to folks back in high school."

"Doesn't matter, does it?" she said, with another sniff to pull herself together. "What folks think. When someone's your person, no matter what kind of person, that's ride or die right there."

"It is," Jackson said softly. "You got a ride or die who will come here and watch your back for a few days?"

The girl—woman, she was probably Jackson's age, but all of that bright hope and possibility in her presentation and he thought of her as young—stared at him in surprise.

"My girlfriend," she said after a moment. "She works security at the courthouse. Why?"

Jackson shrugged uneasily. "Because your instincts are right on about the woman your friend is helping—and about making a deal with the devil. I need to go see this woman in person, and then I'm going to call the police, because she's done bad things. But I don't have any proof that her people will stop bothering you once she's gone, do you understand?"

The woman's mouth parted slightly. "You can get rid of her?" she asked. "We have security, but Cora insisted she take the risk alone. And we don't have much. We keep them at the back and side doors."

Jackson nodded and reached into his pocket for a card. "Okay, hon—"

She flashed him a quick lifesaving grin. "Honey," she said with a little laugh. "I'm Honey Barker. My mom said I was sweet when I came out, but Honey was a natural sweetness."

Jackson was startled into his own grin, and much like his time on the couch with Clive, his new aggressive boyfriend, this moment gave him some backbone and some purpose.

"You're still sweet," he teased. "I'm Jackson Rivers, and this is my card. I work for a defense attorney—"

Her eyes and mouth grew round, and he nodded.

"Yeah, I know for a lot of people here my fiancé could be absolute salvation, but try not to cash that ticket in too much. We're getting married in June. He's busy."

Her grin went radiant, and he inclined his head.

"But if you need to get hold of me, there's my number, and if you've got some emergencies, and I know you know what one of those could look like, let us know."

"Cramer and Henderson," she read softly. "You two went to the wall for that special-needs kid, the one who got assaulted by the police when they tried to pin a crime on him."

"That was our case, ma'am."

"The court reporter drew pictures of your back," she said, startled by the memory. "This here, sir, is a golden ticket." She waved the card. "I'll reserve it accordingly. And Cora is down that hall, up the stairs, and in the room on the left. There's no security, no counselors, nobody there— she cleared the place out as she was taking that fucking troll to check her wounds."

"Thank you, Honey," Jackson said with a nod. "I'll try to make sure your friend Cora stays out of the crossfire. She didn't deserve any of this."

"No, she didn't," Honey agreed. "Fucking troll."

"Let's get her."

Honey gave him a toothy grin and nodded him in the right direction. Jackson, after taking a glance up and down the hall to ensure nobody else was in this area of the building, took the short flight of carpeted stairs, holding on to the wooden stair rail. This really *had* been designed to be a large, multiroomed home. He'd just been in a ballroom that had been divided into what he suspected was a reception area and a cafeteria behind the added wall at Honey's back. The floor *was* a sturdy hardwood laminate, but many of the patches were cheap tile. The baseboards were matching laminate, but the desk had been made of cheap particle board, coated white. The place was a hodgepodge, and Jackson could see how the building repairs alone—not to mention staffing issues—would be enough to make somebody desperate to get the help her patrons needed.

He was halfway up the stairs when his pocket buzzed with Cody's number and the picture Jackson had taken before they'd left.

Meeting about to end. Told people about my phantom boyfriend—let's see what falls out.

Jackson nodded. Good. They needed to know what Shitbag Retty had actually been *doing* in the facility—not just Cowboy's mother but the other people who had come to get help with their addictions and ended up being used by the Stepford Dragons.

Retty might be on premises. Gonna talk to director and maybe to her. If you hear hollering, you know where to find me.

Good hunting.

Same.

No question about it—Cody Gabriel was good. Jackson had no doubt he'd slouched right under the radar into a support group for recovering addicts—the boy had that pretty face and a direct manner that could appeal to the hardest heart. And he really *had* been there, and he had a sort of moral fiber Jackson had rarely seen.

But Jackson couldn't help but miss Henry. No, Henry wouldn't have slouched under any radar. In fact Henry would have been the one approaching the pretty girl behind the Plexiglas, and Jackson had no doubt that Henry would have gotten her life story before he went running hell for leather to find Shitbag Retty and shake the truth out of her—or carry her, fireman-style, back to the car for further interrogation there and a skillful evasion of a kidnapping charge.

Everybody had a style of their own.

Jackson's style, he decided, was a little bolder than Cody's and less savage than Henry's—he wanted to know what in the hell Retty was doing here.

As he grew even with the door, he heard moaning, as though somebody was in pain, and figured he was about to find out.

The doors and doorframes were sturdy wooden structures—he imagined they probably matched the hardwood under the laminate, in a deep blond color that served to make what would probably be a dismal, depressing building at least a little hopeful. Jackson tried the glass knob, and it twisted easily, allowing him to slip inside what had probably been a guest bedroom suite at one time but had been converted into an infirmary with three beds, a tile floor, and a white-tiled bathroom toward the rear of the space.

The beds were gurneys—hospital style with wheels on the bottom— and two of them were stripped down to the vinyl.

The third housed a woman in sturdy jeans, dried stiff around an equally sturdy set of hips. The rest of the woman attached was stout and real— not someone who played tennis on her lunch hour and ate salad, Jackson thought. Like Cowboy had said, someone you'd meet serving your lunch or driving a bus or bagging groceries. This woman had known hard times and hard work.

And right now, she knew pain.

Henry hadn't known the extent of the damage he'd inflicted; he'd just known he'd gotten her through the door.

But her shoulder and the side of her chest were bandaged and seeping, and Jackson wondered if the .22 bullet hadn't fragmented through a beam in the drywall, spraying her with high-velocity pellets as opposed to a single, possibly deadly projectile. A part of him thought *I need to go back to the crime scene and see*, while most of him was thinking, *Oh shit! I found her! Now what do I do?*

Then Retty spoke, demandingly. Her face was, as Cowboy said, red, rough, and blotchy, and her hair was a crispy frizz of graying curls, and her voice was a *deep* Southern drawl.

"Cora, you cunt," she moaned. "You need to fix me up right now."

"I can't," Cora said, bent over a minifridge of medical supplies. "Retty, you've stripped me dry. I have to report where all this medicine went, and I told you—my antibiotics are limited. You will die of sepsis on that table if you don't go see a doctor."

"I'll have this place razed to the ground!" Retty growled. "You fucking drug addicts and perverts—"

"You shut up," Cora hissed, standing and slamming the fridge door shut. "You know what? I'm going to go to the cops, and I'm going to tell them who you are and what you're doing. I *don't care* if they shut us down. At least the world will know about your skeezy fucking organization—"

From far away, it seemed, Jackson heard Honey yelling, "You guys can't just come in here and—*Cora! Cora! They're coming your way!*"

Jackson had come fully inside the door as he'd observed Retty and Cora's interactions, and as he heard the clatter of boots on the stairs and no police identification, his instincts kicked in.

He hauled ass across the room, grabbed Cora's hand, and yanked her into the white-tiled bathroom at the back of the suite. He'd been in big houses before, and he knew that unless it was a master suite, the bathrooms were often shared by two of the smaller rooms, and he almost wept when he saw the adjoining door.

"Key?" he hissed at Cora, who was staring at him with big eyes.

Cora was small, slender, her wrists bony and eyes made gritty with too much work on coffee and good wishes, but she could obviously think on her feet. She produced the key from a lanyard around her neck and opened the door, then darted into what looked like a darkened supply closet that had probably once been a nursery of some sort.

Jackson glanced around and spotted a stack of cots, turned on their sides and leaned up against filing cabinets in the corner of the room. With a hiss he directed Cora to crawl behind the cots, and then he joined her. She was small enough to wedge herself between the cots, the wall, and the filing cabinet, while he lay on his side and scooched his knees up to his chest, his back to the wall and to her feet.

The room was pitch dark, and Jackson had just enough time to bless that he'd remembered to close the door behind him when he heard noise from the medic's suite.

Frantically he texted Gabriel while listening to what was going on in the room next door.

"No!" Retty cried. "No, you guys. I had this. I had it covered. No, you don't need to—" Her next words were muffled as though from behind a gag.

"Was there anyone up here?" graveled a gruff voice.

"I didn't see anybody." This voice was younger and, well, dumber. "Should we ask her?"

"No, dumbass. She'll just lie, like she did about taking care of the kid last night."

Jackson's breath caught. Oh shit. Oh shit. Did they know where Cowboy was? Oh hell.

"How do we know she didn't?" came the dumber voice.

"Fuckin' Dwayne said she never showed with the package. He was waiting all night since this bitch texted. She and Bertie Dunkel are in some deep shit from what I hear."

There were two grunts and some moans of pain muffled by cloth or something worse.

"What do we do now?" Dumber asked.

"First we take her to Twitty, I guess. Look out there and see if that twatty little girl at the reception desk called the cops."

There was a hesitation as Dumber followed directions.

"No," he whispered. "No, she's gone down the hallway somewhere."

"Well, then," MacGruff decided, "time to go. C'mon, Retty—this time *you're* the package."

And then the men were gone, and Jackson was left texting frantically on his phone.

Are you keeping everybody in the rooms?

I'm not stupid, Cody replied. *I got the receptionist too.*

Thanks. She's a sweetheart.

Name's Honey, I've heard.

Jackson listened for a few heartbeats, and far away he heard a door slam.

That them? he asked.

Think so. Three more minutes?

Yeah. I don't think they'd think twice about taking out folks at a rehab center.

Fuckers.

You don't even know.

As his fingers flew, he heard a quavery voice in the dark.

"Can we go yet?"

"Two more minutes," Jackson said softly. "We need everybody hidden until they've pulled away. They're manhandling an injured woman—they might not move quickly."

"Should we call the police?" she asked shakily.

"What would happen if we did?" he probed, although he planned to call Fetzer and Hardison just as soon as they were in the clear.

"I'd lose my health-care license," she said. "I treated that woman without a doctor's supervision. I gave her painkillers I'm only supposed to give addicts when they're having severe DTs, so I misused medications—"

"Why?" Jackson asked, feeling safe enough to straighten his legs and start to scooch out of the tight confines. "Why would you do that for her?"

"She… she kept threatening to pull the license on the facility" came Cora's almost tearful response. "This is the only rehab facility for two miles, and it's one of the most heavily trafficked in the city. She… her friend—"

"Twitty?" Jackson asked, because yeah, he'd caught that.

"Her name is—*was*—Melanie Schnarf," Cora muttered resentfully. "And God, the worst thing that ever happened to me was lending her a pen in an English class we had together at Florida State."

That brought Jackson up short.

"You *know* her? Twitty? The person in charge?" He remembered Cowboy's terror, how "Twitty" had seemed bigger than life somehow, right down to the ridiculous name.

"I *knew* her," Cora said, and Jackson heard disbelief and disgust in her voice. "Just enough for her to remember my name when she moved to Sacramento. God, when I found out her and her fucking Moms for Clean Living were holding up my funding, I almost committed my own damned crime spree." She let out a breath. "They told me they'd push it through. All I had to do was let Retty have access to the facility, to the groups."

They were standing by now, and Cora started to rip off the bloodied gloves she'd still been wearing as they'd hidden.

Jackson held up a finger as he hovered by the door and gave the room a once-over before motioning her back into the infirmary.

"What was she doing here?" Jackson asked as she put on another pair of gloves and started to clean up the bloodied gauze on the floor. Jackson didn't have gloves, so he shook out a trash bag and held it open while she cleaned.

"Looking for blackmail," Cora said without hesitation.

"You know this because…?" He was pretty excited about how much this woman was talking, actually. Perhaps Retty could have not been such a twunt if she hadn't wanted Cora to spill like a waterfall.

"Because it's what they did in school," Cora muttered. "I worked the student union medical office to help pay my tuition, and it got me hours toward med school. I loaned Twitty a fucking pencil, and she said, 'Hey, aren't you the girl who gives out tampons,' and that was it. Her entire fucking clique showed up, one at a time, to get free pads, except they didn't just get pads. They'd stay. They'd slip into the bathroom, or into one of the cubicle stations while I was busy with something else, and pick up on… well, fucking everything. Who was going on the pill, who was getting an abortion, which guy had the clap, how many girls he'd given it to. Next thing you know, Twitty's getting elected student body president and getting into the rich girl's sorority when she didn't have the grades, the brains, or the charm."

Jackson moved the bag to catch a particularly vicious throw, and then whistled through his teeth. "That's harsh. Was that how Retty got into her group? Blackmail?"

Cora ripped the plastic sheeting off the gurney with unnecessary force. "Retty? She's been Twitty's lapdog since middle school. I think—and I could be wrong here because neither of them talks about it—but I think Retty's mom sucked Twitty's father's dick. I'm not sure if it was once, or if it kept going while Retty's parents were still married. I know Twitty's father paid for Retty's tuition, and there seemed to be pressure to include Retty. So Twitty made her the… you saw her. The enforcer. She was *never* smart enough for college, but…." Cora shook her head and shoved the sheeting in the bag.

"What?" Jackson asked, wondering when the rage and the adrenaline would wear off and Cora would quit talking.

"Everyone has pressure points, whoever you are," Cora said shortly, and Jackson got it.

"What was yours?" he asked, no judgment at all.

"I let them listen," she said angrily. "I mean, I didn't *let* them. I didn't realize what was going on at first. But once I realized what they were doing,

I told them to stop, and they just laughed and told me if I didn't want to lose my job, my scholarship, *everything*, I needed to help Retty pass her sophomore year so they could get out of my hair. And I caved. I…."

She rummaged under the sink by the window and came back with cleaning supplies and paper towels. Jackson continued to follow her around the small space, wondering when Cody was going to get there.

"Did you ever stand up to them?" he asked. He was curious what happened to rebels. He got peer pressure—hell, he even got secret societies.

But he'd been a whistleblower, and his fellow boys in blue had almost killed him.

Multiple times.

What happened to a girl in med school trying to pay her way?

"I… not at first," she said, scrubbing at the blood Retty had shed until her paper towel shredded. "I-I might not have, but when my favorite professor…." She let out a sigh, her shoulders sagging as she pitched the savaged paper towel mass into Jackson's bag. "My favorite professor—hell, everybody's favorite professor—he didn't do anything," she said, giving a twisted smile. "One of Twitty's crowd accused him of getting a girl pregnant. The school nurse—remember, *my* employer—called him in to see if there was truth in the matter." She shook her head, and the expression on her face was so heartsick Jackson wanted to hug her. But he needed to hear the story, and Cody had already texted that he was on his way.

"What was the truth in the matter?" he asked softly.

"The truth was they made up the rumor when he wouldn't sleep with the girl. He was gay!" Cora said bitterly. "And I overheard him say it—my receptionist desk shared a vent with my boss, and usually this wasn't a problem, because I didn't *tell people* other people's secrets. But this time Retty was in there, in the bathroom, borrowing a pad—for real—and the next thing you know, it's all around campus and…." She shook her head. "It was thirty years ago," she whispered. "Thirty years ago, when people didn't understand. Not in the South. They were going to fire him, but he… he hung himself instead."

"Oh God," Jackson said, his stomach knotting just hearing something like that. "That's… that's terrible—"

"The day I heard, I lost my shit in the nurse's office. I told her about Twitty's 'sisters,' coming in for blackmail. About how I hadn't realized that's what they were doing at first, and how Retty had been in the bathroom that day. She must have heard." Cora shrugged. "I lost my job. Lost my scholarship. My parents managed just enough money to move me as far away as possible, and I got a degree in social work instead of medicine." She glanced around the now pristine medical room, her face twisted again. "I thought I was doing some good," she said hollowly, "and then… oh goddammit. Retty walked into the room and told me Twitty hoped I enjoyed my break. And the next day, my funding was under threat."

Long-suppressed tears began to fall from the woman's exhausted, hollowed eyes. "That's me. Just one more weakness to exploit. Nothing more."

"That's not true," Jackson told her, his own rage seeking to explode in his chest. "Don't give up—"

"But maybe save the pep talk," Cody muttered, slipping into the room. "Honey's calling the cops, and I don't know how you want to play this."

Jackson grunted. "*Shit*. We can't be found here," he muttered. "Cody, they came in and took Shitbag Retty—"

"The guys in masks and Kevlar? Well, that was nice. Did you get a chance to talk to her?"

"No," Jackson told him. "But this nice woman *did* give us some good information. The thing is, they're taking Retty somewhere—the guy said *she* was the package now, and I told you about that kid, Caleb, and—"

"And you're worried Retty's people are making kids disappear," Cody said grimly. "Yeah, I get it. If Retty's the package, we need to find the package. Why aren't we telling the cops, again?"

"Because what happens to our witness if they know he's a witness?" Jackson demanded. "What almost happened to *you*?"

Cody's eyes got big. "Not a cop anymore," he muttered. "Things to remember when you're not a cop anymore."

"I've got some cops who won't push us on the wit," Jackson told him, and outside he heard the unmistakable squawk and rumble of a radio. He could almost see the flash of the strobe light coming through the wall.

"But we don't know if they're outside," Cody said. "Got it. What do we do now?"

Jackson grimaced. "Cora?"

Cora, social worker and font of information, turned her tearstained face to him. "You've got to go?"

Jackson pulled out his card. "You only get this if you promise not to give it to anybody coming through that door."

"Are you going to bring Twitty down?" Cora asked, her eyes and jaw hard.

"Like the giant on the beanstalk," Jackson promised grimly. "You'll hear her hit four states away."

Cora's smile was unpleasant, but Jackson figured she got to be bitter at this point. "Let me know what I can do to hack that thing down."

"I promise," Jackson said. "Now *please* tell me there's a trellis outside the storeroom window."

"Watch out for spiders," she said, without the slightest bit of play. "Black widows love that shit."

"I fucking hate spiders," Gabriel muttered. "And I hate you, Jackson, for making me do this."

"Too bad," Jackson told him, darting through the infirmary and toward the storeroom. "You fed me and let your cat make sweet lurve to me—I think we have to be friends now."

"Only if we live," Cody promised direly, closing the storeroom door behind him as Jackson opened the window. Together they stared down, and Jackson realized that they weren't *two* stories up—the bottom story had a vaulted roof. They were nearly *three* stories up.

"No promises," he muttered. The day was still gray and cold, but at least it wasn't pouring rain. He leaned over, scenting the damp breeze and realizing how stifling the rehab center was inside—it felt like his entire day had been dogged by stale tobacco and urine.

Using the fresh air as a goad, he reached for the trellis under the ivy and tugged, grateful when it held tight to the crumbling mortar of the brick façade that took over for the stucco in the back.

"It's a good thing we're both scrawny as fuck," Cody muttered, watching anxiously as Jackson slid out of the window and shoved his feet through the foliage to find the ladder. "If either one of us were fighting weight, this thing would collapse."

"I'll have you know," Jackson said, his words coming carefully as he chose his hand- and footholds, "I haven't weighed this much in a year and a half."

"What happened—" Cody was watching him, scrambling down the same way Jackson was, only letting Jackson go first. "—a year and a half ago?"

"Dirty/Pretty Killer," Jackson breathed.

"Oh my God," Cody muttered.

"What? You're going to fall?" Jackson glanced up in a panic, partly because he didn't want Cody to break something if he hit the ground from this height and partly because he was afraid the other man would take him down.

"No!" Cody panted. "I just remember that case. I forget sometimes. I got rescued by a legend."

"Ouch!" Jackson jerked his hand back as something scratched it. Anxiously he searched the dusty, twisted vines of ivy for a tiny black nightmare with a red splotch on its back, and he breathed out a sigh of relief when the real culprit revealed itself.

"Spider?" Cody asked, his voice rising in a way to let Jackson know they were a particular fear for his new partner.

"Nail," Jackson muttered, wincing at the jagged little cut. "Don't worry." He took a step down and then sideways. "I'm the proverbial canary in a coal mine. If it gets me, it won't get any—"

"Ouch!" Cody exclaimed. "Vicious sucker. Does that make us blood brothers?"

"Holy Jesus," Jackson muttered. "No. Yes. Whatever. I think it makes us dangerous in close quarters. God."

"What does that—augh!"

Jackson watched in horror as Gabriel's foot slid on the wooden slat his own had just vacated, and Cody Gabriel went flailing, falling past Jackson to land on his back with a solid *oolf* on the wet pile of leaves that had been pushed up against the house.

"Well shit," Jackson said, finishing his clamber down and leaping the last couple feet to the ground. "Gabriel? You okay? Speak to me, man!"

Cody blinked up from his back with the air of a man counting ribs. "That was fun," he said. "I think I'm okay. My back might be feeling it in the morning."

"You okay with ibuprofen?" Jackson asked. Some people in recovery refused it—he did on principle, because watching his mother spend her life down the rabbit hole had left a mark.

"Yeah," Cody said, reaching up his own wounded hand for Jackson's, both of them dripping blood onto the loam. "Pain relief is perfectly acceptable." He winced as he stood, and Jackson went to brush leaves from his back.

"We can probably get you a hot/cold pack while we're at it," he said. "It's time to check in with Ellery and let you change." He grimaced. "You're gonna want to—"

Cody grimaced, his shoulders twitching, probably because he felt the damp seeping in through the ragged hoodie he'd put on over his grubby garden clothes.

"Tell me there's no cat shit," he begged. "I can take anything but cat shit."

"Nope," Jackson said, flicking two tiny slugs off his shoulder. "Nothing but this snail on your ass."

"Ew!" Cody swept his hand down, and Jackson grimaced as the he heard the shell crack, and then the poor thing went flying against the house.

"I could have gotten it," Jackson told him. "You didn't have to kill it."

Cody Gabriel grunted. "I'm sorry, Rivers, but if you're not going to grab my ass romantically, I'd rather you not touch it professionally."

"I'm not that kind of private detective," Jackson said, taking a step back with his hands up. "Now come on before the cops sweep around the house."

With that they took off across what was a reasonably vast yard, fenced off by hedges and peppered with picnic tables, empty now in the cold and damp wind.

"Not a bad place," Cody panted at Jackson's heels. "Can think of worse facilities to recover in."

"Yours was better," Jackson said, his wind better. "You running in the morning?"

"Yoga," Cody replied on a burst of wind.

"Add some cardio," Jackson told him as they scrambled around the hedge so they could loop around the block and get Jennifer. "If you only run when something's chasing you, you're gonna get caught."

"My God, you nag," Cody breathed after a few steps. "Do you nag Henry like this?"

"Henry was in the military for eleven years," Jackson told him, his blood thrumming happily under his skin. "I do five miles in the morning to keep up."

"Brag, brag, brag," Cody muttered and then was silent as he struggled to keep up with Jackson.

Jackson used his time to think, mulling over the possibilities of what they'd learned from Cora, and the weird, oddly deep relationship Twitty (who would always remain Twitty even though Jackson knew her real name now) and Retty (whose real name he *still* didn't know) seemed to have.

What would it take to do somebody's dirty work for over thirty years? he wondered. Retty had shown no remorse, no worry for the people she'd been after. Her entire focus, even when the cleaners had come to get her, had been to finish up with Twitty's orders.

Did Twitty share the same weird devotion? he wondered. Where did it stem from?

Had *she* issued the order for Retty to be the next "package," or had that come from somebody else?

So many questions—Jackson *really* needed to check in with Ellery to see what he'd discovered.

He felt the pull strongly enough that he'd started the minivan and pulled out his phone before Cody even hopped in.

"Don't leave without me—hey!"

Jackson took a picture, reveling in his surprise and, keeping his foot on the brake, dialed the number, putting the phone on speaker so Cody could be in on the planning.

Which they never got to because two sentences in, he could hear the glass breaking and Ellery's obvious concern, and then the line went dead, and Jackson was standing on the accelerator, shoving Jennifer across town while Cody still scrambled for his belt.

Little Karmas

JADE HAD grabbed the fire extinguisher and was working on the small fire in the reception area before Ellery had even cleared the hallway. He took in the billowing drapes and shattered window with a glance, as well as a poor-man's Molotov cocktail smoldering on their pretty blue-gray carpeting.

His vision washed red.

To his knowledge, this had only ever happened two other times in his life, and he hadn't seen it coming now, but with a roar, he swung the door to the office open, absolutely hell-bent on finding whomever had *done this thing* to this office that he and Jackson and Jade had painted, carpeted, decorated, *loved*, and shaking them until their teeth rattled out of their teeny tiny head.

What Ellery saw when he hauled open the door brought him up short, enough of his fury draining to allow for breath, thought, and—his best weapon—words.

There was a giant standing in front of the door.

Six feet, six inches tall if he was a centimeter, with muscles on top of muscles on top of muscles, the bodybuilding menace with the blond mullet standing on his doorstep would have been terrifying enough, but struggling in his grasp was….

Well, an urchin.

Filthy dirty—his stench filled up Ellery's entire office, and his face was a study in dirt and blotches. His hair hung to his shoulders, and as Ellery stared, he saw not one but *five* tiny creatures crawling across the matted locks.

His clothes were rags, and he had chafing sores at his wrists where his jacket had rubbed him raw.

On top of the stench of urine and trash and unwashed body, there was the overwhelming smell of gasoline.

"We saw him do it," said a much smaller—thank God, *familiar*—man at the giant's side. Lewis Barnard was a software engineer who worked at the headhunting agency in the corner of the upstairs complex. Five eight or so, with a mop of blond hair and an irrepressible smile, Lewis had done some piecework for Jackson and their friend Burton over Christmas.

Ellery stared at the behemoth holding the struggling urchin.

"You must be Nicky," he said after a beat. "Thank you, by the way."

Nicky the bouncer grimaced, still holding his charge by the scruff of the neck. "No worries, dude. I'd shake hands, but…." He shuddered. "Gonna need some *soap*."

Ellery nodded grimly and noted that Jade—flustered and ruffled and a bit ash-bespeckled—had finished with the fire.

"Listen, how about if we take this young man outside while Jade finishes up? Nicky, if you could keep him contained, I'd be obliged. Lewis," Ellery bit his lip, eyeballed the kid up and down, and then took a calculated risk. "Could you have the place next door call child services? This young man needs a good meal and a change of clothes and a place to stay. I'm sure we can do better than we've done to date, yes?" For the first time he made eye contact with their young reprobate.

Ellery almost expected animal noises—the boy's eyes, a light gray, darted furiously, and his expression was terrified and angry. Feral.

But when he spoke, his words gutted Ellery like a gaffing hook.

"Don't make me go back. You can't make me. She promised me food. I had to do it. Don't make me go back."

Ellery gasped a little, and with a nod to Nicky, they moved the boy out to the front stoop, taking advantage of the breeze on the concrete walkway.

"Go back where?" he asked, keeping his voice even and direct.

The boy's eyes darted like fish. "The place. The big house. They look pretty, and they make us be clean but…." He shook his head. "No. No, no, no. I can't go back." His face crumpled. "But she knows where I am, and I was so hungry…."

Ellery took a breath and another one. He was piecing this together, and he realized that as much as he wanted to glove up and shake this little monster until his teeth rattled, what he was dealing with, in its entirety, was a traumatized child.

"Lewis," Jade said from behind him, "hold up."

Ellery glanced at her and then at Lewis, who had paused with his hand on the door to the teacher's union, ostensibly to ask for child's services.

"Young man," she said, and she didn't have to bend down or make the kid crane his neck, because she was five three on a good day, with heels, and this kid may not have hit his growth spurt yet, but it was close.

"Yes'm," he said, eyes big.

"Do you want to go to child services? They will treat you right there. They will give you a bath, and clothes, and find a foster service for you, and get you a lawyer to deal with this thing you just did that we're all ignoring for the moment. It could be a good deal for you."

"Will they make me go back?" he asked fearfully.

"To the Moms for Clean Living?" she asked and shook her head. "No. But they are going to ask you questions about it. We will ask you the same questions, baby—not gonna lie. But if you come with me, I've got a spot in a bed and some big brothers who will take care of you. They'll feed you and let you get clean, and they've got some clothes, and they will keep you safe until you're ready to talk."

"Jade?" Ellery asked, and she glanced over her shoulder at him.

"We've got room in the duplex," she told him. Jackson owned and operated—with Jade and Mike's help—a small halfway house for young men who had gotten out of prison and were trying to *stay* out of prison. Jackson vetted most of the occupants himself, and Jade and Mike had the last word, and between the lot of them—with some help from their friends— they found jobs, helped with transportation, medical benefits, and general "adulting" skills that the young men might not have had when they first turned eighteen and found themselves without a home in the first place.

Jackson had established the place over a year earlier, and it had gone through a number of young men—including AJ's current boyfriend—and so far the results had been encouraging.

Oddly enough, creating desperate citizens resulted in them doing desperate things. Giving them a safety net—including an emotional one, with people all striving toward workable goals and trying hard to live stable lives—resulted in fewer desperate citizens and fewer desperate actions.

Ellery gazed thoughtfully from Jade to the young man.

"If you took him to the halfway house," he said slowly, "they wouldn't have to contact his parents."

"Eventually we would," she said, making sure the young man could see her. "But not until he was ready."

The boy closed his eyes, and tears leaked out, leaving tracks through the grime.

"Food?" he asked weakly.

"We've got some sandwiches in the fridge here," she said. "Ellery can go get them. I'll go put some tarps in the back of the car and text Geordie and Nilas so they can get ready for him."

She looked to the young man again. "Geordie and Nilas will watch over you, make sure nobody can get to you," she said softly. "And you will have all the food and clean laundry you need."

The kid's eyes went crafty. "Video games?" he asked wistfully.

"Of course," she said. "But tomorrow morning, before I come to work, I'm going to come talk to you. I'll only be there for a little—remember, I'll need to leave—and you can spend the day with Geordie and Nilas again, and all the video games you want, but we need to talk, young man. Do we have a deal?"

He considered carefully, and his eyes darted to the window. He closed them and swallowed. "Will you punish me?"

"No," she said gravely. "But we will find a way for you to work that off. Is that acceptable?"

He swallowed and nodded again. "Food?" he all but begged. "She told me she'd feed me, but I had to do a thing first. I'm sure she's gone by now."

"Baby," she said frankly, "between you and me, I don't think she ever meant to give you any food. But don't worry. I do. Nicky, you stay here with him, Ellery's going to get some food, and I'm going to go prep my car. What's your name, son?"

"Otto," he said promptly. Then, a little bit embarrassed. "Don't laugh," he whispered. "My parents were German."

"Nothing to laugh about," she said, and Ellery found himself nodding soberly with Lewis and Nicky. "It's a fine name. Nilas's parents are from Norway, and Geordie's parents were from Africa. Sacramento is a pretty lively mix here—it's not a problem."

"Good," he said, shooting them all a nervous smile. "I like 'Otto.'"

"What's not to like," Ellery said diplomatically. "Let me get you a sandwich."

TEN MINUTES later Jade drove off with Otto in the back of her vehicle, and Ellery provided Nicky with generous amounts of soap and a sink in which to wash up.

"Dude," he said plaintively to Lewis. "Could you run and get my extra T-shirt from the car? I gotta, like, shove this whole thing into a trash bag." He indicated his jeans, sport coat, and T-shirt, all of which stretched over his muscles in alarming ways.

"I texted Killian already," Lewis said, sitting on Jade's counter with the sort of blissful ignorance of somebody who didn't realize he was courting death. He glanced over at Ellery. "He's got some plywood in his trunk for your window," he said, "so you can keep the rain out until you get it replaced."

Ellery—who had been contacting a glazier on Jade's computer—glanced up gratefully.

"Thanks," he said. "I don't think they can get here to replace it until next week."

"Yeah, that's bullshit," Lewis said. "Let me talk to my boss—he tends to motivate people." He hopped off the counter. "I think I hear Killian now—"

"Ellery!" Jackson hollered from the base of the stairs. "Ellery, are you okay?"

"Wrong boyfriend," Ellery said dryly. "Mine tends to—"

He must have levitated up the stairs, because Ellery barely heard a clatter.

"—freak out," he finished as Jackson burst through the door. "Jackson, calm down. We're fine. Everything's fine. Nobody's dead. Believe it or not, we *can* handle a crisis without you."

"Who's we?" Jackson asked suspiciously before catching sight of Lewis. "Hi, Lewis—are you and your—whoa! Hi, Nicky! Are you two 'we'?"

"Jade helped," Lewis said before glancing over at Nicky, who stood without his shirt, only Ellery's towel wrapped around his shoulders to ward off the chill. "God, Nicky, you could put an eye out."

Nicky gave a good-natured chuckle. "'Cause my nipples?" he asked. "Yeah—my girlfriend likes to say they could cut glass."

Ellery fought the urge to scrub his face with his hands.

"Heya," came a voice behind Jackson. "'Scuse me. I've got clothes for my friend in there—oh my God, Nicky, your nipples—that's amazing."

Ellery and Jackson turned toward the tall, quietly handsome man with dark hair in a queue bearing a bag of clothes in one hand and a few planks of wood under his arm. "Mr. Rivers?" he asked. "Hey."

"Hey, Killian," Jackson said, stepping aside. Ellery had no idea how Jackson would know Lewis's boyfriend, but he was not surprised either. "Here," Jackson continued, "you make Nicky decent, me and Cody will put the window in, and Ellery will come and explain *everything*. How's that?"

"Deal," Killian said, handing off the particle board. "I've got more in the car." Then, to Ellery's amusement, he cast a rather beleaguered glance at Lewis. "Every time," he said, to which Lewis gave an unrepentant grin.

"Wait till I tell you how Nicky got to be a superhero. *Epic.*"

A FEW minutes later, after Jackson started the window thing and Killian and Cody Gabriel took over, he managed a moment of quiet conversation.

"You didn't have to worry," Ellery said softly. "It was just a—"

"Brick and a Molotov cocktail," Jackson said, indicating the two objects the boy had thrown through the window. "I think the brick was to crash through and the cocktail was to set the place on fire. Why did you let Jade park him in the duplex *next door* to where she lives, again?"

Ellery glared at him. "It was her idea," he said for the umpteenth time. "And I think she did it for the same reason you turned Cowboy over to Sean and Billy—to keep the kid out of the system. This kid would have done *anything* not to go back to Moms for Clean Living, and I don't know how he ended up there, but he started to tear up when Jade mentioned his parents. So like Cowboy, he needs food and a bath and a haircut, and he needs some peace, and he needs to not be badgered for a little while. Jade also offered him a chance to work off the damage, and he seemed pretty excited about that." Ellery shrugged, some of the starch leaching from his shorts. "I don't know what to tell you, Jackson. This kid just… needed someplace to land. I think Jade trusted the kids next door more than she trusted protective services. Given *your* experience in the system, I can't say I blame her."

Jackson grunted. "I imagine the system has cleaned up a little since I was a kid," he said, "but I see your point. Yeah—Jade probably had the right of it. And Geordie and Nilas are good kids. They'll probably be thrilled to have a baby to care for, and Otto—"

Jackson stopped short.

"What?" Ellery asked.

"Otto!" Jackson pulled out his phone where he'd taken notes from his day's adventures. "Otto is one of the kids who escaped with Cowboy— Cowboy thought he'd gotten hurt and had needed to be returned to the compound. Okay, then. Let's hope this kid is there tomorrow. I'll go talk to him with Jade."

"He will be," Ellery said softly. "Jackson, he… he was almost grateful to be caught. God, what these kids are being put through—"

A darkness flickered in Jackson's green eyes that made Ellery draw up short. "What?" he asked.

Jackson shook his head. "Nothing. A hunch. I've…." He let out a breath. "I've got a lot to tell you, but Cody and I were going to scout out the mansion first. Can you wait?"

Ellery narrowed his eyes. "Aren't those the last words before the hero goes out and gets killed or maimed or something? Jackson, it's nearly four in the afternoon. Aren't you ready to quit yet?"

Jackson grimaced and nodded his chin to Cody Gabriel, who had changed into clean *fitted* jeans and a T-shirt and navy hoodie.

"Ellery, he cleaned up and everything. And he's helping to fix our window—" Jackson paused. "By the way, I had no idea Killian was Lewis's boyfriend. Aren't they adorable?"

Ellery gave him a flat look. "And you know Killian from…?"

Jackson smiled toothily and then relented, his cheeks turning pink. "I had to fish somewhere, Ellery—Killian's a bartender from one of my favorite fishbowls. You know, Catches?"

Ellery tried not to groan. So… many… puns…. "Yes," he said primly. "I know the place. I'm apparently defending their friend Nick—"

"Nicky," Jackson corrected. "Hey, don't glare at me—he's the bouncer."

"—pro bono," Ellery finished smoothly. "And I'm grateful for the help." He sighed and was honest. "And for the company. With Jade gone, it's only me in the office." He sighed again. "It's been quiet today. Yelling at that Bertha Dunkel woman was the most exciting thing that had happened—"

"Until she offered young Otto food to bomb the place," Jackson supplied dryly before sobering.

"Well, yes." Ellery gave him a sideways glance. "What is it? What are you thinking about?"

"Something Henry said," Jackson told him grimly. "About Shitbag Retty having a getaway driver—that she called *Bertie*. Can't prove anything but…"

Ellery looked grim. "Oh, but we've got one more link, don't we."

"There's more," Jackson said, "but do go on about being bored."

Ellery gave him a half-embarrassed look at his needling tone, but he couldn't put a front on it—not today. "I… I hadn't realized how much richer Henry and Galen have made our lives. Can you at least tell me more about your visit to see Henry before you go?"

Jackson gave him a quick, tender touch on the cheek, one that possibly got by under the radar of the now-bustling office, and said, "He was alert enough to tell me what had happened, and to give me a description that matched Cowboy's of Shitbag Retty. I managed to track Retty to a rehab center in North Sac—she was wounded and blackmailing the director for help. We might have to jump in and lobby for the place to get their funding, Twitty—Melanie—"

"Schnarf," Ellery said at the same time Jackson did, and they grinned at each other.

"So we both got that little tidbit," Jackson said, looking pleased. "Yes—well, Twitty wasn't happy that Retty had gotten shot and let Cowboy get away. She apparently sent two goons to fetch her."

"Oh my God!" Ellery gasped. "Seriously?"

"It's fine," Jackson said, waving a hand. "I got to listen to their conversation from a convenient hidey hole. It was great. Cody went to a meeting, we made a couple of new friends, and I heard something really important."

Ellery stilled. "What?"

"They—and I don't know who they are yet—but *someone* was 'waiting for a package,' Ellery. And now Retty is the package."

Ellery's heart thundered in his ears, and he had to remind himself that not only was there no danger anymore, he and Jackson were surrounded by able folk willing to help.

"And last night—" he began.

"Cowboy was the package," Jackson finished. "This isn't done yet. So it's important that Cody and I go do some spy shit." He glanced around. "Have you talked to Nicky yet?"

The giant man had emerged from behind the receptionist's desk wearing cargo shorts that fit, as well as a short-sleeved polo shirt that *barely* fit and a hooded sweatshirt that looked like it was size 4X just to accommodate Nicky's arms and shoulders.

"No," Ellery said. "He was on his way in when he caught our second wayward boy."

Jackson nodded. "Don't get mad. I'm going to have him and Lewis walk you to your car, and *you* are going to drive to Mike and Jade's and stay there until you hear from me, okay?"

"Jackson—" he said, irritated, but Jackson cut him off.

"No. This is serious. Bertha Dunkel—aka Piper Lutz—was the *getaway driver* for Shitbag Retty. These people got nothing if not commitment. And then you were shitty to Piper Lutz/Bertha Dunkel, and they retaliated by sending one of their rejected boys here with a *bomb*, Ellery. The kid might have botched the delivery, but you *do* understand that's what Molotov cocktails are, right?"

"I do," Ellery murmured reluctantly.

"Good. So this is serious. Henry is *in the hospital*, and you know he's *very capable*. Yes, I know you have a weapon, and yes, I know you're not stupid, but…." Jackson gave him a pleading look. "Just do this for me, okay? I do all your stupid crap—I eat, I tag you between runs, I try to sleep. It's your job to pony up and go somewhere safe while I'm doing my thing. You understand?"

Ellery bristled. "It's not 'stupid crap,' as you so eloquently put it—"

Jackson cocked his head, and that's all it took. Ellery was a lawyer. Logic was his forte. If what he asked Jackson to do wasn't "stupid crap" then Jackson was making a perfectly reasonable request.

"Fine," Ellery muttered with little grace. "Fine. You and Cody go out and skulk around corners. I understand. But before you go, you should know my mother was talking seriously about buying property along the coast, the better to be here with five hours' notice, and as it is, she and my father are flying out in two days to visit Henry. So enjoy knowing that while I *ask our clients* for protection."

Jackson scowled at hm. "You are a petty, savage little man, do you know that?"

"And you love me," Ellery told him smugly. Then he made little fluttering motions with his fingers. "Now go. Scoot. Vamoose. You and Cody have 'things' to do."

Jackson swooped in for a hard kiss, but then, at the last moment, he softened. Pulling back a little, he smiled and tapped Ellery on the cheek.

"Stay safe, Counselor," he said, meeting Ellery's eyes with his own glass-green gaze.

"Same goes for you, Detective," Ellery said softly. He glanced over Jackson's shoulder. "Mr. Gabriel?"

Cody was in the middle of sweeping up the last of the available mess, and he paused. "Yeah?"

"You got one job to do. You understand that, right?"

Cody snorted. "Better men than me," he said, giving Jackson a meaningful look. "But I'll give it a go."

"It's all I can ask for." Ellery sighed. "You'll eat?"

"I'm still full from lunch!" Jackson protested.

"You'll call or text?"

"Whenever I can."

"Take care."

"Will do."

And he was gone.

Ellery was left staring at the plywood neatly duct-taped to the broken window on both the inside *and* the outside, and the duct-tape-and-towel "patch" that Killian and Cody had put down on the burned spot on the rug.

He turned toward Nicky, Lewis, and Killian and said, "Well. That was some unexpected excitement. Nicky, what am I doing for you again?"

Nicky grinned. "Wow! I'd almost forgotten why we were here!"

"Well, I haven't," Killian said dryly. "Hey, so our manager at the bar says that Catches can help with Nicky's legal fees—"

Ellery waved his hand. "Only filing fees for the motions," he said. "The rest is my treat." He looked meaningfully at the emergency repairs. "Overall, you all have paid for yourselves already. Now come, let's hear about this man trying to assert you assaulted him. Was he a bad man?"

"Dude," Nicky said sincerely, "he was the *worst*. Would you believe he threw cats out of a moving vehicle and then *bragged* about it!"

Ellery blinked at him. "That's horrendous!"

"Yeah—they were in a crate, and they're fine, but this guy—bad news. Popped Killian in the nose out of nowhere, man, and I had to chase him out of the bar."

And then Nicky made a sound that Ellery knew well.

"Heh heh heh heh heh…."

And Ellery was given to know that what had happened *then* was the tricky part of the defense.

"I've heard that before," he said pleasantly. "Let's retire to my office. Lewis, Killian, you may want to remain here while Nicky and I conference."

"Plausible deniability," Nicky said soberly. Then to his friends, "See? I told you. Don't worry. Me and Mr. Cramer got this. I'll be out in a sec."

And Ellery proceeded to his office, feeling strangely content about his job.

Fish in the Dark

THE SKY was getting that soggy concrete sort of gray that happened as shadows drew long during a damp and rainy day. Jackson piloted the minivan through rush-hour traffic, trying to picture the block where the Stepford Dragon Castle sat and wondering where to park.

"The church," Cody said, breaking into his thoughts. "There's a church about four blocks away. They have meetings at night and sort of a ragged-looking batch of attendees—you know, like me—and this...." He swallowed, probably because Jackson had done a good job of impressing the temperamentality of their ride upon him. "This wonderful vehicle will not stand out like the shining star she is."

Jackson nodded approvingly. "Nice one," he said. "We want to keep her."

"Of course we do," Cody told him, nodding along for good measure. "A, uhm, flashier vehicle that, say, your boyfriend could afford certainly wouldn't do, now would it?"

Jackson could hear the question in his voice.

"Those vehicles don't have Jennifer's... shall we say, strength of karma," Jackson said diplomatically.

He watched Cody play with that one a couple of times before he absolutely had to ask.

"How many cars did you go through?"

Jackson wrinkled his nose. "Four? Wait... five. No, four and a half. Because one got rebuilt and then it got taken out, and then we shipped it down to SoCal to get rebuilt again. I don't think it's coming back."

"Wow," Cody said, sounding truly stunned. "And this one's lasted longer?"

"Than any of the other two combined," Jackson confirmed, slowing to let a couple go by. They were both androgynous under their rain gear, but they were huddling under a giant pink-and-yellow flowered umbrella. Jackson would *guess* female, but he wouldn't put money on it, and he smiled a little when they cleared the intersection and he could go.

"Impressive," Cody told him sincerely. "I'm still tooling around in the Sportage I got a couple of years ago. It was paid off, so it was one of the few things I could keep after I got out of rehab."

"Can't shit on a vehicle that works," Jackson said, patting Jennifer's steering wheel so she'd know she was included. Something was niggling him, something about what had just happened with Ellery, and he realized he was gnawing at his lip as he was gnawing on the problem.

"What are you thinking about?" Cody asked, and Jackson grunted, realizing it was sharing time.

"How? How did that woman that Ellery pissed off know where to find that starving kid? I mean, we're going to assume that poor Otto was like Cowboy. He was indoctrinated into the pray-the-gay-away thing, and then he ran away. Well, Ellery said he looked like he'd been on the streets for as long as Cowboy—and Cowboy said that Otto had gotten recaptured during the great escape. When did he escape again? And how did that Piper Lutz/Bertha Dunkel woman know where to find him? I mean, the pray-the-gay-away camp obviously has a problem keeping kids—have they simply kept replacing them as they bleed away? Or do they know where they go? And what happens to them once they return and piss off Shitbag Retty or her friends again? Because I was *hoping* if a kid was coming back out of the woodwork, it would be Caleb—but Otto mentioned Caleb and started to cry, so…." He shuddered, his stomach in knots.

"No happy ending for Caleb," Cody said soberly.

"I'm really thinking not," Jackson muttered. "It's why we gotta check inside this compound. I need to see some papers or something, or talk to some of the inmates still there. This feels… bigger somehow. Like this isn't just the story of one kid, or one rogue piece-of-shit enforcer nailing Henry, but like there is something *big* that everybody is afraid is going to come out if Cowboy talks to somebody who will listen. Am I making any sense here?" he asked, a little desperate for affirmation. It occurred to him that his head was starting to pound with a sleep headache from hell, and while he wasn't hungry, he could *really* use a soda or a coffee or something. "And is Starbucks still open?"

"Yes," Cody said. "Turn right at the next intersection, my treat. It's not Starbucks, but it's close and independently operated."

"Fair," Jackson said. "So I'm making sense?"

"If I was still on the force, with an entire department at my disposal and the DA on speed dial?" Cody prefaced.

"Yeah?"

"I'd be giving out assignments in a briefing room and having search warrants started. Why haven't you contacted the po-po again?"

"Because Cowboy would have to testify," Jackson said grimly. "And once a kid hits the system like that…."

"Gotcha. And now it's not just Cowboy, is it?"

"No. It's anybody these monster-twats have ever touched. I want to find out what they're doing and who they're doing it for. I want them wrapped up and arrested and in cuffs and put away where they don't have a chance to even see where we got our information before our witnesses talk to a single person with a badge."

He didn't ask if he was making himself clear now, because he didn't care. Goddammit, he knew who he worked for.

Cowboy. Otto. Isabelle.

And Henry. Who would fight to the death for any of them—and almost had.

"Wow," Cody said with a sigh.

"What?"

"A year ago, I would have argued with you until you kicked me out of the car. But then, a year ago…."

His brothers hadn't turned on him and used him as a scapegoat to mask their own corruption.

"It's a shitty lesson," Jackson admitted, pulling into the queue at a kiosk that had a big placard on the front announcing the Midnight Bean. "But lucky me, it means tonight I've got somebody riding shotgun who knows about a brand-new coffee place. I'm stoked."

"Are you stoked enough to get one of their sausage/egg empanadas?" Cody asked hopefully. "Because it's teatime. You know, not dinner, but still…."

"You're feeling a little peckish," Jackson said dryly. "I hear you." His headache throbbed behind his eyes with his pulse, and he thought about Ellery asking if he'd eaten again. "I might join you," he conceded. "It might be our last chance to eat for a few. We should take it."

Oh my God. I must be a grown-up. I didn't even have to fight with myself!

Besides, sometimes carbs could substitute for sleep when one was desperate enough.

A few minutes later, a jumbo-sized sugar caramel pistachio latte with some coffee in it in the drink holder, he munched at the flaky crust of the breakfast pastry at five in the afternoon and decided Cody had good instincts for this kind of thing.

"I've never been there before," he said through a full mouth. "I'm gonna have to…." He trailed off before he could say "take Henry there" because it felt rude and also like he might jinx Henry's recovery just suggesting it.

But Cody wasn't stupid. "Don't worry about it. He'll be fine, and I'll be benched in no time."

"No reason to be benched," Jackson said. "I mean, *we're* tapped out at present, but you know. We're not the only game in town."

Cody shook his head. "I don't know if I could do cheating spouses and workman's comp fraud. It feels so…."

Jackson blew out a breath, because he was well aware that he'd lucked out. Jade had been a paralegal for Lyle Langdon, and she'd talked Jackson up after he'd gotten his license. Since Pfeist, Langdon, Harrelson, and Cooper had been one of the premiere criminal defense firms in the area, Jackson had been able to cut his teeth on more action as a PI than he might have gotten as a flatfoot, if he hadn't been given to a corrupt trainer.

But then… "There's more than one criminal defense firm out there," he said. "And Fingerling, Loser, Hamster, and Cottonmouth might take a recommendation from Ellery."

"Didn't they, like, *fire* him?" Cody asked uncertainly.

"Well, yes," Jackson said. "But reluctantly. Jade and I, on the other hand, left sort of an impression upon exiting."

Cody snickered. "I saw the picture behind Jade's desk when I changed. Jade's ass is, of course, fabulous, but it's good to see you've put on a little weight since then."

"I was *stabbed* in the *liver*," Jackson retorted grumpily. "And I got back to Langdon telling me they were going to let Ellery go but would be happy if Jade and I stayed on. I mean, we *made* him the guy who would go to the wall for the little guy. We couldn't very well let him go out on his own, right?"

"And you personally were in love with him," Cody said dryly.

"There was that," Jackson returned. He smiled a little. "I don't think any of us have regretted it since. But what I'm saying is there are some good defense firms out there who would give you a break, and if we don't have any spare work for you, Ellery and I will write odes to your godlike abilities after Henry gets back, so… you know…."

"There's life after the force," Cody said dutifully. "You've been telling me that since November, Jackson. Don't worry. I've drunk the Kool-Aid. I'm a believer."

Jackson chuckled without humor. "Good. Just be careful. Being a believer got Henry an intestine full of lead."

"And like you, I'm sure he'd agree it's worth it," Cody told him firmly. "And thank you. I'll keep up hope you suddenly add partners, but I honestly hadn't thought of other defense firms—or even your old one. Silly me."

"Out of the box thinking," Jackson said absently. They were passing a row of small businesses and coming up on an alleyway. An employee was hefting a rather large cardboard box down the sidewalk, heading for the alley, and Jackson—who had been pondering how they were going to get into the Stepdragon Fortress of Solitude and Death suddenly had an idea.

He had to cross two lanes of traffic—and return an extended middle finger in greeting—in order to swerve to the side of the road and into one of the "outside of the bike lanes but hopefully not in traffic" parking spots to do it, but he managed to cut off the surprised man hefting the box.

"Do me a favor, would you?"

"Wha—"

Cody was busy clutching the chicken stick, so Jackson threw Jennifer in Park with a silent apology and hopped out. "Wait here, sweetheart," he said, making sure he left her automatic keys in the drink holder. "I'll be back."

He trotted out into the drizzle and hailed the surprised employee. "Hey! Can I have that?"

The man—young, with line tattoos up and down lean arms—eyed the minivan dubiously. "Sure, man, but you got a vehicle to sleep in. Are you sure you're going to need one?"

"I'm not sleeping in my car!" Jackson retorted, and then double-checked his outfit, grumpily pleased that both jeans and hoodie appeared washed and worn but intact. "This is for a… uhm… art project." He smiled winningly.

"Glory hole?" The clerk asked, balancing the enormous flattened box on his head to keep off the rain.

"If that's what makes you want to throw it in the back of the van, sure," Jackson told him, raising the hatch.

"No, seriously, dude," said the thin-faced clerk. His straw-colored hair was plastered around his eyes and neck, and he was starting to shiver, so Jackson handed him a beach towel as he grabbed a canvas bag filled with various uniforms he and Henry used to, uhm, blend as they worked. "Are you moving? What?"

"I'm pretending to be a UPS worker so I can see if a bastion of toxic white women are holding LGBTQ kids hostage," Jackson told him flatly as they shoved the box in over the dolly lying crosswise in the back for this very reason.

"Seriously?" His helpful friend had wide hazel eyes, and he appeared to be charmed. "So, like, I'm helping superheroes?"

Jackson shrugged. "Sure," he said. "It's your good deed for today!"

The kid laughed. "Naw—fuck that, dude. I'm adopting a puppy today. You saved me five minutes of unnecessary work breaking that down so I can get out in time. Have fun storming the castle!"

And with that he turned and jogged back to the store as the sky opened up.

Jackson hung back for a moment, sheltered by the lifted back of the minivan, before slamming it shut.

"Hunh," he said, climbing into the driver's seat, aware that Cody Gabriel was staring at him.

"Just like that?" Gabriel said. "You… you told him the plan just like that?"

Jackson stared back, his hands fastening his seat belt automatically. "Was it a secret?"

"Well, I would have figured it out!" Cody told him. "But… but I wasn't expecting you to tell people!"

"Who's he gonna tell? His girlfriend? His parents? His roommate?" Jackson shrugged. "Man, he was trying to make a gray crappy day a little bit more magical. I got no problem with that. I thought I'd help."

Cody chuckled. "I'd say mission accomplished, but he already had you beat."

"Yeah," Jackson said. "I know. That man was gonna get himself a puppy!"

THE DOWNPOUR had let up as night crept in, and Jackson took a risk when he found a parking place the block *behind* the Moms for Clean Living house instead of the church. For a moment, the two of them sat in the shadows, since there were few sodium lamps on this block. The grounds of the house extended to the backside of the lot, and Jackson could see security cameras up on the trees, but he was pretty sure they wouldn't extend to the minivan's position.

"What are you thinking?" Cody asked.

"For one, I'm hoping the rain holds off until we get the dolly around the block. For two, I'm wondering what we could possibly put in that box to weight it down."

Cody stared at him. "Well, I was thinking *me*," he said, but Jackson shook his head and threw one of the brown shirts he'd grabbed from the back at him.

"No, we need to be able to go in there, find the office, look around. One of us can use the head, get lost, find the other one of us. That doesn't mean it's not a good hiding place to get *out* of there, but we need to come in and be a team."

"Are they gonna see our faces?" Cody asked uneasily, but Jackson reached behind the passenger seat and into the little mesh carryall there and produced two hats with logos.

"Nice," Cody said appreciatively, slipping one on. "Does it got Henry cooties on it?"

"I'd say yes, but he bathes pretty scrupulously, and he gets his hair cut so short you can see his sunburned neck. Zero cooties on Henry's hats."

"No, seriously, how many outfits like this do you have in here?" Cody was glancing around the minivan's interior like whole closets might open up, and Jackson had to chuckle.

"Some basics—scrubs for hospital areas, lab coats, same. Blue chambray with fake name tags for HVAC workers or pest control. A few other outfits. I mean, nothing beats the posture of somebody who belongs where he is." Jackson paused and thought about it. "And a certain resistance to embarrassment," he said after a moment.

"Resistance to…?" Cody frowned at him.

"Chief, we just climbed down a trellis from the attic of a big rich-looking house in a rich-looking area, and I had to flick slugs from your back when you fell. If you'd been more afraid of being embarrassed than you had been of talking to the cops about our witnesses, you would have been too afraid to pull that off. Don't worry. You're good."

Cody was still chuckling as Jackson pulled some postal tape from a compartment in the back and started to fix up the box.

THEY GAVE their acting chops a workout on the stairs up the porch of the building, calling out to each other as Cody balanced the package and Jackson pushed it up. The porch was wide and protected from the rain, with classic Victorian peaks and gables and large french doors that probably let in the light during the day. The outside of the place was really very handsome, with dark blue wood paneling in the front, cream trim, and a stone façade beginning about midway along the back, its origins obscured by myriad hedges and flowering trees that flanked the house itself and obscured the great yard in the back. Behind, where they'd parked the minivan, Jackson had seen a lot of wrought iron and hedges as well, and he was pretty sure in the spring and summer, the place would be abloom with pink flowers, and half the people inside would be high off Sudafed and Benadryl because that was how allergies in the Sacramento valley went.

But now, in the sodden early March, everything was dark and shiny and dripping, even though the downpour had eased, and Jackson wished he'd brought his hoodie to throw on over his ugly brown shirt, because he was shivering as he and Cody danced on the porch, trying to get somebody to come open the door.

The woman who answered had artfully streaked ash-blond hair framing a face made of cheekbones and disdain. She wore navy slacks with a cream Chanel jacket over a navy blouse and pearls and, fortunately for Jackson, a laminated ID that read Piper Lutz.

Oh. So *this* was Bertha Dunkle/Piper Lutz.

Good to know, Jackson thought, as he turned on whatever charm reserves he had left that day.

"I'm sorry," she said, peering out at them from the half-closed door, "we're having a meeting right now—"

"But I've got a delivery for a Valerie Trainor?" Jackson held his tablet like it gave him needed information. "Is she in?"

"Oh, I can sign for it," Lutz said, looking annoyed and half afraid. "Just leave it there—"

"In the rain?" Jackson protested. "Ma'am, they would have my job for leaving this package in the rain. You go ahead and sign for it, but it has got to see the inside of the foyer first."

"You can't leave that thing in the foyer!" Piper Lutz gasped.

"Well, we'd offer to put it in an office or something, but you seem to think we want to come into your place and steal your stuff!" Jackson protested. "And Jack here may have to piss in your pot, but we do *not* steal people's stuff."

"How rude!" Piper complained as Jackson got a foot in the door.

"You think he's rude now, you should hear him if we have to get back in the van and he hasn't had a chance to pee," Jackson told her seriously.

"But that's neither here nor there. I can't leave the box on the porch 'cause it's gonna start whizzin' down rain like a cow pissing on a flat rock, if you know what I mean. I don't got no idea what's in here, but if it's paper goods or something, no good can come of it sitting out on the porch and soaking rainwater up like a sponge."

Piper's eyes flickered from Jackson's face to the box and back again, and Jackson could see her weigh her boss's displeasure against the contents of the box—whatever they were—being ruined or the box itself being somewhere visible in the building.

"All right, Jacky," Jackson said to Cody, "let's leave this thing here and take a picture along with Ms. Lutz here, so they know we tried—"

"Oh very well," Piper said with little grace, opening the door and allowing them to push the crate inside. "The office is down the hall and to the left. There should be room in the back."

"And the can?" Cody asked, sounding desperate.

"Keep going. It's around the corner and to the right," she told him, not even trying to conceal her disgust.

"Thanks, lady!" Cody called as he and Jackson maneuvered the oversized box through the corridor. Cody was a little too tall to be walking backward and pretending to balance the box, and he awkwardly hit the wall with his shoulder, knocking the framed certificate on the wall off.

Jackson caught it deftly and paused before replacing it.

"Hunh," he said, staring at it for a moment.

"What?" Cody asked. Jackson put the certificate back on the wall and, with a glance over his shoulder to make sure Piper Lutz had left them alone, took a picture of it.

"It's one of those award deals," Jackson said. "For organization of the year or buttplug of the century or douchenozzle empress or whatever. Left here."

Cody reached out and opened the door of the office they'd been directed to, and Jackson noted the name on the door—Valerie Trainor—with satisfaction.

The Big Cheese-esse. There should be something to learn here.

"Why'd we take a picture of the Douchenozzle Empress award?" Cody asked, as together they plopped the giant empty box right in the middle of the big room with the pink-champagne-colored plush carpet on the floor. "Also, this area rug is giving me a yeast infection."

Jackson grunted. "It would give *Jade* a yeast infection, and she is not afraid of pink. And we took a picture of it because Ellery's mother told him that places like this are usually an arm or a pinky or a foreskin of a political party or…."

He paused in the act of folding up the dolly to tuck under his arm, and Cody finished the sentence.

"Or a certain politician," he said, pulling out his own phone to take pictures of the stuff on the desk. "I hear you. Do we have any ideas?"

"Well," Jackson muttered, rifling through a filing cabinet. He paused at a file marked Property Taxes and Mortgage Receipts and pulled it out.

"Well, what?" Cody asked, and Jackson glanced up from what promised to be a very interesting slog through something that could prove *very* important, to remember what he'd been talking about.

"Well," Jackson continued, reasoning hard, "Sacramento is more liberal than you might think. Most of the right-wing politicians try to cloak themselves—hide the crazy. You have to look for certain phrases. Things like 'give parents control of education' or 'protect our children from unwholesome influences' when you look at the ballot. And sometimes they hide the crazy under fiscal conservatism. So I'm thinking that whoever is giving these women 'Douchenozzle Empress of the Year' will also have connections to whatever politician is currently involved in trying to hide the crazy. You know, a big right-wing circle jerk."

"Oh!" Cody said, brightening. "Got it. Wow, you and Cramer—big brains. Maybe I *should* stick to taking pictures of cheating spouses and workman's comp fraud."

"Ew!" Jackson replied, genuinely put off. "Hell no. Henry and I wouldn't do a friend like that. No, stick with us. We've got contacts, son, and we've got a little bit of job knowledge." He frowned. "Speaking of which… I really do need a few minutes with these files. How about you go get lost looking for the head."

"What am I looking for instead of the head?" Cody asked.

"Kids," Jackson said grimly. "Try to get lost on the second or third floors, okay? And if you can't spot kids, take a look at their back garden and see if there's any place to stash a body."

"Oh wow." Cody sobered. "God. Yes. Okay. What do we do if we get busted?"

Jackson grimaced. "Well, first play stupid, and if that doesn't get you out of the sitch, yell my name and start charging for the exit. Remember you don't have a badge—cut and run first. I mean, we're both in good enough shape to scale the back fence. If I'm at the car first, I'll fire up the engine and start circling the block in the place I think you'll exit. How's that?"

Cody Gabriel gave him a fierce grin. "Batshit insane. Looking forward to it. Back in ten."

He "wandered" off, and Jackson spent a moment wondering at Cody's undercover experience. He'd never gotten that far in the force—was much of it scripted there? Of course the television perception was of an agent—male or female—walking into giant drug deals with nothing but their brains and a swinging cod, but having spent some time in the department, Jackson imagined Cody had been given a great deal of structure, even when he was undercover.

It made sense, Jackson thought sadly. Cody's job had gotten stressful. He'd been forced to make decisions he hadn't liked—unethical decisions given to him by unethical people. And he'd been surrounded by product in his cover as a drug dealer. The temptation would have been *amazing*. No wonder he'd succumbed.

Watching him now, cheerfully throwing himself into scenario after scenario—the sense of *fun* pulsing from Cody Gabriel was seriously soul-sustaining. Henry had that same sense, and in the quiet of this stranger's office, Jackson took a moment to check his phone for messages.

Galen had texted—it must be his turn on deck—with a quick, *Henry wants to know if you're sitting on your ass crying or actually doing something.*

Ha, ha. Jackson texted the picture of the "Civic Group of the Year" award, along with a *Pull your weight and tell me who runs this and which politician thinks it's a dandy idea.*

Ooh, research. You are giving me an erection, which is both improper and titillating. I shall tell Ellery you're being naughty.

Jackson held back a chuckle. Galen was being his charming self—with a dose of IDGAF, probably aided by sleep deprivation.

Well, good. Jackson was right there with him.

Do that. But do what he's doing and make sure you are not alone. He thought of Piper Lutz, bribing poor Otto with food. How had she known where he would be? How many "errands" had she had the boy run for her before?

Jackson heard voices coming down the hallway and shook himself, realizing with a start that he'd almost fallen asleep during his woolgathering. Okay, then. He'd pushed himself pretty damned far today—this had to be his last adventure before he went and picked Ellery up from Jade's house. Hurriedly he sank to the inside of the desk, the property management files on his lap, and he started rifling through them, taking pictures of any document with a signature and sending them to Galen and Ellery without any more banter.

Galen would know what to look for, and it was time to get to work.

HE'D GOTTEN most of the property management file, as well as a couple of Miscellaneous Expenses files, none of them on computer, all of them neatly done, by hand, in triplicate. Sometime as he took his umpteenth picture it occurred to him to wonder why he hadn't made a beeline for the laptop. Plenty of women were amazing at technology, he thought, trying to follow his gut instinct back down to its root. It wasn't a misogyny thing. What was it about these *particular* women….

They all know each other.

He blinked, the thought important enough to take a moment with it.

Retty did what Twitty said. Piper got a guttersnipe to do her bidding. Cora was blackmailed by Retty and Twitty for a mistake she hadn't even made a million years and three thousand miles ago.

The ties that bound these people wouldn't be in the computer. Of course records could be subpoenaed, and there would probably be a list of employees on the payroll, but that wasn't going to prove anything. There were *personalities* at play here, things that were understood and not said.

Now she's the package.

Things like that, which would make their henchwoman so terrified she'd fight against going with people who clearly worked for the same outfit she did.

Those things wouldn't be on computer, but proof of them *might* be in tax records and property records, and those were the things people kept on paper. And *these* people would make sure the paper trail was clean and pristine. Nobody could get them on back taxes—no they could not.

It was the people those papers might connect them with that would bring this batch of snakes down, Jackson had no doubt.

He'd made his way through the property records, the employee records, the Miscellaneous Expense files, and was searching the file cabinet for one more thing—anything—when he stumbled upon it without even thinking.

Permission Forms.

Oh. Oh fuck. Yes.

Kids.

His movements quickened, any trace of hesitation and pondering what he was looking for and why dissolving as he realized he was dealing with a *huge* stack of paperwork, and he might not be able to photograph everything.

He'd already been girding his loins for plowing through a whole lot of data that night, and he was torn between taking *all* the pictures or maybe just, well, *stealing the file*, when he heard a clatter from upstairs and Cody Gabriel bellowed, "*Plan B now!*"

Jackson shoved the file under his shirt and into his waistband, hoping that was enough to keep it secure, grabbed the portable dolly, and bolted out of the room.

And right into a gaggle of women so thin and brittle they reminded him of uncooked linguini.

He identified Piper Lutz on sight, and most of the other women—they were all one of many shades of blond—scattered, but one woman, midsized, with the slim, powerful physique he associated with tennis players and dancers—stood in the middle of the hallway and shouted "Stop!"

Jackson had never been great at taking orders.

"Nope," he said, dodging around her and staying well out of arm's reach of her smaller form. Not that he didn't think Twitty couldn't kick the shit out of him, but hitting women was not first on his list of defense moves, no matter how much he might have hated this one.

"Get back here!" she screeched, but while she might have been in superior fighting shape, Jackson had meant what he'd said to Cody about running every day so you could escape what chased you. Still holding the dolly under one arm, he leaped off the porch, clearing the steps in one go and collapsing into the soft, wet ground when his feet hit it. He rolled, dropped the dolly, bounded up, and kept running, cutting through the trees on the grounds since he didn't have to take the sidewalks anymore and trying not to slip on the wet leaves behind the front of the main house. He kept to the shadows, dodging behind trees and staying well out of reach of the sodium lights that ran the length of the street.

He watched as the crowd of women, all in dress flats and sweater sets, went charging down the sidewalk in search of him. He assumed they'd separated, since none of them had been through the door before he'd darted behind the topiary to skirt the wrought iron fence behind the foliage. He kept running, keeping one eye on the lit street where the enemy was scurrying, crying to each other with shrill voices.

His favorite cry was, "What in the hell do we do if we catch him?"

He'd decided he wasn't going to hang around to see what would happen if somebody came up with an answer to that question when he saw—lagging behind the women but still pretty fast—two big shadows in dark uniforms.

Security guards, he thought. *Upstairs—not downstairs.*

They knew what they were protecting—and it wasn't paperwork.

Jackson continued to hug the shadows, wondering if it was lack of imagination or if everybody had the same aversion to snails and slugs Cody did but still finding it easier to move in the darkness than to outrun a witch hunt.

A thing he thought smugly to himself until he slid behind one last hedge on the corner and ran into a solid body, the *oolf* of the collision as quickly hushed by the body he'd squashed as it was by himself.

The *rancid* body he'd squashed.

Oh God. He stared down and found that yet another child, Cowboy's age, but this one female, was staring back at him, her eyes wide and terrified, darting to the street and then back to Jackson in the shadows.

Jackson held his finger up to his lips and breathed deeply, The girl—thirteen, fourteen at the most—let out a long breath with him, and he nodded.

"Come with me," he whispered. "I'll get you out of here."

The girl glanced behind her shoulder, underneath a holly bush, which made Jackson's skin shrivel at just the sight of it, because the dark leaves, glossy with rain, were exquisitely pointed on each terrible end.

They must be so scared.

There were two other young people down there, androgynous with dirt and fear, all of them wearing thin sweatshirts with the Moms for Clean Living logo barely visible on their shoulders.

"Them too," Jackson murmured. "Follow me."

He realized the girl was shaking.

"A warm place to sleep," he all but begged. "A bath. Clean clothes. Food. We won't make you go back home if you don't want to, and we're definitely not giving you back to those monsters in that place."

He watched the girl—God, she was tiny—swallow.

"What would we have to do?"

"Tell the truth," Jackson said softly. "Scream it. Tell the fucking world. I don't even know what they did to you guys in there—I don't have details. But if you all were willing to run away, to live like this, then it had to be bad."

She shivered, hard. "We're all so cold," she whispered. "So cold."

He didn't want to scare her; he couldn't even *imagine* the level of trauma. "C'mon, sweetheart. I've got a minivan, and I can get you to child services and away from this place."

She nodded and started to cry. "I want to go home so badly," she said, her voice breaking. He held out an arm, and she burrowed in. Everything she was wearing was sopping wet.

"We'll see if we can do that." He remembered those parental permission forms. "I can't promise, but we can at least see."

She nodded against him, and he glanced out toward the well-lit street, where their pursuers seemed to have disappeared.

"You ready?" he asked, glancing at the kids behind his new friend.

He got hesitant nods, but at least they were nodding.

"Follow me."

It had almost been *fun* when he'd been running through the underbrush in the dark by himself. A game. What would happen if they found him? His life would be a little harder, he and Ellery might have to get a little bit trickier, but really, what could they do to him? Call the cops on him? He had enough contacts in the department now—and enough cred—that he could probably avoid a night in jail. Hell, just the *threat* of Ellery would be enough to make most cops back down.

But it wasn't so fun now. They were, what? Half a block away from getting these kids to freedom? Every slither through the bushes made his heart pound, and every cough, sneeze, or gentle moan made it stop.

These three kids were sick, he realized. *Very* sick. He'd been thinking about calling CPS, but he thought that maybe he should take them all to the hospital instead and have the pediatric administrators call after Jackson described the situation.

Hospitals had armed guards in the front, and Jackson had the proof that these children had been in the care of people who had mistreated them tucked right over his balls.

And although he hated to admit it, it was time to call the police.

He was sweating in the cold humidity by the time they got back to the minivan, grateful for the pool of darkness they'd left the thing in. There were *no* streetlights on this side of the block, and while it might have made the giant blankness of the grounds creepy as hell, it also meant that the women—probably used to thinking of men as predators—were sticking to the lighted side of the street. He was busy lowering the back seat to let the kids scramble in when Cody ran up to the back fence from the inside and catapulted *his* first stray to the top.

"What in the hell?" Jackson said, before adding to the girl he'd been talking to. "There are blankets in the back. I think all three of you are going to have to squish on the back seat." He paused and took a double take at the number of teenagers Cody had brought with him. "On each other's laps," he added. *"Hurry."*

With a growl he hustled to the fence and helped the first kid— an undersized boy of around thirteen who might never hit his growth spurt—down from the fence, and then a tall, gawky teenaged girl with a buzz cut, and then another, and then another. Around the time Cody boosted his last teenager up—a chubby, deconditioned young man who kept apologizing with every heartbreaking breath—Jackson could hear shouts. They'd been spotted. He helped the young man down with a muffled *"oomph"* and urged him to the minivan, wondering if they'd managed to find a way to squeeze all eight—*eight*—kids into a back seat that only fit four.

He ran to Jennifer while Cody was still clambering over the fence himself, noting that two of the smallest teenagers had squeezed, knees to ears, in the back storage area of the van under the hatch, and that blankets had been tossed to the kids who'd been hiding out in the rain.

He got a glimpse of Piper Lutz coming from one side of the street and Valerie "Twitty" Trainor coming from the other as Cody hopped in, and he hit the ignition.

He'd backed up and was squealing down the street, the minivan's front bumper guard scraping on the ground with every pebble in the road, by the time Cody slammed the door shut and was wrestling with his seat belt.

For a moment, the only sounds were the minivan's straining engine, the panting and whimpers from their full back seat, and the *"snick"* of the seat belt clicking into place.

Jackson took a deep breath and said, "This was *not* Plan B!"

Cody chuckled breathlessly. "Hell, son, this wasn't even Plan *F*, but we pulled it off, right? Where to?"

"Davis Med Center," Jackson told him, driving one-handed while he pulled his phone from his jeans. "But while I'm driving, I need to call in the reserves."

"Oh God," Cody moaned. "You don't mean…."

"Yup. Lawyers, guns, and money, my man. The shit has hit the fan."

THE FIRST call was to Ellery so he could mobilize child services and call Dave and Alex so they could warn the hospital they had an influx of adolescents that needed to be admitted *stat* and not housed in the ER. The third was to Andre Christie, Sean's partner on the force, so he could get Fetzer and Hardison to the ER to help take custody of the kids, since they'd all been briefed on the situation beforehand.

And when all that had been done, he took a breath and finally asked the one burning question in his mind.

"What part of 'look around' did you not understand?"

Cody harrumphed. "The part where our hefty friend back there was locked in a closet, crying, with a clothespin on his nethers, and the kids from the girls' dorm were sneaking food to the boys because they'd been put on short rations that night. Something about 'encouraging his perversion.'"

Jackson blew out a breath. "Okay, so that was something, but I don't know if it'll get us out of a kidnapping charge."

"Jackson, there were pictures of drag queens burning in hell with chopped-off penises on the walls."

"Oh my *God*!" Jackson burst out. "That's *horrific*. What in the actual *fuck*!"

"It… it…." The voice came from the seat directly behind them, and Cody glanced back, but both of them shut up.

"It was what, honey?" Cody asked, the compassion in his voice so natural Jackson figured he could forgive the guy for absolutely fucking up their plan.

"It was to make us want to be straight," said the young woman behind them, one of the ones Cody had helped escape. "It… it was so stupid. One day I was fighting with my mom about my girlfriend, and the next all these Stepford wives were telling me I was going to hell. A van pulled up to my door, and my mom said, 'These people will help you, sweetheart,' and she shoved me in." There was a sound of desolation in the girl's voice. "She was crying. She… she put me in this fucking Jesus van and she was *crying* like *she* was the one getting hurt."

"Often they don't understand," Jackson said, feeling wretched and hopeful at once remembering Cowboy's mother. "I think… I think this group of people *lied* to your parents, maybe made this place sound like summer camp or a private school."

"Ha!" came from a boy huddled on the far side of a seat, with another boy tucked in next to him. Both of them were so slender they fit under the same seat belt. "My old man just needed to rest his beating hand."

"Well, hopefully you won't have to go back there," Jackson said, his head starting to pound.

"May as well," the kid said glumly, staring out the window into the rain. "At least with the old man, he'd leave me alone sometimes. These people… wake you up in the middle of the night going, 'Hey, kid, you thinking about dick?' It's like, 'No, asshole, I'm thinking about *sleep*, but now I'm thinking *you're* a dick.'"

That made Jackson's shoulders stiffen. "So there were men in that house?" he asked.

"Yeah," said the girl right behind him. "Two of them. Fuckers. Liked to think all we needed to straighten us out was *their* penis."

Next to him he heard Cody make a pained noise. Fuck. Yeah, that too.

"They left me alone," said the miserable, sick girl from the back.

"That's 'cause you bit that one guy," said their helpful friend with the buzz cut. "Epic move, Denise—seriously, we told that to all the new kids when they showed up. Told 'em you could fight back and end up on the street, but it might be worth it."

"Wasn't worth it," Denise all but moaned. "They still had us by the clit. Poor Otto—that one bitch grabbed him by the scruff of the neck and said, 'Hey, boy, we got a job for you,' and he didn't even have anyplace to run."

"God, he was pissed he couldn't keep up with Cowboy," said the boy with the attitude. "But…."

The whole car shuddered when he said it. Jackson felt the air itself charge with sadness, trauma, and fear.

"Anything's better than ending up like Caleb," said the other slender boy, next to the boy at the window.

"What happened to Caleb?" Jackson asked, hoping that somehow these kids weren't too traumatized to answer.

"None of us saw," said the one girl—small, but well developed, as some girls had the misfortune to become in the sixth grade—who hadn't spoken up yet. "We just…." That collective shudder again. "Mister, you ever heard the sound a watermelon makes when it's dropped on the sidewalk?"

Jackson's stomach rumbled weakly, and that empanada suddenly felt like a colossal mistake.

"Yeah," he said softly.

"*That's* what happened to Caleb," said the girl. "Those boys all tried to run away, and Jeddy here got hurt falling down the wall, and Caleb got dragged back by the ear. Retty was tearing him a new one in the courtyard and… and *he* went back there. We heard Caleb screaming, we heard that sound, and the screaming stopped. Next morning me and Otto were dragged out to the courtyard to clean up the mess." He heard her take a deep breath, like she was shoring up her courage, but when she let it out her voice was still broken. "It… it was blood and brains. I don't know where the rest of Caleb was, but I know what we had to slop out of the concrete with a mop bucket." He heard another sniffle. "Otto tried to get away, but… but sometimes, when you don't got nowhere to go, you're just as trapped on the outside of hell as you are on the in."

His stomach twisted at that, and beside him he heard Cody make a sound like a quarterback taking a tackle. He was spared from having to think of anything to say by Alex's phone call, telling him to drive around to the back of the hospital where pediatric emergency personnel were waiting to debrief and give aid, just as they arrived, but the girl's words stuck with him.

ONE HOUR, two. What he'd started to think of as the "outside" kids were all admitted for everything from delousing to antibiotics, but some of the inside kids had burns, bruises, marks.

The girls each had a blistering case of gonorrhea, which made both Jackson and Cody absolutely homicidal.

Jackson waited until Andre Christie arrived via the back entrance—which still smelled of stolen cigarettes, because health-care professionals had vices too—before he produced the wad of paperwork shoved into his jeans.

"And I didn't get you anything," Christie said, taking the sodden and sweat-drenched papers with distaste. A neat, dapper man in his mid-forties, Christie was madly in love with his wife and fiercely loyal to Sean Kryzynski. Jackson considered him a friend and an ally—and hoped that would be enough.

"Look," Jackson said quietly. "I am *worried* about what will happen to these kids. It is *hard* to get kids away from their parents and into child protective services, and these kids were *given* to an organization that tortured them in the name of… of.…"

"Religion," Cody supplied helpfully.

"If that's religion, you're Miss Piggy," Jackson retorted, about out of fucks, and Cody choked on his own snicker.

"I am *not*, in fact, Miss Piggy," he said.

"And I'm not Kermit the Frog," Ellery said, walking smoothly in at the most opportune moment possible.

"You say that," Jackson conceded, drinking in Ellery's slim, neat form wearing a pair of—oh my *God*—Mike's old sweats and blue flannel shirt? He looked good. His hair had been washed and was flopping across his brow, and his eyes were tired, but God.… So dear. "But you seem to have brought the whole *Muppet Show* with you."

Ellery harrumphed and gestured to the group of men and women behind him, all of whom were dressed in what Jackson's sister referred to as "bra o'clock" clothes—after bra o'clock, all that mattered was comfort and, for women anyway, there was no bra involved. "I brought the most qualified advocates in the city, so.…" He gave a toothy smile to Andre, who handed the paperwork over to him with a meaningful glance at Jackson.

"Marry this man," Andre said, giving him a smug smile. "He knows how to get shit done."

Jackson let out a tired cackle and sent Ellery a grateful look. "I'll consider it. I understand invitations are already out."

"They RSVP'd last week," Ellery said primly. "Them, the kids—I hope to throw one hell of a party."

Andre gave a toothy grin and then regarded the cadre of advocates with the same gratitude Jackson had felt.

"The kids are in rough shape," he said, and Jackson nodded in agreement, a wave of exhaustion washing over him so hard it almost made him nauseous. He was fine, for the moment, to just let Andre talk. "Their parents signed them over to an institution using illegal behavior modification practices to make them, uhm.…"

"Not gay or trans," Jackson supplied, and while some of the advocates appeared horrified, about half of them took it in stride, so Ellery had probably gotten to that part in the briefing.

"Some of the kids would like a reconciliation, provided the home is safe," Cody supplied.

"But some of them were, like, 'Hey, went from one beating to the next.'" Jackson let out a sigh. "It's a mess. And it's one we don't have the power to fix—" The enormity of the situation swept him again, but now was *not* the time.

"But how did you find out about it?" Andre asked. "I mean, I know you were looking into what happened to Henry, but seriously, what in the hell!"

So Jackson recounted how he and Cody had infiltrated the Moms for Clean Living headquarters, searching for something, *anything*, pointing to why Henry would have been shot by a woman wearing their merch. He managed to avoid talking about Cowboy—although Andre knew, he didn't want pressure from the child advocates until the boy was safe—Jackson was honest about the documents he'd photographed. He wasn't a police officer, and he didn't need a warrant to get evidence. When Andre asked him why he hadn't just taken pictures of the induction paperwork, Jackson gave Cody Gabriel a sour look.

"Because some asshole decided to stage a jailbreak without my knowledge or consent," he muttered.

Cody's grin added a hint of the devil to his angelic features. "What can I say? The kids made me as some kind of LEO from the get-go, and…." He swallowed. "Jackson, they were begging me—I mean *begging* me—to get them out of there. And then I heard that one kid sobbing from the closet, and…."

"I hear you," Jackson said, relenting. He was pretty sure that the entire reason he'd tagged Cody Gabriel for this mission in the first place was that Gabriel would take his plays from the same playbook Jackson favored. He'd been a little disappointed when Cody had needed explicit instructions before he'd gone wandering through the house, but the frantic scream of "Rivers, Plan B!" had given him some solid reassurance that his faith hadn't been misplaced.

"Hey, you found your own lost souls anyway," Cody said, grinning. "Which did not surprise me one bit."

"They were lurking outside of the fence," Jackson told the others. "They're the ones in worse shape. Much like the kid who…." He paused. "Ellery, did you fill them in on Otto?"

Ellery nodded. "Yes. He's got his own advocate."

A tired- but pleasant-looking woman wearing sun-and-moon pajama bottoms and a giant sweatshirt with cats all over it, gave a game wave.

"And Aileen already okayed Otto's temporary residence at your halfway house, Jackson. I hope that's okay. The older young men are being very responsible, and Jade and Mike will be spending the night there for a couple of nights to make sure it's all going well."

Jackson nodded, thinking of the bitter young man who'd thought that Moms for Clean Living had been a change of locale, nothing more.

"There's another kid there—I don't know his name—but apparently his homelife fit right in with the Moms for Clean Living philosophy. We may want to place him at the halfway house too. There's five beds," he said to Aileen. "So the place will take two more, but you may need a social worker willing to sleep on the couch. Like I said, the older kids have been pretty decently vetted—"

"And they're very protective," Aileen said. "We've met. No, it's a good place, and I appreciate the extra beds." She gave a nod to her fellow advocates. "We may need them. Homes for LGBTQ teens are not as plentiful as we might wish, so a place like yours might be the difference between helping these young men and sending them back to their parents."

Jackson unconsciously put his hand on his stomach, fighting the temptation to lean against the wall. "Please, no—"

"They'll do their best," Ellery told him softly. He glanced at the army he'd thrown together with an hour's notice. "Thank you, everybody. I can't thank you enough—"

"We're so grateful," said a slender young man with three piercings and ink on his wrist disappearing into his sweatshirt cuff. "Getting these kids out of there—so often they run away, or—" They all swallowed at the same time. "—resort to self-harm," he finished raspily. "Getting them legal help and social workers and therapists—it all starts with an act of bravery, and you two definitely did that." He paused and said, "What would you have done if they'd caught you?"

Jackson shrugged. "Screamed 'Kidnapper' and run for the minivan anyway?"

Cody Gabriel started laughing helplessly, and Jackson found he had a few chuckles to spare. Unconsciously he straightened. If he could laugh now, he could make it through the next few hours, right?

"We woulda thought of something," Cody said, and they continued on the debrief before Ellery's army dispersed among the kids, taking the paperwork Jackson had smuggled in his pants with them.

"I should have taken pictures of that," Jackson muttered, half to himself. His attention was wandering—he couldn't seem to yank it back.

Ellery entered a text, and a moment later every advocate in the place was pulling out their phones to take pictures of the stack of paperwork they'd grabbed.

Jackson had no doubt in a few minutes Ellery's phone would be blowing up with the evidence they'd need to study that night.

For the moment—just the moment—they'd done all they could do.

He wasn't sure where the yawn started—somewhere between his balls and his toes, probably—but it managed to work its way up past his knees, which grew suddenly weak, rumbled in his stomach, which was a mess anyway, and climbed into his throat and his brain and his eyes.

By the time the yawn was done with him, Andre, Cody, and Ellery were all staring at him.

"Jackson," Ellery said quietly, "it's eight o'clock at night. We've been up more than thirty-six hours." He gave a polite little yawn that barely showed his pointy teeth. "It's time to call it a day and wake up to do it again tomorrow."

"Sure," Jackson said in the middle of another yawn. "I just have to take Cody home."

"Cody, do you have parking for the minivan?" Ellery asked.

"I do," Cody told him. "Think she'll let me drive her?"

"She was pretty good to you at the end of the day," Jackson said, digging out the keys. "I think she appreciates people who are good to kids. And she might remember you from when we met. So yeah. Drive safe."

Cody grinned. "My own car is getting an overhaul—this'll be like a treat. I'll be real nice to our lady, you hear?"

"I hear," Jackson said, laughing softly to himself.

Christie shook his head. "I don't even want to hear it about that fucking ca—"

"Shh!" Jackson and Cody both hissed, holding their fingers to their lips. "Don't jinx it!"

"Oh God," Christie said, shaking his head. "Fine, Gabriel, go. Where can I find you?"

"At Jackson's house, tomorrow around—"

"Ten," Ellery supplied, no bullshit.

"Fine," Jackson snapped. "But first, I'm going to go upstairs and tell Henry about the kids."

There was a moment for everybody to digest that, and then the other three men smiled.

"He'll love to hear it," Christie said, some relief in his tone. "I'll go up and add some details when you're done."

It was great in theory, but Ellery—who had admitted to copping an hour of sleep on Jade and Mike's guest bed before Jackson had called him, and who had also gotten sleep the entire week before—needed to steer Jackson up to the ICU because that yawn had sucked Jackson's last reserves right out of him.

Henry was awake when they walked in, and as Jackson told him about the rescue of the kids from the Stepford Dragon compound, he let out a weak chuckle.

"Damn," he said, his eyes closing in spite of his best efforts to stay awake. "Teach me to get shot. All the good shit happens when I'm out of the running."

"Good reason to get better," Jackson told him soberly.

Henry smiled, his eyes closed, and said, "Don't replace me while I'm out, okay?"

"Cody's not mean enough to replace you," Jackson told him honestly. "He needs to find his own Henry—I've got the one I want."

"Good."

He fell asleep, and as Ellery stood to guide Jackson down to the car, they glanced up to see Dex in the doorway, tired but pleased.

"He's the fourth kid of five," he said softly. "It means *everything* to him that you said that."

Jackson's eyes burned, and he cursed Henry's brother for always saying the brave thing, even though it was also the raw one.

"Well he's the first partner I ever had whom I trusted to have my back," Jackson said. "I mean, Cody Gabriel is a good man, but your brother had to fight for that position. I'm not giving it away anytime soon."

Dex nodded. "Good. Get some sleep. Somebody will be here with him all night. We'll keep you in the loop." He sobered. "His fever is getting up there. He may be here for another few days to fight off infection."

Jackson was suddenly awake and wide-eyed with worry. "We'll cross our fingers," he said earnestly.

"You do that," Ellery said. "I myself will pray."

Jackson startled and remembered the last time *he*'d prayed.

Ellery had been in surgery, and Jackson had been in the bottom of an emotional well so deep it had taken Ellery's mother to pull him out of it.

Maybe he'd gotten less pissed off at the powers that be since then?

"I will too," he added.

Dex nodded, and this time his smile was a little watery. "Couldn't hurt to remember how," he said.

And with that there was nothing else for it but to bid him good night.

Fishbowl Prayers, Ocean Answers

"WHA—!"

Jackson's entire body twitched as Ellery pulled the Lexus into the garage, and Ellery tried not to jerk the wheel. He'd known Jackson had been quiet, but he hadn't realized he'd been nearly asleep.

"If I'd known the car was the trick," he said, lifting one corner of his mouth, "I would have been driving up and down California like new parents with an infant in a car seat."

"Very funny," Jackson muttered, scrubbing his face with one hand. "Changing my diaper would be a *bitch*."

Ellery was too tired to snicker, but his one-sided smile cranked up a little. "Let's go inside," he murmured. "You can hit the shower. I'll make you some food."

He'd showered at Jade's before changing, and his suit was in a garment bag in the back of the car. He was tired, yes, but it wasn't desperate at the moment.

Jackson was desperately tired. He was organ-shutting-down-immune-system-compromised sort of tired, and he needed the shower and the food so he could sleep.

Ellery had seen him through these moments before.

"Believe it or not," Jackson said with dignity, "Cody talked me into eating after we left the office."

"So a snack," Ellery retorted, not put off in the least.

"With coffee," Jackson added.

"But a snack."

"But I'm not starve…." The last of the word was swallowed in a yawn.

"Sure," Ellery agreed as they both walked through the garage door. "Get in the shower now… oh my fucking God, *Mom*!"

His mother was sitting calmly at the table, Lucifer in her lap, Billy Bob curled on the table next to her laptop as she worked assiduously away.

"Holy Lucy Satan," Jackson said blankly. "Ellery, I… I can't—"

Ellery's mother turned calmly toward them. "Jackson, go shower. Ellery will bring you food."

"Yes'm," Jackson muttered before fleeing.

"You broke his brain," Ellery said, staring at her. "You broke *my* brain. We were on the phone *ten hours ago*. How does that even—"

"I had a friend with a private jet flying to Denver to ski," she said pleasantly. "Not that I approve of that much conspicuous consumption or the waste of resources, but it was damned convenient. From Denver, I caught a commuter flight to Sacramento. They do run all day."

Ellery blinked. "So you've been here—"

"For about an hour," she said. "I didn't know you'd gone full lumberjack out here in the West, Ellery. What on earth are you wearing?"

Ellery glanced down at his flannel shirt and sweats and shook his head. "Have you eaten?"

His mother's delicately arched eyebrows made an exquisite little *V*. "You know, I don't remember," she said, and he found himself growling.

"Soup," he said. "We have lots and lots of wonton soup. And some leftover bread."

Her face—a perfect oval with expressive brown eyes, perfect makeup, and all—lit up with genuine appreciation. "That would be lovely," she said. "Thank you, son."

"My pleas—"

"And while you're fixing that, and Jackson's in the shower, perhaps you could update me on your current situation. It sounds *fascinating*."

FORTY-FIVE MINUTES later, his mother was eating, the cats had been displaced to the couch after—apparently—having been petted into twin comas, and Ellery took it upon himself to wonder where Jackson was.

He'd made it through the shower and into his briefs. And one leg of his pajama bottoms.

And then, apparently, he'd sort of *melted* over to the side and fallen asleep.

Ellery paused in the doorway and marveled at him for a moment. He was battered and bruised—there were always bruises somewhere, he might as well have been a longshoreman—and his body showed the signs of hard, hard use in a relatively short amount of time.

Visually, Ellery traced the scars he'd been there for, and then the ones that had happened before Ellery had arrived in his life, and he wondered, as he always did, about the scars within.

And at the same time, he gave thanks.

How this amazing creation, this stunning human being, had become the perfect lover, the perfect friend, the perfect mate for *him*, plain and practical, awkward and meticulous Ellery Cramer, was really one of the wonders of the world.

It was a miracle.

Ellery didn't need to have passed his Bar Mitzvah to understand that miracles didn't always last. Sometimes they were transient. They should be celebrated.

Jackson could be—and almost had been—taken from him at any time. He was trying so hard—witness his half-intelligible story of a four-thirty snack—to make their time together as long as possible.

Ellery would cherish absolutely every quiet moment.

"Shwhyruwookingadme," Jackson mumbled, and Ellery could tell he was trying to open his eyes and failing.

"Sweats on or off?" Ellery asked crisply, moving into the room.

"'Weats?" Jackson mumbled.

"That's off, then," Ellery decided, putting a warm hand on Jackson's thigh before stripping the pant leg off.

"In't your mom here?" Jackson asked.

"Yes, but she understands you need to sleep."

"So do you." It was the most articulate thing he'd said.

"I'll be in shortly," Ellery told him, his own yawn working its way up from his toes.

From the dining room, his mother's clear call came. "Ellery, I'll clean up. You two get some sleep."

"Heh heh heh—ears like a *bat*. Prolly turns into a bat at night. Lucy Satan Bat in the Satan Bat trees."

While he was speaking, he helped Ellery by pulling his foot out of the pantleg and rolling onto the comforter curled up into a little ball, probably cold.

"Jackson, stand up," Ellery ordered, and like a surprised cat, Jackson's long body uncoiled. He rose to his feet in a giant splang and windmilled his arms with his eyes at half-mast.

Ellery ripped the covers back. "Now lie down again."

He collapsed like a marionette with a cut string, resuming his curl with disgruntled, catlike movements until he gradually grew still.

Ellery tucked the blanket around his chin, relieved to see his eyes had gone back to fully closed.

"Evil man," Jackson mumbled. "I've got a heart condition, you know."

"It was either that or go out and get extra blankets so we could cuddle," Ellery told him, smoothing his hair from his forehead. "I need to hold you tonight."

Jackson's eyes finally opened naturally, the sleep still solid under the lids, and he smiled.

"And just like that, my heart is fine."

Ellery smiled and stood, stripped Mike's clothes off, and laid them on the dresser to wash in the morning. Outside their bedroom he heard his mother loading the dishwasher and talking to the cats, something about how Billy Bob *forced* Lucifer to run into walls, which Ellery thought was flat-out favoritism. In Jackson's words, Lucifer did that shit all by himself.

He slid into bed behind Jackson, shuddering as he pulled that miraculous, healing body against his own. He was dimly aware of the door opening, and there was one plop on the bed and then three unsuccessful tries before Ellery reached down with one hand and scooped Lucifer onto the bed as well. Most days he made it fine on his own, but sometimes he needed help.

Just like sometimes even Jackson needed sleep. Ellery tucked his arm under Jackson's so he could hold him closer, and Jackson laced their fingers together.

"I love you," Jackson whispered. "So very, very much."

"Oh God. Me too."

Darkness, comfort, and sleep.

"She's crying! Somebody make her stop! Oh God, she's crying—make her stop!"

Ellery struggled to wake up. Oh God. Jackson was shouting and flailing, pushing himself up and screaming into the darkness of the bedroom, and Ellery squinted at his phone on the charger.

Three hours. Ellery wasn't sure he could cope with this with only three hours of sleep after the day they'd had.

"Baby," he tried to soothe. "Baby, c'mon, calm down."

"*Somebody get the fucking baby!*"

The scream was ripped out of Jackson's throat, and Ellery recoiled for a moment, stunned and disoriented and, yes, a little afraid.

This was tearing from Jackson's *soul*, and Ellery thought he knew where, but the memory was fleeting, a casual confession—as so many of Jackson's worst confessions were—of another atrocity he'd managed to survive.

"Jackson Leroy Rivers!"

Ellery's mother's voice snapped through the air like a whipcrack, and Ellery sat up in bed straighter, his senses whirling from another emotional assault.

"Yes, ma'am," Jackson said, sounding woozy and hoarse—but lucid.

"Why are you making all this noise?" Taylor Cramer demanded, slamming on the lights. Ellery's mother was wearing blue silk pajamas, with her hair pulled back into a braid for sleeping, and Ellery had a muddled moment to wonder how she managed to look like she was wearing a business suit at two in the morning.

"She's crying," Jackson said earnestly. "Can't you hear her crying? She won't stop...." He trailed off in confusion, glancing around, orienting himself, his consciousness catching up to inform him of reality after the dream's terrible lies.

"I'm sorry," he said in the remote voice of an apologetic schoolboy. "I-I didn't mean to bother everybody." He made to stand up, but Taylor's glare held him in place. "If… if you let me go, I'll play some video games to calm myself down."

Ellery's mother looked to him. "Son, does this happen often? I mean, you spoke of dreams but...." She gestured helplessly.

"Something's been riding him," Ellery told her, grateful to have his mother there to talk to—or even simply witness. "For a while this only happened once a month or so." He let out a shuddery breath. "It was nice," he said plaintively.

Jackson turned to him, remorse written all over his face. "I'm sorry," he said, his voice wobbly. "Listen, I'll go get a hotel room or—"

"Oh, don't you fucking dare!"

Both of them stared at Ellery's mother in shock.

"What?" she demanded crankily. "You two use the word like you breathe. How often is this happening now?"

"Almost nightly," Ellery said when Jackson glanced away.

"Absolutely not," she said, and Ellery saw fury—and worry— bubbling under her controlled expression like a volcano under an ice floe. "No. No, you two need to be working at optimum levels, and you absolutely cannot do that if this is what your sleep looks like, Jackson." Her voice altered perceptibly from drill sergeant to the thing Jackson probably feared the most.

A mother.

"Son, what's on your mind. What baby?"

Jackson squinted at her in confusion. "Baby?"

"Yes." Disregarding all propriety, Taylor sank down at the side of the bed, and Ellery yearned to go put on his own pajamas but figured now was not the time. "You were begging us to get the baby. What is riding you, son?"

Jackson swallowed and shook his head. "I—"

"What are you worried about right now?"

He lifted his head, and Ellery thought for the umpteenth time that his mother was a genius. Not the old hurt, not whatever had haunted a boy or young man that he might not have had words for. What was the trigger? What was the *current* hurt that the mature, able man could articulate?

"The wedding," Jackson said, and right when Ellery's heart thought it would drop through the bed and bury itself in the core of the earth, he added, "I'm worried I won't measure up. I'm… you know." He gave Ellery a weak smile over his shoulder. "You know your son's a catch," he said, some of his roguish charm surfacing. "I… I don't want to let him down."

In one of those gestures that were the core of Ellery's mother, she smoothed the hair back from Jackson's forehead. "You are everything I've ever dreamed about for him," she said, and Ellery's eyes burned. "But I want your heart whole and well. From what I can see, you've spent your entire life doing nothing but caring for other people. And not just caring, *doing* for them. Often at your own expense—witness tonight's unexpected rescue."

Jackson glanced away sheepishly. "You told?" he asked Ellery, sounding like a child.

"Yes, Jackson. My mother shows up on our doorstep to help us with a case, and I briefed her on current events. This is all obviously my fault." He kept his voice sarcastic on purpose. He needed Jackson to feel normal.

"I love you like a son," Taylor said primly, "but that doesn't mean that Ellery isn't the *good* son."

Ellery was draped practically over Jackson's shoulder, and he saw the tiny corner of his mouth turn up.

Bless his mother. God *bless* his mother. *Okay, God, I get it now. How we see you in everyday works.*

"Understood," Jackson said, some of the defensiveness bleeding from his posture.

"Good." She had both his hands in hers now, and Ellery knew from experience that they'd be freezing. "So you're worried about letting Ellery down. That's a place to start. Impossible, I think, because you work your heart out for him, but it's a start for what we're doing here. Now think. When was the first time you felt like this? When was the first time you were afraid you weren't enough?"

The silence was four thousand, three hundred and eighty-two years too long.

"This is stupid," Jackson said after a breath hitch. Abruptly he stood and slid off the bed, ducking smoothly out of Ellery's hug and Taylor Cramer's grip. He went to the dresser and began to rifle through clothes.

"Sit down," Ellery's mother said, and while she sounded affronted, she didn't sound shocked.

Ellery was shocked. Nobody—*nobody*—defied his mother.

"Look," Jackson said, and Ellery could hear the fine edge of desperation in his voice. "Lucy, I appreciate the effort, but—"

Taylor Cramer made a bored sound. "You may put on your pajamas, but you are sitting back down."

"I was, you know, thinking of going out for a run," Jackson said, a rather green conciliatory smile on his face.

"And I was thinking of having you restrained," Ellery's mother said, "but I rather decided I respected you too much to do that. Kindly show me the same consideration."

Ellery stared from his mother to Jackson and back, not sure who would win this contest of wills but on one level absolutely fascinated. In his entire memory, he couldn't recall a single human being *ever* gainsaying his mother the way Jackson had, and given that Jackson was *terrified* of Ellery's mother, Ellery had to give it to him in the balls department.

Jackson Rivers would face down any demon.

Except his own.

And that's where Ellery's fascination ended and his terror began.

"Jackson," he said, his voice shaky in the silence. "Jackson, baby, I'll back whatever you do. If you go running, I'll run with you. If you decide to hop on a plane to Rome, I'll go there too. But...."

Jackson had glanced at him and then away as Ellery had first said his name, but now, as Ellery faltered, he gazed at Ellery more fully, a stricken expression on his face.

"But what?" he asked, like the words had been forcibly ripped from his chest.

"But this thing," Ellery whispered, "that's keeping you up at night. That won't let you go. This thing you're so afraid of. It'll get you in the end, baby. Unless you talk about it. You almost passed out tonight, you crashed so hard—because you hadn't had a full night's sleep in a *month*. Please. We've gone through so much. You've done *so much* to make yourself healthy. Don't let whatever this is destroy it all." Ellery's eyes stung, and he thought crying in front of his lover *and* his mother while in his underwear in bed must have been one of the big things he'd feared in high school, but right now it didn't even hit his top ten. "I'll follow you until you shrivel up and fade away, but I'm telling you, that's not what I hoped for when you asked me to marry you."

Jackson made a sound like he'd gotten thumped in the liver. "What are you hoping for?" he asked.

"Sunshine," Ellery said, wiping his cheeks with the back of his hand. "Flowers. Our friends and family there to wish us well. Many more years doing what we love. Hope. New plans. New people. Old friends, old family. All of it, together. Don't you understand, Jackson? I see all these things *in you*."

"But I'm not worth it," Jackson said, his voice cracking. "I told you that from the beginning—"

"You have never," Ellery hissed fiercely, "not once *ever*, let me down."

Ellery could hear Jackson's swallow from the dresser, and he slid the T-shirt in his hands over his head as though his body was functioning without his brain.

"Who is it you think you *did* let down?" Taylor asked, and Jackson swung around to face her as though he'd forgotten she was there.

"Lots of people—"

"Bullshit," she replied evenly. "Young man, you do not have desperate nightmares like I just heard for an amorphous 'lots of people.' Now I am *tired*, and I am *irritated*, and I need for this to be over. You will tell us *now* what is riding you, or I *shall* bind your wrists and ship you off to the nearest psych ward—"

"You would not," Jackson retorted, obviously shocked. "You sort of like me."

"*I love you, you infuriating child. Now sit down!*"

Her voice cracked. Ellery's mother's voice cracked. The only time he could ever remember that happening had been… been… oh my God. *In the hospital room, after Jackson had saved Ellery's life as he lay in recovery and had nearly died himself.*

"Jackson," Ellery said, appalled. "You are *breaking* my mother! Now sit down and help us out!"

Ellery hadn't been aware he'd held his breath until the mattress sank under Jackson's weight and he sucked air into his lungs.

Jackson was staring at his hands. "I'm sorry," he whispered. "I—"

"Whatever you're about to ask me, no," Taylor Cramer snapped. "Spit it out, son. Nothing is worth all of this. Who do you think you let down?"

Jackson scowled at her. "It's stupid. It happened forever ago—"

"*Who!*" Ellery and his mother both shouted, exchanging surprised glances before the word stopped echoing in the bedroom.

"My baby sister," Jackson snarled, his shoulders hunched defensively. "Are you fucking happy now?"

"You have a sister?" Taylor Cramer asked at the same time Ellery said, "Jackson, that wasn't your fault."

"You will explain," Taylor said—hopefully to both of them because Ellery was the one who answered.

"His mother had a child when he was fifteen. It was how he got out of the house. She kicked him out so he could live with the Camerons because she had another source of welfare income."

"Oh, son…." Ellery's mother put her hand over her mouth, and Ellery didn't even want to tell her the worst part.

He didn't have to. The explosion had been detonated. The dam had no choice but to crumble around their ears and let the deluge cleanse them raw.

"Kaden and I," Jackson whispered. "We stayed up. All night, that night. Listening to the baby cry. Celia had stayed in the apartment for a month—trying, I think. But after about four weeks, she… I don't know. Left. Took off. Got high. Whatever she did. And the baby just… she was born addicted. Her screams—they made your heart pound and your palms sweat, and Kaden found me on the couch, crying. And… and I couldn't do it anymore. I was going to run down the stairs and break down the door and get her, but Kaden tackled me. He said, 'Jackson, my mom can't feed anyone else. What can we do?'"

"Oh God," Ellery whispered. He hadn't known this part. The bare bones, but not the… the sheer desperation of the moment.

"And he was right," Jackson gasped. "They…. Kaden and Jade and Toni. They gave up *food* so I could live there. Toni was holding on by a thread as it was. So we called CPS. We told them we could hear the baby through the walls, and the mother had abandoned her. And they came and got her. And they never knew that I was upstairs. I was her brother, and I… oh God. I couldn't. I couldn't take care of her. I… I'd barely gotten used to eating myself. So I gave up. I… swore I'd never give up like that again. I'd find a way. I'd keep all my promises. I'd… I'd…."

He paused, breath coming in painful pants as he made a Herculean effort to keep all of it—the pain, the helplessness, the terrifying regret, all of it—tucked inside an increasingly fragile body.

Ellery and his mother met horrified glances, and Ellery was suddenly fiercely glad she was there. This was so big. It was so awful. No one person could bear it, not if they loved this man like they did.

"You've done all that, son," Taylor said, venturing close enough to reach out to him again.

He recoiled at first. "I'm a mess, Mrs. Cramer," he said roughly. "You keep saying I'm good enough for your son, but I don't see how—"

Ellery wrapped his arms around Jackson's shoulders and buried his face against Jackson's neck. "Shut up," he said, for once out of words. "Oh God, Jackson. You are so much better than your weakest moment. You were a *kid*—"

"But she was my family," Jackson said, his voice thin and thready. "Ellery, she was my family, and I let her go so I could have…."

He flailed for a moment, and Ellery's mother reached out with both hands this time to cup both his cheeks in her hands. "Food," she said simply, and Ellery heard tears in her voice too. "Safety. Love. You need to have them to give them, Jackson. And you didn't have them then. You did what you could. You did an incredibly brave thing—don't think I don't know what consequences you could have dragged down on your head with that phone call. And Kaden was brave too. The two of you were in an impossible place, and you did the best you could. It's time to let it go now."

"But I failed," he said, his face crumpling, and as Ellery held his shoulders, his mother drew his face against her stomach, wrapped her arms around his head as though he was Ellery himself, or Rebekah, or Ellery's father. Somebody beloved to her. Somebody she would hover over, protect, and love.

"You were a child," she said, her own voice trembling. "You were so young, son. You did the right thing, Jackson. You *always* do the right thing. And the more power you have in your life, the more good you do with it. It's okay, Jackson. You can let it go now. We still love you, even though you were young and impoverished and powerless. None of that was your fault back then. You are loved *now*, do you understand me? You are loved *now*."

She might have said more after that, but Ellery lost the thread of it, because they were sobbing, all three of them, the raging tide of the past tumbling them about in an icy torrent until they were left, dry and frail husks, on the sands of the now.

ELLERY WOKE up at 7:00 a.m., his internal clock ignoring the shocks and stresses of the past few days.

Uneasily, he looked to where Jackson slept, eyes closed, chest moving in and out evenly, like the storms that had rocked them all had never blown.

For a moment he expected Jackson to say something—he almost always did, somehow knowing that Ellery was awake and watching him before Ellery had even detected a change in breathing, but Jackson's exhaustion the night before, mental and physical, had been complete. One moment he'd been sobbing in Ellery's mother's arms, and the next, he'd slumped sideways, asleep so abruptly Ellery had almost taken his pulse to make sure his heart hadn't simply stopped beating with the stress of being bared to the world.

With a soft kiss on his temple, Ellery slid out of bed and put on some (thank *God)* pajamas, before following the smell of coffee out to the kitchen.

His mother was there, and it was a testament to how rough the night before had been that she was still wearing her own pajamas and not dressed in a Chanel pantsuit with her hair in its usual chignon.

"Is he still asleep?" she asked, peering over the coffee mug that Jackson had chosen for her especially for her stays at their house. It was enormous and featured a tail-twitching black cat, contemplating mischief with slanted green eyes.

Except for the color of eyes, it was *very* like Taylor Cramer.

"Yes," Ellery said, heading directly for the coffee pot.

"Good," she said, breathing out in relief.

"You…." He paused as he pulled creamer out from the fridge. "In case Rebekah or I have never told you, you are a very good mother."

He heard her surprised gasp as he moved to the counter and his own enormous trough of coffee. How he yearned for the taste of tea again—but not this week.

"That's a beautiful compliment," she said, "from a son who has made me proud every day of his life."

Ellery swallowed hard and moved to the table to sit across from her. "What do we do next?"

"With the Stepford Dragons or Jackson?" she asked, her lips twitching as she attempted to lighten things up.

Ellery grunted. "Since Jackson plans to be up and running in a couple of hours, let's start with the case so he has a thing to do."

She gave him a rueful smile. "You do know him well, don't you?"

Ellery shrugged. "Same way I passed the bar exam in three states."

"Study, study, study," she supplied and nodded to the laptop she'd been scrolling on as he'd walked in. "Which is what I've been doing this morning."

He gazed at her for a moment, at the weariness in her brown eyes. "Did you sleep at all?" he asked.

She flashed him a quick grimace. "Unlike you and Jackson, I've had adequate rest over the last few months." She swallowed and looked away. "I'm not so impervious that last night left me unmoved."

"I…." Ellery let out a short laugh. "It's funny. He spends all his time worrying that he won't be enough for me, but I'm the one who needs help with his care and feeding."

"Ellery, when your father and I met, we were both in law school. We'd both come from prosperous families with a solid work ethic and a trust in the government and in education. I thought he was the dearest man I'd ever met, kindness to my sharpness, and…." She smiled fondly, because Ellery's father, with his wildly curly hair and abstracted air of absolute brilliance inspired that sort of emotion, even in Taylor Cramer. "And falling in love with him was as easy as breathing." Her eyes, dark and sharp and bruised with lack of sleep, met his. "I can't tell you that I couldn't have loved him just as much if he'd had the same damage as your beloved. But I can tell you that I would have called my mother and *begged* her to be kind to him when I brought him home, and if she hadn't been kind—she wasn't always—I would never have spoken to her again. As it was I simply brought him home, and we both got hugs and congratulations, but you…." Her smile turned sad. "You chose a much more difficult path. It's one I'm very proud of, but I couldn't call myself a mother if I didn't help."

Ellery must have been raw from the night before because his eyes burned. "I'm so very glad you do," he said, and then, after clearing his throat a couple of times, he added, "If you get a house on the beach, get it in Mendocino County. It's closer, and there are mountains as well as the ocean. I haven't taken Jackson there yet—I think he'd love to see it."

"I'll make a note of it," she said, and there was a tone of normalcy in her voice as they both tried to shake off the terribly personal confessions over coffee. "I also have some ideas that may help Jackson when he's ready to listen to them. But in the meantime, would you like to hear what I've learned about Stepford Dragon Incorporated?"

Had it only been yesterday? It felt like eons ago that Ellery had asked his mother for information on their favorite pearl-and-twinset-wearing monsters.

"Absolutely," Ellery said, taking a fortifying sip of his coffee. "Although…." He shuddered. "After what Jackson and I saw last night, if you tell me anything short of them drinking the blood of newborn babies on the rooftops of brothels under a horned moon, it's going to feel awfully anticlimactic."

She arched an eyebrow at him. "Have some faith in me, Ellery. I didn't swoop in here just to screech like a dockworker at you and your fiancé in the dark hours of the night. I came with *facts*, and they're important, so listen up."

Ellery took another sip of coffee, pretty sure he'd won the parental lottery—twice.

"I'm all ears."

"First of all," she said, "Do you recognize that name?"

Ellery's eyebrows raised. "Gannett Hoover—guy with two last names and no personality. He's a local politician," he said slowly. "A state assemblyman." Ellery frowned because he *did* recognize the name. "He ran under the auspices of the progressive ticket, but when Jackson and I were doing a deep dive on him—"

"You do a deep dive on your local politicians?" Taylor asked politely.

"Don't you?" he replied. "I like to know who's beholden to whom."

"Indeed," she said. "I couldn't be prouder. But continue…."

"He's getting his money from a conservative Super Pac," Ellery said, the information flooding back. "He was a plant. I remember because it was a scandal two years ago, and he's back up for reelection, and getting out the news that he's a fake Democrat is brutal—people are afraid of betraying the party. Why?"

"Because *he* was the assemblyman who presented the Educational Organization of the Year award to your Stepford Dragons. The award was in the stack of paperwork Jackson emailed you last night, which goes to show your young man knows his scoundrels. What can you tell me about his district?"

"He represents the fourth district," Ellery said, thinking hard. "He's got property out in Sonora, I think it is—some enormous monstrosity of a house. Anyway they're *very* red, and apparently that was how he got elected. Put *D* on his papers, flew a certain candidate's flag on his truck and in front of his house. It was a big joke to his constituents. He's spent his entire term trying to rescind free school lunches and dispossess the already homeless. Ha ha."

His mother's upper lip curled in a devastating sneer. "Hilarious."

"Agreed," Ellery told her. He and Jackson had been distracted during that election, but he still felt the outrage. "So… did he recruit the Stepford Dragons or—"

"Oh, son. Have some faith." She reclaimed her laptop and began to open files. "Now, I looked at what you'd sent me yesterday while I was on the plane. Do you remember where all these women seemed to come from—their point of meeting before they changed their names and started trying to rip books out of schoolchildren's hands?"

"Florida State," Ellery said.

"Do you recall any men involved in their little group? Any names—"

"Conway Schmitt," Ellery supplied promptly, and that made her sit up. "You're sure?"

"Yes," Ellery said. "Because one of the women was known to all the kids as 'Twitty.' And it was driving us crazy until I got Piper Lutz to make the connection. Conway Schmitt, Conway Smitty—"

"Conway Twitty," his mother finished dryly. "Yes, I get it. Poor man. The singer, not this piece of work. But yes. Tell me what *you* know about Conway Schmitt."

Oh God. Yesterday—it might as well have been eighth grade. He sucked in another long draught of coffee and tried to make his brain fire. "He was arrested," he said after a painful moment. "For"—he wrinkled his nose—"—child molestation. He was a preacher who reached out to touch his choirboys. He's in jail—"

"Oh no, he's not," his mother said, and Ellery set down his coffee cup.

"But he was sentenced to fifteen years." Oh God. He saw where this was going.

"In an extremely conservative state in the Bible Belt," his mother said grimly. "He was paroled in five. And… you'll never guess what he did when he got out."

"Left the state and changed his name?" Ellery had a thought. "He's not Gannet Hoover, is he?" And then, answering his own question, "No, no…. Hoover is about ten years too young."

"No, not Hoover," his mother said. She turned her laptop around again. "Here's a picture of Hoover giving his award to the Stepford Dragons. What do you see here?"

Ellery studied the picture, a smiling, dapper Hoover, poster boy for the straight white male with his perfectly coiffed trophy wife next to him as they presented the certificate to Valerie Trainor on stage at a luncheon.

And there in the corner of the stage—balder, paunchier, and not smiling—was the man Ellery recognized from his own research that afternoon.

"Prison was not kind to him," Ellery murmured. The man who had been sentenced to prison had been smoothly handsome, slender, with a high forehead and a rather rakish blue-eyed gaze. The man who had emerged from the crucible was beefier and thicker, from his biceps to his lips, and his bulldog expression did nothing to make him less of a bruiser. His nose had been broken, and a cheekbone as well, and Ellery would make a bet that he was wearing dentures from the small number of teeth the man was showing in lieu of a smile.

"No," his mother acknowledged. "And…." She frowned. "There's… something. Something between Gannett Hoover and Conway Schmitt."

"What's his name now?" Ellery asked, scanning the article and not finding it before returning the laptop to his mother.

"Newton Dwayne," she said absently, and Ellery frowned.

"Okay, that's… that's weird. That both names are *almost* the names of old country singers. Conway Twitty, Wayne Newton—"

"Oh Lord," his mother said, glancing at him sheepishly. "That didn't even occur to me."

"You do need some sleep," he told her kindly, but part of his brain was occupied elsewhere. "What do you mean there's something between Hoover and Schmitt/Dwayne, whatever."

"Well, Hoover was a used car salesman," his mother said. "In Nebraska. But his address was the first address Schmitt listed when he was serving his time as a parolee, which he did for two years before being discharged from the system, when he promptly changed his name and the two of them—plus Hoover's new wife, Virginia—moved to California."

Ellery's eyes went wide. "That's… well, very organized," he said. "Also it implies that Gannett Hoover and Conway Schmitt had some prior association before Schmitt went to prison."

"But Schmitt is at least ten years older than he is," Taylor muttered. "I keep searching for Gannett Hoover's family, but I can't find *them*, and it appears as though the man has changed his own name, but—Jackson, do you mind?"

Ellery glanced up to see Jackson staring over his mother's shoulder. "Lucy," he said, "do we have a criminal profile of Conway Schmitt's victims?"

Ellery and his mother both stared at the man, who was wearing his own sweats plus the T-shirt from last night and one of his oldest, most raggedy sweatshirts—a Sac State hoodie with frayed sleeves and a frayed hood edging and almost no ribbing left on the hem—that he'd probably put on for comfort.

"You are quieter than the cats," Ellery's mother said, sounding stunned, and Ellery thought that she really *should* go back to bed for a few hours.

"Godzilla is quieter than Lucifer," Jackson said dryly. "Please God, tell me there's more coffee in the pot."

"There should be a whole new fresh pot," Ellery said, staring at him as—carefully avoiding everybody's eyes—he made his way to the kitchen to pour himself his own double-sized mug of the stuff. Plus about half a cup of chocolate-caramel-flavored non-dairy creamer that Ellery would be willing to bet could also double as a substitute for formaldehyde.

"Awesome. Lucy Satan, are you looking?"

"For what?" Ellery's mother said, sounding truly off balance.

Jackson shot her an arch glance. "Sweetheart, you have got to be on your game if you're putting together puzzles with Ellery. He'll logic you blind. Now that profile of Conway Schmitt's victims. I know they'll have sealed the identity, but do we know what they looked like? What their age range was? When he picked them out? I know they were all choirboys, and probably white, fatherless, vulnerable…." Jackson grimaced. "There's a definite profile for the boys sexual predators go for, but what's their age? What's this scumbag's specialty?"

"Uhm…." Ellery's mother scanned through files on her laptop. "Twelve to sixteen," she said, and then, as though thinking, "Sixteen is a little old for most pedophiles. He prefers his victims…."

"Autonomous," Jackson said, coming to sit next to Taylor so he could peer over her shoulder. Ellery noticed that he was still carefully avoiding eye contact, and his heart gave a big throb. Jackson was acting as though everything was normal, but he didn't *feel* that way. "He wants the illusion that they were giving consent. I would bet," he murmured, pulling the laptop gently from Ellery's mother's fingertips, "I would just bet that… yes. Here we go. His defense was that the boys initiated the affairs. That's how he phrased it too. Affairs." Jackson nodded and took a slurp of his coffee. "It fits, right? Books turn kids gay, these kids turned *him* gay. I would bet that his wife—"

"They divorced," Ellery said, trying to get some control back over this narrative, which was getting uglier and more convoluted by the heartbeat.

For the first time Jackson met his eyes. "If you believe that, I've got some beachfront property in Kansas to sell you," he said. "She's *in Sacramento*, and he's not far off." Jackson made a few more clicks on the computer and turned the picture back to Ellery and Taylor. "See this? This happy little function? These people know each other. I would bet—and Lucy Satan, you'll have to back me up on this because this isn't my forte and I wouldn't know where to look—but I would bet this award was cooked up *by* Gannett Hoover's campaign staff *exclusively* for Valerie Trainor's organization. I would bet it came with a big fat monetary grant—"

"Three million dollars," Taylor said, proving that she was awake *now*, although she'd been close to sleep before Jackson had surprised them both.

"Some of that probably *does* keep that organization running," Jackson agreed. "But *some* of that is laundered money. For what? What are they selling that would get them extra cash?"

"Trafficking?" Ellery asked, the word hurting his mouth. They'd worked with traffickers before, and that case had fucked *hard* with both of them.

"Mmm… no," Jackson murmured.

"Probably not," Taylor said at the same time. Jackson nodded to her, and she took the explanation. "From what you both have said, the children were being religiously programmed. This would be a *very* impractical way to groom trafficked children. While it *would* make them docile and subservient—to a point—it would also make them resistant to things they'd been told were perversions. And," she murmured, "more easily broken. If you've just been programmed that sex is *bad*, it doesn't matter who's telling you to have it with whom, you're not going to respond well when forced to do a one-hundred-eighty-degree pivot, particularly when your personhood is being violated *again*."

"A bad idea all around," Jackson agreed. "No. The kids are… well, I don't know what they are yet. You've got the Stepford Dragons, whose mission is to 'clean up' local schools and, of course, to spread the word that the alt-right should have control of the minds of young people. And you've got the young people themselves, who've been conned from parents to be indoctrinated. As gross as it is, this smacks of… of *belief* somehow. It takes some solid *belief* to rip a book out of a kindergartner's hand while you're telling your own class full of teenagers that they're going to hell. There is some zealotry here, and it's gross and disgusting, but at least it's *sincere*, you know?"

Ellery and his mother both nodded, staring at him. Ellery was, as always, in a bit of awe of his reasoning, and he could see the same awe in his mother's eyes.

"What about Gannett Hoover?" Ellery asked, not wanting to interrupt his flow but unable to put it together himself.

"Hoover and Schmitt are something else," Jackson muttered. "They're a sort of unholy alliance. They give money to Trainor's causes, but *they're* in it for… well, the money," Jackson said, sitting up straight. "Quick, Lucy— we know Hoover's funded by a Super PAC, right?"

"Yes," she said. "An alt-right one."

"Do we know anybody *else* giving his campaign money?" Jackson asked. "Any cause? Is he the NRA's favorite camper? Big oil? Mineral rights? I mean…." Jackson frowned. "Sonora. Known for wineries, railroad museums—"

"Right-wing documentary films," Ellery said, having pulled out his own phone.

For the first time, Jackson stared at him in surprise. "Really?"

Ellery shrugged and held up his phone. "Some guy out there making those icky ones, using AI to make rotting old white guys appear virile and potent. You've seen them on clickbait, right?"

"Oh my God," Jackson said, his brain obviously whirling on super-coffee speed. "Okay. Okay. We're cooking. We need to ask Crystal to check into Hoover's financials and to see if there's anything hinky going on with that film company—Russian money laundering, anybody? Or something equally Bond villain, but I'm feeling it."

Ellery and his mother simply nodded. He knew *he* felt a little bit like he'd been picked up by a tornado and shaken, *hard*, but then Jackson's brainstorms were frequently, well, *stormy*.

"Okay," Jackson continued, standing up and pacing. "Good. Good. While Crystal is looking into that, somebody needs to go have a chat with Gannett Hoover to have a gander—"

"I can do that," Ellery's mother said smoothly. "Ellery, you come with me. Jackson, what will you be doing?"

Jackson grunted. "Checking out the grounds. Henry and I—"

Everybody stopped. Stopped breathing. Stopped moving. Stopped everything but staring at each other, big-eyed, waiting for that wound to open, waiting to accommodate the near miss, the worry, the fear. There was a collective gulp, and Jackson's jaw firmed.

"Cody," he said with a deep breath. "When Cody gets here, he and I will go take a look at the grounds. Scout around the outside. You two scout around the inside. See if you can get a bead on Conway Schmitt or whatever his name is. Because, people, we know the following things."

He straightened and ticked off on his fingers.

"We know Cowboy witnessed a murder, and the body was taken somewhere. We know Shitbag Retty was taken to the same place— probably a good place to hide a body. There's a lot of empty property out in Sonora. It fits the bill. We know that the pray-the-gay-away bullshit was *not* the Stepford Dragon's primary business. They are getting political money, probably laundering it, but it's coming from somewhere and going somewhere. We know Gannett Hoover and Conway Schmitty—goddammit, even *I* am doing it—have been in bed together...."

He stopped, like he'd been hit by a sandbag.

And then Ellery got hit by the same sandbag.

"Oh my God," Ellery said softly.

"Welp...." Jackson shook his head.

"I'm sorry," Taylor Cramer said. "You lost me on that last one, son."

Ellery stared at his mother, and she scowled back.

"It happens," she defended. "What do you mean by that?"

Jackson gave her an expression of compassion. "It means," he said softly, "that if you look back at Hoover's history, I'll bet you find he was one of Conway Schmitt's original choirboys. And whether or not the sexual exploitation has continued—and sometimes these relationships can span decades—the Nosferatu/Renfield thing might still be up and running."

Ellery's mother wrinkled her nose. "That's horrendous," she said and shook her head. "I mean... that's *horrific*. But it also makes sense. Schmitt gets out of prison, reaches out to his groomed companion, and Hoover gives him shelter."

"And Schmitt is educated," Ellery noted, remembering the information that Jade and Crystal had fed him. "He may have been a choir director, but he has a degree in political science. By the time he gets out of jail, he's got a *plan*."

Jackson went very still.

"What?" Ellery asked, turning to him, for the first time in a few moments reminded of the awkwardness between them.

"Nothing," Jackson said cagily. "I thought you were going in a different direction, but no—you're right."

Ellery and his mother met eyes. "Where?" Ellery demanded. "We said he came out with a plan, ostensibly to make money and to gain power. Where did you think this was going?"

Jackson let out a breath and gave Taylor an uncomfortable look.

"Spit it out," she commanded, sitting gracefully and frowning at what was probably a now-empty coffee cup.

Ellery took the cup and moved back to the kitchen, keeping an eagle eye on an uncomfortable Jackson.

"Cody and I were going to talk to Otto first," Jackson said, "and maybe debrief some of the other kids we broke out of the place yesterday. If nothing else I need to talk to your advocates, Ellery, to see what sort of pattern Moms for Clean Living used for recruitment. And I've got Toe-Tag looking into something—"

"I thought you said this was two different things?" Ellery's mother reminded him. "There was the 'service' organization, the political affiliation, and the children. You said the children weren't being groomed for trafficking—"

"But they *were* being groomed," Jackson explained. "Don't you understand? They were vulnerable. Some of the girls had been abused. I would imagine the boys were being used. Think about it. Moms for Clean Living. It's a *catchall*. They implement the political agenda at a grassroots level. They make a handy receptacle for money laundering. And they're so wholesome, so hell-bent on protecting children, that they protect them right into the hands of...." He shrugged.

"Whoever wants them," Ellery said, getting it. "Including Conway Schmitt and Gannett Hoover. Not for money, but simply to be used."

"And discarded," Jackson whispered. "I don't think Caleb was an accident."

"You think he was a byproduct," Ellery said, feeling cold.

"It's like any other abduction," Taylor Cramer said, sounding equally numb. "It *is* trafficking—but it's for personal use. They're using the pray the gay away as an excuse to get children for their own needs."

"I…." Jackson exhaled. "I have some suspicions," he agreed.

Ellery's stomach roiled, only now understanding what Jackson must have been carrying with him all of the last night. Toe-Tag. Toby Tagliare would *literally* know where the bodies were buried.

And where they surfaced.

"When were you going to tell me?" Ellery asked, feeling betrayed. It was stupid. They'd been so busy, and so exhausted the day before. But this… this was so awful….

This was why the dream, Ellery realized. *This* was why that memory had been so close to the surface that touching him had scraped the skin raw. Because he was wondering where his sister had gone.

He'd already seen the worst the world had to offer. He'd thrown it in his minivan the night before and driven the victims to the hospital and hoped—*hoped*—it would be okay.

He probably knew this feeling, Ellery thought sickly. He probably lived it, in a tiny corner of his heart, every day.

"When I'd found the bodies," Jackson said, staring sightlessly at the cats on the couch. "I'd tell you then. That's why I want to be at the property when you're there. I just… I *am* really hoping I'm wrong."

And this was why he hadn't told Ellery. *This* was why he'd risked everything to break the kids out.

"Mother," he said, feeling very off balance as he set her coffee cup down in the sink instead of refilling it. "How about you go take a nap. We can't leave for Sonora until one. It will take us until at least three to get wherever Hoover's little mansion of delights may be, and you will be far more dangerous with a little sleep."

"I…." For a moment she was going to argue—he was well aware. Then she peered carefully between the two of them and said, "Of course." She stood then and walked to Jackson to place a kiss on his cheek. "Be kind to each other," she urged, and then she turned toward the guest bedroom, putting noise-canceling earbuds in as she moved.

Jackson grunted and watched her go. "Why is she doing that?" he asked. Ellery strode out of the kitchen and past him, grabbing his hand and dragging him to the bedroom as he went.

"Because you and I have some business to discuss," he said crisply. "And she's giving us as much privacy as she can manage." He gave Jackson's hand a tug. "Come on, Jackson. We've got a little bit of shit to sort before Cody gets here—"

"He's got two hours!" Jackson complained.

"Good," Ellery muttered. "You should be in the shower by the time he arrives."

"We're having sex?" Jackson asked, sounding legitimately rattled. "With your *mother* here?"

Ellery hauled him into the bedroom and shut the door, careful to make sure there were no three-legged furry creatures in the way.

"She put earbuds in, Jackson. She won't be able to hear us having sex unless we bring the roof down. But that's not the point."

Jackson scowled at him. "What's the point?"

Ellery kissed him, hard and inescapably and without equivocation. He kissed Jackson senseless, until Jackson was backed up against the bedroom door, thrusting his hands under Ellery's pajamas, cupping satin handfuls of Ellery's bare ass with one hand and scraping his fingers across Ellery's shoulders with the other.

Ellery pulled back and made sure he had Jackson's complete attention.

"The point," he panted, "is that you look me in the eyes. The point is that you're not afraid to tell me *anything*." Jackson tried to protest, and Ellery kissed him again, dominating him, taking him over heart and soul. He pulled back again, to see if Jackson was understanding the point, and Jackson was leaning against the door, mouth slack, eyes clouded with passion, and suddenly the passion *was* the point.

Jackson's eyes focused on him then, and he shook his head, as though trying to clear his thoughts. "Ellery—"

"You didn't tell me," Ellery growled, so angry and so hurt he wasn't sure he could get the words out.

"I didn't know—"

"You suspected!" Ellery accused. As he fumed he kept his hands busy, ripping Jackson's T-shirt off, squirreling underneath the waistband of his pajamas.

"It's so awful," Jackson gasped as Ellery struggled out of his own shirt. Jackson helped him by grabbing the lapels of his pajama top and ripping it open, scattering buttons everywhere.

"I know it's awful," Ellery said, rubbing his hands along Jackson's bare torso. "Baby, it's *horrible*. You *needed me*."

Jackson closed his eyes and pulled Ellery against him so they were skin to skin. "Oh God, I did," he whispered. "All yesterday. I needed you so badly. But we had to keep going—you know that—we *had* to keep going."

Ellery kissed him, hard, angry, because he was *right*. They'd *had* to keep going—someone they loved had been *hurt*, and the stakes were so fucking high, and they'd *had* to keep going, but the cost....

Ellery wouldn't think about Jackson's screams, his *whimpers* in bed the night before, or the sobs that had wracked him until he'd fallen abruptly asleep. He wouldn't think about the nagging ache in his chest and the way his head pounded as he'd tried to battle the *wrongness* of their day.

Right now, in this instant, he didn't want to think at all.

The kiss ignited, their hands everywhere, their need for each other insatiable.

Jackson needed him. Ellery needed Jackson to be okay.

Ellery turned him, maneuvered him, kissed their way to the bed. The rest of their clothes were pushed and wiggled out of, and then they were bare skin to bare skin, Ellery's body covering Jackson's on the still-rumpled sheets.

Ellery could smell his sleep and despair and his quiet on the sheets, and the heat and vitality and living, pulsing physical desperation in the man underneath him.

He wanted to devour it all.

He kissed his way down Jackson's scarred chest, stopping just long enough to suck hard on each nipple. He paused around his soft-skinned, lightly furred stomach to command, "Grab the lube." He felt Jackson reaching under their pillow as he wrapped his lips around Jackson's cock.

"Oh God," Jackson whispered, his hips arching. "Jesus, Ellery—"

But Ellery was beyond pleas. He *couldn't* keep Jackson safe on the street as he did his job. He *couldn't* protect him from whatever hells his past had buried in his heart and scarred psyche. His whole life he'd been led to believe that with reason and hard work he could change the world, but he couldn't change Jackson's pain.

This, owning him heart and soul, being the man who *knew* his demons, who helped Jackson Rivers arm himself against darkness—*this* was how he controlled his universe. *This* was how he changed the world. By protecting this one man, by keeping him safe and keeping him sane and letting him know he was loved.

Jackson made a soft sound as his hips stuttered, and Ellery kept sucking, pulling his cockhead into the back of his throat and swallowing.

Jackson beat at the mattress with one hand while fumbling the lube into the hand Ellery *wasn't* using to squeeze and stroke his cock.

Ellery took the lube and paused when Jackson made that sound again, that soft sound of surrender. He tasted the sweetness of precome and squeezed Jackson's base before lowering his head and swallowing again. The next sound Jackson made was muffled, and as Jackson spurted in his mouth and came, Ellery knew he was screaming orgasm into his cupped palm.

Ellery swallowed, his own arousal amping up with every swallow, with every grunt. He whined around Jackson's pumping cock as he sought to get a handle on himself before he spent his climax in the sheets.

With one hand he snicked the lube tube and squeezed some onto his fingers. As Jackson pushed his feet against the bed and thrust his hips up, Ellery parted his buttocks and thrust his slick fingers into Jackson's pucker.

Jackson groaned, the sound still muffled, and Ellery clicked the tube shut and shoved his body up, positioning himself and thrusting inside, letting out a grunt of his own, not bothering to muffle his sounds.

Yes, there was somebody in the house, and *He. Didn't. Care.*

Almost violently he knocked Jackson's hand away from his mouth and kissed him to muffle their noises. Jackson's hands gripped his shoulders, slick and dripping with sweat, and Ellery fucked him savagely in short, powerful strokes, wanting to claim him, to heal him, to soothe him from the inside out.

Jackson groaned into his mouth and raised his legs to wrap around Ellery's hips, and that was it. That's all Ellery needed. Keeping their mouths fused together, he thrust one more time, a short charge of dynamite, and came.

Between them, he felt Jackson's hot spend coating their stomachs and thighs as Ellery fucked him through a second orgasm—or a continuation of the first.

Ellery didn't know, couldn't keep score. He let out a small groan before collapsing on top of Jackson, knowing his lover, his *mate*, could bear his weight.

The roaring of his own blood in his ears receded, and the sound of their panting, the smell of their sex, filled his senses, and he rested his head on Jackson's collarbone, welcoming Jackson's palms on his sweaty shoulders.

"Soundproof?" Jackson asked hopefully into the silence.

"Yes," Ellery said. He remembered his mother being very excited about the gift from her husband. "She'll probably listen to briefs or a book or something while she goes to sleep."

Jackson nodded and covered his eyes with his hand. "I have no idea why I let that happen."

"Let?" Ellery was affronted. He pushed himself up, still inside Jackson's body, and thrust a little. "I hate to tell you, buddy, but that was consensual."

Jackson's lips curved up into his first real smile since… well, since two nights ago before Henry had been shot. "Are you sure I didn't seduce you, baby boy?"

Ellery grunted. "No, no, the blame for that one lays squarely on my shoulders." He grew serious and moved Jackson's hand from his eyes. "I mean it, though," he said, making sure Jackson met his gaze. "No… no holding back. Not even when the world is tumbling about our ears. Not even when you suspect the worst. I need you to…." He squinted, watching as Jackson's hectic color from their lovemaking faded, leaving the rusty blotches on his skin, tipping his eyelashes, smudging his mouth and his forehead, to show themselves.

"What?" Jackson asked, blinking like he was getting something out of his eyes.

Ellery closed his and rolled out of bed with a sigh. "I need you to go to the bathroom, take a shower, and let me dress your hand."

"What in the—" Jackson actually *looked* at his hand, and his face washed red again as he saw the perfectly bite-sized ring of punctures on the bottom of his palm. "Well, that's embarrassing," he muttered, rolling out of bed and searching for his T-shirt.

"You're not putting that on!" Ellery protested and then watched as Jackson wrapped his hand in it. "Oh. Okay. Wow. You… you had to work *that* hard at keeping quiet?"

Jackson gave him an unfriendly look. "*Somebody*," he emphasized, "thought it would be a great idea to have angry sex while his mother was here." He assumed an air of dignity that almost—but not quite—blanketed his shoulders. "I thought one of us should maybe uphold decorum."

Ellery blinked at him, nonplussed. "Decorum?"

"Yes," Jackson said, starting his grand exit to the bathroom.

"*You're* our representative for decorum now?" Ellery stood with his hands on his hips, his cock still dripping with come, and felt his own dignity clapping over his naked body like armor.

"Yes," Jackson said without any particular irony or remorse. "Prove me wrong."

Ellery's behavior of the last half hour played in a dynamic, steamy X-rated slideshow behind his eyes. And now that his fury had passed, and Jackson's self-recriminating spiral had been halted, he realized that after living together for more than a year and a half, *this* had been the first time they'd ever had sex when his mother was in the house.

That had been a mutual decision—their horror at the thought of doing something like they'd just done when Ellery's mother might hear it had been considerable.

But it hadn't been equal to Ellery's belief that sending Jackson out today, to do the dangerous things he often ended up doing, without the emotional catharsis, without Ellery leaving a mark on his very *soul*, would have been wrong.

Jackson had needed what they'd done, and so, apparently, had Ellery.

"Well, then," Ellery said, sweeping past Jackson into the bathroom. "If you're the one with the decorum, you can make sure you got all your blood off my back in the shower. I would hate for Mother to suspect we had sex in our own bedroom."

"Yeah," Jackson muttered. "That could really throw me off my game for the rest of the day."

"Which would be a shame," Ellery said, starting the water. "And we haven't had breakfast yet. Hurry, hurry." He added that last primly, and was rewarded with Jackson's snort.

And then, in the chill of the bathroom, he was rewarded by Jackson's long body sliding alongside his and Jackson's arms wrapping around his waist.

Ellery tilted his head back against Jackson's shoulder, and Jackson whispered, "Hey, Counselor."

"Hey yourself, Detective."

"Good job."

Ellery gave him a demure glance from under his lashes, not able to meet his eyes at this angle, but then, not really *needing* to meet them either. "Why, thank you. I'm rather pleased with it myself."

Jackson chuckled and nuzzled his cheek, and a part of Ellery relaxed just a tad.

They were okay now. Jackson's head was back where it should be: focused purely on getting their bad guy and making their case.

And Ellery was in his lover's arms without any barriers, not even the fears that Jackson held on to in order to keep Ellery safe.

Together, he thought during that three-heartbeat break, being held and tended to by the man he loved more than life, together they could do anything.

Pond Skipping

"YOU WOOK chippew," Cody said through a mouthful of homemade blueberry muffins.

After they'd gotten out of the shower, Ellery had gone on a cooking bender, making sure there was frittata for everybody, and because frittata didn't travel well—or age well, and his mother was apparently still *very* much asleep—he broke out the blueberry muffin mix and whipped up two dozen while Jackson scanned his morning email.

Jackson had to admit the smell and taste of a freshly buttered blueberry muffin really did sustain a man, both in body and soul.

The sex helped—and so did the coffee.

And so did the sleep.

That last one was something he didn't want to think about. The open wound in his chest may have been purged and dressed, but it was still raw and red, and Jackson knew from experience that some wounds had to be healed again and again and again before the scar tissue formed.

"I managed some rest last night," Jackson admitted, piloting Jennifer toward his old duplex on Elvas. "After forty hours of *not* sleeping, it's like I opened a whole new dimensional plane."

"Ouch," Cody said. "But then, you know. Job well done."

Cody sounded damned proud of himself, and Jackson cast him a sideways glance. The former undercover cop appeared happy and eager to roll, and a little like an Australian shepherd, face turned toward the sun and the wind, looking forward to going out and harassing the sheep until they fell in line.

"Yeah," Jackson said, trying to remember what they *had* accomplished last night and not what he feared had happened long before they'd been brought in on this in the most awful of ways. "Can't let my demons get in the way," he said.

Cody grunted. "I got me some of those," he admitted. "Living on the streets—the things I did for a fix. God, all of it." He shook his head. "I wake up screaming more times than I want to admit."

Jackson's breath caught just *hearing* that.

"Same," he admitted, and something about admitting it to somebody else who had been there… it mattered. "Sometimes the shit we cannot control, the things we should have done but couldn't—it's *crushing*."

Cody may have been a happy puppy, but he also had a shepherd's sensitive hearing.

"What's got your panties in a twist, boss?" he asked.

Jackson blew out a breath. "Well, my past stuff is a massive tangle you do not want to—"

"Sure I do," Cody said, not even batting an eyelash. "I mean, we're partners on this gig, right?"

"Yeah," Jackson said, bemused. It had taken him and Henry *months* before he'd realized they were partners, and how awesome it was to have somebody who had your back but who didn't have all of those… *tangling* emotions that a lover did.

"Aw, c'mon, Rivers. I haven't had a partner in crimefighting for *years*—tell me we're partners!" And then, to reaffirm every instinct Jackson had about him being an Australian shepherd, Cody held his hands in front of him like paws and panted. "Please, please, please, please, *please*…."

Jackson had to laugh. "Okay!" he confessed. "Okay, okay. You and me are partners."

Cody sighed. "Until Henry's okay, it'll do."

Jackson's heart gave a twist. The wistfulness in his tone had been unmistakable. "Listen," he said, matter-of-factly, "like I told you, someday we'll have a third law partner in our office and we can afford to throw you more work—"

"Really?" Cody asked, so excited Jackson almost felt bad for saying it.

"Well, *yeah*," Jackson said with a laugh. "Right now it's Ellery and Galen. They each carry about thirty cases at any given time. Some of them are easy come, easy go, and some of them are, you know—"

"Like this one," Cody said. "All hands on deck."

"Yeah," Jackson confirmed. "In most firms the PI to lawyer ratio isn't quite this high but—"

"But you guys are more interested in the truth than the payout," Cody filled in, and Jackson had to give it to the guy. He got it.

"Yes. We were going to make AJ another PI, but he's really more comfortable as our tech guy, and we borrow Crystal sometimes—"

"Why borrow?" Cody asked.

"She works for our old firm." Jackson lowered his voice and glanced around, which was stupid because they were in the car, but he still felt like it should be hush-hush. "They have resources we don't always," he said. "Access to some of the crime databases, easy entry to do financial runs. AJ can get that stuff done—hell, *I* can get that stuff done—but if we want it quick and deep and dirty…."

"Gotcha," Cody said, nodding. "She's your gal."

"Yeah," Jackson said. "But we can't afford her, really, although she keeps promising that we'll have the perfect employment opportunity for her. We just don't know it yet."

"And she would know that how?" Cody asked, sounding doubtful.

Well, he was passing out a lot of secrets, wasn't he? "She's the second most powerful psychic I've ever met," Jackson told him.

Cody sucked in a breath, and Jackson wondered if this was when they lost this guy, right when Jackson was starting to hope they could find a place for him.

"Who's the first?" he asked.

Jackson let out a chuckle. "I'd tell you, but then I'd have to kill you. His existence is so secret, the government thinks he's dead."

"Good," Cody said, absolutely sincere. "The government can fuck up things like a good psychic."

"They nearly did," Jackson told him seriously. "Which is why we don't tell anybody who he is or where he lives. Anyway, Crystal's pretty awesome, and she loves to help, and someday, we'll be able to pay her as much as she deserves."

Cody laughed softly. "And I'm in the queue. I get it."

"Hey," Jackson said seriously, "I'm pretty sure you're getting paid for this little job. I mean, not *enough*, but I know I saw Jade make you fill out a W2 yesterday."

Cody chuckled. "You got me." Then he sobered. "And as much as I'd love to ask more questions, now that we're in this shitty neighborhood—"

"Hey!" Jackson protested, "I own that duplex!"

"Oh, seriously?" Cody managed to sound apologetic like an eighteen-year-old boy who'd just shoved his foot in his mouth. "Okay. Uhm, why?"

Jackson eyed the duplex critically. It had gotten a new coat of paint and some landscaping on the postage-stamp lawns the year before, and Mike kept the gutters clear, the lone fruit tree watered and growing, and the driveway was kept oil-stain free.

"Well," he said, "after I got shot in the name of truth and justice, I went and got my degree and bought this place. I rented out one side of it to the guy who's now sleeping with Jade, who's like my sister, and I love them both, so that's fine."

"And the other side?" Cody asked curiously.

Jackson wrinkled his nose. "So you know, I'm sort of a kept man. Ellery won't let me help with the mortgage, he won't let me make a car payment, and he keeps paying me a salary. It's embarrassing." He pulled into the driveway of the side that he used to live in. "He was literally moving all my shit into his house without asking, and when I complained, he told me to do something good with this side. So I made it sort of a stopping place for young guys getting out of jail and trying to get straight. Jade and Mike and me and Henry work as mentors. We talk to the POs. We look for kids who just need a frickin' break. We get them jobs and try to find junker cars and stuff and help them move on to a place of their own. It only holds, like, five people, and we were waiting on some recommendations to fill all the beds, so I think some of the boys we rescued are going to end up here. One of the child advocates took the couch last night to make sure everything is kosher between the first two residents—who are barely eighteen, by the way—and the kids who got placed."

Cody was staring at him. "Wow."

"Shut up," Jackson muttered.

"No, seriously. Fucking *wow*."

"I don't want to hear it!" Jackson said, turning the minivan off and unhooking his seat belt.

"I've been *picking my nose* for six months, and there was all this glorious public service here waiting for my help?" Cody demanded. "How could you?"

"You were getting your shit together!" Jackson protested.

"*My* shit is *boring*," Cody told him, absolutely sober as a judge. "Somebody else's shit? My God. That's *so* much easier to sort."

Jackson had to laugh. "That, my friend, is the honest-to-God truth. Okay, fine. Come in, meet the guys. We'll see what we can do. Henry's usually pretty timed out as it is, and these guys will miss him, so it's probably a perfectly wonderful idea."

"Damn straight," Cody said, and they both slid out of the car.

JADE HAD left for the office, and Aileen, the patient advocate, was supervising instead.

Jackson had a moment to glance around his old home, appreciating the changes. He'd had pictures of his family—Jade, Kaden, Kaden's wife, Rhonda, and their children—on his walls. He even had, treasured and on the dresser of his bedroom, a photo of the four of them and Jade and Kaden's mother, Toni, at Jackson's graduation from the academy only a few weeks before her passing.

Thanks to Ellery, the photo had been copied, and the copy formatted on a plaque in the living room, with a dedication to Toni Cameron's Home for Hope, along with pictures of the new residents as they'd graduated from work programs or working jobs they were proud of. There were new apartments and first days of junior college. Jackson hoped for college graduations someday in the future, but hey, the place had only been open for a year and a half.

And yet it was still doing good.

The furniture had been bought used, but it was sturdy—sturdy leather couches in the living room, afghans culled from thrift stores piled on top, and a solid wooden table with chairs and new pads on the seats in the dining room.

As Aileen let them in, Jackson smelled coffee and pancakes, and he had a moment to grin at Aileen, who was no less frowzy and sleep deprived now than she had been in the hospital the night before.

It had apparently been a long night.

"You made them breakfast?" he asked.

She shook her head. "No. Your young men made breakfast. They've been…." She looked over her shoulder at Geordie, who was slight and Black and moved like a dancer—or a pickpocket, which is why he'd been in jail—and Nilas, who was also not tall, but thick and muscular, with pale skin and black curly hair. Nilas had been a fighter—probably still had it in him—but he'd been put away for assault. Jackson always suspected the other guy had it coming, because he hadn't seen even a flash of temper in the gentle Nilas.

He was standing over the stove now, wearing a gingham apron over his white T-shirt and jeans, flipping pancakes.

"I said I didn't need any!" Geordie protested, elbow deep in a dish tub.

"And I said you're too skinny," Nilas retorted. "Look, I finally got good at making the faces, and we've got extra sausage. Let me show off here."

"Trying to make me fat," Geordie *tsk*ed, and then glanced at the table. A fourteen-or-so-year-old adolescent whom Jackson had never seen sat there, his newly shaved hair a pale yellow and his bright blue eyes darting from one young man to the other, a hesitant smile on his face.

"Otto?" Geordie asked. "You want some more?"

"It'll make me sick," he confessed, staring down at his plate in embarrassment. "Ask Danny and Enrique."

Jackson recognized Danny as the slight, bitter young man who had gone from a bad home to the Moms for Clean Living, and Enrique as the other boy who'd been strapped to the seat with him. They sat close now, although it was clear they'd both been bathed and had made use of the clothing stores, and while they were less emaciated than Otto, they were clearly appreciative of the food.

"I'm fine," Danny said, although judging by the surreptitious looks he kept sending Nilas at the stove, he probably hadn't eaten in peace in a long time.

"I'm starving," Enrique said bluntly. "I mean, yeah, I just ate twice what we usually got fed at that fucking place, but I could eat way more."

Nilas laughed. "So two more portions. Excellent. Aileen, you good?"

"I'm eating some of the fruit in the fridge," the woman said. "But you are *really* nice to ask." She glanced at Jackson and Cody. "I have to admit, I was expecting to get here and go all den mother on this place, but Nilas and Geordie have been trained up."

"Miss Jade wouldn't let us get away with that," Geordie said, and Jackson had to smile at "Miss Jade." Her mother had been "Miss Toni" to Jackson, because you showed respect to someone when they made sure you were cared for, and he was glad to see the tradition passed on.

"This is a good place," Aileen said, smiling at the boys. "If I can get some funding for a supervisor for these kids, I think, and if Nilas and Geordie don't mind, we'll keep taking your beds for a little while, Jackson. I know you usually have adults here, but…." She grimaced. "This is an unusual situation."

"She means we're all queerbies," Danny said. "Gay. Gay, gay, gay, gay, gay." He chuckled, like it was a sort of victory to just say that.

"That all you got?" Enrique asked. "Your dad did not have *nearly* the imagination of my mom. Fudgepacker, cocksucker—"

Jackson cleared his throat meaningfully. "Please don't," he said when the boys glared at him, defiance plastered all over their faces. "Your language is your own, and I get it. You want to make your identity your own, and you take charge of those words that hurt you. But right now you're using them to hurt *us*, the adults who are trying to protect you. It's not kind."

Enrique's face was made of points, whereas Danny's features were rounder and softer, but their expressions were mirrored as they glanced at each other and swallowed.

"Sorry," Enrique said. "Just…." He shuddered. "Those women. We couldn't even say fucking *gay* there, but we all knew that's why we were stuck in those awful rooms with those awful pictures, learning Bible verses on our knees."

"That's no way to learn Bible verses," Geordie said, coming to the table and drying his hands off on his apron. "I mean, my mom had her flaws, but we were always taught to sing them. I know whole tracts of the book."

Enrique shook his head. "Man, I've been force-fed about as much of that book as I can stomach."

"Don't eat books," Nilas said, coming to the table with a griddle in one hand and a spatula in the other. "Eat pancakes!" Carefully—and artistically—he spatula'd three minicakes and a banana-shaped cake onto each of the boy's plates, and then, using bowls on the table, added a ladle of strawberries across the "mouth," along with whipped cream eyeballs, nostrils, and teeth.

While the boys were cracking up over the "food faces," Geordie had gone to the stove and come back with a plate of sausages and made sure each boy got two more. He turned to Otto and held out two more in tongs. "You sure you don't want more, big O?"

"Later," Otto whispered with a smile. "You fed me lots last night."

"It's been lonely," Nilas admitted, taking the griddle back to the stove and pouring more batter on it. "I know you've been trying to vet more guys for the place, Jackson, but seriously, hanging out with these little dudes is way more fun."

"You're right," Enrique said, meeting Jackson's eyes. "You all have been kind. You forget, you know? People aren't always shitheads." He frowned. "Can I say that?"

"Yes," Jackson told him. "The other stuff was being mean to yourself. It's fine to say shitheads when they've been shitheads." He grimaced. "But because they *are* shitheads, I need to get some more information from you. Not that I don't want to see how you're all doing," he added hastily.

"He checks in on us all the time," Nilas said. "Just so you know."

"Thanks," Jackson said, smiling at the kid. It was nice to have backup. Then he turned his attention to the young people around the table and pulled up a seat. "So here's the thing. We're trying to bring down the shitheads. We need your help."

"Bring them down?" muttered Danny, who seemed to be the kid who could hold on to a grudge with two fists. "What the hell do you mean bring them down? You *found* us in there. Isn't having us all there not bad enough?"

"We need proof," Aileen said. "Specific incidents, examples of behavior modification and child abuse." She sat down next to Jackson. "And we need it corroborated by the other kids from the place."

Jackson grunted. "That's what Miss Aileen needs. And that's going to bring down the whole house of cards that held you guys—make no mistake. But I'm trying to bring down the money men. The guys that funded that nightmare. The guys that put them up to it—"

"Nobody had to put Retty up to *nothin'*," Danny muttered, eyes narrowed. "That bitch was on us every day. Liked to administer punishments, loved to take away rations. And when anybody made a break for it, she would fucking run you down. She wouldn't even always take you in, you know?" He gave a chin jerk to Otto. "Sometimes she'd just stalk kids, let them know she knew where you were. Then when she needed something, she'd throw them scraps of food and have them go do shit. Pick some guy's pocket. Put out for somebody. Whatever it was that you got poor Otto here on."

Jackson caught Otto's eye and winked. He was going to make this kid a legend.

"Molotov cocktail through a lawyer's window," he said boldly, just to watch Danny and Enrique's impressed expressions. "Fortunately, I know the guy, and he's not pressing charges."

"Knows the guy." Geordie chuckled. "Look at him, getting all modest. Knows the guy."

"What do you mean?" Danny asked, suddenly suspicious.

"They're *engaged*," Geordie told him patiently, popping the last of the sausages in his mouth. "They're, like, made of good works, these people. Knows a guy."

"Anyway," Jackson said, rolling his eyes, "I need more dirt. Who gave Retty her orders?"

"Engaged?" said Danny, obviously stuck on this point. "Like, to a guy?"

Jackson grimaced. "Thanks, Geordie, for totally derailing this conversation."

"It's important," Danny said, his voice rising, and suddenly Jackson had nowhere to focus but on this kid.

"It is to me," Jackson said softly. "It is to Ellery—the, uhm, guy."

"It's important," Danny said again, like he was struggling for purchase, emotions windmilling.

"Okay," Jackson said, exchanging glances with Aileen. "You're right. It's important. I know why it's important to *me*, Danny. Why is it important to you?"

"Because we spent *weeks* in that place. Where they didn't give us food unless we said their stupid prayers. Where they threatened to cut off our dicks if we liked who we liked. Where we weren't allowed to talk to each other because they *listened*, but they could walk into our rooms any damned time they wanted, just to check to see if we had boners or not. And you—you're going to *marry* a guy, and you're not ashamed of it, and you're kickass and not stupid. *You're* who we all want to be, and you gotta *front*, man, like, wear that shit! We gotta *see* you're fronting, and you're wearing that shit, and it's *not* evil, and it's *not* something that should get your dick put in a clothespin, and it's *not* the fuckin' devil. I don't give a shit if your guy's a fuckin' *troll*, man—you fuckin' *front*."

Jackson slow blinked and swallowed, suddenly seeing how self-deprecation, self-annihilation—all of the painful, twisting his guts shit that he put himself through on a regular basis, up to and including his memories of that terrible night when he and Kaden had called child services, could be offensive to this kid.

As far as Danny and Enrique and Otto were concerned, Jackson had *made it*. He hadn't just "made it out," he was *doing* the thing they'd just been tortured for, and getting married in a park on a sunny day in June— which had been his only requirement for a wedding—was the dream they'd dared not dream.

It was his job to make it a worthwhile dream, until they had their own Ellery to cling to.

He managed a little bit of swagger and a wink. "Do you *think* I'd be marrying a troll?"

Danny, who had been on the verge of tears, stopped on a gulp, and next to him, Enrique snickered.

"You saw him last night," Aileen said softly. "He came in with the rest of my team, remember?"

"Flannel-shirt guy?" Enrique asked dubiously.

"He usually wears a suit," Jackson said, keeping his voice firm. "And he's kickass enough to pull Aileen and her team out of their, uhm, pajamas—"

"Oh, they know about bra o'clock," Aileen said dryly.

"Okay," Jackson said, sending her a grin. "He managed to pull five professionals to the hospital after bra o'clock. And he did it for you." He sobered. "How kickass is that?"

"This place ain't bad," Enrique said. Then, his voice aching, "How long can we stay?"

Jackson and Aileen met eyes. "As long as you need to," Jackson said. "Assuming we can get some supervision for you all."

"Nilas and Geordie are over eighteen," Danny said on a shrug.

Nilas and Geordie, who were both at the "wiping the counter" stage of cleaning up, stilled.

"Yeah," Nilas said carefully, glancing at Geordie, "but we're convicted felons over eighteen. They, uhm, might not trust us with you guys."

"Sex crimes?" Enrique asked, like this was only passing consideration.

"No!" they both replied, stung.

"Well, then…." Enrique waved his hands. "I mean, that's better than the last *two* places I stayed, and my mom's house before that. You're fine." He turned to Aileen and Jackson. "They're fine. We can stay, right?"

Jackson shrugged. "Aileen is the one who needs to cross t's and dot i's," he told them. "She knows I'm fine with whatever you all need. Now, I hate to rush you all, but…." He looked pointedly to the clock on the mantel, a mental list of the things he needed to do and the people he needed to visit before he and Cody had to leave for Sonora.

"Yeah, yeah…." Danny said. "What can we tell you about Retty and Twitty."

"And Piper," Otto muttered, from near his elbow. It was possibly the first thing he'd said in the last few minutes, and Jackson glanced quickly at him.

"And anything you can tell us about the people at the Moms for Clean Living," he said grimly. "Including Piper." He paused and remembered Danny's point about "fronting." Sometimes it helped to state the obvious.

"You guys were given a raw deal," he said softly. "I mean, the people at Moms for Clean Living served you up a giant shitburger, told your parents it was ground beef, and threw you in the trough to eat that shit for *weeks*. And they hurt your friend Caleb. And my friend Henry, who you guys haven't met, but he's awesome."

"As awesome as Cody?" Danny asked, giving Cody an appreciative look.

Jackson watched Cody's ears tinge red and thought about the man's heroics the night before. It would figure there would be a teeny bit of a crush going on there.

"Yes," Jackson told him seriously. "I have nothing but awesome friends."

Cody snickered. "If I didn't know that was true, I'd say you were flattering me." And then he sobered. "And to help Jackson's awesome friend, we need your guys' information. Can you help?"

The three kids nodded soberly, and Jackson heard Cody let out a breath.

It occurred to him that the easy part of his morning was over.

"So," Cody said to him nearly an hour later, "what'd we learn?"

Jackson grunted, feeling wrung out. "A couple things," he said, maneuvering Jennifer in a neat three-sixty as he left his old neighborhood. "First of all, Retty was the *kids'* nightmare, but she was the *company's* dog. We sort of knew that already, but the kids confirmed it—and the extent of it."

"And she's not that bright," Cody said.

The kids had tales of tricking her—sneaking food in, stealing her windbreaker, which she wore with a sort of obnoxious pride.

"Like it made her a cool kid," Danny had said in disgust.

"And she's a sadist," Jackson added. Retty had been the classic example of shit rolling downhill. From what the kids said, the other women would be shitty to her, ordering her to do the grunt work—blackmailing mothers, recruiting kids, intimidating anybody who got in their way. And Retty would turn around and share that sadism with anybody below her, which usually meant the kids themselves.

"So she's got enemies," Cody said. "But...."

"She's disposable."

They both grunted in agreement.

"And she rode herd on the escaped kids, even after they escaped," Jackson said thoughtfully. Because that had been interesting. Otto had been the one to point it out.

"Retty would give us jobs," he'd said quietly. "Throw food at us from her car and tell us to go do things. Talk to this kid or that kid. She had a list. She wanted to know who sucked dick—"

"Or dove in the wrong muff," Enrique added, a sardonic twist to his lips.

"We were her spies," Otto said. He looked away, and Jackson felt a terrible pang in his chest. "She'd... hold food in front of our faces and make us do things—trick kids into coming into the house, trap kids, get information…." His voice trailed off, and Jackson wondered whom Otto had betrayed for a hamburger because his stomach had been gnawing away at his conscience, at his personhood, like a rabid weasel. "We… we ratted out other kids so she'd feed us."

"You did what you needed to, to survive," Jackson told him, waiting until the boy met his eyes.

Otto nodded once and swallowed, and Jackson had wondered how long it would take to untangle the secrets harbored in that thin chest.

"I told her," he whispered. "Where Caleb was hiding, after he and Cowboy escaped. She…." His voice broke. "I hurt my leg falling out of the window when we tried to escape, and she had medicine for it, and she wouldn't give it to me unless I told her where he was hiding." He wouldn't look at Danny and Enrique. "My leg hurt so bad," he said on a sob. "And I didn't know… didn't know she was going to… to make him make that sound."

"Otto…." Jackson didn't know how to comfort him.

"And then when I could, I escaped, but I didn't know where I was. I was out, but she always fed us just enough to keep us coming back…." He put his face in his arms then and sobbed, and Aileen had given Jackson a speaking glance and taken the boy back into one of the bedrooms to work with him.

Jackson's heart hurt for the kid. Food or loyalty. Integrity or pain. Hard enough choices for a man to make, but for a kid who'd had his identity broken down for weeks beforehand?

He hoped Aileen had a cure for self-hatred in her child advocate's bag of tricks, because Otto would need one.

"Also," Jackson went on, hoping to shake the terrible sadness of a stick-thin, barely adolescent boy named Otto. "We know that, as suspected, Twitty answered to a higher power."

Next to him, Cody made a disgusted sound. "One she… how did Enrique phrase it?"

Jackson breathed out through his nose and quoted, "She would have sucked his dick through the phone if she could have."

And Enrique had been their font of information on that front. Enrique's superpower, Danny had told them bitterly, was his ability to pass for whatever adults needed.

His parents had thought he was straight until they'd caught him with the neighbor's boy, and he was *very* good at looking like he had his head down and was doing menial tasks in the office when, in fact, he was picking up all sorts of "stupid, gross information."

As Danny called it.

Information like the fact that Valerie Trainor still talked to her ex-husband like Renfield talked to Dracula. And he still called her "Mel," which meant she went by three different names in the compound.

Jackson, who knew Ellery and his mother would spend part of their morning poring over all of the documents he'd sent Ellery the night before, had made a mental note to text Ellery to keep their eyes open for a combination of all three names—Melanie, Valerie, and Twitty—along with Schmitt, Trainor, and Schnarf, in any combination.

And Schmitt's aliases too.

The thought of that made Jackson's head ache fiercely, but then, it was supposed to. These were not honest people. The more names, the more LLCs, the more properties and charities and businesses and organizations they owned, the more chances to launder, sucker, and process money without ever getting noticed.

But that wasn't all they'd learned.

Gannett Hoover's wife was a "whining, puling bitch" who, according to Schmitt, needed to "get with the program."

Retty was in hot water for whatever had happened to Caleb, and Piper Lutz had been assigned to "reorganize" the "off-campus residents." Which was why Piper had been so hot to recruit Otto for Molotov cocktail hour.

And, Enrique knew, Piper was in trouble now because Otto had not returned.

"I wonder," Jackson had speculated as Enrique spoke, "what kind of hornet's nest is going on back at the Moms for Clean Living mansion."

The two boys snorted with pure meanness, and the sound did something to heal Jackson's soul a little.

"Who do you hope is getting chewed out the worst?" he asked. He was expecting to hear Retty, Twitty, or even Piper named, but the answer surprised him.

"Those two jagoffs who keep coming in to bother the girls," Danny snarled. "Fuckers. The women know too. I heard that Piper twat laugh about 'heterosexuality hour' when the guys came up. I hope they get their heads broken open like cantaloupes, just like Caleb."

The silence at the table was electric.

"Otto thinks Retty did that," Jackson said softly.

"Otto was hiding behind the building and didn't have a fucking second-story-window view, did he?" Danny retorted bitterly. "Not that Retty wouldn't have fucking done it—don't get me wrong. She talked about splitting our heads open all the fucking time. But the two guys—Jo-Jo and Teddy—they're not as afraid of Gannett Hoover and that… that fucking enforcer he brings with him when he comes. The one who gropes Twitty all the time and then looks at her like she's shit."

And hello, Conway Schmitt.

"They didn't want Caleb hurt?" Jackson prodded. Part of him wanted to caution Danny about his language, which was stupid, because Jackson remembered swearing like he breathed, particularly when he was a bitter fourteen-year-old, but part of him was almost gratified.

He *had* used the F-word like most people used "the"—but it had purged some of his anger, some of his hatred for the world at large, when he had. He hoped that if Danny got the opportunity to pour some of that poison, that toxin, from his system, he'd free up his heart to grow strong and pure.

Both boys being *so angry* at Jo-Jo and Teddy for abusing the girls was a good sign. The girls had been kind to them, sneaking them food when the boys had gotten in trouble, talking to them—even singing to them— when they'd been locked in the closet. Danny and Enrique were *grateful* for simple human kindness, and *furious* that it had been paid back in filth.

Good kids, Jackson thought sadly. All of them: The girls, the boys, and the two trans-folk who had been difficult to spot because of the shitty, thin cotton scrubs they'd all been forced to wear. Kids trying to find their identities—only to find that their identities were despised by their parents and stripped away by their captors.

"Caleb was pretty," Enrique said when Danny proved strangely silent. "Caleb… he had this look. Like an angel. Cowboy showed up, took one look at the lot of us, and said, 'Oh no, fuck this,' and Caleb took one look at Cowboy and…." He and Danny met eyes, and Danny glanced away.

"It's funny," Danny said gruffly. "I didn't follow them out the window because I was pissed that Caleb stared at Cowboy the way I knew I stared at Caleb. But… but once Caleb got caught and… and made that noise"—and now his voice broke—"I didn't care how he looked at Cowboy. I just… I just wanted him alive to look at me any way he could."

Jackson's heart cracked, shattered, turned to dust, and for a moment he was grateful because that meant he wouldn't need it anymore. He could do this job without a heart, and nobody would ever know.

But the shock of numbness faded, and his chest ached, and apparently a powdered heart could still beat and still hurt, and this kid was walking around with a pain in his soul that no young person should ever endure.

"It wasn't your fault," Jackson said.

"I know it," Danny snarled, still staring at the now-clean kitchen.

"No, you don't," Jackson told him, and his chest was suddenly too tight, and he hated himself for what was going to come out because who wanted to burden a kid with this but… but…. "You think you know, but you don't. My friend Henry got shot two nights ago, keeping Cowboy safe from Shitbag Retty. I wasn't there—none of us knew *anything* about what you guys were going through, about Retty, about any of this shit. But I've been telling myself that it was my fault. *My* fault, because Henry was my trainee, my work partner, my *friend*, and I dragged him into all sorts of shit because…." Jackson let out a strained chuckle. "Well, because he wanted to go," he said, his voice thick. "And he wanted to help people, and he wanted to make sure Cowboy and the nice lady taking care of him were both safe. But he got shot, and it *felt* like my fault—"

Danny met his eyes. "It wasn't," he said gruffly. "Shitbag Retty would have done that crap for free."

Jackson felt a small smile creeping around the corner of his mouth. "I know that now," he said. "Because of you and Enrique, and, well, a whole lot of other people who will be justifiably pleased if that woman drops off the face of the planet." He sobered. "But you need to know that, just like Otto, you were in an impossible situation. Getting fed, having a place to sleep? That's not small potatoes. Not wanting to risk that to follow Cowboy? That was a judgment call. You're not the reason Caleb…." He didn't want to say "died," but he was starting to think there was no other way. "Made that noise. You're not the reason he didn't come back. The people who put you guys in that situation are the reason. You were just doing the best you could."

Danny put his face in his arms and wiped his cheeks on his bicep before meeting Jackson's eyes. "Is your friend gonna be okay?" he asked.

Jackson thought about his next stop at the hospital. "I hope so," he said. "We're going to see him next."

"What about Cowboy?" Enrique asked. "You said he got away?"

"Yeah," Jackson told him. "Cowboy's in a good sitch for the moment. We…." He sighed. "We wanted to keep him out of the system for a while."

"Why?" Enrique asked, and Danny gave him a pitying glance.

"'Cause he was probably sucking dick for food," he said before looking at Jackson. "You don't want that shit down in writing."

"The system has its drawbacks," Jackson admitted. "And the people who helped him out aren't exactly police favorites either."

Danny and Enrique exchanged titillated glances. "What? Did he get saved by, like, thieves? Like in those books? *Blood and Bone*?"

Jackson laughed. "You like to read?" he asked, hoping to get Danny off the scent before he found himself spilling about Johnnies and the whole enchilada.

"Yeah," Danny muttered, suddenly dispirited again. "That's how I got in trouble at home. Old man thought books were for faggots."

"Well, lucky you," Jackson said. "We *believe* in paperbacks here. Nilas and Geordie can show you to where the bookshelves are, and if you tell me the name of your favorite series—"

"Me too?" Enrique asked, feeling like a kid for the first time. "Because there's this robot assassin thing that I was *hot* for going around school."

"Absolutely. You guys get with Aileen to make a list—sky's the limit."

"Otto too?" Enrique asked eagerly, and Jackson could hear the same thing in his voice that Jackson himself felt. Something small and happy. God, these kids needed it.

"Otto too," Jackson told him. He glanced up at Nilas and Geordie. "You guys too. Geordie, get out—" He was going to say "pen and paper" because, well, he was over thirty, but Geordie had his phone out.

"On it," he said, fingers a blur.

"Send it to me ASAP," Jackson said. "I'll have them sent as soon as I get the list."

"Cool," Geordie said, taking Jackson's vacated seat.

Jackson and Cody had left then, after checking on Aileen, who was still comforting an exhausted Otto, but their information gathering had left its mark.

"God," Cody said now, sounding as wretched as Jackson felt. "This group of people is pure fucking corruption, aren't they?"

"Oh yes, they are," Jackson said grimly.

"Where we going now?"

"First to visit Henry," Jackson told him. "You can go grab us some sandwiches if you want. I've got about half-an-hour's business in the hospital—gonna say hi, give him an update, and then gotta go visit my friend in the morgue."

"Morgue?" Cody asked, sounding hesitant.

"Yeah." Jackson let out a breath and told Cody something he'd only discussed with Ellery so far. "Yeah. I had… well, let's just say I've had a bad feeling about Caleb since I talked to Cowboy about him two nights ago. And the more people I talk to, the more I think…."

"He can't be the only one," Cody said softly.

"No." Jackson took a deep breath. "These fuckers have been in our town for a year and a half. Cowboy's been on the streets for about a month, which means Caleb 'made that sound' about a month ago. Where's the body?"

Cody blew out a breath. "You checked the morgue?"

"Yup," Jackson told him. "And they haven't had anything like that nearby, so…."

"So it's got to be out of the county," Cody followed. "Where do you think it is?"

"Sonora," Jackson said. "Because that's where Gannett Hoover's estate is, with what probably amounts to vast amounts of acreage. And it's probably not the only one." And with that he walked Cody through their line of reasoning about Conway Schmitt, Gannett Hoover, and the unholy alliance of Moms for Clean Living and the politician who lived in Gold Country with a D by his name and everything but a Nazi flag in front of his house.

And Conway Schmitt, aka Newton Dwayne, aka The Creeper Thug Who Would Not Fucking Leave.

"So," Cody said slowly when he was finished, "when those two assholes who abducted Shitbag Retty said 'she's the package now,' that means…."

"It means I wish we knew somebody with a cadaver dog," Jackson said grimly. "Because I don't think you and me are going to have to do a thing to hold Retty accountable, but her body sure will make for some nice evidence of political corruption."

Cody grunted. "Well, shit," he said. "On the one hand, that sounds a little ghoulish."

Jackson grimaced. "It does."

"But on the other hand, it couldn't have happened to a shittier person."

"No, it could not have," Jackson agreed. His heart was bruised and raw from the last two days. From the worry about his friend, from the opening of old wounds, and from the raw, painful reality of a bunch of kids who could as easily have been him. That core of empathy in him felt like it had been pounded and stretched and pounded and stretched until it blanketed everybody involved in this case with a thin layer of his sorely abused heart muscle.

To stretch it to accommodate the woman who'd shot Henry through a wall, who had taken children from their homes on false pretenses, who had dangled hamburgers in front of their faces until they betrayed their friends….

He could feel that muscle unraveling like a frayed cloak, great gaps in his well-being disintegrating as he tried to be kind to the woman who had cost so many so much. It didn't seem to matter that she was a flunky, probably as emotionally abused as the kids held captive in their sick little religious scam. What mattered was, unlike Otto or Danny or Enrique or the terrified girl trying to protect her two friends the night before, Retty had forsaken everything human that had once mattered about herself and used it to hurt other people.

He just didn't have one more fuck to give.

"What if she's still alive?" Cody asked.

Well, maybe *one* fuck. "Moral dilemma solved," he said optimistically.

"We can always hope," Cody agreed, and they headed for the hospital for the umpteenth time in the last three days.

Muck Swimming

"ARE WE just not running a business anymore?" Galen asked crossly when Ellery answered his phone. "Is that why Jade and I are the only ones here?"

Ellery grimaced and excused himself from the kitchen table where he and his mother were sorting frantically through the documents Jackson had sent and putting together a brief for the ADA on the fly.

"I usually don't have appointments on Thursdays," he said. "And since I don't have court, I'm working from home."

"I know you are," Galen said. "You're working on Henry's case, and not once has either of you two assholes filled me in."

Ellery winced. "Apologies," he said sincerely. "There was—"

"Chaos," Galen said with satisfaction. "Jade has updated me on the chaos." He chuckled. "So you sent Jackson into the ether, and he rescued a hundred kids? Is that how it went?"

"Eight," Ellery told him. "And he had Cody's help. And Jade rescued the one who threw a Molotov cocktail through our window."

"You should know that the Thornton kid—"

"Killian?" Killian had been at least thirty, Ellery thought in bemusement.

"Yes. Anyway, somebody somewhere is missing a fixer, because he has hired a glazier and repaired our carpet. He said it was in payment for keeping his friend out of jail, but I'm saying, if he doesn't mind working for the mob, he could find a whole different profession."

"I think he'd mind," Ellery said dryly. "He and Lewis seem very earnest."

"More's the pity." And like that, Galen switched topics. "Who are we hiring as our third member?"

"What?" Ellery asked, a little surprised. "You're worried about that *now*?"

"Yes," Galen said. "Yes, I am. Because Jade just made four appointments for you for next week and three for me. I'm thinking we don't need a new partner—we need a partner and *two* new associates. They can share an office. That way while you and Jackson are using the law firm's resources to save the world on a grand scale, we can have backup to bring in the money."

Ellery grunted. "I thought that's what *you* were for?"

"And I do my part," Galen informed him. "But truthfully, your ADA friend called me to make sure Henry was okay—"

"Arizona?" Ellery asked in surprise. Arizona Brooks was in her early fifties and one of Ellery's fiercest adversaries in the courtroom.

But she was also fair-minded and had gone to bat for Jackson and Ellery more than once in the name of what was right as opposed to what politicians thought they could get away with.

"Yes," Galen said. "And she sounded… hurt. I'll say it. She sounded hurt that she hadn't been notified beforehand. And if you people are on that kind of ground with your nemesis—"

"I thought only superheroes got a nemesis," Ellery said, his mind racing.

"Sure, you think that like you're not. Anyway, call her up, tell her Henry looks like he may live—"

"Does he?" Ellery asked, because Galen's sudden topic switches had almost twisted past the thing he'd needed most to know.

Galen slowed down. "Yes," he said gently. "He does. He's got a mild fever, but they're pumping him full of antibiotics, and he seems to be responding. His insides do not seem to be springing any leaks, and things are looking good."

"Thank God," Ellery said with feeling. "Okay. I didn't mean to hurt Arizona's feelings. I'll call her—"

"And offer her a job as an associate."

"She won't take anything less than full partner," Ellery told him, surprised. "She shouldn't!"

"I know that, and you know that, but she'll be suspicious if you offer it to her off the bat. Anyway—"

"But you said we should have two associates!" he protested. "To share an office."

"Oh, yes," Galen said. "The teachers union told Jade they're moving quarters."

Ellery's brain bounced off the floorboards for a moment while he tried to put that together. "I sleep in for *one day*—"

"Oh, sleep in my *ass*," Galen retorted. "I know you, Ellery Cramer, and you and Jackson were probably working on the case all fucking night."

Ellery thought about how they'd *really* spent their night and said, "You got me," because he did not want to talk about that right now.

"Or not?" Galen said, curiosity tinting his voice.

Ellery fought the temptation to bury his face in his hands. "Galen, you are a *very* good friend, and I will never regret making you my law partner, but you are *making me dizzy*. Can we stick to a subject—one subject? I'm starting not to care which one."

Galen's evil chuckle slowed the conversation down a little, and Ellery took a breath.

"Okay, then," he said. "First things first. The teacher's union is moving to a new office building closer to the state office of education. They told Jade so we could put a bid in for the property, which I have."

"You have?" Ellery asked, his voice squeaking. "Galen, we are hardly in the black—"

"You worry too much," Galen said breezily. "We've been making our nut since I joined the practice last year. It's fine. So we have added offices now. We don't just have the spare in *this* corner, but we have three smaller ones in the old teachers' union. It's a much smaller space, but do you see?"

"Two associates," Ellery said slowly, "and what's the third office for—"

"Our private detectives," Galen said, as though Ellery was an idiot to miss it. "Think about it, okay?"

"They get their own office?" Ellery asked, surprised. He and Jackson had always worked quietly in the same space, which was something they'd done since they'd gotten together.

"Your boy," Galen said patiently, "needs a place to change, a place to organize, and a place to hold all that weird paraphernalia he keeps showing Henry how to use. It's shoved back behind the reception counter right now, but…." Galen's voice shifted, and Ellery had a sudden sense that this man would be *devastating* in the courtroom. "You must admit that Jade deserves an entire space to herself, as well as an aide. If we put a connecting door in from your office to the last one in the hallway of the new space, you can work together, and he can have a place to store stuff and computers for Henry and AJ and anybody else he wants to employ to use."

"And Arizona is a partner," Ellery said, feeling a little numb from all this planning. "Gotcha."

"Good," Galen said. "Make it so."

Ellery burst into hysterical laughter, because it was such a *grand* plan, when they'd all been cruising along just fine, and Galen jumped in and saved him from being overwhelmed.

"But before you call Arizona, tell me everything." Suddenly he was laser focused. "I am *dying* to hear about the case."

Ellery told him everything, including what Jackson had guessed about and had relayed that morning about the former inhabitants of what Ellery now knew was called the At Risk Youth Prayer Group, which was the term on the paperwork that the parents had signed when they'd given Moms for Clean Living custody of their children.

"Is the paperwork legal?" Galen asked.

"Not in California law," Ellery replied with grim satisfaction. "The paperwork promised schooling, and according to the child advocates who conducted the first interviews and placements, there were no regular classes. Withholding food as punishment as well as corporal punishment as a matter of written policy are both enough to get a place claiming to be a school shut down, not to mention the other offenses…."

His fading voice said it all.

"Of which I take it there were many?" Galen asked, sounding angry.

"There were," Ellery told him, feeling that same anger in his gut. The more he took in the statements taken by the advocates, the more he knew where that terrible nightmare had come from, the one that had clawed Jackson apart.

Yes, the resulting wound may have cleansed some of the festering sickness from Jackson's soul, but the wound itself was so huge. Ellery's own hands shook thinking about it. He couldn't imagine the strength it would take for somebody with Jackson's past to walk around bleeding like that.

"So," Galen said, his voice icy with control, "what are we doing about it?"

"Well, Mother and I are still scanning the paperwork," Ellery said. "Mother is trying to assemble a brief on the fly to present to the state attorney general—she's got more than enough for a full investigation and warrants. However…." He sighed, knowing full well the limits of the system they were working within.

"That could take months," Galen answered for him.

"Yes," Ellery acknowledged. "And Jackson suspects the most damning evidence will have disappeared by then. In fact, Mother and I were discussing it, and I'm not sure if it will be there by the end of the day."

"Where do you think it will be?"

Ellery explained the connection between the Moms for Clean Living, one very shady politician, and a Machiavellian ex-preacher man currently named Newton Dwayne.

"Sonora?" Galen asked, sounding puzzled. "I've heard of the place, but I'm afraid I haven't lived in your fair state long enough to really know all its venues."

Ellery snorted. "It's… well, from what I understand, there's a lot of trees, it's ungodly hot in the summertime, and there's a railroad museum and tour that can take you on a route that's been seen in over one hundred television shows and movies."

"Really?" For once Galen was neither dry nor sardonic. "How do you know this?"

Ellery gave a short laugh. "Jackson. He, Kaden, Jade—they grew up watching old movies on an old TV. Apparently it's one of the places he's always wanted to visit."

"Well," Galen said, as though still putting that together. "That's special. Do we know where this Gannett Hoover *is* in Sonora?"

"Indeed we do," Ellery said, feeling a little smug. "Why? Because the property deed was in the stuff Jackson photographed and sent us. And why was it in the Moms for Clean Living files?"

"Please, tell me…," Galen breathed.

"Oh yes. Because it's deeded to *them* as part of the convoluted money-laundering scheme that it's going to take an entire platoon of forensic accountants to piece together."

"Oh, who cares!" Galen dismissed. "What matters is the connection! You know that, right?"

"No, Galen, I was born yesterday." Galen wasn't the only one with a corner on the Sahara-dry commentary market.

"But you can get *in*," Galen said excitedly. "You can get a warrant, and you can go in there, and you can find…." He trailed off. "What do you think you'll find?"

And this was where the paper trail failed, because this was all hearsay. "Bodies," Ellery said, his own voice suddenly serious. "As in more than one. Jackson suspects that this is where Moms for Clean Living has been taking… packages."

"Packages," Galen repeated numbly. Then, "*Packages* such as Cowboy's friend, Caleb?"

"Yes," Ellery told him, rubbing his stomach as it rebelled against the thought. "And some of the missing children who weren't kept around the mansion as a sort of army of thieves, to do dirty work for the organization so they didn't starve."

There was a stunned silence on the other end of the line.

"And," Ellery added while Galen was digesting, "we suspect the woman who shot Henry might be there as well. Jackson and Cody found her getting treated for the gunshot wound Henry inflicted, but she was spirited away before they could question her. They heard her captors talking about 'packages,' and Jackson...."

"Put it together," Galen said, as though he had just done the same thing. "And then you found out who was funding the organization, and you came up with Sonora. I get it. It's a serpentine mess, but I get it." He paused. "I'm starting to get a lot of things, in fact."

"Like what?" Ellery asked, not sure what he meant by that.

"Like why the two of you never talk about the Dirty/Pretty killer," Galen said frankly. "I've read all about it—I've spent nearly a year wanting to ask you how that happened. But now... I can see why the two of you wouldn't want to even remember it."

Ellery let out a harsh bark of *something*. Sure as shit wasn't laughter. "Oh, Galen," he said brokenly, remembering the way Jackson had come apart the night before, fracturing so completely it had taken Ellery *and* his mother to put him back again. "There's even more to that story than you can imagine. And I'm not sure if either of us will *ever* be ready to share it."

"Well, that is a shame," Galen said softly. "Because I was hoping you'd have some tips on dealing with the... the *awfulness* that I'm feeling here."

"You stop it," Ellery said grimly. "That's all you *can* do."

"So," Galen said after a pause, "I ask again. Do you have a *plan*?"

"We do," Ellery told him. "But it all depends on Mother. She's throwing together the brief, and she's got a phone appointment with the AG at noon, right before the woman's lunch. Hopefully it's enough to get us a meeting on the property."

"And?" Galen asked, sounding eager.

"And if we can get *on* the property, we can sneak Jackson and Cody inside the perimeter. Mother's very good at things like wording—she can make it legal for all the occupants of a vehicle to enter the premises for some preliminary fact-finding without mentioning—"

"Your fiancé and a freelancer popping out of the trunk of your vehicle," Galen said with satisfaction. "Excellent. When do we leave?"

"I'm sorry?" Ellery asked, wondering if Galen had awoken from a full night's sleep and thought, "Hey, yesterday was a shitshow. How am I going to freak Ellery out today?"

"Your mother, with her ties to the higher powers, will be questioning the congressman," Galen said. "You can be her right-hand man, or you can hold back and observe and poke around. I can do the same. And I have the handy, dandy disability, which is a *wonderful* distraction. Somebody looks at you oddly, and oh no, poor Mr. Henderson needs to sit down. And could you get me a glass of water while you're at it? And do you have an appropriate men's room?" Galen chuckled wickedly. "Trust me, Ellery. You'll want me there. On top of everything else, I want…." His voice thickened. "I want *blood* here. That kid—he came to *me*. Henry was under *my* orders to watch him. And the kid was torn apart and terrified for what these people had been doing to him and his friends. I-I can*not* sit idly by here at the office and pretend this has nothing to do with me."

Ellery pulled in a breath, and then another, and thought of the space requirements to sneak two full grown men into a compound while not being seen.

"Fine," he said after a moment. "But see if you can get the Lincoln from John, and…." He chuckled evilly, because Jade had done this before and done it *well*. "And fill Jade in and ask her if she wants in on the action. The last time she played chauffer, she murdered the role."

Galen took a surprised breath and then let loose a chuckle. "Good. Good. I like this. You tell your mother we're in. I'll take care of the office today while you and your mother take care of all the big scary warrants and briefs. We're big guns this afternoon."

"Fine," Ellery said, rubbing the back of his neck. "We can only hope this works."

"Not a doubt in the world," Galen said grandly, and Ellery was reminded that, with a few blithe words that morning, Galen had pretty much changed the entire direction of a business he and Jackson had built from the ground up.

But it hadn't been a *bad* thing, either.

"Sure," he said, feeling weak.

"You worry too much," Galen said, his usual arid condescension back in place. "I, for one, am looking forward to the outing. It's going to be quite… stimulating."

"Sure."

HIS MOTHER found him a few minutes later, sitting on the edge of his and Jackson's bed, staring into space. Billy Bob was on his lap, and Lucifer was trying gamely not to slide off the bed next to his hips.

"Stop that," his mother said tenderly to the black cat. "And come here." With an almost absurd gentleness she lifted the sleek black cat into her arms. "Aren't you getting chonky, yes? These boys need to feed you two something less fatty."

Ellery stared at her. "Chonky?"

"Rebekah's children use the word frequently," she said, sitting next to him and, disconcertingly, resting her head on his shoulder. "What are you thinking?"

Ellery let out a small laugh. "Galen has completely rewritten our business plan, and he wishes to *caravan* up to Sonora so he can be a distraction once we get inside."

"Which one of these things bothers you more?" she asked, with nothing more than curiosity.

"The trip to Sonora," Ellery said with a small smile. "Businesses fail—or succeed. I think he's right. Ours has potential to grow. But what we're going to do in Sonora is—"

"Dangerous," she said, apparently not bothered. With a sweet smile, she allowed Lucifer to rub his whiskers against her nose. "This cat is a charming creature," she said, using her opposite hand to scritch the base of his tail. With a stern scowl, she chastised Billy Bob, who was currently drooling and nursing on Ellery's shawl-collared sweater, which he was wearing over his pajama bottoms. "Why can you not take lessons?"

The battered Siamese mix's purring filled the room.

"It would help," Ellery said, smoothing Billy Bob's whiskers back with his thumb, "if Jackson wouldn't call him terrible names."

"Like what?"

"Like no-thumbs-having motherfucker," Ellery replied, smiling a little.

As if recognizing those words for the terms of endearment they were, Billy Bob's purring amped up a little.

"You and Jackson," she said, "have created a good life together."

He glanced at her, surprised. "I think so," he said.

"I think expanding your business is a good idea. While not every case is as large as this one," she gestured with her chin toward his dining room table, where their laptops both sat in a sea of scanned copies and paperwork, "I think even the small ones you take on help change people's lives."

Ellery thought of Killian and Lewis's friend Nicky, who seemed like three hundred pounds of muscle with an extra twenty of pure good will.

"I hope so," he said.

"A law firm based on helping people and finding the truth is a good thing," she said.

"Well, yes," he agreed.

"Who were you thinking of as your third partner?" she asked, almost idly.

"Galen suggested ADA Arizona Brooks."

"Hmm…." She stood, Lucifer still cradled in her arms. "A decent suggestion. Make sure she wouldn't mind sharing an office. Your kitchen table is impossibly small, Ellery, and if I'm going to be bicoastal, I would like a place to work."

And with that, his mother exited his room, back into the paperwork fray that might help stop a couple of monsters, and Ellery stared after her.

And then he picked up his phone again and called ADA Arizona Brooks to fill her in on Henry—and ask her if she wanted to switch sides.

The Holes Fish Dig

HENRY WAS still in the critical care unit, mostly because the dumb asshole had gotten himself a fever.

"Look at you," Jackson all but snarled, taking in the bright crescents of heat next to his pale skin. "You look like shit. You people tell me that sitting by your bedside and *willing* you to be better won't work, but I haven't seen a damned thing to prove it wouldn't have better results."

Henry peered at him through half-open eyes. "Look at you, all big with ego. I didn't get shot to piss you off, sensei—it just fucking happened."

Jackson scowled and threw himself into the vacant chair by the bed. There were two very nice chenille throws in blues and golds on the chairs, and Jackson picked one up and frowned at it.

"Did Lance do this?" he asked, his temper cooling for a moment.

"Galen," Henry said, smiling through cracked lips. "There is no emotional path so fraught that Galen can't approach it with a little bit of retail therapy." Jackson managed a weak smile, and Henry added, "Where's Cody? I got a whole earful about how you two went out and rescued children without me last night. Rude, is all I'm saying. I'm out of it for a little bit, and everybody gets delusions of grandeur."

Jackson's smile got a little stronger. "Take it easy, Han Solo. Cody stayed in the hallway in deference to your doctors, who only want one visitor at a time. I came in to tell you…." He paused, not sure how to phrase this. "To tell you that what you were doing? Taking care of that one kid, watching Isabelle Roberts and keeping her safe? That was a big deal, Henry. Nobody expected it to be such a big deal. We all knew Cowboy probably heard a… a murder. But it's so much bigger than that. Just, you know. When you're all better and getting pissed off because healing *sucks* and I know it, remember you did a big thing."

Henry grunted. "That's sweet," he said. "Now get to the part about how you look worse than I do."

A harsh sound escaped Jackson's throat. "Buddy, in a week, you're going to be at home, and I'm going to be playing video games with you so you don't die of boredom. I'll tell you about my shitty childhood—"

"Now," Henry muttered. "It's been eating at you for weeks. Now."

"The difference between you and Ellery," Jackson said, hoisting himself out of his chair, "is that—"

"I don't want to see you naked," Henry interrupted. "Now spill."

"I was going to say, Ellery can tell me what to do," Jackson said with dignity, falling back into the chair.

"Please?" Henry asked. "It's been bothering me. You know all my secrets, Jackson. You know about my abusive ex-boyfriend, you know how I betrayed my family—"

"He did that," Jackson said harshly.

"Yeah, and you believe that. So you should know I won't hold this against you. Maybe you tell one person besides Ellery—"

"And his mother," Jackson muttered.

"Ouch," Henry commiserated. "Come on. I've been lying here, trying to keep Lance from losing his shit, and it occurred to me that I know how to handle boyfriends, but you're my first *real* friend. Please? Let me be a real friend too."

Like with most big painful secrets, this one was easier to tell the second time. Jackson finished the story about how he'd called child services on his one living family member in a relatively short time and then stood, avoiding Henry's eyes.

"So see?" he said. "Not too much to tell."

"Jackson?" Henry said softly.

"Yeah?"

"You're still my first real friend."

Jackson gave him a wicked grin. "Well, I've got scads of them. Millions. I could go to the corner and find another Henry Worrall and—"

"Shut up," Henry said, and he was falling asleep, but he was also laughing.

"Only because that wasn't true," Jackson told him. He didn't want to get too close—he was wearing a mask, but one never knew what kinds of nasty bugs occupied space with a person just walking around. He did take Henry's hand, though. "You hang in there, brother. I've got plans to drive you batshit insane when you're getting better. I owe you."

"You gonna bust Shitbag Retty?" Henry asked plaintively, and that made Jackson pause.

"What if I told you I think she's already dead?"

Henry's eyes popped open, and he grimaced. "My head hurts like a motherfucker, and you're springing that on me *now*?"

Jackson shrugged. "Henry, they took her yesterday, and she was 'the package.' I get the feeling her other 'packages' have been… you know…."

"Dead teenagers," Henry muttered. "Oh fuck me. Yeah. Okay. I hear you. Revenge isn't the deal this time."

"Wish I could tell you it was."

"Live teenagers are a better outcome," Henry rasped and then coughed.

"Live Henry is also important," Jackson murmured, touching Henry's burning forehead lightly. "Heal. Forget the rest of this bullshit. Shitbag Retty's not gonna bother anybody anymore."

"Get 'em, brother."

"Will do."

CODY WAS sprawled out in his chair, texting like an old newsman on a typewriter, grunting to himself, as Jackson emerged from the CCU.

"How is he?" Cody asked.

"Fighting infection," Jackson muttered. "God, this phase of it sucks. It's so scary. It can turn on a dime."

"It's *amazing* how much you know about healing," Cody pronounced, eyes still glued to his screen. "And yet you are still apparently a neurotic mess."

"Seems to be the consensus," Jackson said sourly. "Did you want to stay and finish your conversation while I go down to the morgue?"

"No," Cody said, with unexpected vehemence, and Jackson realized he'd probably typed the word too. "No, no, no, no, no, because don't be an asshole, that's why." With a final savage poke at his phone, Cody shoved the thing in his pocket and stood.

"Anything I should know about?" Jackson asked, leading the way to the elevators.

"US Marshals are assholes," Cody replied as the thing dinged.

"All of them," Jackson asked carefully, getting in, "or just the one?"

"Only the one. Delicate constitution my ass," he muttered, shifting to the classic voice of mockery. "'Oh, but Cody, this is a delicate time in your healing journey.' You know what's a delicate time in my healing journey?" Cody asked rhetorically.

"Conversations with yourself?" Jackson hazarded.

"Fucking *boredom* is a delicate time in my healing journey," Cody blurted as the door opened on, oh, hey, the maternity ward. "Beg your pardon, ma'am," he said to the woman getting onto the elevator with a car carrier in one hand, a baby bag over the other shoulder, and a bemused partner on the other side of the elevator doors who had apparently just watched the mother of his child leave without him.

"No, no," the woman said, sounding as put out as Cody. "I'm with you. Lying around waiting for shit to start does nothing for me. If this kid is going to start driving me crazy, I want it to happen in my own damned home."

The elevator door opened on the ground floor, and she got out, and Jackson and Cody continued down to the basement, chuckling a little.

"Apparently you are not alone," Jackson said softly.

"No," Cody muttered and then sighed. "No. And that's all he wants me to know. I'm not alone on my 'healing journey.'" He used finger quotes, and Jackson felt his deep disgust.

"You know," he said, "you can tell him to stop calling it that."

Cody grunted. "Recovery is fine, thank you. Worst thing about being a recovering addict is the… the *lingo*. It's like once you put a title on it, you feel like a fraud. You can't live with a title to your own stupidity—it gives it too much gravitas."

Jackson had to chuckle. "You know," he said, "I am a *fan* of that philosophy." Then he sobered, remembering the night before and Henry's request that Jackson actually confide in him—like a real friend—that afternoon. "But giving voice to the things that hurt you?" he said thoughtfully. "That shows somebody that they're part of your circle, you know? Even if it's just a circle of two."

Cody grunted. "Why? Why would he want to be a part of my circle of two?"

Jackson smiled to himself as he remembered Cody shouting, "Jackson, Plan B!" the night before, just as all hell was breaking loose.

"Because when you're sober and in full control of your faculties, you are a *blast* to be around," he said, feeling that in his bones.

Cody chuckled a little. "That *was* one of my finer moments."

"Tell him that," Jackson said. "Let him know you want more of them."

"Speaking of…." Cody let out a breath.

As they'd been talking, the elevator had let them out on the basement floor, and Jackson had begun leading him through the echoey, chill, and labyrinthine corridors of the basement floor.

Now Jackson took that right, directly into Toby's offices, where Josh, the assistant, and Toby huddled over what appeared to be a prehistoric desktop computer.

"Jackson, hold on a sec," Toby said, without glancing up. "I know you're on a deadline, and I almost have your information."

Jackson and Cody exchanged glances. "Toby, doesn't the rest of the hospital have tablets and shit?"

"Nobody wants to give money to dead people," Josh said, proving once again that he had the tact and diplomacy of a doctor who needed to be nowhere near the living.

"He's right," Toby said, hitting a key on the keyboard repeatedly. "As my son keeps telling me—"

"Parker?" Jackson asked, because that was the gay son that Toby had been trying to set him up with for years.

"No, the youngest. Niles."

"Isn't Niles a *baby*?" Jackson asked, appalled.

"He's in high school," Toby told him, rolling his eyes. "And he's very smart for his age. Anyway, he tells me repeatedly that the morgue is not a consumer-driven business, so it doesn't get consumer-appropriate equipment."

Jackson blinked. "High school, you say?"

Toby gave him a rather wolfish grin over the computer monitor. "Terrifying, isn't it?" He stepped away from the desk with a "Keep working on it, Josh," while he pulled out his phone and tapped frantically.

"And we need the computer why?" Jackson asked as Toby approached.

"I'm *trying*," Toby said with some frustration, "to get you a *map*."

Oh. "A map of *what*?"

Toby glared up at him, all hints of playfulness gone. "A map of the location where a friend of mine was training cadaver dogs last month and found the bodies of three teenaged boys at the bottom of an old mine. It's up in Gold Country somewhere, not too far from Twain Harte."

Jackson blinked slowly. "Near Sonora?" he asked carefully.

Toby gave him a grim nod. "You expected this?"

"Let's just say the place keeps coming up, and…." He let out a sigh, thinking about Caleb and his suspicion from the very first that the boy wouldn't be found alive. "Well, there was a reason I asked you. But…." He swallowed. "Three?"

Toby nodded and didn't force him to ask. "In various stages of decomp, I'm afraid. And on a tricky bit of land."

"Tricky?"

"Well, this is why I wanted the damned map," Toby said. "See, this area has *some* really nice houses, often placed by one of the small lakes in the area. But it's also got some desolate stretches of oak trees with absolute bupkiss. Sometimes there's farms, sometimes there's mansions, sometimes there's forest land, and sometimes there's fuckall, you understand?"

Jackson's eyes widened. "Great," he said. "Because I'm sort of a city/ suburb cat myself. Cody, you?"

Cody was peering over Jackson's shoulder as the doc tried to show Jackson the map, and it might have been super crowded, but Cody was tall enough to make it feel not quite so claustrophobic.

"I've got some backwoods experience," he said. "There's no snow there this time of year, but there sure is a lot of mud."

"Well, I'm wearing hiking tennies," Jackson said. "And we've got rain gear in the car." He peered at Toby's phone and played with the picture for a minute. "Okay," he said softly. "This here—what's this?" He pointed to what appeared to be a residential road, but one that was solidly in the middle of nowhere.

"That's a property," Toby told him. "Josh, did you look up the address?"

"Yup. It's 22000 Ward Lake Road," Josh said. "It's one of those big mansions that front the lake, but you can see the fire roads and such in the rear of the property. That backs up against federal woodland."

"And right here?" Jackson traced up to what in the satellite photo on Toby's phone looked like a UFO landing spot, because it was an almost perfect circle. "This is a mine cap, right?" The mine caps were a leftover from the gold rush days, in an effort to repair the damage done to the hills after the miners had come through. The mines—some of which were no more than ten or so feet deep—were filled in with rocks and soil so the land could be used again. The mines weren't always covered responsibly, though. Most of them were solidly packed, but sometimes there were air pockets or shafts that could be dangerous to anybody who walked the land.

"Exactly," Toby said. "It's on the federal land. The cap itself should be pretty solid. But back here…." He pointed to a copse of trees that hid *everything* from the satellite view. "This, according to my friend, is where the mine shaft opens. Dirt had fallen in on the top of the elevator car, but they had to send spelunkers in, their guide ropes attached to trees, in order to retrieve the bodies. Once they were there—" Toby rolled his eyes. "—apparently there was a much easier way down."

Jackson frowned. "So on federal land. Why didn't we hear this in the news?"

Toby shrugged. "For one thing, it's in a whole other county—and not even one that's adjacent to Sacramento County. For another—" He gave Jackson a bleak look. "—they haven't identified the bodies yet. It's one of those things. Nobody wants people to find out about their loved ones on the news, and you don't want to scare people. My friend says the press release was confined to 'lost hikers sadly recovered,' in the hopes that families would reach out. But, like I said, a month."

Jackson, suddenly claustrophobic, thrust the phone back into Toby's hands and strode away, trying hard to think.

"It's been discovered," he muttered. "*We* may not have heard about it down here, but you can bet damned sure anybody living on that residential mansion road has."

"Are you wondering if they'd use it again?" Cody asked, and Jackson blessed him, because he *had* spent time on the streets, and he could think like a cop *and* a criminal.

"Yeah," Jackson muttered. "If Ellery and his mother can find Caleb's name in that paperwork I gave them, and *we* can find the body on that property, we've got them. We've got *all* of them, dead to rights." He felt fury roaring down his spine as he scowled up at Cody. "I want them to *pay*," he snarled, feeling it in the pit of his balls. "They… they begged, borrowed, stole, cajoled, and cadged kids away from their parents by selling them bad religion, and *this*—" He stabbed his finger at Toby's old, hapless phone. "—*this* is what they do to them."

Cody gestured for the phone, and Toby gave it to him.

"What are you looking for?" the older man asked, and Jackson saw Cody's fierce grin.

"A similar spot," he said, glancing at Jackson. "See, if I was the bad guy, I'd look for another place like the first—like, say, see? This one? Or this one here?"

"I hear you," Jackson muttered. He pulled out his phone and texted Ellery. *Quick. Need Hoover's address.*

24000 Ward Lake Road, Ellery texted back, and Jackson grunted in satisfaction because that was pretty much what he'd expected.

Thought so, he replied. *How much property?* Out loud, he said, "Okay, so the mine cap where they discovered bodies is the closest one to where our suspect lives. Which is right here." He pointed to the address, and even through the grainy depiction of the satellite photo, he gave a low whistle. "Nice digs."

His own phone buzzed, and he glanced at it. *Only ten, which isn't much considering all the land in the area.*

Much of it is federal owned, Jackson sent back, the thought making him bounce on his toes.

"What's got you so happy?" Cody asked.

"Hoover only has ten acres," Jackson said. "So all of this? This area with the three different mines where he could have been disposing of bodies?"

"Is free for us to search," Cody said, catching on.

Jackson grunted, still staring at the phone. It was a lot of area—and they didn't have a lot of time. "My God, I wish *I* knew someone with a cadaver dog."

"Oh," Toby said, as though surprised to hear this. "I know somebody who could meet you there. He's training a couple of them right now. I bet he'd be happy to help."

Jackson cleared his throat. "Toby, we're not exactly legit right here. I was hoping to find the bodies, call the authorities, and then confront the bad guys."

Toby shrugged. "You got a lot of territory to stake out—and he could help you do it before it gets dark. When were you planning to leave for Sonora?"

Later, Jackson would remember how much faith Toby had in him, and it would give him strength. "Twelve thirty," he said, because Ellery had texted him earlier. "Why?"

"Because it still gets dark fairly early," Toby said frankly. "By the time you get there, it'll be around three, and you'll have less than three hours to search. I'm assuming you're on a time crunch?"

"Yeah," Jackson said, thinking hard. "Actually, we're going to leave *now*. I'm changing the plan. See this road?" he still had Toby's phone, and he indicated a small winding snake of a road.

"Yes?" Toby said.

"It bottoms out right where our first searching position starts. Send me that map, and get me in touch with your dog friend. Cody and I are taking off right now!"

As he and Cody tore out of the morgue, Cody said, "Are we even going to tell Ellery?"

Jackson snorted. "Of course we are. I may be reckless, but I'm only a little bit stupid."

ELLERY SEEMED to think differently.

"The plan was," he explained patiently, "that we would all go up together—"

"And I appreciate that plan," Jackson replied, glad he'd entrusted the driving to Cody. "It was a good plan. But it did not accommodate for how soon it gets dark or the fact that there have already been bodies found up there."

Cody took a hard left, and Jackson found himself pressed up against the passenger window. He tried not to say something sarcastic because his original assessment of Cody needing his hand held had not only been dead wrong, Jackson was starting to suspect that little noises like, "Oh my God, we're all going to die!" would only egg the guy on.

"But that's the point," Ellery said, and it sounded like he and his mother were doing a paperwork roundup on a massive scale. "We can give their coroner some pictures of some of the missing children and see if they match the identities of the young people we haven't managed to round up."

Jackson let out a long breath. "Ellery, I asked those kids at the table this morning how long was their longest stay in that place. Do you know what they said?"

"Oh my God," Ellery muttered. "I… I hadn't even thought to ask that. Or to ask the advocates. Or to—"

"We've been busy!" Jackson told him. "But I asked, and you know what he said?"

"What?"

"Three months. The longest any of them could recall a kid being there was from three months ago. Now I may not have time to study that paperwork I was scanning for you, but you know what I *do* remember seeing?"

"Oh God…," Ellery rasped. "They've had that part of it up and running for over nine months."

Jackson hoped his voice wouldn't break. "Where are they?" he asked. "Yeah, some of them escaped, but we saw how well that *didn't* work for a lot of them. Some of them, I hope, made it back to their parents—in fact, I would bet a *lot* of them made it back to their parents. But at least four that we know of didn't end up on the street and didn't end up back at their parents' houses, and you know what we have to ask now, don't you?"

"How many more are out there," Ellery whispered. "Oh Jesus, Jackson. What do we do?"

"Fetzer and Hardison were in the ER last night," Jackson told him. "They know the basic story. You need to call them and tell them you need help screening all those parent forms to see if the parents know where their children are. You said your mother was talking to the state AG—which is great. I'm glad we have contacts. Your visit to Hoover and Schmitt will be very necessary, and getting warrants will be very necessary, but right now we have a way to search for more proof and more...." He worked hard to stay strong for the missing and the dead. "More lost children," he said. "There's also some outbuildings back along the property line," he added, because he'd been studying the map Toby had sent to his phone since he'd buckled in. "Cody and I can check those out too, while everybody is focused on your little lawfare excursion."

"Where will you be?" Ellery asked, sounding disconsolate and, for lack of a better word, young.

Jackson gave him directions, sending the map Toby had pulled up for him to Ellery's phone.

"Cody and I will be along the back edge of the property," Jackson told him. "If you can come up early, there's a small picnic area with a parking lot and some restrooms and picnic tables on the west side of the river. Cody and I have a two-hour head start on you—we'll be ready for a break in four or so hours."

"Jackson," Ellery said, sounding wretched. "We can't even call in any police. We're supposed to be a fact-finding mission!"

"Well, we *are* on a fact-finding mission!" Jackson argued back. "And Toby hooked us up with his friend who's training a cadaver dog—*he's* got all of the law enforcement contacts for this area and a satellite radio to boot." There had been good reasons for making all those other phone calls before he called Ellery, he thought virtuously.

"Oh God," Ellery muttered. "Jackson, do I have to tell you to—"

"Be careful?" Jackson finished for him. "Take care of your property? Come back okay? No, baby. You do not have to tell me that. Do I have to tell you the same thing?"

"I'm not going to be in *any* danger."

"You're going to be facing off against a child molester and two killers," Jackson snapped back. "And whether you're doing it with guns or computers and fake smiles, it's going to be a grim, dirty business. Tell Lucy Satan to keep her wits about her, and make sure the whole world knows where she's going and why or you two need to stay the hell home."

"And Galen and Jade," Ellery added, from what Jackson could tell, for pure meanness.

"Now why would you put so much of my family in one fucking basket and dangle it over a fucking cliff?" Jackson snapped, out of patience. "You had better meet us in four hours—I don't care if you have to stand on the accelerator and put a light and siren on top of the goddamned Lexus. If we've found enough evidence, there might be no reason for you to go in there and face off against Hoover and Schmitt and fuckin' Twitty and the Dwaynes at all. Neither of us have the easy job today, Ellery, so maybe… you know. Have some faith in me, and be careful yourself, okay?"

"Of course," Ellery replied with dignity. "And I'll be sure to pass along your regards to my mother."

"She's a good broad," Jackson said, knowing the anachronism would make Ellery smile.

"She is indeed. Take care of my Detective."

"Take care of my Counselor," Jackson replied, and they both hung up. He glanced around, and realized they'd hit the freeway and Cody was taking Highway 50 to Sunrise Boulevard.

"Wow," Cody said. "That was intense. You have those conversations a lot?"

Jackson grunted. "You spend enough time in the CCU, for yourself *and* others, getting hurt on the job becomes a real possibility. It's rough to live with."

Cody looked stricken for a moment, and then he seemed to shake himself out of it. "It was good," he said after a moment. "What you two said. You made it clear why we had to go hauling ass out of there. You two are quick." He let out an almost melancholy sigh. "I was never that quick. I mean, I could think on my feet undercover, but you two, digging up information, putting it together—it would have taken me weeks to get what you've gotten in, what? Two days?"

"It's not only me," Jackson told him, feeling this in his stomach. "You haven't met the whole team, but we've got people running down leads on computers, and we've got Ellery and his mother—and they've both got more brain power than I could even think of, and *she's* got connections out the yang. We've got Jade, who is keeping our world running while we go off and try to find out why our friend got hurt. I mean, everything from the people taking care of our first witness to Ellery's child advocate army— that's, you know, pulling out all the stops, calling in all the favors, going balls to the walls, and leaving nothing behind. Henry was hurt. The guy's my partner—I need to have his back."

Cody let out a sigh. "Man, I would give ungodly parts of my soul to work with your operation full time."

"Enjoy it now," Jackson said, giving a wolfish grin. "I mean, I was lying my balls off to Ellery. For all I know, we won't even make it through the day."

Cody perked up. "That's the spirit. I'm totally in."

Fish on the Surface

"Ellery," his mother asked as he was piloting the Lexus through traffic, "did you forget product in your hair?"

It took every bit of concentration Ellery had to not wreck the car. "Did I do what?"

"I'm simply saying," she told him as though commenting on the weather. "You're usually impeccably groomed, and while you've shaved and plucked and bathed and combed and done all the usual things, your hair appears… unruly."

Ellery actually felt a little sick. He and Jackson had emerged from the shower, and he'd done the usual things, but… but… he'd been planning to put on casual clothes afterward, and he'd *forgotten* to put product in his hair. It had been water-combed, but not… not *sealed* to his head.

"My God," he said, shaken. "It's like I'm wearing mismatched shoes."

She laughed a little and pulled something from her purse. "Don't worry, dear. I have some. You can comb it through when we park."

"Thanks, Mother," he said, feeling humble.

"You're nervous," she said, as usual cutting through to the heart of things.

"I'm scared," he amended. "Jackson is out there doing scary things, we're talking to the DOJ and getting the FBI involved, for God's sakes, and we have"—his voice trembled—"no idea. No idea how far this goes or how bad this is." Which was why they'd discussed the FBI's involvement after Jackson had hung up. No, Jackson didn't know about it—and he probably wouldn't approve. But this was kidnapping, and it spread across more than one county, and the FBI had a claim on jurisdiction. Add in the prominence of Gannett Hoover—and the ex-con who'd been paroled in Ohio and turned up in California with a different name—and the FBI was their best bet for law enforcement.

But that didn't mean getting their approval or their help would be easy—or timely.

His mother let out a long breath. "I… I don't know if this will help to know, Ellery, but this particular case is a special sort of awful. I know you and Jackson have dealt with some bad guys—the Dirty/Pretty killer brought you together, for sweet heaven's sakes. But this…. There is a heartbreaking sort of evil here, the kind that preys on children, that seeks to break all the bones in their soul and rebuild them, like how in some cultures, women were required to bind their feet, starting at a very young age. This is the same thing, but worse somehow. They're requiring young people to bind their identities." She took another breath. "All I can tell you is that this started when you and Jackson wouldn't stand by and just let things happen when your friend got hurt. And when you discovered he was collateral damage in a larger war, you didn't just hunt down your one soldier. From what I can see, Jackson had a chance to bring in Henry's assailant, and he didn't. You never questioned him on it either."

"We needed to see where the kids were being kept, like Cowboy said, and we needed to see if Caleb was really dead, and if he was the only one, and—"

"And you needed to stand for people whom nobody knew about, because they had nobody else to stand for them," she said with a small, pained smile. "Is it any wonder I want to work in your office, son? That I love throwing myself so much into your battles? I am a *very* good lawyer, Ellery. I have done some things I am *very* proud of. But you and Jackson, working in concert, are a true and mighty force, and yes. I will stick my unwanted mother-in-law nose into anything you'll let me so I can be a part of it, because I have done things working with the two of you that feel almost magical. Don't be nervous, Ellery. You walk in there and own the room, because the state's attorney general and the FBI are here to protect the public, and your tiny law firm has been doing their goddamned job for them. It's time they pony up."

Ellery felt his spine stiffen and his chin lift as his mother spoke, and just in time because parking was full in front of the DOJ and he had to negotiate the parking by the levy. First, though, he dropped his mother off so she could start the meeting on time if he couldn't find any, and as she stepped out of the vehicle, he leaned over so she could hear him.

"Mother?"

"Yes, dear?"

"I love you dearly, which you know. But you should also know that Jackson adores you and is secretly grateful for every moment you spend embroiled in our cases."

She thew her head back and laughed as she was slamming the door behind her.

He was in no way discouraged—it had needed to be said.

Parking really *was* a bear midday, and Ellery hustled up in time to be ushered into the AG's office along with his mother, and he tried to control his breathing.

"You're barely out of breath," his mother remarked.

"I have to run in the morning with Jackson," he reminded her, keeping his voice low. "Keeps us both in shape."

"Mm." And then, as though flipping a switch, his mother's head tilt, her smile, the way she held her shoulders, even the way she wielded her briefcase, all of it assumed the fearsome edges of a shark's tooth, a steely sharpness that drew the attention of every eye in the room.

The AG—a tall sixtyish woman wearing a wide-legged gray pinstriped pantsuit, with her gray hair pulled back into a smooth twist—swung toward them from her desk, her hand extended.

"Taylor Cramer!" she said, delight oozing from her very pores. "I have heard *so* much about you, but I never thought I'd have the pleasure."

"Maudie Arthur," Ellery's mother said, her tone set on "polite enthusiasm." "I'm so glad our paths have finally crossed. I've heard quite a bit about you as well."

Ellery kept his own polite smile on his face, but while he didn't speak "female catfight" that well, he had a feeling his mother and Maudie Arthur were in the process of exposing their claws and inspecting each point for sharpness.

"And is this your son?" Ooh…. Ellery heard it then. The hint of condescension, as though Ellery was a third grader at "take your child to work" day.

"Ellery Cramer," he said, sticking out his hand with the assumption she would shake it. "Of Cramer, Rivers, and Henderson. It's a pleasure."

She shook his hand, her own cold and bony, and regarded him with some sharpness. "Oh," she said, as though just putting two things together. "I *have* heard of you. The Dirty/Pretty killer? That Russian mob thing this summer? And, wait…." She gnawed her lower lip. "The city DA who had to resign last fall, and the sniper at the college. It seems as though your law firm had a hand in all those situations, didn't it?"

"We try to stay busy," he said blandly.

"You try to stick your fingers into everybody's pie," she said, sounding sharp, and his chin went up in defense.

"I've been taught not to let injustice slide by because fixing it gets my hands dirty," he said. "That Russian mob thing, by the way, restored a busload of trafficked children to their parents—"

"And put you and Jackson in the hospital," his mother added.

"You are fucking welcome." Ellery smiled with all his teeth, his irritation at the woman making his hackles rise.

Nobody was more surprised than he was when she actually took a step back.

"No disrespect intended," she said, blinking slowly. "Who's Jackson?"

Ellery couldn't explain it. It was like being a bird of prey and ruffling his feathers—or being a dragon and puffing up his mantle, ready for the attack. What he *wanted* to scream was, "Keep his name out of your whore mouth!" and he was grateful for his mother when she spoke instead.

"The PI at his firm."

Ellery didn't dart his eyes to meet hers. The fact that she hadn't said, "My son's fiancé," with full parental pride, told him that this woman had set her hackles in place as well.

"Well, my goodness—I hope you're giving him hazard pay."

"He's very dedicated," Ellery said blithely, "and it's been lovely to take a trip down memory lane, but we have some rather urgent business today. I'm sure you've been briefed?"

"Your mother has given me a bare-bones explanation of why you're interested in Gannett Hoover's property, but I fail to see the urgency of the request. Why can't you wait one more day—or even a week—before you search his property?"

Ellery *needed* a yoga breath, but he didn't have time, and he definitely couldn't appear weak in front of this woman.

"My mother explained to you the links between the Moms for Clean Living and Gannett Hoover's advisor, Newton Dwayne, who lives on Mr. Hoover's property, am I correct?" Ellery asked, trying to keep his pulse from roaring in his ears.

"Yes—I understand the director of the service group—"

"Hate group," Ellery said grimly. "Moms for Clean Living is in the process of being classified as an alt-right hate group." He reached into his briefcase and pulled out a folder. "Here are copies of documents with which they claimed they were taking custody of—and I quote here—'recalcitrant students' from parents, in order to 'school them in Christian methods.' And here," he pulled out the folder of faxed reports from the child advocates who had been placing children and intervening with parents and counting bruises and atrocities since eight o'clock the night before, "is a folder full of what was *actually* done to those children when they were supposed to be 'in school.'"

"These are all notarized," the state district attorney said numbly.

"They are," Ellery confirmed. "And they're horrible."

"But Gannett Hoover—"

"And here," Ellery said, pulling out the copies of the property that Jackson had copied the night before. "These are copies of the holdings controlled by Moms for Clean Living, Valerie Trainor, Newton Dwayne's ex-wife, as chief signatory on the first line."

"Which means—"

"And this holding, specifically," Ellery said, pulling out the specially annotated copy, littered with Post-it notes, most of which had big black arrows on them. "Which is the property Gannett Hoover lives in and calls 'his California ranch'—"

"In spite of the fact that he still owns a house in the Midwest," Ellery's mother added helpfully. For some reason, that had burned them both.

"So that's a problem for the election board—" Maude Arthur tried to interject.

"Be that as it may," Ellery said smoothly, "it establishes a direct connection between Valerie Trainor's criminal child abuse in Sacramento and the potential for the same sort of child abuse in Sonora. And here," he reached into his briefcase once again, and Maude Arthur was beginning to eye the battered leather receptacle with a great deal of dread, "is the list of children unaccounted for from the Moms for Clean Living so-called school." Fetzer and Hardison had come through in a big way. Apparently they'd put their entire squad room on a phone canvass, and he hoped this folder would be much smaller in a few hours. "We rescued nine last night—"

"Rescued?" she asked, seeming to pounce on the word.

"As they are quoted many times saying in the course of the advocate reports," Ellery replied, his voice hard. "So we rescued nine, we know of the whereabouts of two more, but I have a folder here with *over forty* names. Now, some of those kids may live on the streets—the child advocates are compiling a list—and some of them may have returned to their homes."

"We have people working right now on calling the parents' homes," Taylor Cramer said, and Ellery nodded, giving thanks for Jade, Crystal, and AJ, who compiled the contact numbers for the police to use. "But so far, there are at least eight children unaccounted for there."

"What makes you think that they might be in Sonora?" Maude Arthur asked, and it was clear she'd been caught in the web of logic, so Ellery hoped he could close his case.

"Besides the personnel overlap," Ellery said, "we have this." And with that, he pulled out his tablet, opened to the small news story about finding the bodies of three adolescent boys in an abandoned mine off Old Ward Road. "This is less than fifty yards from the property line of Gannett Hoover's residence. We have two men and a cadaver dog up in the hills at this moment, checking similar locations."

Maude Arthur's face swept bone white. "Bodies?" she said faintly.

"Yes, ma'am. We were hoping to go up to Hoover's place and gain entry, look around, and see if we can discover any places for another 'school' like the one in Sacramento." He paused. "Or worse."

She stared at him. "What could be worse?" she asked faintly.

Ellery had saved this last as the cherry on the shit sundae. "Gannett Hoover's chief advisor is his old pastor and choir teacher, formerly known as Conway Schmitt. Mr. Schmitt—Valerie Trainor's ex-husband—served five of fifteen years for sexually abusing his choirboys, of which Gannett Hoover was one. Given that the bodies found in the mineshaft were adolescent males—"

"Oh dear God."

It was not his imagination. Maude Arthur looked like she was going to throw up.

"Do you need a trash receptacle, Maudie?" his mother asked solicitously.

Arthur shook her head and took a hurried sip of water, and then another, seeming to get herself under control. "Yes," she said, her voice weak. "You need FBI backup—"

"We'd prefer it if they waited on the edge of the property," Ellery said quickly. "We'd rather obtain evidence and, you know, snoop around a little. My law partner is coming. We would like to question Gannett about the property and the holdings—my partner studied the deeds and seems to think the LLC apparatus that binds them is particularly unsavory. It appears very… money-launderingey to Mr. Henderson, and he'd like to take a look around."

Arthur nodded, not apparently listening, which was why Ellery wasn't stressing too much about making "money laundering" into an adjective.

"Of course," she murmured. "Whatever you need. Just…." She stared up at Ellery's mother with bleak eyes. "Taylor, you should know. These people—the Moms for Clean Living—donated heavily to my campaign. I will give you all the manpower you need, and all of the backup I can, but…." She glanced around the office, which was nicely appointed in cream and chrome, with wood accents and a plethora of houseplants dominating one sunlit wall.

She had made this place hers, Ellery realized, and for a moment, he felt remorse for what he and his mother had just done to her, without realizing they were firing a killing shot into her career.

"Yes," she said with a sigh. "But better to go down doing the right thing. I just might not be able to help you once this gets out and my constituents demand my head."

"We'll take whatever help you can give us," Ellery said, slightly less cold than he had been a moment ago. "But if you're going to call in a special agent in charge and put a unit together, I'm afraid it's got to be now. If our search party finds anything, they're going to need us there."

"Oh Lord," Maude Arthur whispered. "Yes." She gave a soft little sound of surrender. "Let's get this done."

SAC Gerald Manning was not happy about being given fifteen minutes to assemble a team—and even less excited to be told they were to "wait outside" the fences of the mansion's extensive grounds while Ellery, Taylor, and Galen went inside to question the congressman and his chief of staff.

"Why even call us?" Manning was a squat, muscular, *very bald* man in his fifties who wore his disgruntlement like a Halloween mask. It was possible this man had six kids and spent his weekends grilling by the pool, but Ellery didn't want to *ever* be invited to that pool party.

The thought made him miss Jackson, and he remembered the other thing he had to tell Manning that he wasn't going to like.

"We don't have a warrant yet," Maude Arthur said, her cell phone held to her ear. "I'm trying to get hold of a judge who will issue one, but it's going to take a lot of talking and a lot of presenting the case."

"So why go now?" Manning asked.

"Because we have reason to suspect there are young people in danger there," Maude Arthur told him bleakly. "And we have statements taken by licensed advocates that indicate the people at the estate are engaged in active child endangerment, if not actual harm." Her eyes slid to Ellery's mother's implacable face. "Don't say it, Taylor."

"I wasn't going to," Ellery's mother replied, but Ellery could hear a thousand position papers these two women must have been mentioned in about how damning rhetoric and demonization of vulnerable communities could result in real-life harm.

Ellery's mother believed firmly that hate speech caused irrecoverable damage, and the case they'd both laid out in front of State Attorney General Maude Arthur proved her right.

"Wait a minute…." Gerald Manning cocked his head. "Does this have anything to do with the teenagers who were rescued from that weird Karen-compound in the middle of the city?"

"Moms for Clean Living," Ellery said dryly. "Our paralegal has forbidden the use of the appellation 'Karen' in deference to the very *nice* women named Karen that she knows."

"Are you that afraid of your paralegal?" Manning asked, frowning at him.

"Yes," Ellery and his mother said in tandem.

Manning took a hasty step back, and Ellery tried to clarify. "She's my future sister-in-law."

Manning's eyebrows went up. "Oh," he said. "Then I fully understand. Is the bride working for the firm as well?"

"No," Ellery said, hating this conversation in this moment with so much else at stake, "but the other groom is. In fact, we need to get this show on the road *now*, because he and our other PI are currently chasing down leads with a cadaver dog on the federal property *right outside* of our target in Sonora."

Manning stared at him. "Who *are* you people?" he asked, and there went Ellery's last nerve.

"Us? We're the people who took down the Dirty/Pretty killer," he snapped. "And the guy who made him. We're the people who helped bring in a busload of children about to be trafficked by the Russian mob. We're the people who weeded out the choirboys, that group of corrupt police officers who tried to get an undercover agent to commit murder and then beat up a disabled man in a public park. We're the people who found kids being abused in the name of God and got them the fuck out of there, and *we're* the people who are perfectly willing to walk into the goddamned lion's den to help you get your hands on some real fucking psychopaths, but *nobody will get a goddamned move on!*"

Manning gaped at him, and so did Maude Arthur, and so did his mother.

For a moment, all Ellery could hear was the ringing in his ears.

"Is there anybody else you needed on this little jaunt?" Manning asked, seemingly out of the blue.

"My law partner and my sister-in-law," Ellery said grimly.

"Go arrange to have them meet us here," Manning replied. "You can have two SUV's in your entourage, and they will stop, as you requested, outside the grounds. We can equip you with listening devices so you'll never be without backup. And as soon as you get what you need—or Ms. Arthur here gets a go-ahead on a warrant—we'll get you out of there. Is that good enough?"

Ellery blinked. "Well, uhm, *yes*. Thank you. That's exactly what we needed. Thank you."

Manning shook his head in what looked like disbelief. "Am I really gonna meet the other guy who helped you take down the Dirty/Pretty Killer? Because my behavior analysis coordinator is going to think I'm a total badass."

"He's the guy out with the cadaver dog and its handler," Ellery said weakly. "If you've got something more fitting for tramping through the wilderness than that suit, you can help him yourself. We're meeting up before Mother and I go through the front door."

Manning—who had displayed an impressive poker face until now—perked up. "Really? Let me go alert my unit."

He left, and Ellery tried to control the whirling of the room—and recent events—as he pulled out his phone. He was about to tag Jade and tell her what was up when he caught his mother staring at him in fascination.

"What?" he asked grumpily. "Was that too ostentatious?"

"Not at all," she said, giving him a pleasant smile. "I've just never heard you list your resumé like that before. Between you and Jackson, you really *are* badasses."

Ellery snorted. "Leave the badassery to Jackson," he muttered. "I'll be waiting for my medal for lawyering to arrive in the mail for the rest of my life."

"I'll have one made for you as a wedding gift," she said with a straight face, and he gave her a sour look before hitting the Call button.

Jade picked up before the first ring had even finished, and they were on the move.

Fish in the Hole

"WHAT DO you mean you've been there for half an hour already?"

Ellery's voice took on that tinny timbre that often meant either a) he was panicking about Jackson a *lot*, or b) his own day had gone batshit insane and he was taking out his stress on Jackson because, well, Jackson usually deserved it.

In this case, Jackson surmised, it was probably both.

"I mean we made good time," Jackson downplayed, but he was scowling at Cody as he said it.

Cody grinned back unrepentantly and stroked the enormous head of Preacher, the dog who had been training far from Napa when he'd found the original three bodies, and who had returned by helicopter at Toby's request to work with Jackson and Cody. Preston, Preacher's handler, had seemed absolutely unflappable, but after watching him work with Preacher for a few minutes—and then interact with the helicopter pilot who had landed his craft in a big stretch of flatland near the picnic area and who also seemed to be Preston's significant other—Jackson surmised Preston was probably neurodivergent more than he was unflappable.

But while his affect remained unruffled, that did not mean Preston wasn't "flapped" at the idea that the bodies of three adolescent boys had been found nearby, and that they would be searching the two nearby mine caps to see if others had been dumped.

"Preacher prefers rescue work," Preston had said, the intensity of his voice sounding *angry*, although his expression remained neutral. "Nobody likes finding cadavers. It's *sad*, and just because he's a dog doesn't mean he won't get depressed."

Jackson had held his hand out to the dog to sniff, and Preston had all but growled at him. "He is *working*."

"Yes," said the helicopter pilot, who had the dark hair and brows and the fine facial sculpting of a native islander, probably Hawai'i. He walked with a slight limp but didn't seem self-conscious in the least. "Yes, Preston, he *is* working, but so are these two men. They need Preacher to trust them, which means *you* need to trust that Preacher needs to smell their hands in greeting."

Preston emitted a hurt sound, while Jackson and Cody—after a glance at each other to confirm that what was going down was what they thought was going down—both held their hands out for the dog to sniff. And—with a surreptitious glance at his handler—to lick, because Preacher seemed like that kind of dog.

"Kids, Damien," he said, sounding heartbroken. "And Preacher has to find more."

"I know, baby," Damien said softly. "C'mere."

Damien had engulfed Preston in a hard, soul-nurturing hug then, and Cody sighed a little.

"You want one of those?" Jackson asked with a smile.

Cody shrugged. "Need to find the right donor. I think that one's taken."

And that's when Jackson's pocket had buzzed. He'd walked a few feet away and huddled in his windbreaker to have the conversation, but that didn't mean Cody wasn't listening. Shamelessly.

"Good time?" Ellery asked in disbelief. "You only left two hours ago! What does 'good time' mean?"

Jackson grunted. "It means keep an eye out for my eyebrows and parts of my stomach when you hit Mokelumne Hill," he said honestly. "And I think I have a cramp in my shoulder from yanking on the Oh Shit bar."

"Praise Jesus," Cody said with a smile.

"Oh shit," Jackson replied reflexively, because who didn't like a good "fear for your life" joke?

"You and Cody appear to be getting along okay," Ellery said, sounding irritated.

"Jealous?"

"That you're in the field with a wildly handsome man who seems to think you're awesome? No. Not at all. Doesn't faze me a bit."

Cody's bark of laughter carried to the phone, and Ellery said, "Am I on speaker?"

"Yes, Ellery—the copter is still winding down, and it's windy *and* rainy here. You're on speaker. Sorry. Cody is laughing because he wouldn't shag me on a dare. Now I love you, but we're about to start heading for the first mine cap on our path here as we work around the property, and our dog handler is, well, un*happy* that we're looking for corpses and not rescuing kids, so we need to get this shitshow on the road. What can I do for you?"

Ellery grunted. "I'm about to let the FBI track your phone," he said, and Jackson fought the temptation to sit down in the middle of the mud and overgrown grass of the field and kick his heels.

"I fucking beg your fucking pardon?" Every instinct of hatred for organized law enforcement colored his voice, and he realized he was somewhat reassured. He'd been afraid he was getting… conventional or something.

"You heard me," Ellery replied, steel in his voice. "We're dropping off Gerald Manning and his partner, Laura Crowder, to come assist you on the search. We get three guys to sit out in front of the property surfing their phones unless they hear suspicious activity."

"Suspicious activity?" Jackson repeated, feeling dumb. "Like what?"

The insouciance in Ellery's voice, even over the speaker phone, was telling. "Loud words, disagreements, gunshots…."

"No," Jackson told him, angry they were even having this discussion. "Absolutely not—"

"Mother's here with me," Ellery said, all pleasantness. "Would you like to tell her the same?"

"It's not necessary—"

"What if there are kids in there, Jackson," Ellery said. "You knew this was the plan when you left the house this morning."

Jackson scrubbed at his face with his hand. "It was a stupid plan, and I should be beaten for even letting you think of it."

"Well, same. Manning can track your phone now."

"Can he clone it, Ellery?" Jackson asked. "Because…."

He didn't have to finish that thought to remind Ellery that their phones had the personal numbers of some people who didn't need to be found.

"No," Ellery said. "He gave me his word. I'm going to take it."

"That's *great*," Jackson snapped. "Oh, Jackson, what if your new partner *doesn't* kill you and wants to shag your ass, and by the way, I just met a strange man who may or may not *betray people we gave our word to*!" Oh God. So many people. They'd *promised*.

"Is this Jackson Rivers?" The new voice on the phone had him exchanging puzzled glances with Cody, who approached to listen with even less shame.

"And this is?" Jackson's feathers were on permanent ruffle.

"This is Gerald Manning, Special Agent in Charge. I'm leading the investigation into the missing minors and—"

Jackson hung up.

Cody stared at him in surprise as Jackson actively struggled not to chuck his phone across the vast muddy field.

"What was that for?"

The phone rang again, and Jackson punched the Answer key. "You're in charge of shit," he said. "Absolute jack shit. Do you understand me? Ellery, can you hear me? Take his phone and throw it out the window!"

"Apologies!" came the almost frantic answer. "I'm sorry, I phrased that wrong—"

"You sure as shit did. You absolutely do not have my permission to track my phone."

The voice—mature, assured, and obviously used to giving orders—softened. "All I want to do is be able to find you on the field so you don't have to return to the picnic area in the middle of your search. I'll sign whatever Mr. Cramer gives me to sign that guarantees your privacy in this matter."

"Make sure there's a work order for new phones included for everybody I know so they are *never* put in this position again," Jackson snarled.

"Yikes," Gerald Manning muttered. "Okay. Absolutely understood. I promise you, Mr. Rivers, all I am interested in is being able to find you in the field."

Jackson blew out a breath. "Fine. What's your ETA?"

"About two hours," Manning told him.

"Pansies," Cody muttered.

"Put Ellery on the phone." Jackson ordered, and Cody raised his eyebrows.

"Wow."

"Don't even start," Jackson told Cody, right before Ellery's voice came across.

"You almost made that nice man cry."

"Ellery...."

"Yes, yes, I know, Jackson. But... but think of it like this. Even if people we care about are compromised, do we know a single person who wouldn't think this is worth it?"

Jackson grunted. "No," he said after a minute. "I just hate—"

"I know you do, baby," Ellery soothed. "You hate to be in the position where people might be exposed. But...." Something in Ellery's voice shifted. "I don't know if it's occurred to you, but we're in the middle of a big one."

Jackson gave a somewhat fractured laugh. "Yeah, I know. Weird, right?"

"Very." Ellery's dry tone helped to ground Jackson a little. "So you understand. No meeting up at the picnic spot. Mother, Galen, Jade, and I are all going in, wired for sound, and the FBI is our backup. Your job is to look for more"—his voice dropped—"proof." He paused. Then quietly, he added, "Jackson, do you remember how Lacey went?"

Jackson's blood ran cold. He and Ellery had been crouched behind an aluminum-sided airplane hangar while Lacey had monologued about how the men he'd destroyed were too weak, that was it, that was the problem. They were so weak that the mind games and tortures he'd inflicted on them had twisted them beyond humanity, but with a little more work, he could do it, he *could* make the perfect soldier.

And that was when Ellery had taken the gun he'd only recently learned how to use and had blown a hole through the thin wall in an effort to shut that motherfucker up.

And Lacey had returned fire.

Jackson had killed Lacey to defend Ellery, who had been lying in a pool of his own blood.

"Yes," he said, feeling queasy and awful and scared with that one word.

"We're both smarter than that now," Ellery said. "I wouldn't lose my temper this time. I wouldn't take that shot. Do you understand?"

Jackson grunted. "Yes, I understand," he muttered, "and no, I won't take the motherfucking shot."

"Good," Ellery said. "June. Flowers. Sunshine. A fitted suit. Everybody who loves us. Remember the endgame, Detective."

"Will do, Counselor. What does Manning look like, by the way?"

"Five feet, eight inches, one ninety—"

"Hey!"

"I beg your pardon—one seventy, uhm…."

"Bald," Manning filled in dryly. "I'm very bald."

"G-man suit?" Jackson asked.

"Jeans, those boot things you wear when you're hiking a lot, and some sort of… insulated blue fleece vest over a maroon hoodie."

Some of Jackson's temper dissipated. "He doesn't sound completely stupid," he said bluntly. "Manning, ping me when you're on the ground."

"Will do."

Jackson signed off and turned toward Preston and Preacher. Preston was busy telling Preacher what a good boy he was and letting him sniff what looked like a hotdog. Preacher grinned, tongue lolling, and Damien, the pilot, approached with packs from the plane.

"You both can help carry water," he said, and while his voice rose politely, Jackson knew it wasn't really a question.

"Of course." Jackson had a canvas satchel hanging from his side with a soft-sided water bottle, trail mix, and beef jerky, and he'd equipped Cody with the same. He understood, though, that while he and Cody might be good with three liters of water apiece, the *dog* was doing most of the heavy lifting. He took the pack from Damien and started rearranging the contents, adding his own to the emergency foil blankets and thin wool pullovers that he found there, in addition to protein bars and another two liters of water. "Does the dog wear the sweaters?"

Damien grinned at him. "You laugh, but those are fine alpaca. If you layer those between a T-shirt and an outer layer, like fleece, they can help insulate your body in some pretty brutal temps. A sweater much like that saved my life a few years back. We put them in all the packs now when the weather's inclement. It's like a lucky charm."

Jackson nodded. "Can't argue with what works," he said. Then, soberly, "I know Toby didn't give you much time to do this. I appreciate your service and Preston's—and Preacher's."

Damien nodded. "My flight partner and I haul a lot of celebrities, so we can afford to help when it's needed. I'm just glad I was home today so I could be the one to fly Preston here." He gave the big blond man a sympathetic glance. "He and Preacher *really* hope they find somebody alive this time."

Jackson nodded. "I wouldn't argue. I checked out the map, although I don't know the terrain. Do we have time before the dog tires to check out the first dump site, or should we skip straight to the others."

"There's a rough path between them," Damien said, "and if I understand it right, somebody is going to try to find you out here in the field. It would be best if we stuck to the path to help your backup."

"Fair," Jackson said, mostly because he didn't want to drag this nice man into the backwash from the giant chip on his shoulder. He glanced around the area, seeing copses of trees growing in clusters, giant clumps of grass that were nearly waist high, and an uneven walking surface across the field that would only get worse when they hit the various clusters of trees. Then he studied the clouds, hovering pewter and angry over their heads.

"Think it's gonna rain?" he asked so he could know how bad this would suck.

"We brought ponchos," Damien said, probably meaning that was a yes.

"Think there's snakes out there?" Cody asked, and Jackson sent him a sharp glance because this was a new wrinkle.

"Count on it," Damien told him. "We let Preston and Preacher go first. Preacher hits off snakes—he'll be able to tell us we're coming up on one, and Preston wears steel-toed boots. We'll be fine."

Damien strode back to Preston for another one of those soul-affirming hugs, and Cody muttered, "Yeah, sure, we'll be fine. This is rattlesnake country, but it's *fine*."

More of Jackson's irritation slipped off his shoulders. He missed Henry—much like he was going to miss his eyebrows, which he was positive had been left back on Mokelumne Hill—but Cody had his own merits.

He settled his pack, turned his face to the gray drizzle, and closed his eyes for a moment. Time to push on through.

IT TOOK them less than an hour of tramping down the overgrown path, and while the threatened rain never really delivered, the whipping March winds were *not* fucking around. The hiking kept them warm, but every so often they would clear a copse of trees and the wind would hit and hit hard.

The second time he heard Cody gasp and swear, Jackson pulled a rust-colored knit hat from the pocket of his fleece and handed it over.

"How's your jacket equipped with a... is this crochet?" Cody demanded.

"Ellery's sister made it for me," Jackson said, a little surprised himself. "His family's big on Hanukkah gifts *and* Christmas gifts—it's weird. Anyway, Ellery gave me the jacket for Christmas, so I got the matching hat for Hanukkah—" He shook his head as they worked to keep up with Preston and Preacher while Damien took up the rear. "Whatever. It'll keep your ears warm."

Cody grunted—probably while he was putting on the hat—and Jackson concentrated on the dog. Preston hadn't given the command to search yet, but he'd assured Jackson that if there was something dead out there when they were simply hiking the woods, Preacher would definitely hit on it. He hit, Preston explained, by going down to his belly while staring at the direction the dead smell came from, and after Preston rewarded him, he would give the command to search, and Preacher would keep looking.

"I read somewhere," Jackson told him, "that dogs like this are often rewarded with playing and comfort objects. Not Preacher?"

Damien's snort of laughter was reassuring. "Most of Preston's other dogs use play as a reward," he said. "But Preacher's old-school. That dog don't get out of bed if there's not a hotdog in it for him."

Preston's mouth flattened, but not like he was mad at Damien. "Between hotdogs and Colonel, I almost doubted my calling for a *year*," he muttered before turning toward the first mine cap and soldiering on.

"Colonel?" Jackson asked Damien.

"The only dog that has ever flunked Preston's training," Damien said, keeping his voice down. "Although I'm pretty sure it's because he fell in love."

As they'd hiked, Damien had regaled them with the story of a German shepherd who had been *supposed* to hit on drugs, but who had somehow confused one of the other pilots in their private search and rescue and transport outfit with cocaine.

"Spencer was going to *kill* us because we kept asking him why he smelled like cocaine," Damien had chortled, "but it turned out, the dog was just *in love*."

Jackson and Cody had laughed at that, the good story making the trip go faster. Cody had started to talk about his tiny dog, Poppy, and how for such a little thing it was as loyal as they came, until Jackson had realized he was getting cold.

Now as the wind picked up even more, Jackson turned to Damien—obviously the communicator of the couple—and asked, "I got only a sketchy look at the map. How much farther—"

"Preacher, *scent!*" Preston called, and Jackson turned toward where the trees opened up.

It looked almost like a volcano with a cap of dried lava, except it was green and soft, about the size of a volleyball court, and Jackson noted some stakes driven in that probably made that a reality. The depression the mine cap left was only about six inches deep, and there were picnic tables and even a spigot up closer to the next copse of trees.

Jackson and Cody glanced around the small clearing for a moment, and then Jackson spotted the series of boulders off to the side.

"Is that it?" he asked.

Damien nodded soberly. "Yes. It's not a pit, really. At least not the part we know we can access *now*. The boulders hide a sort of… ramp. The ramp goes underground, and you can see that underneath the cap, there's still tunnels left by the mines." He shuddered. "Small places are *not* Preston's friends, but Preacher was hitting *so* hard." He didn't appear the tiniest bit sheepish when he said, "Man, we really hate to hear that dog cry."

"Well, he's a good dog," Cody said, as though that sealed the deal. "Good dogs get treats, not crying."

Damien grinned at him. "You are just too precious for this life, aren't you?"

Jackson grunted. "Do *not* say things like this around me," he ordered. "You have no idea what sort of grief you could open us up for. Cody, you and me gotta go check out that tiny enclosed space with the dog."

"If I whine a lot, can I get out of it?" Cody asked dubiously.

"No," Jackson told him, voice stern. "Because *you* have thumbs and *you* can hold a flashlight."

"*I* can get bit by a snake too," Cody muttered, "but I don't see that as a plus."

"That's 'cause it's not," Damien offered helpfully, and Jackson may have kept walking, but he made a mental note to buy that fellow smartass a beer.

"THIS IS bigger than I thought it would be," Cody said, and to his credit, the whining over the mine had eased up, and what was left as they aimed their beams over the roughhewn walls of the pit was pure professional curiosity. "Preston, where were the bodies originally found?"

"Here," Preston gestured, and as they progressed, first through a narrow passageway and then through a small chamber, he aimed his beam toward Preacher, who was circling a recently cleared area, complete with crime scene tape, sniffing unhappily.

With a final circle, he gave a dejected little flop, and Preston told him he was a good boy, he *had* found the dead things, but they'd just been taken. Then he gave Preacher a piece of hotdog.

Everybody had their price, Jackson figured, and hotdogs were at least honest.

Then, after Preacher took the rub to the ears and the hotdog, and a few minutes sniffing Damien's crotch (Damien bore it with good will— apparently he was used to being Preacher's reward for a job well done), Preston took a gander around the cave and issued the command again.

Jackson cocked his head, staring, and as Preacher began another odyssey of smells, Preston said, "They discovered some tunnels back behind this main compartment after our original find. We haven't been back here, and I thought we'd see if Preacher could find any other… interesting things."

Jackson and Cody exchanged glances, surprised, and—mindful of the uneven floor of the mine, which could pose a hazard for the most sure-footed hiker—they both turned their attention to the giant dog.

Preacher took the new command to seek like Cody had taken the challenge to get them to the search site "as fast as you can." Not only was the dog dedicated to his task, it gave him *great* joy. He began snuffling in corners, and then he stood in the middle of the main chamber and turned around three times, as though orienting himself like a compass.

Then, keeping his nose in the air, he trotted in the direction of the other passages.

"Sure," Cody said, his voice determined. "It's only claustrophobia and a lifetime of nightmares. Let's follow the dog!"

With that, they reshouldered their packs and soldiered on.

"So," Gerald Manning said carefully as Ellery piloted his Lexus down Sunrise Boulevard, leaving Rancho Cordova in their rearview. "What doesn't he want us to track?"

"None of your fucking business," said Ellery's mother from the back seat, and Ellery couldn't see Manning's expression, but he did catch the man's quick, terrified glance behind his shoulder.

"What she said," Ellery told him mildly.

He felt Manning's regard and didn't know what to do with it. When Manning had insisted that someone from his crew would catch up with Cody and Jackson in the field, Ellery had chosen Manning because he felt as though Manning, at least, could be trusted. But Manning had seemed to hold him and Jackson with a sort of curiosity that made Ellery itchy.

"My mother," Ellery said, prevaricating with all his considerable skill, "has *many* contacts in the DOJ for her job. Jackson and I have utilized a few of those, and we simply wish for them to remain anonymous, thank you. My mother's work is important enough that we don't want her friends to be bothered."

Manning appeared to be mollified, and Ellery thanked the God he only seemed to believe in when he and Jackson were in serious danger.

"You could have just said that," he muttered, sounding hurt.

"You could have backed the hell off," Ellery snapped, not caring about his feelings. "I get that we had to appeal to the state's attorney general to make this legitimate and to get help, but Jackson and I have been working this case for….” He faltered.

“This is two days, dear,” his mother said.

“My God,” Ellery muttered and then found his fury. “Our friend got hurt—got *shot*—and told everybody who would listen that the woman who shot him was wearing a Moms for Clean Living windbreaker. He described her to the police minutes after surgery, and we filled them in with what we knew. And yesterday? Jackson and Cody found imprisoned children by following the breadcrumbs. And in the meantime, while our friends in the department are pushing to investigate, do you know what they’re getting?”

He’d spoken to Andre Christie and Adele Fetzer that morning.

“Nothing?” Manning hazarded.

“Not a goddamned thing. They can’t even get an okay to make an inquiry, because Moms for Clean Living put a cross on their logo, and suddenly to mess with these ogres in twinsets is to put their immortal souls at risk. The departments’ hands are *tied*. Their *pensions* were threatened, and that sounds like a small thing to you, but if someone’s been on the streets for thirty-five years, having their retirement money threatened is like putting a gun to their head.” Adele Fetzer’s fury had been hard to miss. “And these are good cops, sir. The *best*. They would have gone AWOL and come here anyway, because everybody on our list—that phone list you’re all hopped up about getting your paws on, by the way—owes me or Jackson in some way, and they’ve got our backs. So suddenly you’re on board our little law-and-order train. In Jackson’s words, fucking bully for you. You’re here because cowards stood in the way of better soldiers, and there’s no changing that.”

Manning took a deep breath. “So you’re not going to give me a chance?” he asked.

“You’re in the vehicle,” Ellery told him. “And I’m heading for Jackson’s last known to drop you off. Consider it a chance.”

Gerald Manning made a surprising sound then—almost a chuckle. “Fair,” he said, as though surprised. “I’ll try not to let you down.”

“THIS IS insane,” Cody muttered, and Jackson had to agree with him.

“Did you guys have any idea how far these mines went?” Jackson asked. The tunnels were narrow, shored up often with giant square creosote-saturated support arches, and after a good half hour, Jackson was starting to feel a little bit of the claustrophobia Cody had been valiantly trying not to complain about.

That last corner had shown nothing but more zig-zags ahead, and Jackson had suddenly thought of the hospital. It had taken him a few yoga breaths to figure out why, and then it had hit him.

After so many years—and so much time spent—in the places, being in the hospital always felt like an *accretion* rested on his chest. A gathering of years, of heartbeats, of breaths, of the concrete and rebar that made up the structure itself—all of that rested on Jackson's diaphragm and his shoulders and his throat.

Here in the mines, with their exit so far behind them, he was feeling that *accretion* again. How many supports, how many feet of earth, of rock or granite, of trees and their roots gathered between him and his first deep breath in an hour?

And just like he'd done when he'd gone in to visit Henry and to talk to Toe-Tag, he breathed through it.

"You know," Cody said, and Jackson didn't mind him talking because Cody's idle—and frequently amusing—chatter distracted him from his increasing *accretion*. "I keep thinking this dog is either batshit insane or absolutely amazing. Your verdict?"

Jackson grunted. "Has it occurred to you that if the dog is absolutely amazing, there's a dead body at the end of this maze?"

"Oh Jesus. You can be a real fucking asshole sometimes, you know that?"

Jackson felt some of the accretion dissipate from his chest. "I do my best," he said.

Ahead of them, he sensed two things.

One was fresh air—but that was a light, almost over-scent to the miasma of… not of decay, not yet, but of active infection. The sickly sweet, gangrenous smell of flesh that was rotting while it still had a blood supply.

Almost imperceptibly, the ambient light of their tunnel went up one or two shades of gray, and in the chamber around the corner, which Preston, Preacher, and Damien had disappeared into, Preston's voice same sharply, "Preacher, *sitzen.*"

And Jackson heard a raspy female moan.

"YOU SURE you've got them?" Ellery asked, and Manning pointed to the tracking app on his phone.

"I promise you, Cramer, I'll find them. Now are *you* set?"

Ellery's Lexus, Galen's Town Car, and two FBI SUVs all gathered in the parking lot of the picnic area near the abandoned mines, and if it wasn't for the refurbished Bell 407 that sat in the biggest part of the lot, they'd look like overkill. Right now Ellery was adjusting the fit of his suit jacket, trying hard not to pat his pocket square.

He was wearing a bug in that little pocket, and apparently patting it made the FBI Agents in the SUV scream and cringe.

Galen was standing by the Town Car, getting the same pat down from *his* pet agent, and Manning was lacing up his boots and making sure he had enough water to hike.

He glanced up at Ellery with an expression of distaste on his face. "Must we take two vehicles in? I realize we were coming from two different parts of town to get here, but really, Ellery, ostentation has no place here."

Ellery nodded. "If Jade doesn't mind, she can drive the Town Car from here. We'll leave the Lexus in the parking lot. Jackson has keys."

Manning gave him a look. "You don't mind leaving the fancy car here?"

"In a parking lot dominated by a search-and-rescue helicopter?" Ellery asked him, surprised. "No. Besides…." He gave his vehicle's roof a fond pat. "This thing has survived some adventures. It'll be fine."

Manning grunted. "I don't know. That ratty minivan we parked next to has to belong to somebody. Are you sure you trust another vehicle here?"

Galen and Jade's eyes widened and Jade reached out and patted the minivan's back quarter panel fondly. "It's okay, girl, he didn't mean to hurt your feelings. Don't pop him in the head. We need him."

Manning stared at them. "Your entire firm is batshit insane," he said.

"Yes, we are," Ellery told him. "And we also need to get a move on. Arthur was able to get us an appointment with Gannett Hoover in half an hour. With any luck, you'll be caught up with Jackson by then, and you all can scope out the back entry onto the property to see if there are any other kids there or anything suspicious. The rest of us will take a look from the big house in the middle, and Jade will stay out with the car and do her own, uhm, assessment."

"Snooping," Jade said, a rather smug smile on her face. "You can be honest."

"I don't want to use that word with Hoover and Dwayne," Ellery said primly. "Remember, our entire strategy is that they won't notice you."

Jade smiled contentedly. "Because I am a Black woman," she said, tapping her temple. "Why you get paid the big bucks."

Ellery snorted and shook his head. "For the last time," he began, embarrassed in front of Manning.

"I don't want to be a lawyer because I couldn't do what you do," she finished, and he narrowed his eyes at her. Oh dear Lord, so much bullshit. Times like this, and he could see the family resemblance between Jade and Jackson and nobody could tell him different.

"Well, this time we can't do what you're going to do," he said. "But be careful. If they *do* notice you, they'll be more likely to shoot you, and Jackson would never forgive me."

"Neither would Henry," Galen intoned dryly. "Do stay safe."

Jade grinned up at Galen and patted his cheek. "Now from you, it sounds like you care."

"But… wait… I'm not saying—" Ellery sputtered, and then she patted *his* cheek and turned to the FBI agent still fussing over his pocket square.

"Are you about done?" she asked, and the young agent, dressed in the traditional black suit, held his hands up and backed off. "I thought so. Let's drop this dude off and motor."

And with that, Manning did one last check-in with the two follow cars before he and his partner lit out across the field toward the little flashing dot that represented Jackson on his phone, while Ellery and his mother gathered their briefcases and loaded into the Town Car, Ellery's mother in the front.

"Don't be nervous," Galen reassured next to him as Jade took the car smoothly through the rolls and turns that this part of the country seemed to require from its roadways.

"I'm not," Ellery retorted, trying not to think about why they hadn't heard from Jackson during the drop-off.

"Then don't be pissed off," Galen said.

"These fuckers shot Henry," Ellery told him, uncompromising. "I *am* pissed off."

Galen blinked. "Well, then, so I shall be too. Because you're right. These people aren't here to play."

"And neither are we," Ellery said. And something about that consensus seemed to drive all the nerves out of his belly.

As they turned into the next chamber, the reek of infection threatened to take Jackson and Cody out at the knees.

Then Preacher gave a happy little woof, and Preston praised him, and as Jackson and Cody entered the area—blessedly lighted from another path that appeared to creep up toward the surface—Damien said, "Guys, c'mere. He's not hitting on a cadaver."

And then they heard a small, faint moan.

Jackson's eyes, which had become accustomed to the dark and the artificial beams of their flashlights, were now adjusting to the half light filtering in from the rise upward, and he could make out two crumpled heaps in the corner of the chamber, almost obscured by some stubborn granite boulders which probably hadn't been shifted during the original mining.

Jackson sank next to the one that was moving, and he fought hard not to gag with the smell. As he pulled the mass of graying frizzy hair from the woman's face, he could see the green pus seeping from the wound on her arm, and that alone would have confirmed her identity.

Retty had indeed become the package—and odds weren't great that she'd make it out of here to be anything else.

"Retty?" Jackson murmured as Cody and Damien moved to the other body crumpled in the cave. Damien grunted in distaste, and Cody shook his head. Whoever it was—and from Jackson's angle he could still see a slight feminine form in slacks and a green cardigan. He had no idea who this was, but nobody deserved to be dumped in a cave to die.

Preston was telling Preacher what a great dog he was, and Jackson wanted to second that, but at the moment, he needed some answers.

"Retty?" he said again.

"Loretta Jane," she muttered. "Betty. My mom called me Betty."

"That's sweet," he said, because as awful as she'd been to the kids, he'd gotten the sense from the investigation that shit truly *had* rolled downhill. She thought that's how subordinates were treated because that's how *she* had been treated, probably her whole life.

"Melanie called me Retty," she said, almost dreamily. "When our folks got together. So I was Retty. Everybody called me Retty." She let out a little sigh. "Melanie said we were sisters."

"That's why you did what she asked," he said. "Isn't it, Retty?"

"Yeah," she sighed. "Melanie…? Mel? I'm sickly. My arm hurts like fire, and I'm so dizzy. Schmitty said I'd be put out of the way, but can I get out of the cave? I… I think Schmitty shot poor Ginny Hoover. I don't know why."

"Probably so she couldn't tell Valerie Trainor what happened to her sister," Cody said softly in Jackson's ear, and Jackson nodded. It looked as though Conway Schmitt had been trying to get rid of his ex-sister-in-law for once and for all. Loose ends? A recognizable person of interest? Whatever the reasoning, it was clear that everybody's favorite shitting hill had suddenly become very expendable.

It was also clear that there was a rift between Conway Schmitt and Valerie Trainor that only Schmitt was aware of.

Jackson took a deep breath and tried to factor in the implications of the two women, one dead and the other dying, in what was apparently being used as an alternate dump site after the other site had been found. Conway Schmitt and Gannett Hoover hadn't factored in Retty's death—or Ginny Hoover's for that matter. Cowboy's escape from Retty's clutches, Retty's shooting—and Henry's—had obviously mobilized law enforcement, and the escape of the "students" the night before must have Hoover and Schmitt and even Trainor on the run. Jackson couldn't even imagine the atmosphere in the house right now, particularly since Ellery's mother was well known to have DOJ ties. It occurred to Jackson that the state's AG should be the one asking the questions today, not Ellery. Perhaps Taylor Cramer would be invited along for the ride, but why? Why would Ellery and Galen and Jade be needed to—as Jackson put it—dangle his entire family in a basket off a cliff?

"The AG's connected to the same money people," Jackson muttered, remembering that. Well, shit. On the one hand, sending other representatives into the lion's den kept the investigation from being tainted with Super PAC money.

On the other hand….

Holy God. What were his people walking into?

"What do we do?" Damien asked.

Jackson unzipped his pack and pulled out a foil blanket, a bottle of water, and a couple of tablets of ibuprofen, pleased when his hands didn't shake. "Let's try to get this into her," he said softly, "and then cover her up. I take it you have a backboard and some first aid equipment in the copter?"

"Yeah," Damien said. "Preston can stay here and look after them if you want to continue your search. I get that you're searching for other people in danger, right?"

Jackson and Cody met eyes and nodded. "We are," Jackson murmured. "Although at some point, we're going to need to check out that third site and see if it's connected through any other tunnels. Finding Retty is enough to get a search warrant to this place, but something tells me that if they're ready to dispose of her now, they're not done housecleaning."

"Oh, I do not like the sound of that," Cody said, casting an unhappy glance over Jackson's shoulder at the two victims already found.

"Me neither," Jackson muttered. "Damien, is there any way you can land the copter closer? It took us forty-five minutes to get here. I know there was a field right before we hit the mine shaft—would that help get her to treatment faster?"

"On it," Damien said. "Although I wouldn't want to bring the copter too much closer or it might bring the mines down on everybody's head."

"And God, that would be bad," Cody muttered.

Damien nodded at him in appreciation. "Get her set up with what you got, let's leave Preston and Preacher with the girl, and you two take off. Don't worry about us. We're pros."

ELLERY AND Galen both "helped" Ellery's mother alight from the vehicle like the gentlemen they'd been born to be. For her part Taylor Cramer smiled charmingly, taking her son's arm as though they were on their way to visit a friend instead of a deadly enemy.

"How'd you convince the state's AG to let you do this again?" Galen asked as they crossed under the shade of the drive-up carport. Behind them, Jade circled the car around an honest to God fountain, planning to park on a paved section obviously saved for visitors.

The whole setup reeked of gross expenditure, ostentation, and privilege. It wasn't that Ellery hadn't been to houses that used more baroque architecture and building materials—it was that they'd been in an appropriate place. The white Grecian columns and white-painted doors of this particular mansion were coated in red dust—or even redder mud.

As they'd driven the long, winding cul-de-sac that wrapped around a small lake, there had been perhaps five other properties facing the lake itself, and those houses—just as large, Ellery suspected—had accommodated their surroundings. Some had been built lodge style with exposed and stained wood paneling, and some had been stuccoed—red, yellow, or orange—the stucco, Ellery was certain, helpful insulation for a climate that could be brutally hot in the summer, but also cold enough for a moderate amount of snow in the dark seasons.

Gannett Hoover was trying very hard to be a southern gentleman.

"My mother would faint from the vapors before she entered this monstrosity," Galen said, his Savannah accent dripping acidly into the damp air.

"At least it's green," Ellery said, feeling the inanity deeply. In the foothills of California, winter often hit not as buckets of snow—although this far up there was *some*—but as lots and lots of rain. Mudslides were known to close down aortic freeways for weeks. In rural, undeveloped areas, grasses and flowered weeds grew in great swaths. The mansion—surrounded by three outbuildings, one of which appeared to be a mother-in-law cottage far back in the rear of the grounds—only had a partially developed lawn. About halfway to the mother-in-law cottage, the mowed, manicured grass gave way to the thigh-high, hay-length clumps that prevailed out among the trees in the rest of the red-earthed county. Because of the recent rains, the weeds were pressed flat, almost forming little huts of grasses and the husks of plants that had died in the fall. The result was a sort of rank and entropic derision, as though the people who lived in this place no longer cared about appearances or bothered with the niceties, and Ellery suppressed a shiver of fear.

Two nights ago Henry had been shot through a wall guarding a teenaged boy. Last night, Jackson had stormed an enemy citadel and produced witnesses of widespread corruption.

It was late afternoon now, the shadows stretching long from the great oak trees and the chill in the air threatening a dark, dank night. What would happen when night fell again over this place where evil—even Ellery's mother had said it was evil—had settled in to fester?

Green—even in a land as plagued with drought as California—didn't seem as important here in this mud-spattered monument to greed and poor taste.

"Last minute sound check," Ellery said, speaking normally as though offering his mother an observation on the carport extension over the driveway. "If you can hear us, buzz our cell phones twice."

It was reassuring to feel the twitches in his pocket as Galen—leaning on his cane with one hand—reached out to employ the door knocker with the other.

Then Ellery felt another buzz in his pocket and frowned.

"Hold up a moment," he said and fished out his phone. "It's a text from Jackson."

Retty and another woman dumped in the second mine site. Something's going down. OMW!

Ellery forwarded that to his mother, Galen, and Gerald Manning, hitting the Send button right as the door opened.

JACKSON WAS running too hard, the pack jouncing on his back, to do the math. He knew that the mine cap was probably five kilometers from the back edge of the property, and as he and Cody had jogged up the ramp of packed earth from the mine chamber to the sunlight, they'd caught sight of ATV tracks in the mud at the entrance to the mine.

The tracks went off in the direction of the Gannett Hoover property, forming a path that looked as though the vehicles had been out in this area a *lot* over a prolonged period. On the one hand, it made it easier to traverse, and Jackson felt as though they were making good time, but on the other?

It meant that somebody—probably the two henchmen who had come to fetch Retty—had been hacking a trail to the mine caps as quickly as possible. Jackson didn't want to know what was at the third mine cap, but he was reasonably sure it wasn't a moving body at a body dump.

All he knew—all he *really* knew—was that Ellery, Jade, Lucy Satan, and Galen were all walking into a hornet's nest that was *already buzzing*.

"Know what," Cody panted next to him, "I been thinkin'?"

"Tell me," Jackson said, and that whole physical fitness thing he'd been doing since his heart attack the year before seemed to be paying off in a big way today because he wasn't even winded.

"How freaked out do you have to be to dump a body that ain't a body yet."

Jackson grunted. "Same. What the hell is going on in that house?"

At that moment, they heard the rumble of a two-stroke engine, with an excited cacophony of muted voices. The path they were jogging down wove itself through wooded areas and around a particularly winding slough, and as the sound of the engine—probably a motorbike or ATV—grew closer, Jackson nodded toward a stand of trees on the other side of the path itself. He and Cody made for the trees, finding shelter behind one of the copious granite boulders scattered around the area like marbles and was currently being split in two by an old and mighty oak.

They crouched behind the boulder, peering around the tree itself to see where the noise came from, as the sound of the engine—*engines*—drew nearer.

"Wow," Cody muttered, squinting up at the tree that was literally cracking the boulder in two.

"What?" Jackson asked. While they were still, he fished water out of his pack and shared a bottle with Cody.

"See here? This is why I never bottom."

Jackson stared at him, then stared at the tree in the rock and then stared at him again. "Who, pray tell, is the oak tree?"

Cody snorted. "They *all* are. I don't know who started the myth that a man has to have a twelve-inch cock to scare the shit out of someone, but I'm saying, at this point butt plugs make me clench up."

Jackson swallowed, feeling his ears flush for reasons that had nothing to do with running through the backcountry. "You know, I now know things about you I never ever wanted to."

"Yeah. I should have had a gay friend a long time before this, you think?"

"I'm bi," Jackson muttered, disgruntled. "That I fell in love with a man is Ellery's bad luck."

"Fair. I'm just saying. I've only had a couple of men friends before now, and I have questions. So many questions."

Jackson fought the urge to laugh, and he peered over the boulder, barely making out two ATVs struggling along the path through the trees.

"When this is over, I'll hook you up with Henry—he mentors a bunch of porn kids who may not know their belly buttons from a lint trap, but what they know about sex will blow your hair out your ass."

Cody nodded sagely, as though that was the only fair solution. "I would be *very* grateful," he said earnestly, and then Jackson was shushing him as the ATVs finally jounced into sight.

The one in front was piloted by one of the two men who had come in to grab Retty from the rehab facility, and Jackson would guess that his thinner buddy with the long stringy hair was driving the one hauling the trailer.

The trailer hauling three frightened kids wearing the same pink pajama things as the kids Jackson and Cody had rescued the night before.

"Well, shit," Cody said, dropping his pack.

Jackson's was already on the ground, and he scanned the earth under the tree, looking for… for….

He grabbed a hefty tree branch, blown off by the wind, while Cody picked up a fist-sized rock.

"I'll take the guy in front," Jackson said, and they both clambered to the top of the boulder, one on either side of the tree.

Cody stayed on his perch, cocking his arm back like a pitcher on the mound, and Jackson slithered to the ground, thinking unhappily about road rash on his ass as his jeans shredded.

Oh well.

They'd planned their entrance almost perfectly so he was arriving in the first driver's blindside. Jackson braced his giant tree branch like a baseball bat and shouted, "Play ball!" as he swung, and the ATV growled under the arc of his weapon.

He heard a satisfying "*Oolf*!" and the sickening thump of the tree branch probably cracking open a couple of ribs as the ATV pilot sailed off the machine and landed flat on his back slightly to the side of the path of the other ATV, his arms extended, stunned but still breathing.

And then, even over the engine noise of the two machines, one of them still coasting in idle after its driver had been dumped, Jackson heard the kind of *thunk* a watermelon makes when it hits pavement.

Neither of the drivers were wearing helmets, and Jackson grimaced as the second driver's head snapped sideways and he slid off his ATV and directly under the wheels of the attached trailer.

He was still out of it when Jackson and Cody ran to the ATVs, put them each in Park, and then turned toward the teenagers, bound and furious on the back.

But not gagged.

"Who are you?" one of them—a rail thin, tall, and sturdy boy—asked as Jackson pulled his Leatherman tool from his pocket and went to work on the zip ties holding his hands together behind him.

"Random cowboy, hoping to give help," Jackson told him. "Were you guys staying at the mansion up the way?" They'd gotten close enough to see the roof, peeking over a long rise of hill in front of them.

"Mr. Hoover and Mr. Dwayne," the boy said, shuddering, and one of the other two boys began to cry—small heartbreaking sobs that twisted Jackson's heart. They were all male, reinforcing Jackson's sick supposition of why some of the kids had been transferred up to Sonora instead of staying in Sacramento, and they all looked shell-shocked and angry.

"Shit," Cody muttered. "Jackson, we gotta get to the mansion. Can you feel it?" Cody rubbed his stomach, and Jackson had no choice but to nod. First Retty and Gannett Hoover's wife and now these three kids. They were cleaning house, fast and furiously, and *Ellery was walking into that house*!

"I got an idea," Jackson told him, and he pulled out his phone, wondering at the miracle that gave him a strong signal in the middle of South PigBlanket, USA.

"Manning," came the voice of a man who was *not* used to hauling ass through the underbrush.

"You almost at the first site?" Jackson asked.

"Drawing close now," the man confirmed. "Are you here?"

Jackson gave him directions to travel into the cave and through the tunnels. "The dog handler will be staying with two women, one of them still alive, while the chopper pilot tries to land closer. I'd tell you to stay and help them, but we've got a problem about three miles east of the dump site, and you, sir, are our solution."

With that he gave Manning absolute orders to keep heading out, and to follow the ATV path until he found the trailer full of young people eating protein bars and drinking a good portion of Jackson and Cody's water.

"There's two assholes with broken ribs and concussions that will be tied up with zip ties nearby," Jackson told him. "I'm giving the kids sticks and rocks to use to beat the fuck out of them if they try to get away, so you need to get over here before your suspects are beaten to death by sticks and rocks. You understand me?"

"You're *leaving* them there?" Manning gasped.

"*My people are walking into a meat grinder*!" Jackson yelled. "They are *cleaning house*, and if the cleaners are there, your FBI guys aren't going to have enough time to get there. Now shut up and run faster!"

With that he hung up and went to help Cody bind and gag the two injured men, ignoring their groans of pain as they double-bound their wrists and ankles in zip ties.

Then Cody surprised him by pulling out two lengths of paracord from his own pack and helping Jackson bind their feet to their wrists—and then wrapping a length of P cord around their throats and making the hogtie complete.

"Only hit them if they escape," Jackson told the kids.

The boys, busy gulping down fresh water and huddling under some more of those foil blankets, all nodded.

"You swear," one of them whispered. "You swear help is coming? 'Cause… 'cause we all screamed. In that house. We screamed and screamed and help never came."

Jackson squatted, putting himself near to the boy. This one was young—not twelve yet—and small, and Jackson's stomach lurched at what the kid must have been through. "I've got family in that house now," he said softly. "You're out. You're safe. We've got help coming. I need to go help my family so they don't have to scream like you did. Is that okay?"

And the hell of it was, he meant that. God, he was leaving these kids in the woods and—

"Go," said the oldest. "I'll take care of them." He gave an unpleasant grin, one hand wrapped around the rock Cody had used to incapacitate one of the captors. "I sort of hope they break their zip ties."

"I do not," Jackson told him. "But there is help on the way." He glanced at all three kids, and Cody held out his pack for the older boy. "Stay safe. Hide behind our rock if you want. It's dry there because the tree kept the water off."

"No worries," said the oldest kid, turning his face toward the sky. "A little rain won't hurt a thing."

Jackson and Cody took off then, free of their packs and much lighter now.

Particularly since Jackson and Cody had both unzipped their weapons from the compact nylon-and-foam carry cases, and holstered them in the pancake holsters they'd worn just in case.

Jackson hated guns—had always hated them, even when he'd been on the force. But the chafe of the holster in the small of his back was a great comfort to him as the two of them made *spectacular* time sprinting through the wet grass and the mud.

ELLERY GLANCED around the foyer as they entered, unaccountably disturbed by what he saw.

He understood what the setup was supposed to be. A grand entrance hall, with two staircases rising up on either side to take the family into the private parts of the house. Underneath the first landing, where the staircases met, was a grand door leading to a receiving room, and behind that there was probably a kitchen and a dining room. He figured the receiving room might be adjacent to a ballroom used for parties, but while he'd always come from money—and had gone to a few parties in his time—he had no head for the peacocking architecture of the disgustingly rich.

What worried him was the stripped-down furnishings of a house that was being very quickly disassembled, its most expensive items packed away first.

There were two niches on either side of the grand french doors leading to the receiving room, which were bare, although small silk area rugs, each one bearing the four-point imprint of what had probably been a pricey antique display stand, remained.

It was a small detail—but it was a telling one. The house was being stripped, and judging by the hastily rolled rugs—all of which bore the mark of a fine silk/wool blend on the back—stacked against the far wall of the foyer, it was being done in a hurry.

Almost as though the residents had maybe a day's warning to clean house and get the hell away.

Ellery, Galen, and Taylor all exchanged uneasy glances.

"Perhaps," Galen said, his drawl as unhurried as it always had been, "we are disturbing the people of this house at an inopportune time."

Ellery's mother turned toward the man who had opened the door for them. Thin and nervous looking in real life, Gannett Hoover bore himself like somebody who was used to making his soul disappear. Although he was dressed in a men's catalogue of leisure clothes befitting a wealthy man in his "rustic country residence"—khaki slacks, loafers, and a cashmere zip-up sweater in an odd color between mauve and granite—Hoover, who should have been a lean, confident man with a politician's polish, appeared harried and, well, almost *gray*.

"I'm sorry, Congressman Hoover," she said, "I know you had some warning we were coming. We weren't told you were in the process of moving."

The smile Hoover gave them was a ghastly pulling back of thin lips to expose white teeth.

"Not at all," he said faintly. "We're just…." The corners of his mouth twitched up like a muscle spasm. "Cleaning. Spring cleaning. The living room is, uhm, relatively undisturbed."

From the corner of his eye, he could see Galen shaking his head while trying to appear unalarmed.

Ellery was not that good of an actor.

"Sir," he said bluntly, "are you well?"

Another one of those terrible smiles. "I'm fine. Fine. My, uhm… wife, she's not well. She's usually so good at uhm…." His face fell. "Greeting people. So good. I shall miss her today!" His voice cracked on the last word, and Ellery suddenly knew who one of the women in the bottom of the mineshaft had been.

And that made up his mind. "You know," he said decisively, "I think we'll go. We can come back tomorrow." He spun on his heel and was pulled up short by a squat man, dressed impeccably in a suit, who might have been handsome a lifetime ago.

His once-blond hair was now a translucent stubble, and his sweet, disarmingly round face had gone jowly and hard in prison, but Ellery still recognized Newton Dwayne, aka Conway Schmitt.

"I think you should stay," the man said, and his voice was absolutely transcendent, a lovely baritone, mellifluous and kind.

The voice of a murderous choir director, and it gave Ellery the shivers.

"Why is that, Mr. Dwayne?" Taylor asked sharply. "We're here to discuss some of your current business dealings, and you are obviously in disarray. We do realize we're here at the attorney general's request, but I'm sure if she'd known there was illness in the house she could have—"

Dwayne made a short slicing motion with his hand in an attempt to cut Ellery's mother off, but he didn't really know who he was dealing with.

"We are not your enemy, Mr. Dwayne," she said, her voice reasonable. "We are merely here to—"

And that's when he pulled out the gun.

"I knew it," Galen muttered. "Fucking cowards all."

Dwayne closed in, grabbed Galen's arm with what must have been a cruel grip, and Ellery was about to cry out when Galen swung with his cane, first smacking Dwayne in the shin and then, with a truly prodigious swing as the man was crouched down assessing the damage, he landed a solid blow on his back. Dwayne went down with a grunt, and Ellery's mother caught at Ellery's hand and dragged him and a stumbling Galen through the doorway to the receiving room, slamming the door shut behind them as Dwayne scrambled to his feet.

"Hide," she gasped. "Quickly. He's got no choice but to shoot us, particularly if the FBI storms the place."

She tapped the bug that had been put under a tacky flower on her tweed Chanel jacket. "Hello," she muttered. "Are you people there at all?"

Ellery had a sick feeling in his stomach, and he pulled out his phone. Unlike the reception under the carport, which had been stunning, stellar, the Wi-Fi among the gods, their bars had gone down to zero once they'd crossed the threshold,

"Blocker," he muttered. "Or a dead router. Or he killed all Wi-Fi in the house. Whatever was powering our bugs is dead."

They heard shouting in the foyer, and Taylor gave them both grim looks. To Ellery's right was a small staircase, probably a servant's passage, leading up and away toward the back.

"You go there," Ellery pointed, because it was small and immediately hid anybody going up from view.

"What about you?"

Ellery gave Galen a speaking glance, and Galen grunted. "I'll take the closet. Ellery, follow your mother."

"I'll take under the desk," he said. "Everybody *go!*"

Normally, hiding under a desk would be a really bad idea—but in this case, Ellery thought he could swing it. A truly massive antique, a mix of ebony and cherrywood, the desk sat back in the corner by the staircase. If somebody went up the staircase in pursuit of Ellery's mother, Ellery could tackle him, and if they saw him huddling underneath, Ellery was certain his mother would be on the assailant's back like a vicious killer primate out for blood.

And hiding underneath it was like scooting back into a deep, dank cave.

One that stank of sweat and wet metal and semen, Ellery discovered with a roil of his stomach. Oh God. He eyed the stained leather cushion of the rolling chair in front of him and spotted suspicious crusty blotches.

The antique carpet under his hands was as rank as a movie theater, and he wanted to vomit.

Whatever had been going on here—*whoever* had been going down here—this ostentatiously tacky mansion was being treated like a brothel, and the man in power didn't appear as though he was in charge of a damned thing. The *real* power was the man with the gun.

The sudden splintering of wood toward the french doors was the only indication Ellery had that his mother must have locked the things behind them as he and Galen had scoped the room. Clever woman, his mother, and absolutely bloodless in a crisis, but Ellery didn't want her anywhere near the damned gun.

"Where'd they go?" The voice was smooth, cultured—Newton Dwayne, the choir director, whose face no longer matched his cherubic mask from before his stint in prison.

"I have no idea." Gannett Hoover sounded… well, out of it. Shocky. As though he couldn't have recognized the people they were pursuing even if they'd been in the same damned room. "Maybe they went out the rear, toward the ballroom."

"I'll check there," Dwayne muttered. "If you see any of those people, *use this!*"

"Why?" Hoover mewled. "Why should we shoot them? They could have come in, asked their questions, and left, and we could have *fled*. Why would you even pull out your gun?"

"*Because they knew*!" Dwayne growled. "All those kids escaped last night—how long do you think it would be before they connected us, huh? How long before every domestic in this whole hornet's nest blabbed?"

"But my wife…," Hoover breathed. "She wasn't a threat. She… she…."

There was a rustle, and Ellery had the impression that the men had shifted position. He could picture the shorter, squatter Dwayne grabbing Gannett Hoover by the fine cashmere sweater. "You may be a sniveling pile of shit, Gansy, but don't you ever forget who you belong to. That screaming cow was going to take you from me, and that was *never* going to happen. She was just as much deadweight as fuckin' Retty, and Mel should have gotten rid of *that* dumb cow back in college. So yeah, I shot your wife, but it's not like you were fuckin' her, Gansy. Face it—your teeny weenie can't get it up unless I'm balls-deep in your ass."

"I hate you," Hoover breathed. "I loved her. She was kind. But I hate you. You… you turned me into this *thing*, and I kept getting you kids to feed you because I was just… oh God… you're going to fuck me for the rest of my life, aren't you?"

Dwayne's next words chilled Ellery to the pit of his groin. "If. You're. Lucky. Now *stay here*!"

There was the sound of pounding footsteps, and then, to Ellery's horror, a sort of meandering step, not to the couches, which Ellery had first assumed, but toward the desk.

Without peering into the dank cave where Ellery crouched, Gannett Hoover collapsed into the stained leather chair.

"I know you're somewhere in here," he said, loudly enough to carry. "Up the stairs, the closet—do you think you're the only ones who've ever needed to hide from him?"

Ellery breathed very lightly through his nose, and didn't twitch a muscle.

"I didn't send him out to find anybody," Hoover continued, in that same lost shocky voice, and Ellery heard the words again. *I loved her. She was kind. But you turned me into this* thing….

"Why *did* you send him away?"

Ellery thought he was going to die, because that was his *mother* talking to Gannett Hoover, and he had a *gun*!

"I wanted space," Hoover said softly to Ellery's mother. To Ellery's simultaneous relief and horror, Hoover turned the chair so he was facing the hidden staircase and scooted the chair a little as well. If he lay on his stomach—an appalling thought—Ellery could weasel out and be behind the man in the chair.

The man in the chair with the gun, facing his mother.

Reluctantly, Ellery got to his hands and knees and began inching his way out of the gap between the chair and the desk.

"Space to do what, young man?" Taylor Cramer asked softly. "Because it's not *me* you're pointing that gun toward."

Ellery froze, hoping he was reading her signals right. Oh. Oh no.

"I… my wife never knew," Hoover said apologetically. "But you people—you people know, don't you?"

"That your old choir director sexually abused you?" Taylor's voice was kind, Ellery thought in a panic. So kind to this man who had done so many terrible things.

To this man whose level of choice had been arrested, as he probably had, in the moment when his agency and innocence had been stripped away.

"I was a bad boy," Hoover whispered tearfully. "And… she was so sweet. She… she didn't like Schmitty, but she kept saying he could stay at our house. That's what good Christian women did, right? Offer a place for the disenfranchised. And he kept… he kept…."

"And you were like a little boy," she said. "You felt like you couldn't say no."

"I couldn't!" There was a sob, and Hoover muttered, "Oh God. Oh God…."

"Son, I wish you wouldn't do that with the gun," Taylor said, and Ellery's stomach lurched. He'd paused, because his mother had sounded like she had it under control, but at the throbbing note in her voice, he started to creep out from under the desk again.

"And then he came up with a scam—that's what he called it. A scam. That I should run for office. He said it was the greatest grift of all time. We had a president who did the same thing, right? And I couldn't say no, and he… he sold Bibles and gold watches that never came, and I cashed in my retirement, and we came out here, and I ran for office and… and it just got… big. And his wife started sending kids here…. I… God help me, I needed some *fucking space*."

"So you gave the victimized children to your abuser," Taylor said, and while her voice remained neutral, Ellery could tell she was having problems not saying something awful, not asking him what the hell he was thinking, or not demanding that he find a backbone.

Ellery's mother had always been one to show compassion but also demand accountability—but nobody wanted to see the inside of Gannett Hoover's brain pan. Just *hearing* it was awful enough.

"And it all got so much worse," Hoover whispered. "And this morning… this morning he had his… his *goons* hauling Retty out to the mines, and my wife…. Ginny finally saw. She came out and asked why they hadn't gotten Retty an ambulance, like she'd told them, and he… he shot her."

Hoover collapsed into tears then, obviously distraught, and from Ellery's angle on the floor, he was almost clocked by the gun as Hoover let his hands dangle by his sides.

Very gently, scooting so he was in no way in the line of fire, Ellery disengaged the gun from Gannett Hoover's hand, and still holding the thing—safety on, mindful of the many times Jackson had taken him to the gun range in their off-hours—he managed to scramble out from under the desk.

His mother let out a breath. "You know what you're doing with that, son?" she asked.

He nodded, adding, "It's *horrible* in there."

She grimaced. "I… I get the feeling this is a place of significance for him."

Hoover was still sobbing, head in his hands, and Ellery shuddered.

"There's just… there's no justice for a guy like this," he muttered. What? They put him in prison where he would continue to be everybody's meat? But he'd facilitated the trafficking of children, and odds were had predated on them himself. There was no penalty, no justice, that would make up for what he'd done, other than the hell he'd been condemned to when he was just a child and had apparently lived in ever since.

"We should move," his mother—ever practical—said, before they could start trying to change the world for the unforgivable sinners as well. "Do you hear anything out front?"

Ellery moved to the french doors, which had been shattered at the lock and frame, and peered cautiously into the foyer. "The FBI is completely absent," he muttered. "Whatever jammer they've got working apparently starts at the threshold and doesn't budge."

"What about—"

At that moment two things happened.

One was that Newton Dwayne crashed in through the doorway near the back of the room, wielding his gun. "Did you find them—Jesus, Gannett, get your shit together!"

And as Gannett Hoover's soft moan of total surrender sputtered across the room, Ellery heard the faint roar of ATV engines.

For better or worse, Ellery needed to make his position strong.

While Dwayne was still gesturing with the gun like a rank amateur, Ellery crouched behind the monstrosity of the desk and—after making sure his mother had ghosted up the stairs already—fired a little to the right of his target.

Dwayne whirled, aiming desperately, and Ellery realized that the light was on his side.

The far end of the room had two open doors into what was a wide, well-lit space, so that end of the room had natural light, but not enough to blind.

Ellery, on the other hand, was in a pit of darkness, his mother hidden by shadows up the staircase, he himself nearly invisible behind the computer and stacks of paperwork on the desk itself.

"Gannett, the *hell*—"

Gannett had slid out of the chair and was curled up in a corner of the room, his hands over his eyes. "Schmitty, don't…," he whimpered. "Please… no more…."

"Who's got the gun?" Dwayne demanded, and Ellery stayed low as Dwayne approached, caution in every movement. He wasn't great with guns, Ellery noted with detachment. He hadn't had lessons. He had no stance, no squared spine, no sturdy triangle between his arms and his chest. He held it up in one hand, his wrist shaking, as he scanned the room frantically for other hazards besides his unknown assailant crouched behind the desk.

And still the sound of ATVs got louder.

"I told those punks to shut off the engines," Dwayne muttered. "Gannett, get out here. Did you just shoot at me?"

"No no no no no no no…," Hoover was chanting, and upstairs, on what sounded like the second floor, Ellery heard the sound of shrieking and thumping, and his heart squeezed in his chest.

His *mom* was up there!

But he couldn't peek over his shoulder, the risk was too great, and he kept shifting his crouch as Dwayne swung wide, hugging the sides of the living room, his back now toward the great coat closet that was probably used for guests.

Ellery's vision sharpened, and he steadied his aim, ready to shoot at this horrible person and then defend that action in a court of law, when the closet door exploded open, and before Newton Dwayne could even squawk in surprise, Galen brought his cane down on the back of Dwayne's head.

The roaring of the ATVs grew louder, and there was a crash of glass from the ballroom as the things rumbled in like an exhaust-belching hurricane, and over the din, Ellery heard Jackson's voice—Jackson's?— shouting his name.

And in a spill of Chanel jackets, sensible pumps, pearls, and hose, *two* women tumbled down the stairs, landing in a heap at the bottom, in front of Gannett Hoover, who was still mewling like a kitten. Galen's assault of Dwayne with the cane came to an abrupt end as Dwayne grabbed it and upended Galen, who crashed to the ground with an angry snarl, and Taylor Cramer scrambled to straddle a woman who must have been Valerie Trainor from behind and, using the woman's knotted hair as a handle, slam her forehead into the hardwood floor on the edge of the stained carpet.

Repeatedly.

"Ellery!" Jackson cried, and as Ellery heard his feet thundering down the hallway and into the sitting room, he saw that Dwayne had turned toward this new assailant with his gun, however inexpertly held, aimed at the lighted end of the doorway.

"*Jackson, he's got a gun!*" Ellery screamed, and as Jackson burst through the same door Dwayne had charged through, another shot rang through the house, this one from Newton Dwayne's weapon.

"Ouch, *fuck!*" Jackson snarled, and his momentum through the house was derailed as his body wrenched sideways.

Oh fuck. He'd been hit! He was still running, but Newton Dwayne's entire attention was turned toward Jackson and Cody as he tried to fix his aim to take another shot.

Ellery was done with shooting.

With a rush at Dwayne's back, he used the heavy Berretta in his hand to clock Newton Dwayne on the back of the head, and their opponent went down in a bruised, concussed pile of debris.

"We're right here!" Ellery yelled, dodging the body as it crumpled. "Jackson, get your ass over here! *Somebody* needs to go fetch the *goddamned FBI!*"

Galen had regained his footing and was beating the shit out of Newton Dwayne with his cane again, and Jackson, probably following his voice, sprinted through the great sitting room to Ellery's side and took in the situation.

"Galen, stop," Jackson said automatically. "If you kill him, you might get disbarred."

"Fucker," Galen muttered, but he staggered a little, the move forcing him to put his weight on the cane, and Ellery figured he'd about exhausted his strength.

"Cody," Jackson called, "could you zip-tie that guy?"

"On it, boss!" Cody had followed Jackson into the great room, and Jackson—clutching a wound in his arm—turned his back on that situation, giving Ellery some faith that it was well in hand. He'd dropped his briefcase in the hallway as the situation had gone to hell, and now he turned to grab it, reaching for the first aid kit he'd started carrying since, well, he and Jackson had become a couple.

"Lucy!" Jackson snapped, and Ellery's mother put both her hands on her opponent's shoulders and shoved, although the woman was mostly groaning now. "Who in the fuck is that?"

"Valerie Trainor," Taylor said with a sniff. "She tried to hold a gun on me, and I introduced her to my briefcase."

Ellery sucked air in through his teeth. "The leather is steel reinforced," he said.

Jackson chuckled meanly. "So she's going to need some new cheekbones and a new set of teeth," he said. "Lucy, stand down. Cody—"

"I'll get there," Cody said.

Jackson had drawn near Ellery's side by this time, and gently—oh so gently—he tugged the gun from Ellery's grip and held it, safety on, down by his thigh. Ellery could see the trembling in his hand now, the clenched jaw he used to disguise the pain, but he could also see that the wound in his arm was superficial—a graze—and while they probably had to settle themselves in for some stitches and a fever—Jackson always ran a fever after an injury—Ellery felt an almost giddy sense of relief that he might be okay.

"Who's the guy sobbing in the corner?" Jackson asked.

"Gannett Hoover," Ellery told him. "He, uhm, told us that Dwayne killed his wife."

Jackson grunted and gestured with the gun, since his other arm was being held gingerly to his ribs. "I can vouch for that. Retty's still alive—she told us who was in the pit with her."

"Still alive?" Valerie Trainor muttered thickly. Cody was on her now with the zip ties, and with some help from Ellery's mother, Jackson's new partner pro tempore rolled the woman over to her side so they could talk. "Retty's not dead?" she asked, the hope in her voice pitiful.

"No, ma'am," Jackson said. "Although you all tried your best."

"Schmitty did it." She sobbed weakly, tears cutting through the grime and blood on her face. "Our whole lives together, that was my one request. He not hurt Loretta Jane."

There was a groan from "Schmitty's" place on the floor, and Ellery winced as Galen gave him one last thump with the cane.

"This sadistic asshole broke a promise?" Galen asked, his usually even tones dripping with fury. "I am fucking surprised."

"My daddy said I had one goddamned thing to do," Trainor continued, as though the rest of them weren't speaking. "I had to watch out for Loretta. And she tried so hard to help, but Schmitty said she'd fucked up, had ruined the entire goddamned operation. Nobody would notice a dead kid, he said, but when females start shooting up apartment buildings, somebody's going to sit up and pay attention."

Ellery's vision went red, and at that moment the FBI crashed in through the foyer *and* through the ballroom entrance, crying out, "FBI, put your weapons down and step away from the civilians."

Jackson cocked his head at Ellery and said, "Really? You thought we needed these bozos?"

Gerald Manning, who had come racing in from the ballroom—probably, Ellery realized dimly, because it faced the back of the property and led to the paths that went between the federal land and the mansion itself—lowered his weapon, and glared at his black-suited, sunglass-wearing compatriots.

"Really?" he said. "*Really?* How hard is it, you guys, to make me look cool?"

Jackson chuckled weakly. "Are those kids safe?" he asked.

"Yessir," Manning said soberly, holstering his weapon. "I left my partner there and called in reinforcements to come take the kids into custody, and the attorney general is getting hold of Mr. Cramer's child advocates as we speak. Your search-and-rescue people got the wounded woman in the air and are taking her to the nearest hospital, in handcuffs as you apparently suggested to them."

Jackson gave a hard nod. "Fair. Don't worry about these hosers. You're cool."

"Great!" Manning said, perking up and appearing absurdly young for a middle-aged man shaped like a bulldog. "Now could you, perhaps, enlighten me as to what in the *actual* fuck we burst in on here?"

Hoover was still sobbing, Melanie Schnarf/Valerie Trainor was crying quietly, and Conway Schmitt/Newton Dwayne was moaning and bleeding onto the carpet, which, outside of the cave under the desk, appeared to be pristine.

Ellery noted dimly that there wasn't a domestic assistant or housekeeper in sight.

"This," Jackson said with grim emphasis, "is what happens when pure evil meets vanity and weak minds and festers for twenty years."

"Very pretty," Ellery's mother said sharply. "While you're elaborating on that, Jackson, is there any way you could *stop bleeding*?"

Jackson grimaced. "Yes, ma'am," he said, and Ellery held up his briefcase, which was more easily rifled now that he'd set down the gun.

"I've got a first aid kit," he said. "If the Day-Late-and-a-Dollar-Short Surprise Posse could gather up the criminals, we can give you a brief history of bad-guys central."

Manning gave a nod, and the four agents—who apparently had been playing on their phones in their cars until they'd heard the gunshots—all holstered their weapons and began cuffing people.

"What are we arresting them for again?" Manning asked.

"Child abduction, child trafficking, child endangerment, rape, fraud, and—" Jackson took a shuddering breath. "—murder."

"Gotcha," Manning said. While his people worked and Jackson and Ellery began speaking, Taylor assisted Galen up and toward one of the sofas in the living room proper.

Ellery interrupted himself to say, "Mother, uhm, no. No. Galen, trust me. Come sit on the desk." He swallowed back bile. "Trust me on this one. If they blacklight this room for DNA, we don't want to be anywhere near it."

"Make sure they check the closet should they do so," Galen said acidly, the tautness of his voice indicating the pain he must be in after his spectacular assault of Newton Dwayne. Since they had to pass Dwayne's prone body as he was being cuffed, Galen paused to spit on the back of the man's head. "Fucker. Complete and total *fucker*."

"Amen," Jackson muttered. "Ouch—Ellery!"

Ellery scowled at him and dumped a considerable amount of anesthetic wound cleanser on the puffy crease of flesh in Jackson's arm. "Two shots fired in this entire room and you had to catch one in the arm. You weren't even *here* that long."

"Hey!" Jackson protested as Ellery used a gauze pad to clean as much blood and debris from the site as he could. "Cody and I took out *two* guys on ATVs, and I didn't get a scratch on me!"

"That's a lie," Cody said. "You got the same set of bruises I did from trussing those assholes." He laughed, low and dirty. "You secure those bozos, Manning?"

"I did," Manning said. "Unlike you people, I know how to use coms!"

"There's a jammer somewhere in the house," Ellery said testily. "The minute we crossed the threshold, our phones went dead, and your people got sent on vacation while Dwayne here lost his mind." He had to fight the compulsion to spit on the back of the man's head too. He would have to ask Galen if doing so had relieved any of the same rage Ellery felt seething in his belly right now.

"There's another woman upstairs," Taylor said, stepping back as the G-men assumed custody of her own victim… erm, suspect. "I'm afraid she's not conscious at the moment."

"Mother," Ellery said, a bit surprised, "what did you do?"

"I did nothing!" his mother protested. "She was like that when I found her. This one—" Taylor Cramer punctuated the words with a kick to the woman's ribs with her pump. "—was standing over her with the gun, which I assume she used like a paperweight." Taylor scowled. "I didn't give her a chance to use it on me, and we had quite the scuffle."

Ellery recalled the two of them tumbling down the stairs and took in his mother's disheveled appearance. Her hair was in disarray from its usual neat chignon, the sleeve of her jacket was torn, and the pump she'd used to kick Valerie Trainor was the only one she was currently wearing.

"Well done, Lucy Satan," Jackson said with a wolfish grin, and to Ellery's disgust, his mother smiled back, as delighted as a schoolkid after a fight. Then she grimaced.

"Ellery, would you happen to have some ibuprofen in that kit of yours? I've got some water—"

Ellery was gloved up and knuckles deep in blood and gauze, so Jackson did the honors with his free arm, passing the ibuprofen to Ellery's mother, who promptly shared it—and the water—with Galen.

Manning surveyed the prisoners, including Gannett Hoover, who hadn't stopped his quiet, hysterical sobbing.

"Are we going to talk about what in the hell happened?"

Jackson let out a sigh and, as Ellery finished up with the inadequate tools at hand, began to speak.

"This," he said, "is what happens when a bunch of pissed-off entitled people meet when they're young and plot to shit on everybody they meet on their way up the political grift."

"That's not true," Valerie Trainor whined as she was hauled to her feet. "We were *helping* those kids!"

"You were torturing them to feel superior," Jackson told her. "Just like you let your entire sick little clan here torture your stepsister."

"She was so awkward," Valerie sniffled. "Even when we were kids. She was so happy to hang out at my coattails."

"So you made her your lapdog," Jackson said. "And she tortured the kids you took responsibility for, let some of them escape so they had to choose between doing her bidding and starving to death. And she thought she was doing good, so she kept being a sadistic twat because you and your girls got off on it."

"Nobody was supposed to get hurt," Valerie protested. "Those kids—"

"Got fed to your ex-husband," Jackson retorted, and Ellery wrapped his hands around Jackson's arm at the elbow, below the bullet graze, to keep him from jumping on top of her and throttling her. "You let him pick the pretty boys, didn't you? Brought them up here, let them service him. Anything, right? Anything so he'd keep the money train going. Six hundred grifts to keep your whole little tribe in clover, and you had no problem knowing he was sodomizing teenaged boys and killing them when he was done."

"They were evil," she whispered. "Seducing him like that."

"Get her the fuck out of here," Manning told the agents holding her arms, "before I kill her myself."

Ellery stared at him in surprise. "That sounded sincere," he said.

"It was," Manning said, his face twisted in disgust. "Now what about…. Jesus, that guy's in the California State Assembly, isn't he?"

"Gannet Hoover," Ellery said, as the pathetic blob of a man was hauled away. He hadn't stopped sobbing. He could barely breathe. "He was one of Conway Schmitt's—aka Newton Dwayne's—first victims. When Schmitt got out of prison for abusing choirboys, he showed up on Hoover's doorstep, and Hoover and his wife gave him a place to stay. And he came up with the idea of moving to California so Gannet could run for office. Schmitt brought his ex-wife along, and she formed the Moms for Clean Living with all her old sorority sisters, and between her and Schmitt, they laundered Super PAC money and ran real-estate scams and abducted kids from their parents on the promise of 'curing' their sexuality so they could collect school voucher money. And they got to funnel kids—boys for Schmitt, girls for the two gentlemen I understand Jackson took out—to be abused."

Manning looked ill. "This is… gross. Atrocious. Absolutely disgusting."

Ellery felt like the sour expression on his face would never go away. "Don't sit on any of the furniture," he said. "And, uhm, stay away from the rug."

Manning shuddered, and Ellery started wrapping the last of his gauze around Jackson's bicep. "This one's going to haunt me," the agent said frankly, his face bleak.

"Us too," Jackson said, his shoulders seeming to sag. "We never would have known—not any of it—if one of the kids who'd escaped their clutches hadn't tried to solicit Galen and his partner as they were taking a walk one evening."

Manning gazed at him curiously. "Are we ever going to meet this witness? What did he see?"

Jackson shook his head. "Isn't this enough?" he asked bitterly. "You have so much evidence, you're swimming in it. Can't we let that kid go and be a kid?"

Manning nodded slowly. "I'll tell you, normally I'm a by-the-book guy, but you're right. I'm sure there's a way you came by all this information that has nothing to do with that kid, right?"

Ellery felt a small smile twitch at his lips. "It all started," he said softly, "when Piper Lutz came to my office, trying to sell Moms for Clean Living to a law firm populated with a lot of gay lawyers. And I shut her down."

Manning's face lit up. "Did that really happen?" he asked.

"And then she set one of the 'outside' kids on us with a Molotov cocktail," Ellery said. "We have the kid in custody, being tended to by one of the advocates. We've already taken his statement. Will that do?"

"Oh yeah." Manning swallowed hard. "All those kids you guys rescued—the ones from last night, the ones from here—the more we can do to keep them out of the system and just get them help, the happier I'll be. There's a lot of guilt to go around in this hellhole, but none of it is theirs."

Ellery felt like a band around his chest had loosened, and he nodded. It wasn't justice—there could never *be* adequate justice for this atrocity—but Conway Schmitt and his wife were going away for a long time.

It was a start.

At that moment, there was a scuffle at the door, and Jade's voice chimed loudly.

"Would you people let me in? I've got three kids here who were hiding out in that garage with the ATVs, and I promised them some goddamned food. And my brother's in there, and his stupid fiancé, who happens to be my boss."

"Three more kids," Jackson said, his own face relaxing. "Alive." He raised his voice. "Guys, let her in! And for fuck's sake feed those kids!"

Manning snorted inelegantly. "So glad we brought you along," he said. "It's good to have someone in charge."

Blue Fish

THERE WERE more questions, from the FBI and from the state's attorney general and from the police—lather, rinse, repeat.

Jackson, Ellery, Lucy Satan, Jade, Cody, and Galen were finally allowed to be escorted home around ten o'clock that night, long after the kids Jade and Jackson had found had been taken to the local hospital and church to be fed, clothed, and tended to.

All of them fretted about the kids getting adequate treatment, adequate debriefing, adequate care after all they had undoubtedly been through, but Manning had irritably told them that sometimes, the government actually knew what the fuck it was doing and had made them go home.

Sometimes there was only so much they could do. They all knew that.

As it was, the next day was going to be a massive effort at the office as the lot of them tried to deal with the paperwork and postponed appointments that the past two—or was it three?—days had created.

Nobody, Ellery had said, *nobody* was going to go out of the office to do anything or talk to anybody, and none of them were to be there any earlier than ten o'clock.

One of their best moments was on the ride home, when K-Ski had texted them pictures of Isabelle Roberts, her arms around a shyly smiling Cowboy, standing in front of the iconic Disneyland gardens, each wearing a set of ears.

They're inseparable. She's already promised him her spare room when they get back.

Jackson told them that they were free to come home at any time, and made a mental note to ask the advocates to put a speed order on the foster care papers that would let that happen.

Then Kryzynski told him that they were going to stay two more days and sent him another picture, this one a selfie of him and Billy, their own ears perched happily on their heads, in the same spot.

The pictures were so wholesome after what had just happened, what they'd seen, heard, *knew*, that Jackson's eyes stung, and he heard Ellery take a shuddering breath next to him as he peered over Jackson's shoulder in the back seat of the Lexus.

Cody had opted to drive the minivan—alone—without Jackson, which all by itself qualified him for the job.

When they got home that night after dropping Galen off, it was to find Lance in their house, sitting on the couch with the cats, with a giant chicken casserole in the oven and a quart of ice cream in the freezer.

Jackson, Ellery, Taylor, Jade, and Cody fell upon the food like ravening wolves, while Lance explained that after Jackson had texted Dex to tell him that they'd apprehended Henry's shooter and gotten Cowboy disentangled from any sort of witness duties, Dex had suggested—none too gently—that the lot of them had probably had a helluva day and would appreciate a gesture.

"Bobby and Reg are at John's place," Lance said humbly, dishing up some salad to go with the casserole. "But Henry has a key here, and…." He managed to meet their eyes. "I had some amends to make."

"You were worried about your boy," Jackson said kindly, but Lance shook his head.

"No. No, it was more than that. I was *jealous* of all the time he spends, not just with you, but doing this job. And it wasn't fair of me. He puts up with doctors' hours every damned day. I just…." He smiled bitterly. "Being afraid for him is something I need to get used to. It's worth it." He flashed them an honest smile. "I mean, it's *Henry*, right? I forgot, the other night, that everybody in this room—" He gave Cody a confused glance. "Except you—I don't know you—but everybody else here loves Henry too."

"I love the guy," Cody said through a mouthful of french bread. "Trust me—good people."

Jackson chuckled weakly. "Lance Luna, Cody Gabriel. Cody Gabriel, Lance Luna. We met during that case right before Thanksgiving."

Lance blinked. "The… the undercover policeman," he said softly, and if Henry had told him anything about that case, odds were good Lance knew all sorts of things about Cody's past that he could make *very* uncomfortable right about now.

But Lance smiled at Cody instead. "Henry thought you were brave as fuck," he said. "I didn't know you were taking his job while he's out. I'm glad somebody's got Jackson's back." He met Jackson's eyes then. "He's always—*always*—had ours."

CODY LEFT shortly after that, taking the minivan, which he praised affectionately on the way out. Lance offered to give Jade a ride to the duplex and to check in on the kids on the other side while he was there. It was, he said, something Henry would probably take over when he got out of the hospital in a week.

The exhalation of relief that statement caused made him smile.

Taylor, who had been quiet and exhausted—and rightfully so, because weren't they all—had retired almost immediately after. Ellery had given his mother a long heartfelt hug before she turned to the bedroom, and Jackson, keenly conscious of all the times in the past two days Ellery's mother had saved his life by saying the simple words "I love you" time and time again, stepped up before she could turn away.

"A hug?" she asked, eyes wide and glossy. "Voluntarily? Oh, my darling boy, you are *spoiling* me!"

Jackson engulfed her, conscious that she was smaller than he was but that her spirit was mighty. "I love you, Lucy Satan," he whispered. "Your evil plan succeeded. Well done."

She clung to him for an extra moment and then pulled away, wiping her eyes. "You and I have some more talking to do, young man," she said. "But for tonight I'm going to take your poor clumsy kitten to bed and take that as the win it is." She stood on tiptoe to kiss his cheek. "I love you too, Jackson. We'll work at making the words easier to say."

And with that she scooped Lucifer up from where he was complaining *loudly* at her feet and stalked off to bed with dignity.

And a purring three-legged black cat who seemed absolutely besotted with her.

Lance had cleaned up before he left, so after a quick turn in the shower for each of them—and a rebandaging of Jackson's arm, which was, given all that had befallen that day, the *least* of their worries—they fell into bed.

Jackson's need to hold Ellery to his chest and simply *be*, alive, whole, and for this brief moment, *still*, was constricting his breath.

The moment they slid together in the dark, Billy Bob purring and kneading Jackson's head, his lungs relaxed and he could get oxygen again.

"Ellery?" he said softly.

"Yeah?"

"This case was awful. It was… it was almost the worst thing I've ever seen."

One of the three bodies pulled out of the first disposal site had been identified as Caleb Greavy before Manning had given them permission to go home. There were three more—all of which had been discovered by Preacher at the third site after Damien had taken Retty to the nearest hospital—all of them teenaged boys.

"Me too," Ellery said softly.

"After something that awful, hugging your mother, telling her I loved her—that's like a no-brainer. Telling Jade the same thing—God, even texting Henry—it just… I am so grateful for all of our people. I… that thing we're doing. The one in June?"

"The wedding thing?" Ellery said, sounding amused—and tired, but also amused.

"Yeah. I tried to make that not such a big deal today. I was talking to kids who'd been victimized, terrorized, who had seen their friend die. And one of them got so mad. He said we were *important*. They had to see that a happy ever after was possible. They had to see that people like them could be a family, could have a day to celebrate, could have love."

Ellery rubbed his cheek against Jackson's chest, and Jackson could feel the dampness of tears. "What did you say?"

Jackson smiled in the dark. "I said you weren't a troll, for starters."

Ellery chuckled weakly. "What else?"

"I said I was so looking forward to marrying you. God, Ellery, we see some of the worst shit. But we have so many good people in our lives. It makes dealing with the worst shit possible, you know?"

"I do," Ellery said, and he sounded so sleepy that for a moment Jackson thought that was it. It was okay, he figured, because they would wake up like this too. They would work quietly in the office together, like they did, and they would get the grunt work that usually they hated out of the way and appreciate the paperwork for a chance to give them some peace.

Then Ellery said, "By the way, Galen wants us to hire Arizona Brooks as our third partner, and Mother would like to share the office with her when she's in town so she can help us."

Jackson's eyes shot open in the dark. "I'm sorry?"

"And I think we're renting the offices next door—Galen and Mother say you need an entire room for the PI end of the business—one to meet clients and keep computers and clothes and all that other stuff you're currently shoving into Jade's space."

"But—" Jackson *treasured* those quiet moments they worked together in Ellery's office.

"Apparently Galen already checked out the space. It would be right across the hall from my office, once the separating wall is broken down. You'd have the room for you and Henry and Cody and AJ, and then when it's time for you and me to work, we'd still have our space."

"Oh my God," Jackson said, his mind racing. "You… you said *yes* to this?"

"It was the damnedest thing," Ellery said, sounding truly lost. "I called Arizona to apologize to her for leaving her out of the loop, and the next thing I knew, she was agreeing to be a partner, and her part of the buy-in will help cover the cost of a remodel. I… I guess we're expanding, you know? We need two more associates, by the way. And two more paralegals."

Jackson chuckled at the mention of paralegal secretaries. "Jade will have people to boss around," he mumbled. "And new challenges herself. She'll be over the moon."

His sister and Taylor and Galen and Henry and Cody and AJ and even Arizona Brooks, who had been an adversary and was now a friend.

The thought of all of them, working together, doing good—it released the final bit of tension from his chest.

"Wow," he said, falling into sleep. "Ellery, we have so much to do."

"And so many people to help," Ellery said, obviously sinking into his own sleep.

"I never knew what a difference love could make in my life," he whispered, and Ellery snuggled just a little bit closer, and then they were both clutching each other in dreams.

Good dreams, for once. For all the horrors they'd seen, for the physical discomfort in Jackson's arm and the stupid inevitable fever growing in his bones, for the stress and fears of the day, Jackson's demons finally gave him some peace.

Although he was well aware there would be future battles to come.

THE NEXT morning, he was the first one up, making coffee and starting a breakfast frittata even before Ellery's mother arose. Yes, he was feverish, but he'd taken his medication without badgering from Ellery today. Too much to do. Taking care of himself had to be a no-brainer, not a struggle.

When Lucy Satan finally came out of her room, disconcertingly dressed in a classy leisure suit in winter white with dark blue accents, she had left her makeup off and was wearing her thick black hair in a disarming ponytail.

He realized that she was perhaps in her mid-fifties. Her promise to be part of their firm held teeth—she would be whipcrack smart and vigorous for many years to come.

"Coffee?" she said. "How kind." She took her mug to the table and sat for a moment—just sat—and inhaled the steam of a giant mug of coffee with cream and raw sugar.

He was sure that for her this was like dessert in the morning.

"Jackson," she said after a moment, as he fried the vegan sausage for the frittata. "Have you given any thought to what happened to your sister since we last spoke of that?"

Jackson fumbled the spatula, picked it up off the floor and turned the water on it while he wiped the mess up with a paper towel. "I'm sorry?"

She gave him a faint smile. "Don't panic, young man. It's just when she was taken away from your mother, you were a child. I know… I know your life has been such that it probably hasn't occurred to you, but you are very much an adult now. In fact you're an adult with a very select set of skills that might help you find some answers."

"Oh," he said, going back to the frittata and adding mushrooms to the sausage. "Oh wow."

She raised her eyebrows at him, her lips turning up at the corners as though she was fully aware she had blown his mind. "Don't freak out about it today," she said, covering her mouth with a yawn. "Today is for quiet paperwork and takeout. And coffee." She took a sip. "But do keep it in mind."

He nodded dumbly, his brain racing with possibilities.

Ellery emerged from the bedroom shortly after that, wearing his own pajamas and a sweatshirt of Jackson's. Jackson gazed at him fondly as Ellery came next to him and set the teakettle on, hiding his yawn behind his hand. He thought of all the wild changes in the firm Ellery had told him about as they'd fallen asleep the night before, and it hit him.

It could happen, he thought. He was *very* good at his job. After the dust settled, maybe he could give Henry some leads he could pursue while still sedentary so he wouldn't go insane. Maybe while he and Cody were chasing around, doing a thing the three of them seemed to love a lot, Jackson could add in some inquiries of his own.

Maybe, he thought plaintively, just maybe, that one chapter of his life, the most awful, sordid, and painful one, might not have a terrible ending after all.

"What?" Ellery asked on another yawn, and carefully, so he might not burn the frittata—or burn Ellery with the frittata—he leaned forward and kissed Ellery on the cheek.

"Oh, Ellery," he murmured, nuzzling Ellery's temple. "We have *so* much to do."

Fishlets

A Brief Fishlet Interlude that Is Absolutely Positively Not in Canon

IYKYK

I'm pretty sure if there was anybody yet to be offended by my politics, they've already bailed from my reading list. I'm sorry—I tend to be opinionated, and sometimes it jumps out. In this case, I needed to write a catharsis for myself, because while I am fat and slow and arthritic and too old to run around doing shit like Jackson, I still have the heart of a juvenile delinquent, and I had to fight the urge to stomp my little foot and scream, "It's not fucking fair!" at the moon this November. It turned out, while I was writing a catharsis for myself, I wrote one for so many other people.

This makes me happy.

We all need to howl at the moon sometimes.

P.S.—The surprise hero of this one was John, who, as we saw in Black John, *was a bit of a goofball with a heart that hasn't completely matured, but only in the best of ways.*

Amy Lane

"YOU'RE GOING out?" Ellery asked plaintively.

Jackson leaned over Ellery's shoulder and kissed his temple. "I'm sorry, baby. This… I just can't sit here and watch this on the TV. You know I love you, right?"

"Of course," Ellery said. That Jackson loved him had never been in doubt.

"Then let me sulk and take my bad mood out by baying at the moon, okay?"

"Okay." Ellery sighed. He personally planned to watch wildlife documentaries and listen to REM's *Eponymous* until the urge to cry and scream gave him room to breathe.

Jackson's pocket buzzed, and he didn't bat an eyelash, just kissed Ellery's temple again, patted his shoulder, and left.

Ellery wasn't fooled a bit. Jackson's pocket had buzzed just before he'd stood up and stalked to the kitchen to put on his shoes and pull on his most ragged hooded sweatshirt.

Something was afoot. Something Jackson felt like Ellery wouldn't approve of.

Jackson was usually right about things like that, but Ellery had no idea how this particular idea would manifest itself.

Ellery heard the door slam, and then his pocket buzzed twice. He frowned and pulled out his phone, surprised to see texts from Jade, Galen, and Lance.

Okay, I give. What are those assholes doing?

Ellery, could you be so kind as to tell me where my significant other might have gone?

What has Jackson sucked him into now?

Ellery blinked. Oh dear.

He made a group chat that he was worried he might have to use more often than he'd ever planned and texted, *I have no idea where they went, but given the state of politics right now, I've got a very bad feeling about this.*

Jade: *Fuck me. I'm calling K-Ski.*

Galen: *Oh dear God. I'm tracking his phone.*

Lance: *No, seriously, Ellery, what do you think they're up to?*

Ellery: *You know, I think Jade has the right idea.*

Jade: *If they get into trouble, Ellery, we'll need you.*

Ellery: *I'd like to say no jury in the world would convict them but....*

Jade: *Yeah. Holy fuck, I thought there was more intelligence in this country.*

Galen: *As long as our significant others don't add to the stupidity, I shall be content.*

Lance: *There'd better not be blood.*

"JESUS, JACKSON, why are you *always bleeding!*" Henry tried to fuss over Jackson's knuckles as Jackson—piloting Jennifer—squealed away from the crime scene, erm, scene of the altercation, erm....

"Holy shit, boy," Mike muttered, looking behind him, "what in the hell did you do?"

"Way more damage with that portable air compressor and those tools you brought me," Jackson said happily. His knuckles stung, and one of his assailants, erm, victims who'd caught him behind the trucks as he'd worked, had managed a solid clock to his jaw, but the adrenaline pumping through his veins—through *all* of their veins—was way better than that bitter, acidic syrup of despair that had overwhelmed the four of them while being gobsmacked by the state of politics on television.

"I haven't had that much fun since I did coke," John said with some satisfaction. "I mean, apart from Galen, and running the business and being Uncle John to all those screaming toddlers… but, you know. Delinquency. It's a rush!"

"Oh God," Henry muttered, trying not to laugh. Lance's old boss was a helluva nice guy for a porn mogul, but seriously.

"John," Jackson said, sounding pleasant. "If we get pulled over by the police, don't speak."

John cackled, and Jackson wondered if he'd heard those words before.

"Seriously," Mike said, smacking his ballcap—thank God he leaned toward his home sports teams now and not the hated red hat he'd recently burned in protest. "You three worked mighty fast. I'm most impressed."

"The trick," Jackson said, spotting the wrecks in his rearview mirror just before they rounded the corner that would get them away from the, uhm, incident, "was to figure out which truck was leaving that lot first and taking it apart thoroughly. Everything else was just physics."

John cackled some more. "My favorite class!"

Mike stared at him. "Boy, are you still high?"

"I've been sober four years," John said indignantly, and then he deflated a little. "But you know, I *did* do a whole lot of coke for a long time—maybe this is a flashback."

"I'm so gonna tell Galen on you." Henry's laugh was a little strained, but if Jackson knew his boy—and at this point, he and Henry had been through enough shit that he did—Jackson figured he was riding his own adrenaline high. "But I haven't had that much fun since me and Mal went out and tipped cows!"

"That's a myth," Mike—who had grown up in rural West Virginia and would know—protested. "You can't tip cows over!"

"Tell that to the multiple fractures in my leg," Henry grumbled. Then he added, "But the cow was on a hill, and I think Mal had dumped a shit-ton of beer into its feed before we went out to try."

Jackson—who had heard this story—grimaced. "You went out and tipped a drunk cow onto your leg," he said. "And I trust you with my life why?"

"Jackson," Henry said with patience as Jackson tore through the midnight-quiet streets of the city, "do you have any idea what you just got us to do? There has got to be felony mischief and destruction of property charges waiting for all of us if we get caught."

At that moment, *everybody's* phone buzzed.

Jackson couldn't grab his—he was driving too fast as it was—but around him he heard a collective groan.

"What?" he asked. "What is it?"

"Well," Henry said, "I think we may have escaped charges—"

"But I'm pretty damned sure we're all caught," John added.

"Fuck me," Mike muttered, and Jackson had no choice but to keep his foot on the pedal and the pedal to the floor.

SEAN KRYZYNSKI and his partner, Andre Christie, were having the worst fucking night.

Of course election night was going to be bad enough, but given who was winning… oh Lord. It was a nightmare. Petty theft, vandalism, assholes with a three-year-old's vocabulary telling any cop they ran into that it was okay, there were no cops now because they'd all become defunded.

Sean and Andre were so tired of explaining that "defunding the police" didn't work the way everybody thought it did.

And now… well, what the hell did you call *this*?

"Okay," Sean said, his notepad at the ready. "Sir, could you explain what happened?"

The older guy he was talking to had a face chain-smoked to leather, and maybe three teeth. He could have been anywhere from thirty to sixty, and his wispy ginger/gray hair stuck out from under the hated red hat in clumps.

"Well, we were on the corner here, just waving our flags," the guy said, pulling hard on his ever-present cig, "like it's our God-given right in the constitution, no thanks to you commie fuckers tryin' to stop us—"

"Nobody's trying to stop you, sir," Christie said, sounding bored. "So you'd all parked in the back lot behind us and were here on the corner, protesting—"

"We was celebrating!" snapped another man—bald, with a long, graying ZZ Top style beard tucked in the stretchy waistband of his khaki shorts. "Weren't we, Shep?"

"Tha's right," Shep told him. "Me and Curly and Moe—"

Next to him, Sean felt Andre's whole body tense up, and they eyed the bald guy with the beard down to his waist and the scrawny guy with long black bangs in his eyes and then exchanged glances.

"Curly, Moe, and Shep," Andre said, with absolutely no inflection in his voice at all. "Keep going."

"Well, we was out here celebrating our righteous victory," Shep continued, "and some guy—first we thought he was one of us, cause he had the hat and all, but he walked up and threw the hat on the ground. Said he'd worn this eight years ago and learned so much more about the world, and he was fuckin' ashamed of the hat and ashamed of the choices and ashamed of *us*!"

Sean and Andre exchanged another glance. "And then what'd he do?" Andre asked, at the same time Sean said, "Wait, what'd this guy look like?"

"He had this young face," said Moe, who was twenty-five at the most. "And this white hair, which was weird. And these bright blue eyes. And he had an accent… like a good ole boy accent." Moe paused for a sec. "Was purty," he said upon consideration.

Sean blinked and tried to keep his eyes from widening. Couldn't be. Right? He'd met a guy like that a couple of times, but… really?

"And then he covered the damned hat in lighter fluid and set fire to it!" Curly raged and pointed his finger at a smoldering heap of what used to be nylon and cardboard.

"Wow," Sean said, rather impressed. "So he's the one who damaged your, uhm, vehicle?" He stared at the street in front of him where the remains of the giant truck lay on its side, bits of exhaust pipe and various flags all scattered around it as its engine hissed and smoked and died.

"Naw," Moe said. "But we weren't too pleased with the guy who burned his hat, so we were giving him what for, and then, well, Curly here got *really* pissed and took a swing and…." He wrinkled his brow. "And this other guy popped out of nowhere like the goddamned thing on the box of Lucky Charms."

"A *leprechaun*?" Andre asked, stunned.

"Yeah!" Moe told him, absolutely baffled. "He was redheaded and not too tall, and Curly went after the guy with the white hair, and the leprechaun kicked him in the back of his knee, and he went *down*."

Sean swept his eyes up and down Curly's squat, stout frame and noticed the road rash on his knees and palms. "I see," he said. "So J—the redheaded guy took apart your truck."

"No," Curly said, scowling. "But these two fuckers'd dissed us and we couldn't let that stand, so we took off chasing them, and then our friends over there—" He pointed to another crowd of assholes who looked just like Curly, Moe, and Shep. "—started screaming because a blond-headed fella had run by and stolen their banners." He grunted. "He threw them on the fire with the hat."

"The smell was prodigious," Moe told him soberly.

"Good word," Sean noted, although he'd stopped taking notes as the story itself took shape. "So what happened to the first two guys you were chasing?"

"Well, they… uhm…." Shep wrinkled his brow. "I guess they got away, because we went after that blond fella, and he…."

"See," Moe said, "he went 'round that pet store there, and then he disappeared."

"Disappeared," Curly said. "We couldn't catch him."

"So what happened to your trucks?" Sean asked. All three of the men had bloody foreheads and were cradling their wrists—the three-truck accident hadn't been his imagination.

"Well, it was weird," Shep said. "We all came back here and stamped out the fire, and then this brown minivan pulled up alongside us and the guy driving stuck his head out and screamed, 'Come and get me, you cousin-fucking morons!' and we had to go." He nodded, and Curly and Moe all nodded too.

"So he hung out there at the corner, and we all jumped into our trucks, and then he took off and we followed," Shep said. His excitement dimmed, and he appeared crestfallen. "And then my baby… she fell apart at the seams. The tires came off, and the exhaust ports toppled, and we went over like a tipped cow, and…." He gave Moe and Curly unhappy looks.

"We was drivin' in formation," Moe said staunchly. "We done it plenty of times." Then he glared at the pileup of trucks in the middle of the road. "And I practically drove over poor Shep."

"And I plowed into the back of Moe," Curly said unhappily. "You know, I thought them trucks was better made than that. But it was every damned one of our welds shattered like plastic. It was no damned good at all."

Sean and Andre had both frozen, stock-still, at the mention of the brown minivan. "So," Sean said. "This minivan. Did you guys catch the license plate?"

"Naw," Shep said, spitting. "Ain't that what cameras are for?"

"You shot out the cameras," Andre said. "When you claimed this corner to electioneer on. Remember? We have you on tape."

"That wasn't me," Shep said automatically.

"On camera," Sean said through gritted teeth. "Do you remember anything else about the minivan?"

"Yeah," Moe said glumly. "I think the other three guys who'd given us such a bad time were in the back, laughing."

Sean rubbed the back of his neck. "Well, we'll see what we can do," he said.

As he and Andre were striding toward their department-issue vehicle, Andre said, "Really? Are we really going to see what we can do?"

Sean muttered, "Let me give them time to get their stories straight first, okay?"

"Fair," Andre said. He sighed. "You know, if I'd been twenty years old tonight, I bet I could have taken the bumpers off too."

"Oh yeah," Sean told him. "And I definitely would have stripped off the chrome rims."

ELLERY GOT the text from Billy and was obliged to pass it on.

Everybody was home tonight. Everybody. Was fucking home. Nobody went nowhere. Like me. I went fucking nowhere, when I wish I'd been out with everybody else. Don't leave me out of shit because I'm with the cop now. He can bail me out of jail same as everybody else. But it doesn't matter because EVERYBODY WAS HOME.

Ellery stared at the text and then forwarded it to his new text group.

Jade: *I'll kill him.*

Galen: *I'll maim him first, then kill him.*

Lance: *I won't kill him. But he'll wish I did.*

Ellery: *However you commit murder, remember two things. Number one: We're angry too.*

Jade: *And number two is EVERYBODY WAS FUCKING HOME.*

Ellery: *Because they were.*

And then he got up and poured himself an extra glass of wine and waited for the rumble of the minivan in the driveway.

An hour later—because apparently he had to drop everybody off—Jackson opened the door, and Ellery's reason escaped through the door like a startled cat.

The House on American River Drive

Ellery: Are you crazy? Do you realize what could have happened?
Jackson: You would have bailed me out. That's what you do.
Ellery: Bailed you out from *what* exactly? What were you doing that you absolutely positively have to be home when we're questioned tomorrow?
Jackson: Heh heh heh heh heh

The Duplex off Elvas:

Jade: What the fuck were you doing out there? Do you think you're above the law now?
Mike: Aren't you happy I was burning my hat?
Jade: ….
Mike: Sweetheart?
Jade: Yeah, sort of—but are you crazy?
Mike: Certifiable. Wanna hear how good Jackson is with a power tool? Henry too! I was impressed!

At the Tiny House in Midtown:

John: Galen! Ouch!
Galen: Does that hurt?
John: Yes! Ouch! Would you stop hitting me with your cane?
Galen: *No!*

At the apartment complex that also houses the flophouse:

Henry: Lance, I'm back!
Lance: You never left.
Henry: I'm sorry?
Lance: There's going to be cops here tomorrow—you never left.
Henry: Okay, I never left. Want to hear what I never did when I never left?

Lance: *I don't even want to know you never left!*
Henry: Okay, okay, okay—I'll tell you tomorrow.

And Back on American River Drive:

Ellery sighed, realizing his harangue of Jackson's recklessness was falling on deaf ears. With a sigh he collapsed on the couch and took a gulp of wine, patting the seat next to him.

"Fine," he muttered. "Fine. You're proud of yourself. Do you feel better now?"

"Yeah," Jackson said with a sigh, leaning against him. "Definitely."

"You can't go out and commit acts of vandalism and destruction of property every time you get pissed in the next four years. You know that, right?"

"Yeah," Jackson murmured, leaning his head against Ellery's shoulder with such profound weariness. "But… you know…."

"Yeah," Ellery said, getting it. "Sometimes, you gotta howl at the moon."

"Awooooooo!" Jackson said, his head getting heavier on Ellery's shoulder. Ellery realized that the unthinkable was going to happen.

God. Odds were pretty good there would never be cops at their door for this incident, but even if there were, Ellery would consider the whole debacle fair if only, just this once in what was sure to be a shitty four years, Jackson could get some sleep.

Jackson's soft breathing made Ellery wonder if maybe Mike could show *him* how to use the power tools with the air compressor. He was going to need a way to sleep as well.

Mrs. Bobby's Mom

By Amy Lane

In an embarrassment of riches, I had Randy's book, Jackson's book, and Eric Christian's book floating around my head at the same time. Jackson and Randy's books were going to coincide, and they might even have moved down south, except I wrote this little ficlet, and the next book changed shape overnight.

Yes, for those of you wondering, I think there will definitely be a short at some point, showing Isabelle and Cowboy making a home together, because they both have so much more love to give.

"G'NIGHT, MRS. Bobby's Mom!"

Isabelle Roberts turned toward the *very* attractive young men who had just escorted her to her car and smiled gently. "Thanks, guys. You know, you don't have to walk me to my car—"

"Oh no," the first one—a young blond Viking who went by the stage name of Ricky—said soberly. "It's a rule."

She held back a smile. They were all so sober and responsible—and so young. Even the twenty-five-year-olds were young. "A rule?" she asked, although she sort of knew.

"It's one of the first things they tell us," said the Viking's friend. "Rudy" was his stage name at present, and he was smaller—nearly her height—and was probably not quite nineteen. He'd tried hard to work out enough to mask his slender grace, but unless he did steroids—and Johnnies prohibited it—that wasn't going to happen.

"They?" she prodded, remembering when her Vern was this age. He'd had a lot of the same secrets as these young men, and getting things that *weren't* secret out of him had been like pulling teeth. He was a little older now—twenty-three as opposed to nineteen—and as always, preternaturally mature for his age, but she still had her arsenal of tricks to get him to come clean.

"The older guys," Rudy said, nodding like it was a secret society. Well, in a way, it was, right? "And the bosses. Dex and John. They always come by and say 'Remember to make sure Mrs. Bobby's Mom gets out okay. We need to keep her.'"

Isabelle laughed, the sound coming much easier than it had four years ago. Yeah, it had been hard to get the hell out of Dogpatch, California, and she was still *not* okay with the sacrifices her son had made for her to come down here and live a better, *freer* life, but she *was* free now, and she could laugh or smile or even flirt at these sweet, *highly* unavailable young men who made her feel like she was a queen and would never, ever let her go out to her car alone, even in broad daylight.

"Well, you're all very kind," she said, allowing her smile to reach her eyes. "But you both need to get home safely too." The shoot had been in the hands of a new photographer today, and while the feedback had been pretty good—his videos did well, with a quick-cut style that apparently appealed to today's younger viewers, and the models all said he was professional and even funny at times—the guy was also "Not Dex or John." Dex and John had over two decades combined with shooting porn, and they were *very* good at getting in and out (pun *always* intended) as quickly as possible. The new guy—Vic—tended to close down the office around eight, and the escort from the models as the sky grew dark in early May was welcome.

"No worries." Rudy grinned at her. "We're staying at the flophouse now. It's pretty awesome!"

She didn't even want to know what awesome meant. Bobby had stayed there for a couple of months, and when she'd asked him about it— since so many of John's models spent time there—his response had been a sort of grunt about, "Too much testosterone, too many penises, not enough clothes."

She didn't need to know any more. She *did* know that Dex's younger brother and one of the former models had taken on a sort of unofficial supervision of the place, to make sure the kids—eighteen did *not* make them adults—stayed healthy and hopefully on some sort of track that would help them realize a life *beyond* porn. It had taken her a while to get it, that some of these young men weren't here for the money. Whether it was for the acceptance, the challenge, or being the star of their own lives, there were other reasons to be in the business. Some of them, she'd figured, were just *really horny* and had the judgment of lemmings, so there were worse places to end up than a porn studio that tried to keep kids from losing their nut in a totally tragic and nonsexual way.

It was weird how some parents freaked out about their kids having sex, or who they were having sex *with*, as though doing a thing with their bodies before their smarts kicked in somehow made them older or dirtier or more sinful. It simply made them *kids*, oftentimes going, "Hey, what does *this* button do! Oh wow! That was fun—let's do that *again*!" The rest of their emotional needs were not automatically met because they found that humans sometimes had magic buttons. In fact sometimes the magic buttons got in the way, and it was the *adults'* job to look out for their kids when they were off chasing magic buttons and threatening to get plowed over by trains.

So she was glad that Rudy and Ricky had both found the flophouse— and that there were other people watching out for them who might understand the needs of people with their specific buttons. But she really *didn't* want to know what went on there.

"That's wonderful," she said kindly. "You enjoy your stay. Tell Henry and Lance hello for me." Henry was Dex's little brother, and Lance was his boyfriend—the flophouse supervisors.

"Oh wow!" Ricky said, his eyes as big as a little kid's. "We're totally late for our scene dinner."

"Oh my God!" Rudy, too, a little freaked out. "I'm *starving*. We gotta go, Mrs. Bobby's Mom—bye!"

And with that they took off into the night, leaving her to start her vehicle to head home to her cross-stitching and her murder mysteries and her cats. Vern and his boyfriend, Reg, had gotten her two kittens for Christmas—Cornish rexes, who had the shortest, most tightly crimped fur. She adored them and had tried to ask where they'd gotten such expensive animals, but Vern and Reg had been sort of vague about the whole thing.

She loved the creatures—they were affectionate and playful and made her little two-bedroom apartment so much less lonely. She'd originally thought that Vern might stay with her when she'd chosen the place, but it had very quickly become evident that once he and Reg had gotten back together, they were partners for life. It was okay, though. John Carey, her employer, paid her more than enough money to keep the place, and she had benefits too.

And of course the special assignments that John sometimes asked of her that they didn't tell anybody about.

It was funny that she would have thought of that *now*, because as soon as she pulled out of the Johnnies parking lot, her phone rang. She hit the button on her dashboard and John Carey's voice came through, quiet and tense, and she was instantly on alert.

"Isabelle?"

"Mr. Carey, are you okay?"

"Oh yes—"

"Galen?" she asked. She did love John's boyfriend—he was just so charming with his suits and his southern drawl.

"We're both fine, Isabelle," he said, his voice taking on that gentle timbre that was probably why all the kids seemed to worship him. "It's just… I'm going to need your help tonight. We've got another one."

"Oh my," she said. "What size? I've got a closet full of clothes, unless he's bigger than Vern or smaller than Reg."

"Closer to Reg than Bobby," John said. "But he's going to need a long bath and a haircut. Galen is sending Henry over with some antifungals and some lice treatments. Prep the bathroom and start dinner—we've fed him a burger, but he needs something real."

"Oh my," she said. Her voice dropped. "How young, John?"

"Fourteen," John said softly. "Hit on Galen and me as we were coming out of a meeting. Swears he's drug free, but I don't think that's always been the case. I'm going to have Henry sleep on your couch tonight, if that's okay."

"Of course," she said, because sometimes it was necessary. "But fourteen! John, where is he going to go?"

"We'll find a place," John said. His voice lightened a little. "We always do, right?"

"Of course," she said. "I'll go get things ready."

"Thanks, sweetheart. We'll meet you there."

Fourteen was young, she thought unhappily. Usually when John got hit on by a street kid—and because the NA meetings he and Galen attended once a week were held in a battered church in a sketchy neighborhood, it happened far more than it should have—the kid was at least sixteen—old enough to understand how to behave in at least a transactional way. "Here, kid—we've got a place to squat, three hots and a cot, but you need to be nice to Mrs. Bobby's Mom. We'll try to find you a place that'll let you get a real job and get back on your feet."

Sacramento had one of the few shelters for LGBTQ youth in the state, and oftentimes, the kids had ended up there. If the kid was over eighteen, John offered him a job—not in porn, unless they asked, but at Johnnies or one of the other businesses he'd been developing to help the kids who either were ready to quit porn and needed a helping hand, or who had been out of the street and just needed a job and a place to stay. Isabelle understood that this was how the flophouse had started, although John had sworn her to secrecy about the fact that he paid the lease, and if any of the kids there couldn't make rent, he made up the difference.

Isabelle knew that some of John's favorite kids were the ones who'd jumped in to the business with both feet to try to "pay their own way." She also knew, because John had confessed to her one quiet, melancholy night that this was one of the primary reasons John had stopped shooting scenes himself.

It just hadn't felt right, when the eighteen-year-old who'd seemed too damned young to hit on him was suddenly naked and having sex in his camera's lens. If Isabelle hadn't come to regard John so highly already, that confession alone would have done it for her. It wasn't only the kids who "aged out" of porn—John had matured beyond it too. He still thought it had its place, but the place was not for him.

So he'd passed the torch, and he and Dex had taken the business in a direction that gave the kids who'd fucked themselves silly on camera a place to now be mature, sober adults without the spotlight. Someday, she thought wistfully, Vern wouldn't feel the need for that harsh glare showing the world who he was.

She knew that he was so much finer a man than the body God had gifted him with, but that was something he'd figure out eventually.

So Isabelle had become John's way station as he was trying to place kids. Not every placement was a success, but she liked to think that having a kind voice, a place like a home—even a home they'd never had—and some good meals meant something to those who'd stayed with her.

And of course, she and John had gotten a routine together.

SHE BEAT John to her apartment by about ten minutes, which—after greeting the kittens and then confining them to her own bedroom with the litter box and food and water in her adjoining bath—gave her time to put a trash bag in the foyer to gather the old clothes and to throw some plastic-coated liners on the couch and one of the kitchen chairs and the bed. She got the ones with the flannel on one side, so the liners were comfortable to sit on—and didn't creak—but she'd had to get rid of a couch early on in this endeavor because lice were nasty little creatures who *didn't go away.*

She had the paper gown, booties, and shower cap on the counter in the bathroom—Henry would probably do the honors of shaving the poor boy's head—and she'd laid plastic on the floor.

She'd also put a variety of bubble baths in the room with cartoon-character bottles. It was surprising and heartbreaking how a SpongeBob bottle would sometimes break down the kids with the hardest, most "been there done that" façades.

So very often these kids hadn't had a chance to be children. They'd jumped right into sex work and trying to make a living on the streets because anything was better than being at home.

She was rummaging through the closet, deciding on a brand-new T-shirt and some gently used flannel pajama bottoms and briefs for the boy when there was a knock on the door.

The young man huddling in a used towel behind John was skinny, naked, and shivering—and yes, crawling with mites.

"Come in," she said, gesturing to John and the young man, and Henry and Galen behind him. "Henry, I've set everything out in there. You may want to run the bath. Your change of clothes is in the basket in the hall by the washer."

"Thanks, Ms. Roberts," Henry said, because he tried to be humble. She knew he could be pugnacious and stubborn and irritable—but he was also a good boy, and she gave him one of her best smiles.

"No problem, Henry." She lowered her head and looked their new friend in the eye. "Hello there," she said. "I'm sorry—we'll get you all cleaned up in a second. I've got some food in the fridge—I was planning on potato soup, homemade, and some homemade bread. Does that sound good when you're out of the bath?"

The boy stared up at her, his mouth round and inviting in spite of chapped lips, his cheeks red and burned from days outside, but still fair. He swallowed a couple of times and said, "That sounds really good, ma'am," and she saw his eyes welling up. "I… I shouldn't be in your home."

"Nonsense," she said. "But let's do get you clean. I've put covers on the chairs and couch and the bed, until we're sure all the crawlies are gone, so wherever you see red flannel, that's fair game. I know it sounds fussy, but as I'm sure you know, these things aren't fun at all, and its best to get them before they get you."

She smiled at him, and he smiled back—a small miracle of grimy teeth she was still proud of—and then Henry gestured with his chin. "Come on, Cowboy. Let's get started. Mrs. Roberts makes really good soup."

They moved out down the hallway, and she turned to John and Galen with raised eyebrows. "Cowboy?"

John grimaced. "He swore it's his real name. I don't... I mean, you know. He's fourteen—that much we got out of him. For all we can tell it *could* be."

She grunted. "Well, to hear my son talk, it's still better than the one I gave *him*. This one looks like he's been on the street for a while—will Lance be by in the morning?"

John nodded. "Yeah. And don't worry about coming in tomorrow. I already asked Kelsey, and she can come in for the day." John's old receptionist had quit work at Johnnies to get her degree in child development so she and an ex-model named Ethan could run a day care out of the home they shared.

"Bless her," Isabelle said. "But I'm sorry to miss the baby." One of the perks of the job, she'd realized very quickly, was that gay, straight, or bi, young people tended to procreate—or have siblings that procreated. When Vern had come out, she'd quietly mourned the loss of grandchildren she'd never have, but now, in addition to the Johnnies models who treated her like the mother they'd never had, she was pleased to be surrounded by children who adored her. *She* got to be the nice lady with cookies in her drawer, or who could be counted on to babysit, or who got to give away presents at Christmas and sew samplers for birthday gifts. All the love she'd been too exhausted and frightened to shower on Vern when the two of them had huddled in the shadow of his abusive father, she was free to strew around her like flowers down a garden path, and her son told her—often and with feeling—that he was so proud of her for doing it.

"She'll make it up to you," Galen said warmly, and she glanced at him.

"Galen, please sit," she said. "My recliner is waiting for you." The poor man was white-knuckling his cane, and the fatigue of pain tightened around his eyes.

"Thank you, Isabelle," Galen said, "but John and I were hoping to leave you here while we made some more calls. I'm afraid our young friend told us some *very* concerning things while we were on the way over, and I need to consult with my law partner for a bit. That's best done at his home."

He approached her as she busied herself in the kitchen and kissed her cheek. "We treasure you, Isabelle Roberts. If anybody can help this young person, it's you."

She gave him a rather watery smile. "Be careful, Galen. You and John are very much in danger of being philanthropists."

"Hush your mouth," he said gently, before turning to his partner in kindness. "John?"

John offered his arm to Galen before saying, "Isabelle, if you do not expense any of the things you need, I shall feel free to reimburse your check with sheer guesswork."

She gave him a sharp look as she carved up the loaf of homemade bread she'd baked the night before. There was plenty, and she thought Henry and Cowboy would enjoy some of it toasted with cheese. "Your guesses are terrible," she told him. "No mother in the world needs that much money to feed a child."

"I wouldn't know," John said blandly. "I was raised by wolves. You do it or I will. Now please call us if you need us—and definitely update me in the morning."

The first night he'd done this had been with Cotton, and John had spent a sleepless night on Isabelle's couch, making sure the sloe-eyed, hurt child he'd brought in wouldn't turn on Isabelle in the middle of the night.

There'd been others since—Randy and Vinnie included—but none this young. She knew that leaving Henry here was John's best investiture in safety.

"We will," she said. "Now go, get Galen home. You two let me know what's going on with him. He can't feel safe here if there are going to be surprises."

They assured her that they would—and that they'd take the bag of clothes from the porch to be burned—and then left her to prepare dinner. She did so, keeping an ear out for Henry's progress in the bathroom as she worked.

There was a quiet rumble of speech both during and after the electric buzz of the razor, and then the run of water in the bathtub. She was alert for the harsh breath of warm water hitting chafed skin and the quiet sobs that came with it. Living on the street in stiff clothes for long periods of time often generated sores, and that a hot bath was sometimes as painful as it was beneficial. She heard the pouring of water from a cup, which meant that Henry was helping the boy get clean, talking the whole time. She made out something about Henry and Lance's new kittens, and Henry's job working as a PI at Galen's law firm, and how Henry's brother's boyfriend had turtles and snakes and a giant iguana named Mrs. Quincy. She knew all of this, of course, but she was sure that to a frightened boy being promised the world, that hearty rumble of gruff chatter was like being told fairy tales. Real life couldn't be that normal, could it?

Finally, just as she was worried that she'd toasted the bread too early, Henry and the boy emerged from the hallway, both of them wearing the clean pajama bottoms and T-shirts she'd set out for them, including soft, faded hoodies that covered the boy's thin arms. Henry had a full trash bag that he placed outside the door to take to the dumpster in the morning before he gestured to the boy to sit down at the table in front of a hearty bowl of soup and toasted bread with cheese.

Isabelle settled herself down in front of her own bowl and blew on her spoon before tasting. "Mm…," she said, then smiled at her new charge. "I like lots of spices, how about you, Cowboy?"

He swallowed as though his mouth was watering, and he picked up a spoon and sipped, not even wincing at the heat. "I've never tasted homemade," he confessed. A smile spread across his pinched features, something unplanned, she suspected, and marvelous. "It's really good," he said in surprise, before taking a bite of bread and digging in.

"Well, young man," she said, winking at Henry, "you keep praising my cooking and you and I will get along fine."

Avenging Fucking Angel

By Amy Lane

I am not a good parent. My oldest had a communication handicap and was picked on often, and his sister has always been good at defending his honor. And no, she didn't get in trouble once. From us. My favorite moment, though, was when a kid got in her face in the playground, and the two of them got in trouble because all the yard duty saw was my big guy sitting on the other guy, screaming, "Don't hurt my sister!"

I think the point was gotten because that never happened again. And, yes. He got ice cream when it was over.

"ANTHONY!" RIVER called out, her voice furious and hurt. "Go! Get Diamond out of here! Go!"

But Anthony Cameron—that was his last name now, and he loved it—took one look at his sister's face, streaked with blood and tears and snot and rage, and knew he wasn't going *anywhere*. It had been more than a year since Anthony had needed to fight for a meal or a toy or a place to sleep— but those muscles tightened up in his thirteen-year-old body, and he knew they were poised, waiting to be unleashed.

"Let go of her!" he shouted, charging forward. Two boys—his and River's grade, eight—held River's arms, and one of them had been slapping her, taunting her, as he'd neared. He glanced to Diamond, their little brother, who had dragged him out to the back soccer fields of the school when they were supposed to be meeting to be picked up by River and Diamond's mother, Rhonda.

"Go get your mother," he ordered Diamond, who was two years younger than him and River. "Go get her now."

Once, a year or so ago, going for an adult authority figure would have been the last thing on his mind, but not now. Not after Diamond and River's parents had brought Anthony into their home and treated him like family. Not after their uncle—as white as Anthony but just as loyal to the

Camerons, who were Black—had taken Anthony to this place where he was treated like a person and cared for and forgiven for his fuckups as he learned to forgive others.

Nope—they definitely needed Rhonda and Kaden, and since Rhonda would be waiting for them in front of the school, that was the safer bet.

"Go get your mother," one of the boys—Stef Salter—mocked. "Go get your mother, you little—"

And then he said a *very* bad word. A racist word. A word that Anthony, in a million years, would *never* let anybody call his family.

"You take that back," he growled, his vision turning red.

"Oh, get off it, you little faggot," Stef taunted. His buddy, Arnold, got really creative then.

"Isn't their uncle a faggot? So you've got a whole family full of n—s and f—ts!" And that's how Anthony heard the words too, by then. Not the actual whole word, but the beginning and end of the word, because the actual word was sort of whooshed out by blood rushing through his ears.

"Yeah," sneered Stef. "So if your whole family is n—s and f—s, what the hell does that make you?"

Anthony had gotten close enough now to see the bruises on River's arms and that her nose was bleeding and that the pretty pink-flowered blouse that had been her favorite was now torn.

And when he spoke, he sounded older and angrier and meaner, and all those muscles from all those fights before he'd met the Camerons were bursting in his arms and his legs and his neck and his heart.

"I'm an avenging fucking angel, that's my family, and I'm gonna kick your ass to hell."

"So," Rhonda asked Jackson, her voice sounding worried over the phone, "do you think I handled it right?"

Jackson was trying hard not to drive all the way up to Forest Hill and find the little pukes who had *dared* touch his namesake, and Jade's, and the boy who had become family in the last year, so *he* could administer some old-fashioned family justice.

"Was she okay?" he asked, probably for the millionth time.

"Yeah, baby," Rhonda said, her voice soothing like it had been in junior high when it had been Jackson, Jade, Kaden, and Rhonda, having each other's backs like a Doom Squad to survive daily. "She was fine. Once Anthony got there, she got some good licks in—I got there in time to see both of them kicking ass. If the other kids hadn't started it three to one, they never would have gotten her in the first place."

Jackson smiled slightly. Rhonda was a teacher now, at the same school her kids attended, but he noticed how proud she sounded that her kids were nobody's meat. Rhonda had never belonged on the streets—an accident of school placement had put them in one of the shittiest schools in the district, and Jackson and the Camerons had helped keep Rhonda alive until they'd all made it to high school and the honors classes to help keep them safe—but Rhonda had learned to be tough all the way through graduation.

"Just like her mother," he said fondly.

"That's kind," Rhonda told him, "but seriously—do you think I handled it well? Jackson, this is important. I don't want him to feel like he can get involved in violence on a regular basis, but…." She got a little sniffly. "I was really proud of our boy."

"Well, did you take him out for ice cream?" Jackson asked.

"We did. And promised him pizza during the suspension."

Jackson still couldn't believe the "both sides" bullshit of the suspension.

"Did you promise him pizza in front of the administration?" Jackson asked.

Rhonda's laugh was low and mean. "You bet your ass I did. I also told them that I knew the editor of the local paper, and there would be a big fat article on the backward standards of education in this week's issue."

Jackson had a moment of misgiving. "Rhonda… do you have tenure?"

"No," she said with a sigh. "But there's a district not too far away from Foresthill—you've heard of Colton?"

"Didn't they have all those guys stuck in a gravel pit this summer?" Jackson asked, racking his brains.

"Yeah, honey. And two of them were the school principal and the local sheriff's deputy, both men, who got married in August. So I've got an application in there if this place doesn't want me. I've already got nibbles. I'll be the belle of the ball, don't worry. But right now we're worried about Anthony."

"So you've done ice cream, pizza, any gifts?"

"Mm… yes. Kaden got him—well, all the kids, really, but Anthony was working toward this with chores—one of those video game expansions."

"Nice," Jackson said, glad because it meant *he* could play Kaden and the kids on the expansion as soon as they practiced a little. "Okay, then—no, I think you're good."

Rhonda let out a breath. "But… but Jackson. I was *so proud*. I mean, besides standing up for his sister, and having his brother come get me—a grown-up—he was so brave. And did I mention the kicker?"

Jackson grinned. "Yeah. Man, that was some class A banter right there."

"Right?" she said. "I want him to know he was *appreciated*."

Jackson had an idea. A wonderful, awful idea.

"Don't worry about it," he said happily, pulling up his laptop as he spoke to Rhonda and worked on dinner for Ellery. "I've got just the thing."

"ARE YOU sure we won't get into trouble?" Diamond asked. Well, he was young, and Anthony understood how somebody who worked hard at being good would not be excited about doing what they were doing.

"You don't have to," River told him. "You weren't in the fight—nobody will expect you to come back with 'tude."

Diamond furrowed his handsome little brow. "No, no," he said. "It's fine. Anthony stood up for our family. The least I can do is wear the damned T-shirt."

"Heh heh heh heh heh heh," River laughed, the sound a little bit evil, but Anthony approved. "Our uncle Jackson is *the best*," she said, zipping her hoodie up over the T-shirt. It was March, and there was still a crust of snow on the ground, and the hoodie—and the T-shirt—were both brand-new.

"He is," Anthony said, grinning at *his* T-shirt before zipping up his own jacket. They both looked at Diamond, who stared back and then caught the hint and zipped up *his* jacket.

"This way," he said, like the idea was just dawning on him, "Mom and Dad can't see."

"Yup," River said. "They have plausible deniability."

"And we can show the kids not to mess with our family," Diamond said smugly.

"Nobody messes with our family," River affirmed. "Right, Anthony?" She stared at him meaningfully, because she knew of some of the struggles he'd had, letting down his guard to *be* family.

"Right," Anthony said. Then, a little quieter, "I hope you guys don't get into trouble."

"If we do, we can blame Jackson," River told him.

"He won't mind," Diamond said, blithe as a spring day.

"Kids!" Rhonda called from downstairs in the Cameron home, "get down here and get your toast and let's get this show on the road!"

"Listen to your mother!" Kaden told them, and they all ran to their own rooms to grab their backpacks, now that their conspiracy was solid and all.

"SO," KADEN said as the kids ran for the car, jackets zipped securely up to their chins, "are we supposed to not know they're wearing the shirts to school?"

"Yup," Rhonda said, kissing him on the cheek. "We shall be surprised."

"Think they'll be suspended again?" Kaden asked.

"Heh heh heh heh…." Rhonda laughed, and Kaden loved that she and his brother had the same laugh. "Not after that newspaper article hit the stores. Boy, people were mad. Mark Troyar hasn't gotten that many pissed-off phone calls in his entire worthless career."

"I love it when you're evil," Kaden said, *his* kiss landing on her mouth. "Go out and kick some asses and take some names, Buttercup."

She gave him a happy wave as she grabbed her own book bag and ran to the minivan so they could all get to school.

"YOU READY?" River asked, and Anthony and Diamond both put their fingers on their jacket zippers as they stood at the hall entrance. It was not their imagination—the entire junior high was staring at them to see how they'd enter after the three of them had been out for the week. Would they keep their heads down? Would they be the next bullies? Were they predators or fresh meat?

Anthony's family would *not* be meat.

"Zippers down," he said.

Their jackets parted dramatically, and the two hundred or so students caught their breath as they read the big white letters on the specialized shirts.

I'M AN AVENGING F—G ANGEL.

HANDS OFF MY FAMILY.

They didn't even need to see the rest of what was printed on the backs of the shirts to know that the Cameron kids should be well and truly left alone.

Teaching Randy to Drive

By Amy Lane

Note: *This story happens about a month before the events of* Guarding Randy, *which has yet to be written, and* Devil and the Deep Blue Fish. *It was—as so many things are—inspired by a conversation with my bestie as I explained why my Mate was the preferred parent to teach our adult children to drive, and not myself. For the record, Dex's yell was my yell, and Jackson's quiet chiding was how Mate got our kids to make miles upon miles of laps of the accurately described Sunrise Mall.*

Mary, this one is all your fault.

Dex—

"C'MON, RANDY," Dex wheedled, smiling playfully at the big teenager through the door with the chain on it. "You know me. We're friends. I'm your boss, for heaven's sake. We agreed to do this weeks ago. You don't want to quit after one try, do you?"

Randy was turning twenty in less than a month, and the look he gave Dex was agonized. "I'm sorry, Dex," he said, his long-boned face crunched up like a little boy's. "I don't want to let you down, but I can't!"

"But Randy," Dex said, using the voice he'd used to cajole Frances to visit the doctor, get shots, even try on new clothes. "It didn't go badly last time. We just ran into a—"

"*You yelled*!" Randy shouted through the gap between the door and the frame; then he clapped his hand over his mouth. "You yelled," he said through his hand. "You promised not to yell."

Dex sucked air in through his teeth. "It's true," he acknowledged. "I yelled. And I'm sorry. But it was an unusual circumstance—"

"But you were mad at me, and you yelled," Randy told him, almost tearful. "Dex, I can't deal with you yelling at me. I… you're always so nice, and you can't yell!"

Dex let out the air he'd just sucked in and gave up. "Okay," he said. "Understood. I violated a trust. Would you like me to get Henry instead?"

"Can I drive his minivan?" Randy asked hopefully.

Dex stared. "The ugly brown thing?" He would have thought that, if nothing else, Dex's new Forester would have made Randy eager to learn to drive.

"Yeah," Randy said, sounding much more relaxed already. "If I ding that thing on a light post, nobody will know but me and Henry."

Dex squinted a little, thinking. "It's… well, you know the minivan is technically Rivers's vehicle, right? Henry gets use of it a lot, but I don't know if he has it *today*."

Randy's face fell, and Dex—who had promised Randy months ago to help him get a driver's license so maybe he could become more independent, and, hey, get a job *not porn*, which Dex had to admit, would be a lot healthier for this kid, even though Randy made the company Dex helped run *scads* of money—felt the sweet sweat of desperation dew his brow.

"Let me talk to him," he said, and gave Randy's completely naked— and admittedly magnificent—ginger-furred body a once-over through the crack in the door. "I'll be back in an hour." Because Dex felt like he deserved an hour to talk to his little brother. "In the meantime, you need to go put on some clothes. You knew I was coming, Randy—it's forty-five degrees outside."

Randy glanced down at himself. "D'oh! You'd think I'd learn not to answer the door like this!" he said. "Sure thing, Dex."

He closed the door, and Dex closed his eyes. Eight-and-a-half-inches long when erect, and three—*three*—inches in diameter, and that thing showed zero shrinkage in the cold. And yet, Dex could not in good conscience keep this kid in porn any longer than necessary. Dear God, this kid needed to find his head with both hands and position it firmly on his shoulders.

With a sigh, Dex clattered down the steps of the flophouse apartment building and knocked on his brother's apartment door on the ground floor.

Henry answered while pulling a sweatshirt over his bare torso, scowling. "Lance isn't here," he muttered. "I was sleeping in."

Dex said, "Do you have breakfast or coffee? Can I come in and beg a favor?"

Henry's eyes popped open. "You want breakfast?" he asked, sounding excited. "As in, if I *cook you an omelet*, with *cheese* and some sour cream and salsa, you'd eat it? Coffee with cream and sugar? A fruit salad? Yes!

Come in! Please, God, do you have any idea what it's like trying to feed those fuck-monkeys upstairs? Every goddamned one of them has an eating disorder—I can *barely* get Lance to eat enough to fuel his insane schedule, and Jackson and I have been *learning to cook*. Get your ass in here, big brother. I've got such plans!"

Dex found himself at the small kitchen table of the two-bedroom apartment, drinking coffee and looking around at a blessedly adult living space. No blowup mattress on the floor, no, uhm, *stained* couch or love seat in the living room, a television on a stand and not on a stack of cinderblocks and 2x4s, and artwork—actual *artwork*—on the walls.

"I'm old," he said, taking a satisfyingly cinnamon-sprinkled sip of some first-rate coffee. "But I like it."

Henry chuckled. "Who were you visiting upstairs?"

"Randy." Dex slumped in his chair. "I was supposed to take him for a driving lesson today, but he was *not* going."

Henry chuckled. "Well, that's what you get when you yell."

Dex scowled. "Yell? Is that what he said? I *yelled*?"

"It's all we've heard for *days*—how 'Dex yelled at me!' and I had to assure him that the one time you'd yelled at me was when I fell in the pond and then hadn't called for help, so you probably had a good reason."

"Oh, I had a good reason, all right," Dex muttered grimly. "Did he tell you what I yelled?"

"Just that it was a yell," Henry said. As he spoke, he was deftly cutting up vegetables and some leftover pork chops and onions and putting everything in little bowls. Tomatoes, Dex thought dreamily, and chives. Oh, this was going to be a beauty of an omelet.

Dex pulled his attention back to the matter at hand. "Sure—it was a yell that sounded like, 'Turn left here and *don't hit the two garbagemen in the middle of the road*, and *don't hit the can behind their truck either*!'"

Henry barely missed slicing his finger while dicing a mushroom as Dex relived the "yell," and he turned around to laugh at his brother. "So that was the yell?"

"It was hardly unwarranted!" Dex said, hurt.

"Well, yeah—a very necessary yell," Henry agreed. "But, you know, Randy—"

"He won't go with me," Dex said miserably. "Henry, this kid *needs* a driver's license. He *needs* a way out of porn. And I know people can ride the bus for years, but—"

"But he needs to know he can do it," Henry said, nodding like he got it. He turned to whisking a bunch of eggs cracked into a glass bowl, added some milk and some garlic salt, and then whisked them some more.

Dex was at the place now where he needed to man up. "He wants you to do it," he said. "And he wants you to do it in Jennifer."

Henry almost fumbled the bowl and the whisk. He set them both down and stared at his brother in bemusement. "He wants *me* to teach him how to drive in Jackson's haunted minivan?"

"It's haunted?" Dex asked, surprised.

"Oh my God. The other day, it almost dumped Galen on his ass in front of the office because Galen… well, he said one of those mean, dry things that I won't repeat about how Jennifer isn't a lady. Anyway, she didn't take it well, and Jackson's been detailing her upholstery and oiling all those little hinges on the disappearing back seats this weekend. He says it's like a smudging, except Jennifer's a practical girl."

Dex groaned, and not even the smell of the amazing coffee could make it better. "Will it kill my top-billed adult film actor?"

"He's top billed?" Henry asked in shocked. "*Randy*?"

Dex grunted. "Have you ever seen his porn?"

"No. *God* no. It feels wrong."

"Yeah." Dex nodded glumly. "But that's because we *know* him. If you just randomly watched him in a scene, you'd be saying his name as you came."

"*Davy*…," Henry whined.

"Look, I know," Dex acknowledged. "It's wrong when you know him. You know him and you're like, 'Wait—*that* kid is an adult film star?' But on film he's a powerhouse. So here I am, trying to get my powerhouse out of the business, where he is making me lots of money, by the way, because the *little kid in his heart* is not going to do well in this business much longer. And apparently, *I* can't teach him how to drive because *I yell*!"

Henry grimaced and nodded. "Okay," he said. "Okay. I get it. Hold on a sec, let me get this started, and then I'm gonna call my boss."

Dex groaned. "No…."

"Yeah. Sorry, Dex. My specialty is in telling them bluntly that they're fucking up. I am *not* who Randy needs. We're gonna need to bring in the big guns, okay? And *you* are going to need to sit this one out."

BY THE time Jackson showed up at Henry's with a giant box of doughnuts, Henry had finished his very healthy omelet.

Jackson sighed and sat down to eat, admitting Henry's choice had probably been wiser, while Henry ate three doughnuts in front of Dex and Jackson and they agreed that killing was too good for him.

"Metabolism," Dex muttered. "Wait until he hits thirty."

"Little asshole," Jackson agreed, but he was agreeing through a face full of egg, cheese, and sour cream, so he couldn't be too mad.

"So," Jackson murmured, wiping the egg off his face (heh), "where's our victim?"

"Not my victim," Dex told him, still harboring a grudge. "My car's so nice it scares him, and apparently I yell."

"Not my—" Henry started, but Jackson shook his head.

"Oh no. You're in the back seat, chief. I'm not doing this alone. Besides, Jennifer will get all bent out of shape if we let somebody else drive her and we're not both there."

Henry stared at him. "You know that how?" he asked.

"Ernie told me," Jackson said grimly. "As in, he called me at two in the morning to tell me specifically not to let somebody besides us drive the minivan without both of us inside her."

"When?" Henry asked, right to be suspicious. "On what *day* did he call?"

"*This* day," Jackson said, standing up and taking his plate to the sink. "This morning. Didn't make any sense to me until you called. But I was up early, double-checking her engine, in case."

Dex stared at them both. "Have I met—"

"No," they both said.

"Billy and K-Ski have," Jackson told him. "Just... just don't. Don't question it. Let me go upstairs and tell Randy we're going to the mall."

Dex frowned, obviously feeling left out. "What do I do? I blocked out all sorts of time for this!"

Henry shrugged. "Listen, we're going to be gone for at least two hours. You know, I've got an empty house here, an entertainment system... do what you gotta. I swear I won't tell your husband."

Dex got a sort of dreamy expression on his face. "I could watch football uninterrupted...," he almost sang, and Jackson knew he was now fine with it.

At that moment there was a knock on the door. "I'll get it," Jackson said, setting his plate in the sink before glancing at Henry. "You go change."

He opened the door to a giant muscular chest, pale as marble, covered in hearty ginger fur.

"Dear God," Jackson said, raising his chin a little. "How tall are you now?"

"Six five?" Randy guessed. "Six six? Why are you here?" He paused, his angular jaw working as he remembered his grown-up words. "I'm sorry. Good to see you, Jackson. Are you coming driving with us?" He followed that up with a hopeful smile, and Jackson nodded.

"Yeah, kid. But first go upstairs, put on a T-shirt, and then put on a sweatshirt over that." Jackson glanced down at the knobby knees poking out from under a pair of cargo shorts that went mid-thigh. "And maybe find your own pants."

Randy grunted. "To drive?"

"It's forty degrees outside," Jackson pointed out, reasonably, he hoped. "Your nipples could cut glass. Go! And hurry—I need to be done in two hours."

"What's in two hours?" Randy asked, and Jackson grimaced.

"Well, right now Ellery's watching *Meet the Press* and throwing toast at the screen whenever the Republicans talk, and as soon as that's over, he calls his mother for a blow-by-blow breakdown of everything that's happened in politics in the last week."

At Randy's horrified expression, Jackson nodded. "Yeah, it's terrifying. But *after* that, I get to spend the day with my fiancé, and I *like* him, so that's a good thing. Now scoot!"

Randy turned and went up the stairs with enough alacrity to make him slip. He recovered with a hand on the stair in front of him, and Jackson saw one more thing that needed to be addressed.

"And change your shoes! New drivers don't get flip-flops!"

He shut the door and turned around with a breath, staring at Henry with a flat expression. "Somebody owes me for this," he decided. "You, Ernie, Dex—hell, I'll take it up with Jennifer if I have to, but *somebody* owes me."

"Understood," Henry said. "But first, go up and remind him to grab his driver's permit, because I'd put down *money* he doesn't have that either."

EVENTUALLY THEY made it into Jennifer, and as Jackson piloted her down the mostly quiet streets of Sacramento and then Carmichael, he told Henry to be on the lookout for a Starbucks or Dutch Bros. or something, because Jackson had chosen doughnuts over coffee and now he needed coffee.

"You could have let me make you some!" Henry objected.

"Well, we need to get to Sunrise Mall early for what I have in mind," Jackson told him.

"What's at Sunrise Mall?" Randy asked.

"Nothing." Twenty years ago, it had been an active little indoor shopping center, and while the place across from it, Birdcage Center, was now all refurbished and outdoor accessible and busy, the mall itself had not fared so well.

"Literally," Henry said, frowning. "Absolutely nothing."

In the fall, it had pop-up Halloween stores in one of the cavernous old department store shells, but now? Maybe half the venues were occupied, and attendance, even during holidays, was grim. Jackson had seen it on Sacramento's Ten Most Haunted Places lists—many, many times.

"Yup," Jackson said grimly. "Absolutely nothing."

There was a moment of quiet, and then Henry said, "Oh. *Oh*. Nothing. I get it now."

"Yup," Jackson said, sighting a Dutch Bros. on Fair Oaks with relief. "Not a goddamned thing."

The mall was all but deserted when they arrived, and Henry wanted to know where the employees were.

"On the back side, facing the roller rink—"

"Wait! Shut *up*!" Henry told him, enchanted. "A *roller rink*? As in *skating*?"

Jackson grunted. "Straight out of an eighties movie, yes. Skating. On four wheels. I think the popcorn oil is older than I am. But we're not going there." He guided Jennifer to the far corner, where Macy's used to be, and threw it into Park near the curb, near Greenback Lane. "Okay, Randy, I'm leaving the keys in so she doesn't stall. We're going to get out and switch places. It's fine."

Once they were back in their seats, Jackson made Randy put his seat belt on and sighed.

"Okay, we're in Park. The right pedal is the gas—that makes it go."

"I'm not stupid, Jackson," Randy grumbled.

"I'm not repeating this because you're stupid," Jackson told him patiently. "I'm repeating this because you've got acres of nerve endings between your head and your foot, and sometimes you need some reinforcement to make that happen without thought. So, left pedal stops, right pedal goes. Say it with me."

Randy rolled his eyes. "Left pedal stops, right pedal goes," he muttered, but his foot twitched as he said which pedal was which, and Jackson had some hope.

"That's right. So you step on the brake and shift into Drive. Never shift into Drive unless your foot is on the brake. Repeat after me."

"Never shift into Drive unless your foot is on the brake," Randy said, and apparently it only took the repeat ritual once.

"So put your foot on the brake and shift into Drive."

Jackson tried not to hold his breath, but Randy apparently *did* have a connector between his foot and his mouth—and it didn't always work against him.

In this case he shifted the minivan into Drive and waited for further instructions.

"We're going down this lane," Jackson said. "There is absolutely nothing here, not lane lines, not obstacles. I will tell you if you stray out of the lane, and what you might hit if this wasn't the ninth vacant circle of hell, but I will not get excited unless you stand on the gas, jump the curb, go over the sidewalk, take out the stoplight, and head directly into traffic. Anything short of that and there will be no yelling, do you understand?"

"Yessir," Randy said, and his relief was palpable.

"So if I *am* raising my voice, that means simply that I don't want to die and not specifically that I blame *you* for my imminent death. Are we clear?"

Randy laughed a little. "Yessir. I understand."

"Good. Take your foot off the brake, and put it gently on the gas."

The car jumped forward, but, hey, there was nothing in front of them but empty parking lot, made interesting only by faded parking lines and a few plastic bags being pushed around by the wind.

After the jump—and no yelling—Randy pulled his foot off the gas a little, and Jennifer meandered forward, like an old cow smelling flowers.

Right over the faded lane lines, and then back into what would be oncoming traffic if anybody was in that lane, and then into the lane lines again, and into imaginary traffic. After they wandered past the distant hull of the Macy's building, Jackson started to offer mild commentary.

"Okay, so we're taking out cars here. Yup. That was a car. And another car. And another car."

"Oh *shit*!" Randy stomped on the brake, and they all were flung forward, hard enough to leave bruises. "Are you sure?"

Jackson grunted and remembered that promise not to yell. Poor Dex. He'd only wanted to avoid a manslaughter charge, that was all.

"They're imaginary cars, Randy," he said, his voice remarkably even. "Pretend they're giant penis cars, like Trump trucks or something. Get it out of your system. You're wandering into the oncoming lane—you got any grudges you want to take out? Who are we plowing over as we drive?"

"Jackson!" Randy protested, obviously distraught, "I don't want to *hurt* anybody! That's *horrible*!"

From the corner of his eye Jackson saw Henry put his hand on his heart, and he nodded. Too sweet for words. Too dumb to function. It was a *lethal* combination.

"Okay, then, so just Trump trucks? We'll pretend they're empty."

"Heh heh heh, *yes*," Randy said. "You tell me when I'm taking them out."

"Sure," Jackson said, and then, "Take your foot off the brake and put it gently on the gas."

"Oh!" Randy remembered he'd been stepping on the brake, let it go, and this time their acceleration was a little smoother.

"Good," Jackson said, his voice still soothing. "And that's a Trump truck, and there's another, and there's another."

"Shit," Randy said, overcorrecting.

"And there's one in front of us, 'cause it's an oncoming lane," Jackson reminded him.

"Shit!" This time the overcorrection was a little less dire.

"And that's a car, and that's a car, and hey," Jackson said, as he neared a stop sign, "that's a whole family, Randy, because that was an intersection."

"*Shit!*"

And they started again. By the time an hour had passed, they'd made four tortuously slow loops around the mall, and while Randy wasn't ready for the road yet, they hadn't gone over any curbs, and he'd stopped taking out imaginary families at vacant intersections, so that was something.

After their third trip around, as they passed the back of JCPenney again, Henry spoke up from the back.

"Jackson," he said slowly, "remember that case we're working on?"

"Shoplifting?" Jackson asked. "Randy, that was an entire fleet of trucks. I know you can drive on the right side of the road."

"Sorry, Jackson," Randy said, then thrust his tongue out between his lips and resumed driving.

"Yup. Remember our client's defense?"

"That two women dressed like Jersey Shore rejects walked out with—oh holy fuck," Jackson muttered. "Randy, stop. Henry's got to jump out of the minivan and take some pictures."

"Yahtzee!" Henry muttered. "I didn't even know the mall was open!"

"The parking lot here has been filling up," Jackson admitted, checking out the two women with big sprayed hair, tight T-shirts in the cold gray day, and sparkly sunglass frames. "It's getting to be time to go back. Go flirt with those two dumb broads and get some shots of what's in their bags. We'll be around in time to get you as you run away."

"Oh my God!" Henry cackled. "This is amazing!" He paused. "Do you think you'll be back before they get me?"

"Yeah, run through the mall and come out on the first entrance on the Sunrise side. I swear we'll be there."

"Sweet!"

And then Henry flung the door open and trotted out. They were far enough away that the objects of his camera phone hadn't spotted him yet, and Jackson said, "Put the car into Park, Randy—be sure to step on the b—"

"Step on the brake," Randy muttered, suiting actions to words. "Put the car into Park. Get out of the seat, jump in the back."

"That's my boy."

While Randy was jumping in the back, Jackson crawled over the console.

"Seat belt on," Jackson muttered.

"Go!" Randy shouted.

As if on cue, Henry ran up to the women and knocked the giant Macy's bags out of their hands—yes, the same Macy's that had gone out of business—and whirled around, taking pictures of clothes that had all the tags and none of the receipts.

And Jackson stepped on the gas and roared down the street that passed behind the mall and then around to the front.

He got there just in time for Henry—covered in red underwear and a stunning blue formal, all of it draped from his head and shoulders and floating behind him like a banner of shame—to launch himself from the double doors.

Jackson screeched to a halt long enough for Henry to jump in, and they peeled away and off toward the Greenback entrance before the women even got a look at the crap-brown minivan serving as his getaway vehicle.

Jackson cut corners, jumped curbs, and cut off several pissed-off motorists merging onto Greenback and roaring toward Fair Oaks, their empty Dutch Bros. cups rattling in the holders while Henry freed himself from tacky lingerie and finally got his seat belt on.

It took them three miles to stop laughing, and another mile for Henry to start texting the pictures to Ellery so he could use them to bargain for their client's freedom.

"Well," Henry breathed when they finally all calmed down, "put another one in the 'Listen to Ernie' column."

"Who's Ernie?" Randy asked from the back seat, and Jackson had to keep himself from startling, because he and Henry had been in their work mode and had almost forgotten he was there.

"A friend," Jackson told him. "He told me Henry should come along for the ride."

"I wonder what he meant by getting bent out of shape if I didn't?" Henry asked, and Jackson shook his head.

But he was thinking about his desperate peel out around the mall and how several vehicles had been entering a once-vacant side road as Jackson had ripped down the drive.

Several Trump Trucks, on parade.

There was no guarantee Randy would have gunned the engine and gone for it if he'd seen them—after all the "That's a car" exercise had been purely hypothetical.

But no guarantee he wouldn't have, either.

"I got nothing," he lied smoothly, and Henry gave him a look that said they'd talk later.

"That was awesome," Randy said, sounding content. "Can we come here next week and do that? You're both so relaxed. I think I might learn how to drive after all!"

Jackson let out a breath and silently consigned a couple months of Sundays to this enterprise, and next to him, he could hear Henry do the same.

"It's fine," Jackson said. "I really can't stand *Meet the Press*."

"Thanks, guys," Randy said, his gratitude literally on his sleeve. "With you guys, I feel safe as a kitten."

Henry snorted next to him, and before Jackson could send him a "Hush!" look, his seat belt unhooked out of nowhere and smacked his fingers as it got sucked back up into the release mechanism.

"See?" Jackson muttered.

"Yeah, I know," Henry muttered back. "Sorry, Jennifer—didn't mean to tempt fate."

"What's that?" Randy asked.

"Nothing, kid," Jackson told him. He and Henry both shook their heads in silent prayer. "Not a damned thing."

Continue Reading for an Excerpt from
Fish in a Barrel
Book #7 in the Fish Out of Water series
by Amy Lane.

Apple Picking Weather

JACKSON HAD to hand it to the woman; she claimed she was shy and nonconfrontational, but she didn't seem to be afraid to express an opinion.

The courthouse in Sacramento was a newish marble-and-glass structure, the rooms inside were carpeted, and the seats were cushioned. It wasn't exactly designed for comfort, but there wasn't a thunderous echo either, which was helpful when the witness who saw the crime in question hadn't wanted to testify in the first place.

But she had finally agreed because, she said, it wasn't right.

"So, Mrs. Kleinman," Ellery said, looking decisive and articulate in his best gray wool pinstripe. "You say you are absolutely positive that the person you saw holding a knife to the victim's chest was not, indeed, the defendant, Mr. Ezekiel Halliday, seated." Ellery gestured to Halliday in the defendant's chair, still thin from the hospital, dressed reluctantly in a suit that was tight at the shoulder joints and knee joints but loose everywhere else. He had dark curly hair and a close-cropped beard, mostly because it was easier to trim the beard than to shave by himself, and his brown eyes didn't always track the proceedings, although Jackson knew without a doubt he was listening. His narrow face was capable of great joy—Jackson had seen that—but not today.

"Absolutely," Mrs. Kleinman said. Her face softened as she took Ezekiel in. "Zeke wouldn't have known what to do with a knife if he had one."

Ellery nodded. "We'll get back to that. It's important. But how can you be so sure? The police identified Ezekiel after one canvass of the neighborhood. What makes you say it couldn't have been him?"

She gave a *harrumph*. "Well, for one thing, I'd passed Ezekiel about a block before I came to the mouth of Harmony Park, where the incident happened. He was sitting on the sidewalk, holding his foot up to his mouth to suck on a wound."

Ellery had been prepared for this answer—he and Jackson had spent some private time in their office giving voice to the "oogies" as their paralegal, Jackson's sister, called the intense visceral reaction to something gross. But Jackson still saw his wince of dismay when Mrs. Kleinman said it.

"That doesn't sound… hygienic," Ellery said delicately. "Why would he be doing that?"

The woman was plump and doughy, in her fifties, with graying hair and everything from bad ankles to bad knees to a bad back. None of that stopped her from walking three obnoxious Pomeranians two to three miles a day in her little suburb, and apparently Effie Kleinman didn't miss a trick.

"He'd run away from his care home the day before," she said, shaking her head. "His shoe had come off, and he'd stubbed his toe. Zeke's joints aren't properly formed—it makes him very flexible, but not very stable on his feet."

"Did you offer Mr. Halliday help?" Ellery asked.

Effie sucked air in through her teeth. "Well, that's tricky. I've got the number for his care home by my desk in my house, but I didn't have it on my cell. I talked to him for a bit, and he was feeling fractious, so I told him I'd call Arturo—that's the man who usually comes to get him when he's gotten out—and left him to go on my way."

"So that's the last time you saw Mr. Halliday," Ellery responded.

"That day, yes," she said with a grimace, "because then I was walking through the park entrance, and that asshole with the knife was screaming, and I was trying not to shit my pants."

Jackson watched Ellery as he slow-blinked, trying to digest what she *actually* said as opposed to what they'd been *coaching* her to say for a week.

After a stunned silence in the courtroom, Ellery asked, his voice dry as toast, "Were you successful?"

Effie gave an embarrassed snort. "Not entirely. I did feel a powerful need to go home and change my britches, which is one of the reasons I didn't stick around and talk to the police. Besides," she added, sobering again, "I really wanted to call Arturo. If there was a lunatic loose in the park with a knife, I didn't want Zeke out in that."

"So you didn't stick around to answer any questions?" Ellery reinforced.

"No, sir. Not my scene." She gave a shrug. "Witnesses like me are invisible to police anyway. Just another fat brown woman with too many dogs. They didn't want my opinion."

"So what made you decide to come here and testify?" Ellery prodded, and Jackson let out a breath. They had to make this clear now or the prosecution would turn it into a "gotcha" question on the cross.

"Well, your man there," she nodded toward Jackson, who waved, "got my name from one of the other witnesses. When he told me they'd fingered poor Zeke, I had to come forward. I'd called Arturo, and he was going to come get Zeke, but Arturo's got no obligation to me. He hadn't told me Zeke was in jail, which was the stupidest thing I'd ever heard of."

Jackson Rivers had known Ellery Cramer for nearing on nine years now, and they'd been sharing a bed for over a year of that. Ellery had slick brown hair and sharp features—nose, cheekbones, chin—along with hard, flat brown eyes.

Jackson knew Ellery's every expression, including when those narrow lips went slack and bruised with passion and his brown eyes went from hard to limpid with need, and he knew that if he hadn't known Ellery down to the last nuance, he might have missed the fury he was suppressing as they covered this next line of questioning.

"Could you explain why it's a 'stupid' idea to think Zeke should be in jail for holding a knife to the victim's throat." Ellery asked, keeping that fury in check.

"Objection!" Arizona Brooks, the ADA in charge of prosecution, stood up hurriedly. "This witness is not a medical professional, and she is hardly qualified to tell us what conditions the defendant may have had that would hinder his ability to perpetrate a crime."

Ellery and Jackson stared at her. Arizona was a fit woman, known for her zero tolerance for bullshit, who sported a spiky gray buzz cut, big silver earrings, and liked to wear white men's-cut suits when she was in court.

She was sharp, surprisingly compassionate for an ADA, and willing to deal for the good of the victim and the perpetrator if she saw injustice being committed in the name of the law.

And she never, ever made a mistake.

Until right now.

"Your Honor," Ellery said, yanking his gaze to the judge in the front of the courtroom with an obvious effort, "besides having been a teacher of the moderate and severely disabled for over twenty years, Mrs. Kleinman has taken a compassionate interest in our defendant for several years and has an established relationship with his caretaker. While we will call Arturo Bautista, who runs the Sunshine Care Home, as our next witness, Mrs. Kleinman can speak directly to why it would have been impossible for the defendant to be where the police claimed he was at the time of the crime."

"Overruled," the judge said reluctantly, and Jackson caught the glare the man sent Arizona.

And he didn't like it.

Judge Clive Brentwood *looked* like everything a judge should be—tall, broad-shouldered, distinguished, with the tanned skin of a tennis or golf aficionado and a lion's mane of gray hair tamed by the stylist's comb. Brentwood *looked* like he should be wise and educated and fair. His courtroom presence was formal and impeccable, much like the man himself.

But Ellery had groaned and cursed his luck when he'd seen that he'd drawn Brentwood to try the case in front of, because whereas much of Sacramento was progressive and most of the judges were fair and had the best interest of their constituents in mind, Brentwood was conservative down to his Ronald Reagan leather-soled oxford shoes.

Although he'd never been said to let politics get in the way of a fair ruling, it was still a blow to their case to have someone belonging to a party that seemed fundamentally against mental health and disability care. And they hadn't seen much of his greatly vaunted "fairness" here.

The look he'd aimed at Arizona Brooks had not been friendly, although technically Brooks had done nothing wrong. Her mistake had been in giving Ellery a chance to voice Mrs. Kleinman's qualifications as a judge of Mr. Halliday's condition, and Ellery had taken full advantage.

Jackson eyeballed Arizona, who managed to put an apologetic face on things, but who didn't—to Jackson's eyes anyway—look sorry at all.

In fact as she sat down, Jackson saw her give Effie Kleinman a look that bordered on hope. Like she *hoped* Mrs. Kleinman was the answer to Ezekiel Halliday's prayers.

But Ellery was already questioning their witness, and Jackson's attention was pulled—as it always was—to the magnetic personal force that was Ellery Cramer.

"So," Ellery said, rephrasing for Arizona's sake, because she was a colleague, "could you tell us why it would have been impossible for Mr. Halliday to have been the perpetrator who took Annette Frazier hostage?"

"Well, like I said, Zeke was sitting down, tending to his foot when I passed him. He was bleeding, and it looked like a fierce cut there, and Zeke doesn't move well anyway."

"Could you explain 'doesn't move well'?" Ellery prodded.

"He's got something wrong with his muscles and joints—I think Arturo said it was caused by brain damage at birth, so cerebral palsy of some sort. He's very flexible but not very strong and not very coordinated. If he was the dickhead with the knife who terrorized Annette Frazier, he would have needed to pass me up on the park pathways, and he did not. And he would have needed to have gotten a weapon from somewhere, and then done all of the things the witness for the prosecution said he did: wrap his arm around Annette's chest, hold a knife to her throat, and threaten bystanders. His speech isn't clear enough to threaten bystanders, and if he wrapped his arm around somebody's throat it would be to help himself stay standing. I was there. I saw the guy they were looking for. He was young with brown eyes and brown hair, but that was the only resemblance. Zeke Halliday was not him."

The silence in the courtroom was electric, and Jackson saw the witnesses for the prosecution looking at each other speakingly. The four policemen—Jackson had dubbed them "choirboys"—would not be able to actually speak because courtroom rules precluded it, but their eyeballs were talking daggers. Jackson managed to let out a breath he hadn't known he'd been holding for a month, ever since Arturo Bautista had contacted them on Zeke's behalf to try to get his charge out of jail.

"Why do *you* think Zeke Halliday was arrested?" Ellery asked Effie, and Jackson's eyes darted toward Arizona Brooks to see if she'd object to the question. She should have—it called for speculation on facts Ms. Kleinman could not know—but she didn't, which told Jackson all he ever needed to know about how excited Arizona had been to prosecute this case.

"I think the cops got lazy," Effie said, obviously hurt. "I think the bad guy got away, running through the park's underbrush and down the irrigation stream, and whoever followed them encountered Zeke on the pathway and thought, 'Hey, this guy's obviously homeless. Nobody will give a crap if we arrest him, and that way we can say we tried.'"

Effie's words rang throughout the courtroom, bitter and very true, and once again Jackson looked toward the prosecution to see if there would be an objection.

This time, when Arizona remained stubbornly silent, Ellery met Jackson's eyes in question for a brief second before he turned his attention back to the stand.

"One more thing," Ellery said, before turning the witness over to the prosecution. "You said Mr. Halliday had a wound on his foot. Was he wounded anywhere else?"

"No, sir," Effie said, her eyes seeking out the officers sitting behind the prosecution's desk waiting to be called in rebuttal.

"Were there any bruises on his face, neck, or on his arms?"

"No, sir."

"Was there any blood besides his foot?"

"No, sir," she replied, eyes narrowing.

"Objection," Arizona said belatedly. "Where's this leading?"

"We'll have to talk to the next witness to find out," Ellery said smoothly.

"Withdrawn," Arizona snapped out smartly, and again, that glare.

Brentwood had been going to sustain, but Arizona hadn't let him.

Interesting, Jackson thought. Very, very interesting.

The cross-examination went smoothly, and Arizona pretty much stuck to the script, testing Effie Kleinman's testimony in the places it could—potentially—be weak. Could Mr. Halliday have run through the underbrush in order to take a shortcut to where the incident had taken place?

No, Effie had insisted, he could not have. Between the injury to his foot and his lack of physical coordination, Zeke Halliday couldn't have beat her to the park's entrance where the incident had taken place.

Then Arizona had done more of Jackson and Ellery's work for them. Why, she asked Effie, if Zeke Halliday was disabled, would he be allowed to stand trial?

"He's not *stupid*," Effie had protested. "His IQ is very functional, and I understand he really loves audiobooks—he apparently loves to discuss them. But his body makes it difficult to parse his sentences and difficult for him to be self-sufficient. He's cognizant and able to stand trial, but he's not physically capable of committing this crime."

Then Arizona Brooks had put the nail in the coffin of her own case by asking what sounded like a "gotcha" question—but it got the wrong side.

"You say you were going to go home to call a resource for Mr. Halliday," Arizona said, her voice measured, as though she were weighing every word.

"Yes, and I did. I called Arturo as soon as I got home."

"But there were resources all over the park. The police were already there. Why didn't you call them?"

Effie Kleinman visibly recoiled. "Have you ever *heard* the police roust the homeless? Have you *heard* the way they talk to the transient population in my neighborhood? It's dehumanizing as hell, and it's certainly not help of any sort. No, if I'd realized they were going to come get Zeke, I would have sat down next to him and told them to fuck off when they tried to arrest him. I certainly wouldn't have thrown him to the wolves."

And before the judge could call order, Arizona proclaimed herself done with the witness, and Ellery was up to call the next one to the stand.

Arturo Bautista was a trim man in his midfifties with a square, lined brown face and a sweet smile. His family ran several adult-care homes off

Stockton Boulevard, and while the places weren't posh, they were clean, the residents felt safe, and the staff knew everybody by name and talked to them like human beings. Arturo, who'd been sitting next to Jackson during Effie's testimony, gave Jackson a nervous smile as he stood.

"You'll do fine," Jackson mouthed, and Arturo gave a here-goes-nothing sort of shrug.

After being sworn in, he sat, both feet on the floor, and regarded Ellery with bright, alert eyes and a sort of calming presence. Jackson had seen him in action at the care home. Arturo had a big job, taking care of nearly forty residents, each with an assortment of mental and physical disabilities, but he dealt with the challenges using compassion, humor, and a solid dose of common sense.

"Mr. Bautista," Ellery began, "you are the proprietor of the Sunshine Prayers Care Home off Stockton Boulevard?"

"The Sunshine Prayers Care Home for the Moderately Disabled," Arturo clarified. "Sunshine Prayers is the company name. There are different homes for different needs."

"Thank you for the clarification," Ellery said, and Jackson had to keep from smiling to himself. Ellery had originally scripted different wording during witness prep, but once, when he'd been tired, he'd simply left off the remainder of the name. Arturo had made the clarification then, too, and Ellery had liked the way it sounded—as though Arturo was a professional who knew his business and made sure there was no confusion.

"So," Ellery continued, "you're responsible for Ezekiel Halliday?"

"Well, his family is responsible for him," Arturo said wryly, "but we provide the day-to-day care. It's often difficult for a family—particularly one with low income—to provide a suitable peer-interactive environment for an adult with special needs."

Ellery nodded and began to question Arturo about the day-to-day operations of the care home. Jackson's stomach knotted, expecting Arizona's objection at any moment, but none came. In a way, it was a relief; sometimes the prosecution spent the entire trial trying to disrupt the defense's rhythm or vice versa. But as Ellery's questioning—designed for one exclusive purpose—continued, Jackson started getting jittery. When was the other shoe going to drop?

"So your facility sounds very organized," Ellery said. "But that begs the question. How was it Ezekiel Halliday was in the park that day unsupervised?"

Arturo looked sorrowful, as he had during witness preparation. "Zeke's smart," he said with a sigh. "And he gets bored. Some of the residents are cleared to leave unsupervised. They need very little help and are close to being independent. Ezekiel has been begging for the same privileges, but—" Arturo took a deep breath. "—he's easily injured," he said, meeting Ezekiel's eyes in apology. "And his speech is unclear, so it's difficult for him to ask for help."

"How long had Ezekiel been missing from your facility on the day of the incident?" Ellery asked without commenting on Arturo's explanation.

"Two days."

"Is this common, Mr. Bautista? For a resident to be missing overnight?"

"No," Arturo said grimly. "In fact with any other resident, we would have been on the phone to every authority in the book to find him. It's not safe for him to be out there."

"Then why not this time?" Ellery lowered his voice, made it soft, almost invisible, because he wanted everybody to hear the answer. Jackson hated the answer, but it wasn't any less true because Jackson hated it.

"This was his third such incident in two years," Arturo said. "When it happens too often, social services moves residents to a different facility."

"Wouldn't a different facility be a better fit?" Ellery asked. He'd asked that question during preparation to find out why Ezekiel had been in the park that day.

"The state-owned facility is horrible," Arturo told him, voice shaking. "Too many people, too many problems. He could get assaulted, have his possessions stolen, be force-fed medication. He's vulnerable on his own, but that is not the place for him. Neither is jail. There's not a violent bone in his body. He just… just was in the wrong place at the wrong time."

"So you didn't call the police because you were afraid of what they'd do?" Ellery asked.

"Yes."

Ellery pulled a folder from his desk that featured eight-by-ten photos that Jackson had taken when they'd managed to bail Ezekiel out of jail.

"Is this what you were afraid of?" he asked.

Arturo's voice broke. "Yes."

Between the time Effie Kleinman had seen Ezekiel sitting on the sidewalk and Arturo had gone to the jail with Jackson and Ellery to post his bail, Ezekiel had been badly beaten. His face was puffy—one eye swollen almost completely shut—and his jaw had been broken as well. He'd lost two teeth, and there were bruises on his neck and shoulders that showed clearly the outline of hard-soled boots.

Not the soft-soled crocs given to prisoners.

"Objection?" Brentwood asked, looking at Arizona Brooks.

"Of course I object to seeing a man badly beaten," Arizona said smoothly. "And so should you."

"But the pictures are irrelevant," Judge Brentwood protested.

"To why the defendant had a legitimate fear of the police?" Arizona responded. "No, sir, I think they speak very clearly as to why the defendant and his caregiver didn't ask the police for help. It is not your place to object. It's mine. And I don't. I think the defense should continue on."

Brentwood gaped for a moment before looking at Ellery in confusion.

"Mr. Cramer," he said, gesturing vaguely.

"Thank you, sir," Ellery said smoothly, but Jackson could see that Ellery was as boggled as he was. Arizona Brooks was a topflight attorney. Much of the testimony, including the damning pictures that spoke to a painful beating at the hands of the authorities, should have been a tooth-and-nail fight to get admitted.

Arizona was doing everything but leaning back and taking a nap. In fact she was going one better. She was actually putting on her hip waders and helping Ellery cut through the bullshit.

Jackson wondered why. He wanted to excuse himself to go make a phone call or two, but he'd promised both Effie and Arturo he'd be there for the two of them. Effie was sitting next to him now, clenching his knee with stress.

Jackson patted her hand until she let go with a sheepish look, and together they watched as Ellery finished with Arturo's testimony and turned Arturo over to Arizona.

She looked at Arturo reluctantly and continued to give him a very mild cross-examination. Toward the end, she paused and took a deep breath, as though fortifying herself.

"Now, Mr. Cramer showed us pictures of the defendant, and he looked in bad shape. Did you ever, at any time, see one of the officers seated behind me lay a finger on Ezekiel?"

"No, ma'am. I didn't see it happen."

"Then why would we assume that the police are responsible for the bruises?"

"Because when I asked Ezekiel what happened, he said it was 'the bad policemen,'" Arturo said, not backing down.

"But I thought Mr. Halliday couldn't talk!" Arizona was feigning surprise—and not bothering to hide it.

"It's difficult to understand him," Arturo told her. "But not impossible. He knows who to be afraid of."

Arizona nodded slowly. "Good," she said. "It's good somebody does. No more questions for this witness."

The judge looked at the clock. "It's getting close to quitting time. Let's resume testimony tomorrow, 9:00 a.m. sharp."

"All rise!" intoned the bailiff, and Brentwood exited the courtroom, followed by the jury.

Arizona didn't look at them as she packed her briefs into her briefcase and turned to speak to the officers who had been ready to be called as witnesses. The conversation didn't appear to be going well.

The officer in charge, wearing his full blues, hat tucked under his arm, was doing his best to use his six-foot-plus height to loom over Arizona's five eight or so.

True to the woman Jackson and Ellery knew, she sent him a killing look.

"If you didn't want it brought up," she said icily, "maybe you shouldn't have authorized it."

"He fought back!" said a younger officer bitterly. So fair his neck was turning purple with agitation, his voice rang with injured adolescent dignity.

"You were *beating* him," Arizona retorted. "I don't know which part of that you don't understand. I told you this would happen, and I warned you they would introduce the evidence in the criminal trial so they could use it in the civil trial. Well, they have. And when this kid gets let off, expect Cramer's partner to come after you in the most celebrated civil suit in the city. This isn't going away."

"Well, not from anything *you're* trying to do," snarled the taller dark-haired officer. "I swear, it's like you want him to get off!"

"Because even *I* know he didn't do anything," she snapped back. "Now if I were you, I'd go try to find the real perpetrator, or Rivers and Cramer are going to do it for you and make you look even worse. Now go."

They all stared at her and then looked over at Jackson and Ellery speculatively.

Jackson bared his teeth at them in what was definitely *not* a smile. They were working on it. Of *course* they were working on it. But the state was hell-bent on cramming this case through the system, trying their defendant while the bruises from his police beating were still visible and his jaw was still wired, rendering him all but mute.

The witnesses for the prosecution visibly recoiled from Jackson's expression, and the silence in the courtroom thudded like a lead gavel on flesh.

"*Go!*" Arizona shouted, and the clot of cops left, grumbling, leaving a nearly clear courtroom.

"Arizona…?" Ellery began, but she shook her head and held up her hand.

"Win this one," she said. "I can't have any more off days or Brentwood'll declare a mistrial. You know that. See you both tomorrow."

And with that she was gone, leaving Jackson with the distinct impression she was crying.

Ellery met his eyes then, and they had a complete silent conversation that started with "Okay, that was weird" and ended with "We'll talk about it when we get rid of the civilians."

Arturo had already gone around the table to grasp Ezekiel's wheelchair and begin pushing him down the aisle between the banks of seats, and Effie followed him slowly. Arturo, Effie, and Zeke had all come in Arturo's van—he'd been given custody after Zeke made bail, and suddenly Zeke was having to deal with locks on the door to his dormitory and hourly checks to make sure he hadn't tried to fly the coop again.

Jackson got the feeling that after meeting the "good" guys, Zeke wasn't going to want to fly the coop again for a very long time.

Scan the QR code below to order

Writer, knitter, mother, wife, award-winning author AMY LANE shows her love in knitwear, is frequently seen in the company of tiny homicidal dogs, and can't believe all the kids haven't left the house yet. She lives in a crumbling crapmansion in the least romantic area of California, has a long-winded explanation for everything, and writes to silence the voices in her head. There are a lot of voices—she's written over 120 books.

Website: www.greenshill.com
Blog: www.writerslane.blogspot.com
Email: amylane@greenshill.com
Facebook: www.facebook.com/amy.lane.167
Twitter: @amymaclane
Patreon: https://www.patreon.com/AmyHEALane

Guess who's swimming in the same pond...
FISH OUT OF WATER
Amy Lane
1

Fish Out of Water: Book One

PI Jackson Rivers grew up on the mean streets of Del Paso Heights—and he doesn't trust cops, even though he was one. When the man he thinks of as his brother is accused of killing a police officer in an obviously doctored crime, Jackson will move heaven and earth to keep Kaden and his family safe.

Defense attorney Ellery Cramer grew up with the proverbial silver spoon in his mouth, but that hasn't stopped him from crushing on street-smart, swaggering Jackson Rivers for the past six years. But when Jackson asks for his help defending Kaden Cameron, Ellery is out of his depth—and not just with guarded, prickly Jackson. Kaden wasn't just framed, he was framed by crooked cops, and the conspiracy goes higher than Ellery dares reach—and deep into Jackson's troubled past.

Both men are soon enmeshed in the mystery of who killed the cop in the minimart, and engaged in a race against time to clear Kaden's name. But when the mystery is solved and the bullets stop flying, they'll have to deal with their personal complications… and an attraction that's spiraled out of control.

Scan the QR code below to order

There's blood in the water and death in the air...

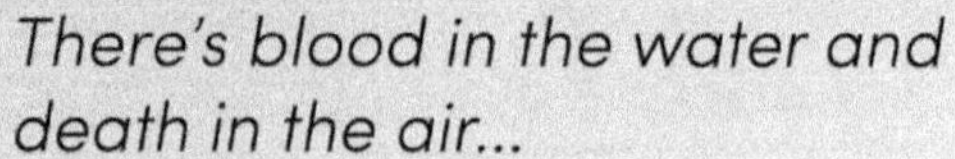

RED FISH, DEAD FISH

Amy Lane

"Deliciously tense . . . a satisfying mix of sweet angst and steamy suspense."
KAREN ROSE, NYT Bestselling Author

2

Fish Out of Water: Book Two

They must work together to stop a psychopath—and save each other.

Two months ago Jackson Rivers got shot while trying to save Ellery Cramer's life. Not only is Jackson still suffering from his wounds, the triggerman remains at large—and the body count is mounting.

Jackson and Ellery have been trying to track down Tim Owens since Jackson got out of the hospital, but Owens's time as a member of the department makes the DA reluctant to turn over any stones. When Owens starts going after people Jackson knows, Ellery's instincts hit red alert. Hurt in a scuffle with drug-dealing squatters and trying damned hard not to grieve for a childhood spent in hell, Jackson is weak and vulnerable when Owens strikes.

Jackson gets away, but the fallout from the encounter might kill him. It's not doing Ellery any favors either. When a police detective is abducted—and Jackson and Ellery hold the key to finding her—Ellery finds out exactly what he's made of. He's not the corporate shark who believes in winning at all costs; he's the frightened lover trying to keep the man he cares for from self-destructing in his own valor.

Scan the QR code below to order

A FEW GOOD FISH

Amy Lane

3

Fish Out of Water: Book Three

A tomcat, a psychopath, and a psychic walk into the desert to rescue the men they love…. Can everybody make it out with their skin intact?

PI Jackson Rivers and Defense Attorney Ellery Cramer have barely recovered from last November, when stopping a serial killer nearly destroyed Jackson in both body and spirit.

But their previous investigation poked a new danger with a stick, forcing Jackson and Ellery to leave town so they can meet the snake in its den.

Jackson Rivers grew up with the mean streets as a classroom and he learned a long time ago not to give a damn about his own life. But he gets a whole new education when the enemy takes Ellery. The man who pulled his shattered pieces from darkness and stitched them back together again is in trouble, and Jackson's only chance to save him rests in the hands of fragile allies he barely knows.

It's going to take a little bit of luck to get these Few Good Fish out alive!

Scan the QR code below to order

Hiding
the
Moon

AMY LANE

Fish Out of Water: Book Four
A Fish Out of Water/Racing for the Sun Crossover

Can a hitman and a psychic negotiate a relationship while all hell breaks loose?

The world might not know who Lee Burton is, but it needs his black ops division and the work they do to keep it safe. Lee's spent his life following orders—until he sees a kill jacket on Ernie Caulfield. Ernie isn't a typical target, and something is very wrong with Burton's chain of command.

Ernie's life may seem adrift, but his every action helps to shelter his mind from the psychic storm raging within. When Lee Burton shows up to save him from assassins and club bunnies, Ernie seizes his hand and doesn't look back. Burton is Ernie's best bet in a tumultuous world, and after one day together, he's pretty sure Lee knows Ernie is his destiny as well.

But when Burton refused Ernie's contract, he kicked an entire piranha tank of bad guys, and Burton can't rest until he takes down the rogue military unit that would try to kill a spacey psychic. Ernie's in love with Burton and Burton's confused as hell by Ernie—but Ernie's not changing his mind and Burton can't stay away. Psychics, assassins, and bad guys—throw them into the desert with a forbidden love affair and what could possibly go wrong?

Scan the QR code below to order

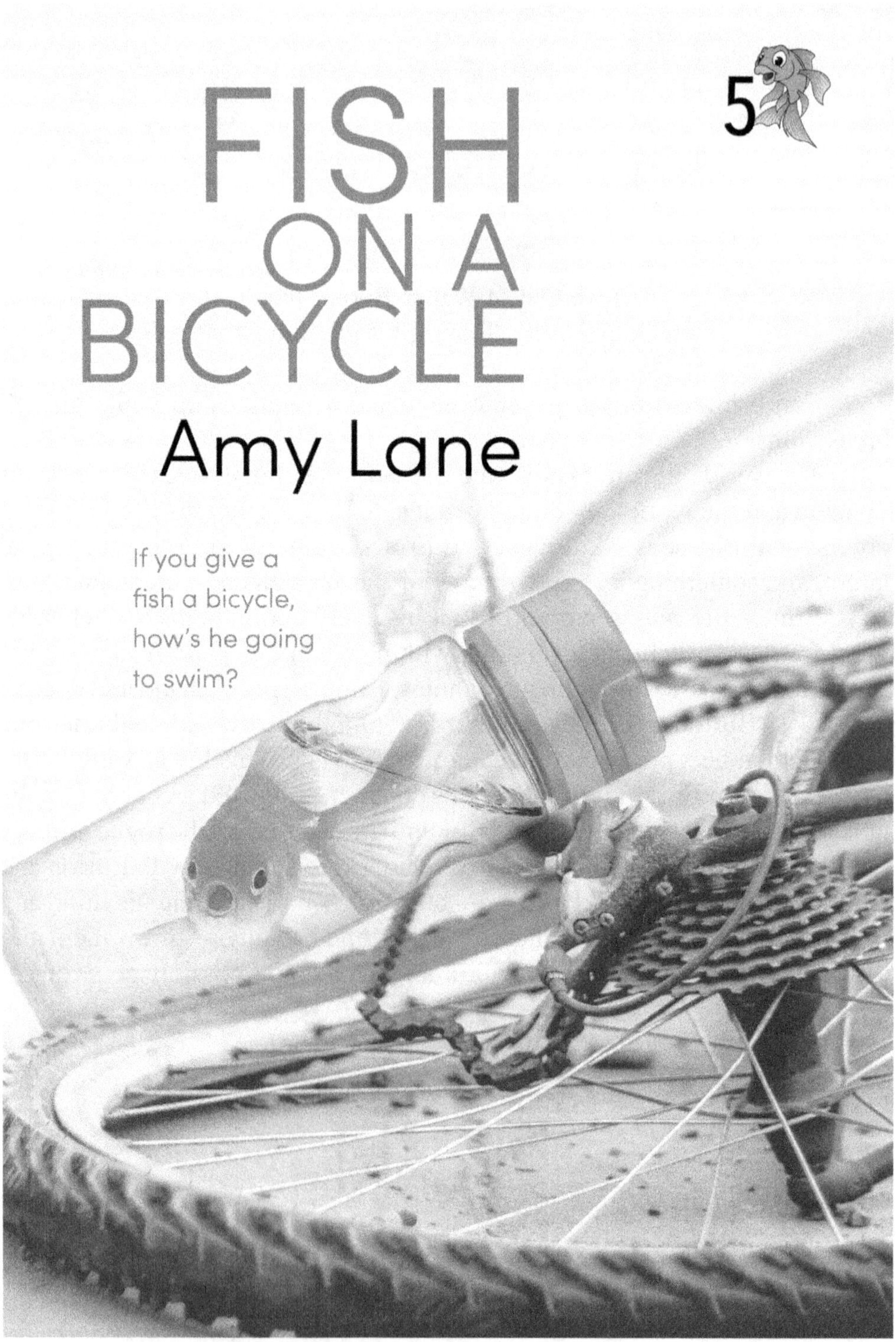

FISH ON A BICYCLE

Amy Lane

If you give a
fish a bicycle,
how's he going
to swim?

Fish Out of Water: Book Five

Jackson Rivers has always bucked the rules—and bucking the rules of recovery is no exception. Now that he and Ellery are starting their own law firm, there's no reason he can't rush into trouble and take the same risks as always, right?

Maybe not. Their first case is a doozy, involving porn stars, drug empires, and daddy issues, and their client, Henry Worrall, wants to be an active participant in his own defense. As Henry and Jackson fight the bad guys and each other to find out who dumped the porn star in the trash can, Jackson must reexamine his assumptions that four months of rest and a few good conversations have made him all better inside.

Jackson keeps crashing his bicycle of self-care and a successful relationship, and Ellery wonders what's going to give out first—Jackson's health or Ellery's patience. Jackson's body hasn't forgiven him for past crimes. Can Ellery forgive him for his current sins? And can they keep Henry from going to jail for sleeping with the wrong guy at the wrong time?

Being a fish out of water is tough—but if you give a fish a bicycle, how's he going to swim?

Scan the QR code below to order

Amy Lane

SCHOOL OF FISH

6

Order out of chaos,
innocence out of guilt,
fish out of water...

Fish Out of Water: Book Six

Jackson Rivers has been learning how to take care of himself so he can be there for Ellery Cramer, but after eight weeks of healing, body and soul, he's itching to get back to work. Finally Ellery gives him a simple task: pick up a file on a kid who probably didn't commit murder but who refuses to participate in his own defense.

Nothing is ever that easy.

A horrifying game of connect-the-dots leads one case to another, to the mob, to the local high school… and a bottomless list of potential suspects and victims. The case has a lot of moving parts, and Jackson and Ellery have to work fast to make sure the machinery of the mob doesn't mow down everyone they care about—or rip them apart.

After a year of living together, Ellery is learning to accept that Jackson can't let an injustice stand. Together they fight to keep kids out of jail while the streets of Sacramento threaten to explode. They'd better hope they've learned enough about each other to keep it together, because for this case, school is the most dangerous place to be.

Scan the QR code below to order

FOR MORE OF THE BEST GAY ROMANCE